THE YELLOWSTONE DIRECTIVE

John S. Shaw, III

Also by John Shaw

Death by DNA

For Carolyn, Carson, and Kendall

And also for Yellowstone National Park,
one of the most magical places on earth.

MAY 27

As Sage and Adam rounded a bend in the well-worn Fairy Falls hiking trail, they encountered a girl sprawled motionless, face down in the middle of the path. Sage dropped her backpack and rushed to her side. Grabbing a long, crooked branch, Sage poked the girl's porcelain cheek, barely visible beneath a tousle of tawny blonde hair, and then poked her a second time, as if testing for doneness. She figured the girl was no more than sixteen, maybe even as young as fourteen.

"Are you okay?" Sage asked tentatively.

Shaking ever so slightly, Adam remained by Sage's backpack. "I think she's dead."

"No, she's not! She's only unconscious. Let's get her to sit up."

After turning the girl over, Sage hoisted her up into a sitting position, but her head and arms flopped around. She placed the girl back down on the trail and shook her vigorously.

"Wake up, wake up!"

As she shook her, a small silver cross danced at the end of a chain around the girl's neck.

"Come on, Adam—give me some help over here."

Adam didn't budge.

Sage put her ear to the girl's mouth. "I don't think she's breathing!"

She started pumping on the girl's chest. "One, two, three ..." She counted to thirty, then performed two rescue breaths. She repeated the cycle twice more, her own chest heaving from the exertion in the high altitude.

"Please breathe, please breathe," Sage said more softly. "Please breathe."

After three more rounds of chest compressions and rescue breathing, she stopped.

"Call the medics!" she shouted at Adam, her voice tinged with fear.

"I'll call Kurt," Adam replied. "He'll know what to do."

Transfixed by the sight of the prone teenager, Adam could barely operate his Park Service radio. He reached Kurt on the second try.

"Is she breathing?" Kurt asked.

"I don't think so. We tried CPR and it didn't seem to work."

"Stay with her. I'll get there as soon as I can."

While Sage kneeled next to the girl, stroking her hand, Adam backed away slowly until he bumped into a lodgepole pine at the edge of the trail. Sliding down the coarse trunk, he landed among the pine needles with an audible thump. The trail was still wet from the spring snowmelt, and the dampness spread across his backside.

Sage and Adam had started as rookie seasonal rangers at Yellowstone National Park three weeks earlier. Although training sessions took up much of their time, they still found plenty of opportunities to explore the many wonders of Yellowstone.

Under a brilliant late May sun, they'd set out together just before noon to familiarize themselves with the Fairy Falls Trail, one of the most popular trails in all of Yellowstone, and they'd been hiking for over three hours when they came upon the girl. Members of the public weren't supposed to be on this trail this time of year—it was in a bear management area in late spring—but this girl had obviously ignored the warnings.

It took their supervisor Kurt almost twenty minutes to reach them. When he arrived, he ambled slowly toward the girl and stood with his hands on his hips. "Was she like this when you found her?"

Sage was still holding the girl's hand and didn't bother to look up. "No, she was lying on her stomach. I tried to get her to sit up, and then I laid her back down so I could perform CPR."

"Did she respond?"

"No."

"Move away from the girl," Kurt said sharply. "Let me take over."

Sage scrambled to the side of the trail and sat next to Adam.

Kurt used his right foot to try to flip the girl onto her stomach but only succeeded in turning her halfway over. Now she lay on her right side, her left arm slung awkwardly across her body and her long blond hair draped over her face. Kurt squatted down to take a closer look and rocked slowly back and forth on his heels.

Sage clambered to her feet. "Aren't you going to call for an ambulance?"

"No use. She's already gone," Kurt replied.

"How do you know?"

"Just look at her. She's dead."

"Don't you think we ought to at least …?"

"What's the point? She's already dead."

"What do we do now?"

"We wait. This is the third body today."

"There are *other* bodies?" Adam broke in, his voice rising an octave and cracking as he spoke.

"Yep. There were two on the Mystic Falls Trail. Found them myself 'bout an hour ago. A boy and a girl, probably teenagers. They were holding hands. So cute."

Sage winced.

"Once the medics arrived, I called for backup and was on my way back to the ranger station to file my report when I got your call."

"What's going on?" Sage asked.

"Don't know. Something weird, that's for sure."

"Was it a grizzly?" Adam jumped up, took out his bear spray, popped the safety off, and did a slow 360-degree turn.

"What do you think? You see any claw marks?"

"No, but I can't really see—"

"Of course it wasn't a bear. There'd be blood and guts everywhere if this was a grizzly attack."

"Then what was it?" Adam continued wielding his bear spray just in case.

"Don't know." Kurt crossed his arms and stood rigidly by the dead girl.

Sage didn't know much about Kurt Becker except that most of the other rangers didn't like him. Short and muscular, with a crew cut that signaled his military background, he had been in charge of Sage and Adam's training when they first arrived at Yellowstone. He barked out orders to the fifteen or so new seasonal rangers like a marine drill sergeant and showed contempt for anyone who tried to upstage him.

Sage walked back to the girl, trying to get a better look at her face. "What did the other bodies look like?"

"Same as this one—face down on the trail, no marks that I could see."

"So what do you think happened?"

"I told you, I don't know. You think *you* know what happened?"

Before Sage could respond, Kurt's radio squawked and he walked thirty feet up the trail before speaking. Sage couldn't hear what he was saying, but he seemed just as brusque with whoever was on the other end as he had been with Adam and her.

Suddenly Sage was startled by a gurgling sound behind her. Turning quickly, she saw Adam bent over at the waist, vomiting in the bushes next to the trail. When he was done, he stood up unsteadily and wiped his mouth with his sleeve.

"You all right, Adam?"

"I'm fine. Just a little scared."

"That's okay. I'm scared too."

Once he'd regained his composure, Adam cautiously approached the girl. "So what do you think happened to ... do we even know her name?"

"No. Let's see if she has any ID on her."

Adam backed away. "No way I'm going to touch her."

"Okay, I'll do it."

Sage knelt down and tried to unhook the small pack around the girl's waist, but the plastic clasp was twisted and jammed. The pack was partially unzipped, so she reached in and pulled out the girl's phone, still attached to the earbuds in her ears. Sage could hear a muffled Taylor Swift song emanating from the tiny speakers.

Sage's face brightened. "That's why she can't hear us! Maybe she's still alive!" She yanked one of the earbuds out and yelled right into the girl's ear. "Can you hear me?"

In the heat of the moment it seemed like a reasonable inquiry, but there was still no response from the girl. Sage thrust her hand back into the girl's pack and pulled out a slim wallet. Not much was in it except for a few dollars, a credit card, and a school ID.

"Abby Bishop. Her name is Abby Bishop. She is ... was ... in the eleventh grade at St. Agnes High in Boise, Idaho. That probably makes her about sixteen or seventeen."

She wasn't just an anonymous dead girl anymore. She was Abby Bishop, high school student. Sage stood up, fighting back tears.

Kurt strode quickly toward Sage, almost stepping on the body in the process. "Don't get all girly on me," he sneered. "We've got a dead body here. Why don't you just leave and let the professionals deal with this. You're just going to mess everything up."

Sage didn't move. "I'm going to stay here with Abby until the medics arrive."

Kurt's eyes narrowed. "I remember you from training class. You think you know everything. I don't care for you and your fancy degrees. They aren't worth much out here. I want you out of here right now!"

"I'll have you know I have a Ph.D. in volcanology from the University of Hawaii, and I did a postdoc with the USGS."

"Like I said, young lady, those degrees aren't worth anything out here. You see any volcanoes erupting?"

"Only you," Sage said loudly enough for Kurt to hear.

"That's enough from you! We've got an official investigation going on here and you need to head back to the village.

"But I want to stay here and help."

"No can do. The medics will be here soon and there will National Park Service Law Enforcement Rangers and probably even local cops. It's going to get very hectic. You need to leave immediately."

"Let's go, Adam. I can see we're not wanted here."

Kurt turned to Adam. "Young man, I need you to stay and help me secure the scene."

"Yes, sir," Adam replied. "Sage, I'll see you back in the village later on."

Sage pulled on her backpack, walked briskly down the trail, and disappeared around the corner, muttering about Kurt.

* * *

It was almost 5 p.m. when Sage arrived back at Apartment 1B, the small two-bedroom place she shared with Anaya Patel, a fellow ranger at Yellowstone working her second summer. Some of the other first-time rangers lived in dorms, and Sage felt lucky to be living in a real apartment. Her brand new building had been cleared for occupancy just a week before she and Anaya moved in. Although the apartment was exceedingly small—the cramped kitchen adjoined a tiny living area that had just enough room for a dinette set, a coffee-colored sofa, a tan overstuffed chair, and a couple of side tables—at least she had her own bedroom.

With sparkling green eyes, a smooth olive complexion, and a cascade of wavy chestnut hair, Sage Maldonado's striking appearance came from her Hawaiian mom and Spanish dad. She was five foot six, but her erect posture made her appear taller. Her mother used to tell her that she could be a model, but Sage had no affinity for fashion or modeling. She wanted to make her mark in the world with her intellect.

She usually pulled her voluminous hair away from her face in a loose ponytail, which is how she wore it under her ranger hat, and she eschewed contact lenses for oversized glasses with dark brown rims, thinking they afforded her a more scholarly appearance. She rarely wore jewelry, except for a small heart-shaped gold pendant her parents had given her when she finished graduate school.

Sage's parents were both college professors, and it was natural for her to follow in their footsteps. Bright and intensely driven, she excelled academically, especially in math and science. Often teased for her nerdiness, she won numerous robotics competitions and math contests throughout high school and college. After graduating from the University of Washington *summa cum laude* with a degree in geology, she earned a masters and a Ph.D. in volcanology at the University of Hawaii, where her parents were on the faculty.

After finishing graduate school, Sage took a postdoc at the U.S. Geological Survey where she studied undersea volcanoes, spending a great deal of time on research vessels monitoring automated submersibles while they explored volcanoes and hydrothermal vents thousands of feet below the surface of the ocean. Despite frequent bouts of seasickness, Sage became intrigued by the extremophiles that lived around the super-hot thermal vents on the ocean floor and wished she knew more about these wondrous life forms.

After two years of bobbing around on the world's oceans, Sage knew her next job had to be on terra firma. Although the seasonal ranger job at Yellowstone was only a five-month stint, she jumped at the chance to study one of the most famous volcanoes of all—the Yellowstone super volcano that had last erupted 640,000 years ago. Her primary responsibility was to look for seismic patterns that might signal increased magma activity beneath the volcanic caldera that spanned much of Yellowstone National Park. This was a little outside her expertise, which centered on the physical and chemical properties of magma, lava, and tephra, but it was close enough. She was a quick learner, and she knew she would adapt to her new job.

It was Memorial Day weekend, so park visitors had just begun arriving in large numbers the week before. Most of the inns and lodges were already full, and the campgrounds were bustling. In about a week, the Summer Ranger Programs would begin, and Sage would be leading hikes and occasionally presenting evening campfire programs about earthquakes and volcanoes. Until then, she had planned to explore the park and commence her research on seismic activity. In addition to her ranger duties, she was also working at the Yellowstone Volcano Observatory, run jointly by the National Park Service, the USGS, and the University of Utah. If things went well during the summer, she hoped to transition to a year-round position with the National Park Service at Yellowstone.

While Sage waited for Anaya, she changed out of her park ranger uniform—dark green pants, light gray shirt, heavy-duty shoes, and wide-brimmed ranger hat—took a shower to wash off the trail dust, and put on a pair of sweats and a t-shirt. She had just plopped down on the couch in the living room when Anaya exploded through the door.

"Did you hear? Four people died in the park today!"

"I know, I was there!" Sage replied. "I found one of the bodies myself."

"Wow! Was it scary?"

"Sort of. Adam was there too."

"Surprise, surprise. You two sure have been spending a lot of time together."

Sage and Adam had hit it off right from the start and had been exploring the park together over the past three weeks, getting to know it—and each other—better. They tackled strenuous trails, such as those to Mount Washburn and Pebble Creek, and also enjoyed more leisurely hikes to places like Beaver Ponds, Storm Point, and Mystic Falls.

They both loved the outdoors, which is what drew them to Yellowstone, and they had both been runners in college—Sage had run cross-country at the University of Washington, and Adam had competed in 400 and 800 meters at the University of Montana. It had taken Sage a couple of days to coax Adam into divulging that he had been state champion in the two events in high school and had set several records at the University of Montana.

What had started as a friendship gradually evolved into something more. Sage was drawn to Adam's athleticism and sense of humor, both of which were on full display as they explored Yellowstone's trails and backcountry areas. She marveled at his agility as he maneuvered around fallen tree trunks, boulders, and other obstacles on the trails, and she appreciated how he laughed at himself when he occasionally stumbled. On a morning hike to Storm Point about two weeks after they first met, Sage had broached the idea of moving their friendship forward.

"But I've heard it's never a good idea to date a co-worker," Adam said.

Sage told him it was a risk she was willing to take, and they finished the rest of the hike hand in hand.

From that point on, they were inseparable. Every evening after dinner they explored the forests, meadows, and geyser basins around Old Faithful Village, taking in the sights, sounds, and smells of Yellowstone and meeting some of its inhabitants. One evening they came face-to-face with a lone male bison that was ambling along the side of the Grand Loop Road near the village. Knowing that bison can be extremely aggressive despite their placid appearance, they slowly backed away and gave the enormous animal a wide berth. The rush of adrenaline triggered by their close encounter culminated in a passionate embrace as the bison disappeared down the road.

On their daily walks they chatted about their families, lives, and career aspirations. Sage explained that she wanted to be a full-time researcher with the National Park Service before eventually transitioning to a faculty position at a prestigious university, and Adam told Sage that he wanted to be a Park Superintendent someday, maybe even at Yellowstone.

Anaya leaped onto the sofa right next to Sage. "Tell me about the body you found!"

"We were having a wonderful time hiking the Fairy Falls Trail when we came across it. I still can't believe I saw a dead person. I've never seen one in real life before."

"What did it look like?"

"I don't know. It looked like a dead person. Adam seemed even more scared than me."

"So where's Adam now?"

"He had to stay with Kurt to help secure the scene."

Anaya crossed her arms tightly. "I've never liked Kurt."

"Me neither ... Wait a second—did you say *four* bodies? I only heard about three."

"Yep, there are four. One on the Fairy Falls Trail, two on the Mystic Falls Trail, and one on the trail to Lone Star Geyser."

"I didn't know about that last one. What's everybody saying?"

"Nobody knows anything. I heard that lots of visitors are leaving the park."

"I don't think it's grizzlies," Sage said. "The girl I saw didn't have any marks on her. What do you think is going on?"

"Some people are saying it's a serial killer. All the victims were under twenty and three of them were girls. Maybe some sort of sex predator."

The words sent shivers down Sage's spine. "Here in Yellowstone? I don't think so."

"Why not? There are sickos everywhere nowadays. What do you think it is?"

"Aliens maybe?" Sage relaxed just a bit as Anaya started to laugh.

The two women had become fast friends when they moved in together at the start of the summer season. Originally from Mumbai, India, Anaya had come to the States when she went to grad school at the University of Wyoming, where she earned her master's in botany. Her plan was to return to Wyoming in the fall to start a Ph.D. program in plant biology.

In many ways, Sage and Anaya could have passed for sisters. Roughly the same size, they often shared clothes, and Anaya's thick, wavy hair was much like Sage's, only shorter. They had a lot of the same interests and could talk endlessly about world politics, the environment, and reality TV shows. Although they occasionally made fun of politicians and celebrities and teased each other mercilessly as sisters often do, at their core they were both kind-hearted, caring, and generous.

"But really, what *do* you think might be going on?" Anaya asked.

"I've no idea," Sage replied. "Maybe it is some sort of serial killer, but I don't know. What I do know is that I'm going to find out. This is *way* more interesting than reading seismograph printouts all day, that's for sure."

Anaya headed to the kitchen. "You want some dinner?"

"I don't know if I can eat."

"You excited or scared?"

"Excited mostly. How about you?"

Anaya paused. "Well, something weird is going on and we've no idea what it is. It is a bit scary."

"So what do we have to eat?"

"Let's see ... leftover Chinese, leftover pizza ..." Anaya's voice was muffled in the open fridge.

"I'll take the pizza," Sage said.

"Okay, I'll have the Chinese."

After finishing her gourmet dinner, washed down with a bottle of Heineken, Sage glanced at her watch.

"I think I'll go up and see if Adam's back yet. Wanna come?"

"No, thanks. I'm just gonna hang out here. Watch out for aliens!"

Sage bounded up the steps to the second floor of the apartment building and knocked on the door to 2D. Adam's roommate, dressed in a filthy death metal t-shirt and jeans that were much too tight for his portly frame, answered the door. He was wearing heavy-duty rubber gloves and holding what appeared to be a dead squirrel. His face was covered in sweat.

"Adam's not here. Want to come in and wait?"

"Uh, no thanks. Just tell him Sage came by." She turned and headed back down the hallway.

"Are you sure you don't want to come in?"

"I'm sure," Sage said without turning around.

As she opened the door to head down the stairs, Adam burst through, almost bowling her over. He grabbed her tightly to keep them both from falling.

"Sage! What are you doing here?"

"I came up to see if we could talk."

"It's been a pretty creepy day, huh?"

"Actually, I think it's been sort of interesting ... but in a creepy sort of way."

"How about we go down to your place? My roommate's a little strange."

"I'll say. I just met him for the first time. I'd always wondered why you never invited me up to your apartment."

"Now you know. Give me a moment to change and I'll meet you downstairs."

As soon as Sage got back to her apartment, she whirled about tidying up, even though everything was already immaculate. Even the food canisters on the kitchen counter were lined up neatly from smallest to largest. Anaya had grown accustomed to Sage's penchant for order but still liked to tease her about it.

"Everything okay, girl?" Anaya asked, smiling.

"Yeah. I'm just straightening up. You mind if Adam hangs out with us?"

"Not at all. Has he eaten?"

"I've no idea. Do we have anything to give him?"

"I didn't finish my dinner. You think he might be interested in twice leftover honey chicken and noodles?"

Sage grimaced.

There was a quiet knock at the door.

"Come on in—the door's unlocked," Sage announced.

"What are you doing?" Anaya's voice was filled with apprehension. "What if it's a stranger? What if it's the murderer?"

Adam strode in, a duffle bag slung over one shoulder, holding a large paper sack.

"See, it's only Adam."

"Anaya's right," Adam said. "We all need to start being more careful."

Adam looked every bit the elite athlete in his crumpled t-shirt and faded sweats. His gait was assured yet smooth, and every movement appeared effortless. Sage caught Anaya checking him out, but decided not to say anything. He dropped his duffle bag at one end of the couch.

"I've got a sandwich and a soda. Mind if I eat while we talk?" He sat down and opened the paper sack. "Your place is always so clean. It looks a lot like mine, only neater. Much neater."

"So, Adam, you're a forestry guy, aren't you?" Anaya said brightly, her dark eyes taking him in.

"Yeah, I'm in grad school at the University of Montana. And you're studying botany at Wyoming, right?"

Before Anaya got too cozy with Adam, Sage changed the subject. "You were such a great runner in college, Adam. You ever think about trying out for the U.S. Olympic team?"

"I considered it, but I didn't think I was good enough."

Maybe *he* didn't think he was good enough, but he sure looked good enough to Sage. Just shy of six feet, he had a lean, toned body, honed from years of running track. Unruly russet hair framed his boyish face, and a light tan complemented his dark brown eyes. What was most attractive to Sage, though, was his self-effacing manner. Many of her friends liked confident, assertive types, but she preferred the quiet ones who were smart and strong, yet had a softer side and were willing to put others first. Adam checked all the right boxes.

After wolfing down his sandwich, Adam told Sage what had happened on the trail after she left. He told her about the medics, the police officers, and the law enforcement rangers. He also admitted that he had thrown up again when the medics put the girl's body on a litter to carry her down the trail to an ambulance.

"That's okay. You don't like dead bodies—I don't like spiders. Let's call it even." Sage smiled gently.

Now it was Adam's turn to change the subject. "Today was even more exciting than yesterday!"

"Maybe," Sage said, "but earthquakes are still pretty exciting in my book, and yesterday's 5.9 quake in Norris was a doozy. It occurred in almost the exact same spot as the 6.1 quake in 1975 and the 4.8 in 2014. Norris Geyser Basin is a very seismically active area, even by Yellowstone standards. Most of the Norris quakes have been related to episodes of ground uplift in that portion of the Yellowstone Caldera."

"You sure know a lot about earthquakes."

"Volcanologists study earthquakes too."

For the next few hours, Sage and Adam speculated about what was going on with all the dead bodies while Anaya sat in the comfy oversized chair and read *Jurassic Park*. They wondered why the young girl on the Fairy Falls Trail had been hiking alone. Dressed in mustard yellow cargo shorts, a brown sweatshirt, and hiking boots, she was clearly prepared for a day out on the trails. But why had she been walking by herself on a closed trail in a bear management area? Adam still thought bears might be involved.

"Can you die from a heart attack if you see a grizzly bear?" he asked.

"I suppose it's possible, but she was just a teenager. It's unlikely she had a heart attack."

"But why would she just drop dead without a mark on her?"

"I think she was attacked by a person, not an animal. Don't forget, we have four deaths, not just one. All teenagers."

"You think it's some kind of serial killer?"

"That's what Anaya thinks. She thinks it might be a sexual predator."

Anaya looked up from her book. "I don't see why not. There are plenty of them out there."

"Maybe it's a crazy person with a weird psycho agenda." Sage's hands were shaking and she sat on them, hoping Adam wouldn't notice, but it was too late.

"Are you okay?" he asked.

"I'm fine, just a bit tired. It's been a long day."

"It's getting late. How about I crash here on the couch for the night?"

Sage flipped her hair in mock appreciation. "How gallant! You want to stay here and protect me?"

"Gallantry my ass," Anaya mumbled from behind her book.

MAY 28

Sage and Anaya were already eating breakfast when Adam woke up.

"It's seven forty! I'll never make it to work by eight."

"Of course you will," Sage said between mouthfuls of bagel. "Where are you working today?"

"The information desk at the Visitor Center."

Adam got dressed quickly, making sure his ranger uniform was as neat as possible.

"You had your uniform in your bag?" Sage smiled quizzically at Adam.

"Just in case," he said, grinning back.

"Today's my day off, but I think I'll join you in a bit 'cause I want to find out what's going on."

When Sage arrived at the Visitor Center thirty minutes later, the crowd at the information desk was ten deep. Instead of the usual questions about Old Faithful, grizzly bears, and day hikes, people were shouting out frantic queries about the deaths the day before. Although Sage didn't have her uniform on, she stepped up to the counter to help Adam handle the onslaught of questions. Somewhat reticent by nature, Adam was happy to let Sage take over.

"How many people are dead?"

"I heard the victims were missing their eyes! They were gouged out or something. Is that true?"

"I heard that too. Somebody told me the victims were missing all their fingers!"

Sage spoke calmly, offering general denials to each of the bizarre rumors, but hardly anyone could hear her over the din. Then she tried a more forceful approach.

"All of these rumors are one hundred percent false!" she shouted. "I know, because I saw one of the bodies."

The cacophony subsided abruptly and every face in the crowd turned toward her.

"You actually saw one of the bodies?"

"Yes, I did."

"What did it look like? What happened? Was it bears? Wolves? Coyotes?"

"No, no, nothing like that," Sage replied.

"Well then, what was it? Why did these people die?"

"We don't know."

"Are you a park ranger?"

"Yes."

"Then where's your uniform?"

Sage didn't bother to answer. The questions kept coming.

"Is it just four people?"

"Did they know each other? Were they related?"

"Were they murdered?"

"I heard the victims were all girls. Were they raped?"

"It was three girls and one boy," Sage said firmly.

"So the three girls were raped?"

"That's not what I said!"

"So what's going on?"

"What are you doing to protect us?"

As the commotion continued, Sage turned away from the crowd and looked to Todd, the supervisor on duty, for help. He offered none.

The crowd pushed closer to the information desk. Suddenly a woman fell and shrieked out in pain. Two men lifted her to her feet and tried to move her toward the door, but they couldn't get through the tightly packed throng.

After more shouting and pushing and shoving, Todd turned on the public address system.

"May I have your attention please! We know you have many questions. So do we. At this point, we don't know any more than you do. As soon as we have additional information we'll share it with you. In the meantime I suggest that everyone calm down and get something to eat. Today would be a good day to just hang out in your lodge or campground—maybe play cards or read a book. If you decide to venture away from the Old Faithful area, I recommend you go in groups."

The last bit of advice opened the floodgates again.

"Why only go out in groups? It *is* bears, isn't it?"

"How many bears? Just one or a whole bunch?"

As the shouting grew louder and angrier, Todd announced that while the Visitor Center would remain open, the information desk would be closed until further notice and park rangers would not be available to answer any questions. Todd, Adam, Sage, and the other two rangers on duty retreated to the back office and closed the door behind them. Todd was visibly shaking.

Sage grabbed Adam's hand. "Let's go outside and get some air."

After exiting through the rear door of the Visitor Center, they walked briskly across the parking lot to the patio tables on the deck outside the Geyser Grill. Adam went inside to get some water while Sage waited at a table at the far end of the deck.

"Do you have a few moments, ma'am?"

Startled, Sage looked around.

"Do you mind if we talk?" A petite woman with short auburn hair was standing a few feet away. Wearing a crisp white shirt and pressed tan slacks, she would've looked ready for a job interview at a bank if it weren't for her well-worn hiking boots.

"Do I know you?" Sage asked.

"My name is Penny Phillips. I'm with the *Jackson Hole Gazette*. I was in the Visitor Center a few minutes ago and heard you say that you saw one of the bodies. I'd like to ask you a few questions, if you don't mind."

"Actually, I'm exhausted and don't feel like—"

"It'll only take a few minutes. Promise."

"Okay, but just a few minutes."

"I'd like to ask you about the four bodies."

"I only saw one of them." Sage glanced down and saw Penny's voice recorder on the table. "Can we keep this off the record?"

"I'm trying to write a story about what's going on here and I really—"

"Never mind, then. I'm too tired to talk right now."

Penny looked down at the recorder and then back at Sage. She turned the recorder off and put it in her bag. "I really want to know what's going on. We can go off the record."

"Thank you."

Adam rushed up with two half-filled cups of water. "Sorry. I spilled most of the water trying to open the door."

"Adam, this is Penny. She's a reporter from Jackson Hole."

Adam nodded toward Penny. "Nice to meet you, but I don't think we should be talking to reporters."

"Neither do I," Sage said, "but Penny promised it would be off the record."

"Well, I suppose ..." Adam handed the cups to Sage and Penny and went back inside to get another for himself. When he returned he sat down and just listened.

Sage told Penny what little she knew. "Now it's your turn. What have you heard?"

"Not much really," Penny said.

"C'mon, you're a reporter. I'm sure you know something."

Penny hesitated. "Off the record?"

Sage smiled. "Of course."

"To begin with, there are now at least *six* bodies."

"What? Where were the other two?"

Adam shifted uncomfortably in his seat and looked down at his water.

"One was by the side of the road between here and West Thumb. It looked like she might have been out for a run."

"How old?"

"Twenty-six."

"And the other one?

"On the trail to Lone Star Geyser."

"That's not new," Sage said. "They found that one yesterday."

"No, this was another girl about a quarter mile further down the trail. They didn't discover her until this morning."

"Where are you getting your information?"

"I can't tell you."

"This is crazy! What do you know about the victims?"

"Not much more than you. All six were young, ranging in age from about sixteen to twenty-six."

Adam chimed in. "And all but one were girls. Some of us have been thinking that there might be some sort of sex killer on the loose."

"That's what I thought at first too," Penny said. "But now I'm not so sure."

"How come?" Sage asked.

"I heard there were no marks on any of the bodies and no evidence they were assaulted—no cuts, no wounds, nothing that anyone could see. Of course, we won't know for sure until they do the autopsies."

"Have you seen any of the bodies?"

"Not really."

"What do you mean, *not really*? You've either seen them or you haven't."

"I sort of saw one of them from a distance."

"Where are they now?"

"Over in the Old Faithful Clinic on the far side of the parking lot." Penny pointed at the two-story building barely visible across the sea of cars.

"The clinic's in the same building as the ranger station," Sage said. "Any evidence they were attacked by animals?"

"No."

"So how did they die?"

"Nobody knows. There's something else that's a little weird. It seems that three of the victims knew each other. The girl you saw on the Fairy Falls Trail and the two girls on the Lone Star Geyser Trail belonged to the same church group."

"But weren't they all alone when they died?" Sage asked.

"That's not exactly clear. Their bodies were alone when they were *found*, but that doesn't necessarily mean they were alone when they *died*."

"So maybe someone in the church group …?" Adam wondered.

"Maybe," Penny said. "But the other three victims—the teenage couple and the woman by the side of the road—had no connection to the church group … at least none that I'm aware of. And there's more. I heard the FBI is on the way."

Sage straightened up. "Is this some sort of terrorist situation?"

"Sounds like it, doesn't it?" Penny said. "I've been told they'll be here by tomorrow. Yellowstone is a tough place to get to on short notice."

"We ought to get out of here before this gets out of hand," Adam said.

"Not yet. I want to find out what's going on," Sage said. "Penny, are you up for some sleuthing?"

"Absolutely. That's what I get paid to do."

Sage turned to Adam. "Want to join us?"

"I can't. I'm working today, remember? I've got to get back to the Visitor Center."

"C'mon. It'll be exciting."

Adam stood up. "I really need to get back to work. You two be careful out there. Who knows what's going on."

"We'll be fine. Let's meet back at my place when you get off."

As Adam walked slowly back to the Visitor Center, Sage turned to Penny. "So, where to?"

"Want to try to see the bodies?"

"Of course!"

They headed across the parking lot to the Old Faithful Clinic. Earlier that morning, Penny had just walked right in and looked around before being asked to leave. This time, though, security was much tighter and Penny couldn't convince the law enforcement ranger to let them in.

Sage stepped in front of Penny and showed her Department of Interior ID card. "Just want to check in at the ranger station. I'm on duty."

"Then how come you're not wearing your uniform?"

"I'm supposed to be off today, but they needed all hands on deck so I rushed down here to help."

"Who's she?" the law enforcement ranger asked, nodding toward Penny.

"She's in training. Starting next week. I need her to come with me."

"I'll let you through this once. But you should always wear your uniforms if you're on duty."

Sage and Penny quickly disappeared into the ranger station and waited by the front window. When the law enforcement ranger started checking the IDs of a large group of people, they made their move. The entrances to the clinic and the ranger station were about twenty feet apart, and it took them only a few seconds to slip next door to the clinic.

Inside, it was a flurry of activity—at least fifteen people were crammed into the small waiting area. Taking advantage of the hubbub, Sage and Penny casually poked their heads into each of the examination rooms. Finally, they struck gold. In a dark room near the end of the hallway they could just barely make out two bodies lying on gurneys. The corpses were covered loosely with sheets that were too short to completely conceal them, and their feet stuck out the bottom. A deep chill surged out of the room, like a storage locker in a meat processing plant. Large bags of ice were positioned around the windowless room, and there were two large, noisy fans at opposite ends circulating the frigid air.

Two armed law enforcement rangers immediately approached them.

"Stop right there!" the taller one shouted. "Do not enter the holding room. Who are you? Why are you here?"

Sage flashed her DOI ID card. "Just checking things out, Ranger …?"

"Little. Ranger Little."

"Checking what out?" the other ranger asked.

"We're scientists with the Park Service and we need to verify that all appropriate protocols are being followed in the handling of the bodies. Where are the other bodies?"

"Can't say," Ranger Little replied.

Penny chimed in. "And these two are?"

"I'm not sure about the young girl, but the other one was Daniels. Did you know her?"

"Who?" Sage asked.

"Ranger Daniels."

Sage gulped. "No, I didn't."

"It's really sad. Out for a run and boom, she's dead."

"Why are these two bodies still here?" Sage asked.

"We're keeping them as cold as possible until the autopsies are performed later today."

Sage started to back away. "We'll return later to verify that all Park Service protocols have been followed."

"And on whose authority are you here?"

Sage turned toward the front door. "Thank you, Ranger Little. Keep up the good work."

Penny and Sage walked out of the clinic, nodding to several

other rangers on the way out. Once they were outside, Sage grabbed Penny's arm.

"I *did* know that ranger. She was a rookie, just like me. Her name was Caitlyn Daniels. Sometimes I go out jogging too. That could have been me!"

"Are you okay?"

"I think so."

Penny changed the subject. "So what brought you way out here to Yellowstone?"

"I love volcanoes, I love the outdoors. What's not to like?"

"Are you seasonal or permanent?"

"Seasonal at this point, but I hope to get a permanent position at the end of the summer."

"Then what?"

"I'd like to work here for a few years and then get a faculty position at a big university."

"You have any dreams beyond that?"

Sage hesitated. "I do."

"Well, c'mon. Tell me."

"You'll probably laugh."

"No, I won't. I promise."

"I want to be known as the Carl Sagan of volcanology. You know, the person who brings the science of volcanology to the masses—write books, host TV specials, that sort of thing."

Penny looked at Sage but didn't say a word.

"See, you *do* think it's silly."

"Not at all. I think that's a great dream."

"So what about you?"

"I was born and raised in Jackson Hole. After getting a degree in journalism at Syracuse, I knew the East Coast wasn't for me, so I came back here to my roots. I took a job as a reporter for the *Jackson Hole Gazette* and I've been there for almost four years."

"You have any dreams?"

"Of course. Most of them involve Johnny Depp."

Sage laughed. "You know what I mean."

"One day I'm going to win a Pulitzer. I don't think the *Jackson Hole Gazette* has ever had a Pulitzer Prize winner."

"Maybe this will be the story that gets you one."

Penny smiled. "Wouldn't that be nice!"

For the rest of the morning, they wandered around the Old Faithful area trying to find out as much as they could. First they tried the Old Faithful Snow Lodge and the Old Faithful Lodge. After learning nothing of substance in the two lodges, they walked over to the iconic Old Faithful Inn. Before they went in, they stopped to read a notice taped to the front door.

OFFICIAL NATIONAL PARK SERVICE NOTICE
MAY 28

```
In order to allow National Park Service
Law Enforcement Rangers to conduct
official business, all park visitors are
encouraged to stay in their rooms or their
campgrounds, unless they are departing
Yellowstone today. Lunch and dinner will
be served in the main dining room from
12:00 to 2:00 p.m. and from 6:00 to 9:00
p.m., respectively. The Bear Paw Deli
will be open from 11:00 a.m. to 9:00 p.m.

Further updates will be provided later
today.
```

Sage and Penny hung out in the enormous lobby of the Old Faithful Inn and spoke with guests as they walked through. Some were on their way to the front desk to check out while others were heading to the dining room or the deli to get something to eat. No one knew anything more about the deaths than Sage and Penny did, and nobody had seen any of the bodies.

Just as they were about to leave, a middle-age couple approached the front desk. The man was yelling at no one in particular and the woman was shrieking hysterically. Penny tried to approach them but was stopped short by a law enforcement ranger. She rejoined Sage at the other end of the lobby.

"Could you hear what they were saying?" Sage asked.

"Not really. All I could make out was that they wanted information. And the man kept yelling about something not being fair."

"Maybe they're parents of one of the victims."

"Maybe so."

As the lunch crowd thinned out, Sage and Penny went to the Old Faithful General Store to see if anyone there knew anything, but no one did. Sage headed back to her apartment while Penny set out to poke around a little more.

* * *

"Three more bodies!" Anaya yelled as soon Sage walked in the door. "Three more!"

"Three? I only heard about two. There was a second girl on the Lone Star Geyser Trail and Caitlyn Daniels. Who was the third one?"

"A twenty-four-year-old woman found somewhere near Morning Glory Pool."

"This is getting scarier by the minute." Adam's voice trembled noticeably.

Sage, Adam, and Anaya settled in for the afternoon and swapped information about what they had learned.

"So to recap—seven people are dead," Sage said. "Four were found yesterday and three today. All were between sixteen and twenty-six years old, and all but one were female. Three of the teenage girls belonged to a church group from Boise. The young couple on the Mystic Falls Trail was here on vacation with the girl's family. The woman by Morning Glory Pool was vacationing alone from St. Louis. And the seventh victim was Caitlyn." Sage paused. "It's weird, but I feel worse for Caitlyn because I knew her. Is that wrong?"

"Of course not. That's only natural," Anaya said.

"What else do we know about the victims?" Adam asked.

"The three girls from the church group were found in three different locations. The girl we saw on the Fairy Falls Trail was about a mile from the trailhead and the other two were on the trail to Lone Star Geyser. One of them was found yesterday and the other, early this morning, about a quarter mile further down the trail from the first girl. Penny heard that the three of them had been on some sort of scavenger hunt. They were working in pairs and had been warned not to go out alone, but several of the pairs split up anyway, probably thinking they would have a better chance of winning. Evidently the two girls on the Lone Star Geyser Trail were working together, and the girl on the Fairy Falls Trail was in a different pair. Nobody noticed they were missing until dinner last night, and by that time two of the bodies had already been found. It looks like the church group has six chaperones on the trip, four women and two men."

"And the other four victims?" Adam asked.

"We don't know much about them," Sage replied. "Except for Caitlyn."

Suddenly the windows rattled, the floor undulated and heaved, and a sharp jolt shook the entire apartment.

"Earthquake!" Anaya yelled.

Sage instinctively started the timer on her watch.

The shaking continued while the walls and ceiling creaked and groaned. The kitchen cabinets flew open, sending their contents crashing to the wooden floor, broken shards of glass and stoneware scattering everywhere. Three food canisters abandoned their designated spots on the counter and quickly followed the plates and glasses onto the floor.

The light fixture over the dinette set swayed back and forth in a looping figure eight, and the sofa transformed into a reeling vessel, tossing its three passengers about. Anaya ducked down, holding a cushion tightly over her head. Adam tried to stand and head to a doorway, but quickly tumbled back onto the sofa. Sage threw her arms around him and held on tight as dust and small bits of plaster descended from a spiderweb of cracks that had opened in the ceiling during the first quake a few days earlier.

When the shaking finally stopped, Sage looked at her watch. "Thirty-seven seconds. Pretty long for an aftershock. Pretty big too. If it was the same depth as the quake two days ago, I'd guess this one was about 4.8 or 4.9—maybe even 5.0."

"Are you enjoying this?" Anaya asked.

"Sort of."

"Well, I'm not. Seven dead bodies, two big earthquakes. What's next—a tsunami?"

Adam looked terrified. "I'm with Anaya. I think we ought to get out of Yellowstone right now!"

"Are you kidding? This is even better than I'd hoped for when I took this job. I love a good mystery."

"Me too … when it's a novel or a movie," Anaya said. "In real life? Not so much."

Sage chattered on about earthquakes and aftershocks, oblivious to Adam and Anaya's growing agitation. After a few minutes, Adam went upstairs to check on his apartment and Anaya poured herself some wine in one of the remaining intact glasses.

When Adam returned, he was lugging a large suitcase. "Is it okay if I stay here tonight?"

"Fine with me!" Sage said brightly.

"Sure. You can stay in my room if you want." Anaya flashed a devilish grin.

"I ... don't think ... that would be such a good idea," Sage sputtered.

"And why not?" Anaya teased.

"I'll just sleep out here on the couch like I did last night," Adam said.

"Well, if you change your mind ..."

"Really, I'll be fine."

The three of them sat down on the sofa, Sage wedging herself between Adam and Anaya.

"So you'd rather sleep on our couch than stay in your own apartment?" Anaya asked. "What's that all about?"

"It's my roommate. He makes me uncomfortable. He arrived about a week ago and we just never hit it off."

"What's his name? Where's he from?"

"Steve Musk ... from Austin, Texas, I think."

"So what's his story?"

"I'm not sure. I think he works in maintenance. There's one thing that's really weird, though. He's constantly bringing dead animals into our apartment. He got an old freezer from the maintenance shed and put it in his bedroom. I think he stores the carcasses in there. Usually they're pretty small, like pikas and birds, but one time I saw him with a marmot."

"So that's why he had a dead squirrel," Sage said.

"What?" Anaya asked.

"When I went upstairs to Adam's apartment yesterday, his roommate answered the door holding a dead squirrel."

Anaya shuddered, "What does he do with them?"

"I don't know, and I don't want to know," Adam said. "I think he skins them or something."

"Maybe he's a taxidermist," Sage offered.

"Maybe."

Anaya changed the subject. "Let's get back to talking about the victims."

"So what do we know about the cause of death?" Adam asked.

"Only what's been ruled out—animal attacks, shootings, stabbings, strangulation …"

"And tsunamis," Adam added.

No one laughed.

"What does that leave?" Anaya asked.

"Suffocation or poisoning?" Sage suggested. "But suffocation seems unlikely given there were no marks on the bodies and no signs of a struggle. That leaves poisoning."

"What about some sort of exotic contagious disease like cholera or malaria?" Anaya asked.

"Or Ebola," Adam added.

"It looks like everyone died suddenly," Sage said, "and all the deaths occurred within a twenty-four-hour period. That looks more like poisoning to me."

"How about we take a break," Adam said. "Let's eat."

Sage shook her head. "How can you be hungry after talking about all of this?"

After consuming a perfunctory dinner of pasta and garlic bread, they spent the next few hours hanging out, playing cards, and chatting. After a while, Sage and Adam cuddled up on the couch while Anaya finished reading *Jurassic Park*.

Just past midnight Anaya decided to turn in. Sage wanted to stay up and chat some more, but Adam agreed with Anaya. "I've got a feeling tomorrow's going to be a long day."

Sage headed to her room, turning around when she got to the door. "Good night," she said softly.

"Sleep tight," Adam replied.

Sage did her best to fall asleep, but her mind was racing. She kept going over everything that had happened during the past two days. Eventually she gave up and slowly opened her bedroom door.

"Adam?" she called in a loud whisper.

"Sage?"

"I can't sleep."

"Me neither."

"Do you mind if I sit out here with you for while?"

"Of course not."

Adam sat up and slid over to one side of the sofa. Before Sage could sit down, there was a loud rumbling outside and the apartment shook.

Adam jumped up. "Another earthquake!"

"I don't think so." Sage walked over to the window and peeped out between the blinds. "I think there's some sort of convoy out on the road."

"But it's two in the morning."

"It looks like army trucks. Come and see."

Adam joined Sage at the window, their shoulders touching lightly.

"It looks like the National Guard," he said. "I see jeeps, armored transports, and a whole bunch of large trucks."

They watched the parade of vehicles in the darkness. Adam slipped his arm around Sage's waist.

"I wonder why there are so many of them," he said.

"It's probably just a precaution."

"A precaution for what?"

"I don't know, but I wouldn't worry about it." Sage yawned. "Let's try to get some rest."

"I definitely won't be able to sleep now."

"Would sleeping in my room help?"

MAY 29

Next morning, Anaya crawled out of bed about seven and shuffled into the kitchen to make coffee. Seeing the couch was empty, she assumed Adam had already left, so she went into Sage's room to see if she wanted to have breakfast.

As soon as Anaya opened the door, Adam sat up in the bed and put his finger to his lips. Sage was out cold, lying face down on the bed, her head partially covered by a pillow. Anaya backed out of the room slowly and quietly closed the door.

After grabbing a bagel and some yogurt, she tried to get some news on her phone but none of the usual web pages would load. She texted two friends in L.A. to see if they'd heard anything about the deaths in Yellowstone, but the texts wouldn't send.

Eventually Adam emerged from Sage's bedroom. "Mornin," he said, yawning.

"Well, good morning to you too!" Anaya said, grinning. "I see you and Sage had a good time last night."

"No, no, it wasn't anything like that. We were both having trouble sleeping and Sage said I could sleep with her ... I mean, she said I could sleep with her in her room ... I mean ..."

"I'm just teasing. Anyway, it's none of my business. By the way, I can't get any cell service and the Wi-Fi is down again." She shook her phone as if that would help somehow. "Can you give it a try?"

Adam retrieved his phone from the coffee table. "Nothing. My phone's never worked here anyway."

Anaya tossed hers on the counter. "I thought the Internet would work here at least some of the time."

"Did you hear all the commotion last night?" Adam asked.

"No. I slept like a rock. What happened?"

"A whole bunch of trucks came rumbling down the road about two in the morning. It looked like the National Guard. You didn't hear them?"

"I didn't hear a thing."

"I want to go check it out. Tell Sage I'll be back in a bit."

"Oh no you don't. You're not going to have all the fun." Sage was pulling on her jeans at her bedroom door. "I'm coming too."

"So am I," Anaya said.

Sage and Adam gulped down some juice and shared a bran muffin, then they all headed out together. The cool morning air was bracing as they made their way toward the center of Old Faithful Village. When they emerged at the end of the path, they all lurched to an abrupt halt—their beloved village had been taken over by an army of National Guard soldiers, at least sixty strong, and had been converted overnight into a quasi-military camp.

The National Guard had set up three large tents and two trailers in the massive parking lot ringed by the Old Faithful Inn, the Old Faithful Snow Lodge, and the Visitor Center. The tents were similar to those found at outdoor weddings, only these were utilitarian beige instead of lustrous white. Enclosed on all four sides, they concealed whatever covert activities were occurring within. A stream of important-looking people flowed in and out of one of the tents. The trailers were without windows, and their single doors were manned by two National Guard soldiers. A generator the size of a minivan sat halfway between the two trailers, and dozens of iridescent orange power cords snaked between the generator and the tents and trailers. Along the far western edge of the village were a dozen olive-colored prefab barrack-type housing units.

On the east side of the parking lot, a gravelly area with bits of grass and a few small trees next to the Snow Lodge was cordoned off with yellow police tape. Dozens of media personnel milled about the enclosure. All the big networks were there—CNN, Fox,

ABC, NBC, and CBS—as well as journalists from many smaller outlets.

Sage saw Penny waving from behind the police tape, stretching her tiny frame as much as she could, and they hustled over to speak with her.

"What are you doing in there?" Sage asked Penny after she'd introduced Anaya.

"The FBI jammed all the media into this oversized pig pen. They said they'll let us out later, but for now we're stuck in here."

"What's that all about?"

"I have no idea."

Sage looked Penny over from head to toe. "You wearing the same thing you had on yesterday?"

"I am." Penny tried unsuccessfully to smooth her rumpled pants.

"Didn't you go home last night?"

"No. I slept in my car."

"How come?"

"I wanted to be here in case something broke overnight and it paid off. When I got up this morning, I heard there were two more bodies."

"Where? When?"

"Don't know. None of us know."

"We're going to go see what we can find out," Sage said. "You hang tight."

"Do I have a choice?"

Sage, Adam, and Anaya proceeded toward the Visitor Center. An exceedingly tall, slender man in dark dress pants and a black windbreaker stopped them as they tried to go in. "Agent Cruz with the FBI. No visitors allowed beyond this point."

"We're not visitors. We're seasonal rangers with the National Park Service," Sage announced.

"You don't look like park rangers to me. Where are your uniforms? Access denied."

They pulled out their DOI ID cards. Agent Cruz grabbed them and disappeared inside without saying a word. When he emerged a few minutes later, he thrust the cards back at them.

"You can enter."

Instead of park rangers and curious visitors, the Visitor Center was filled with FBI agents and National Guard soldiers. While Anaya wandered around the lobby, Sage and Adam went to the Ranger Office where they found Ben Thomas, the Superintendent of Yellowstone National Park, sitting behind a large desk.

Sage knew Superintendent Thomas's story well. After getting his Ph.D. in geology, he had started as a seasonal ranger at Yellowstone and had steadily risen through the ranks of the Park Service over the course of his thirty-year career. After stints at several other National Parks, including Sequoia, Everglades, and Glacier, he finally returned to Yellowstone where he became the first African American to be appointed Superintendent.

"What on earth is going on?" Sage asked angrily.

At six foot six, Superintendent Thomas's bearing was befitting of his senior position, and his massive frame and broad shoulders complemented his booming baritone voice. His round wire-rim spectacles were swallowed by his massive face, which was a peculiar mix of warmth and authority.

"The FBI has set up a command post here in the Visitor Center, and we have to report to FBI Special Agent in Charge Velasquez who's coordinating the investigation," he said. "I don't quite understand all this inter-agency stuff, but I called Washington and they said the FBI is in charge for the time being."

"This isn't what I came to Yellowstone for," Sage complained.

"Me neither, Dr. Maldonado, but we have no choice. I suggest you do what they ask."

Sage was astonished. "How do you know my name?"

"I try to learn all the new rangers' names. Can I call you Sage?"

"Of course."

"I understand you discovered one of the bodies."

"Adam and I found it together." Sage pulled Adam forward.

"I'm sure the FBI will want to talk with both of you."

"Do we have to?" Sage asked.

"Yes ... unless there's some reason not to." Superintendent Thomas leaned forward. "Are you hiding something?"

"Absolutely not, sir."

"That's good."

"So do we report for work?" Adam asked tentatively.

"Normal operations have ceased until further notice. The National Park Service Law Enforcement Rangers will continue to be on duty, and all other essential personnel, including park maintenance, medical staff, and concessionaire food services, will continue to operate. But seasonal rangers and other nonessential personnel will not have to report for work."

"What should we do then?"

"You're free to do what you want—as long as you stay in the Old Faithful area. The FBI will be making an important announcement later today."

"Let's grab something to eat at the Lodge Cafeteria," Adam said.

Sage poked him in the stomach. "You're always hungry. Is that all you ever think about?"

While Adam made a beeline for the front door of the Visitor Center, Sage wandered through the lobby hoping to overhear snippets of interesting conversations. Eventually she made her way to the front door, where she found Anaya and Adam waiting for her, and they all headed to the Lodge Cafeteria.

Just as they reached the lodge, Old Faithful announced it was about to erupt. The wisps of steam rising from deep beneath the surface gave way to bubbling water splashing over the sides of its sinter cone. Sage paused to take it all in. She'd already seen the venerable icon erupt dozens of times during her three weeks at Yellowstone, but it still gave her goose bumps.

Old Faithful wasn't the largest or tallest geyser in the park—that distinction belonged to Steamboat Geyser in the Norris Geyser Basin—but it was one of the most predictable of the large geysers, with an average interval between eruptions of about sixty to one hundred and ten minutes, only slightly longer than when it was first chronicled by the Washburn Expedition in 1870.

Three times over the course of the next ten minutes Old Faithful teased a gathering crowd with increasing amounts of splashing, accompanied by small, playful jets of water, but each time the water receded back into the cone.

Finally the eruption began, and it was magnificent as always, spurting up into the air about a hundred and fifty feet. The wind was blowing briskly from the northwest, and it sent the spray flying almost to Sage's feet.

On a normal early summer morning, a thousand park visitors would gather for each eruption of Old Faithful, overflowing the benches that formed a semicircle around the stately geyser. But this morning there were fewer than a hundred, as many visitors had already left the park, while others stayed in their rooms or campgrounds as instructed. Nonetheless, those in attendance let out a hearty cheer as the eruption grew to its full height. Sage turned to speak to Adam and Anaya, but they were nowhere to be seen. She stayed for the remainder of the show, joining in with the applause when the water and steam finally subsided at the end of the grand display. As the small crowd dispersed, Sage lingered a few more minutes before turning to join her friends in the cafeteria.

Normally the Lodge Cafeteria was jammed during the summer season, but now only a smattering of visitors populated the cavernous dining room. Almost all of them were seated by the large windows facing Old Faithful. After getting her food, Sage joined Adam and Anaya at a table in a corner far away from most of the visitors.

"Did you notice the Superintendent called us nonessential?" Sage said. "I don't know whether to be offended or pleased."

As Sage and Adam dug into their lunch, Anaya pulled two packets of paper out of her backpack.

"What are those?" Sage asked.

"I'm not sure. I grabbed them on the way out."

"On the way out of where?"

"The Visitor Center. There was a large black steel security box sitting on top of the information counter. I'd never seen it before, so I opened it up to see what was inside. There were two stacks of papers, and I took a packet from each stack."

"How on earth did you get away with that?"

"It was pretty easy, actually. All the agents were busy doing who knows what, and I just waited until no one was looking in my direction and went for it. It took about fifteen seconds max. Then I put the packets in my backpack, smiled at the FBI agent behind the counter, and walked out."

"So what are they?"

"Don't know. This first one looks like some sort of classified FBI report."

"We are in soooo much trouble," Adam said. "It's probably some sort of federal crime to be reading these. Maybe even treason."

"Don't be such a baby," Sage teased.

Anaya folded back the cover page and laid the report on the table.

FEDERAL BUREAU OF INVESTIGATION
YELLOWSTONE NATIONAL PARK COMMAND POST
CLASSIFIED REPORT

REPORT NUMBER: YNP.5.28-1

APPROVED BY: Special Agent in Charge Monica Y. Velasquez

TITLE: Backcountry Campsite Incident

SYNOPSIS: Two fatalities occurred at a back-country campsite in Yellowstone National Park. Cause of death unknown at the present time. Autopsies and toxicology reports are pending.

===

INCIDENT LOCATION
Mallard Lake backcountry campsite in Yellowstone National Park.

INCIDENT DATE
May 28

INCIDENT SUMMARY
The FBI Command Post in Yellowstone National Park received information at 18:20 on May 28 that a park ranger had discovered two deceased individuals at the Mallard Lake backcountry campsite. Agents Hyde and MacDonald responded to the scene at 20:05. Upon arrival, they observed a male Caucasian and female Caucasian lying in an oversized sleeping bag. Both bodies had moderate amounts of rigor mortis. The agents estimated their ages to be early to mid-twenties. The female was completely inside the sleeping bag, although the zipper had been pulled

three-quarters of the way down, exposing her torso from the waist up. The male was partially outside the sleeping bag, but still had one leg inside. Neither of the deceased was wearing any clothing. Small amounts of marijuana were found in a plastic bag adjacent to the sleeping bag.

The park ranger at the scene, Susan Rowlands, informed the agents that she was patrolling the Mallard Lake Trail as part of increased surveillance following the recent deaths. At approximately 18:10 she arrived on the scene and found the decedents in the sleeping bag. It appeared that the male decedent had been partially dragged out of the sleeping bag and had bite marks on his head, left shoulder, and left arm. The female decedent had scratches on the right side of her chest. In Ranger Rowlands's opinion, the bite marks and scratches were consistent with a grizzly bear or large black bear. Since both victims were clearly deceased, Ranger Rowlands made no attempt to revive them. She notified her supervisor immediately and stayed with the bodies until the FBI agents arrived.

Agents Hyde and MacDonald called for a coroner to process the scene and transport the bodies for autopsy. The agents entered the decedents' tent and found typical camping supplies. In their opinion, the tent had not been ransacked.

Tentative identifications were made from personal effects found at the scene, but formal identifications are still pending at the time of this report.

On the last page of the report were four photographs of the bodies. Sage, Anaya, and Adam studied the pictures in silence amid the low hum of conversation in the dining hall.

Sage turned the report over. "That's enough for me. Let's look at the other one."

FEDERAL BUREAU OF INVESTIGATION
YELLOWSTONE NATIONAL PARK COMMAND POST
CLASSIFIED REPORT

REPORT NUMBER: YNP.5.28-2

APPROVED BY: Special Agent in Charge Monica Y. Velasquez

TITLE: Preliminary Autopsy Results For Victims A, B, C, & D

SYNOPSIS: This report summarizes the preliminary findings of the autopsies of four bodies discovered in Yellowstone National Park on May 27. The autopsies of Victims A, B, C, and D were conducted on May 28 by medical examiners from Jackson Hole (Victims A and B) and West Yellowstone (Victims C and D). The full autopsy reports are on file at the FBI Command Post in Old Faithful Village, Yellowstone National Park.

===

VICTIM DESCRIPTIONS
- Victim A was a White Female, 17 years old, discovered on the Mystic Falls Trail at 14:40 on May 27 adjacent to Victim B.
- Victim B was a White Male, 18 years old, discovered on the Mystic Falls Trail at 14:40 on May 27 adjacent to Victim A.
- Victim C was a White Female, 16 years old, discovered on the Fairy Falls Trail at 15:30 on May 27.
- Victim D was a Hispanic Female, 16 years old, discovered on the Lone Star Geyser Trail at 18:20 on May 27.

CONDITION OF THE BODIES

All four bodies were initially found lying face down on popular hiking trails in the Upper Geyser Basin area of Yellowstone National Park.

Examinations of the bodies in the field revealed that in three of them (Victims A, B, and D) hypostasis was present on the anterior surfaces of the bodies and had a bright brick-red appearance, which is consistent with the presence of cyanmethemoglobin and excess oxyhemoglobin, both of which can be caused by acute cyanide poisoning. In the other body (Victim C), hypostasis appeared both on anterior and posterior surfaces, indicating that the body had been turned over postmortem.

The general condition of all four bodies was the same. External examinations during the autopsies revealed no gunshot wounds, stab wounds, bruises, or other external trauma on any of the bodies except that two of the bodies (C and D) had scrapes on their elbows and knees, possibly from falling just prior to death. There were no defensive wounds on any of the bodies and no external evidence of strangulation or suffocation. Internal examinations revealed no internal trauma in any of the bodies.

Both medical examiners concluded that the mechanism of death was "internal asphyxia," which meant that the victims' blood was not able to transport oxygen. Because internal tissues in all four bodies were pink or red, the medical examiners believed that the probable cause of death was cyanide poisoning, but they also noted the necessity of waiting for toxicology results for confirmation. Due to the condition of the lungs, brain, and vital organs, they concluded that the doses of cyanide were large enough to cause death within seconds.

Examinations of the stomachs and intestinal tracts were inconclusive with respect to whether cyanide had been ingested, which typically would be in the form of an inorganic cyanide salt such as sodium cyanide or potassium cyanide.

Examinations of the lungs were inconclusive with respect to whether cyanide had been inhaled in the form of hydrogen cyanide gas.

TOXICOLOGY

Blood (heart and peripheral), saliva, nasal secretions, lacrimal fluid, urine, multiple tissue samples (lung, heart, brain, kidney, spleen, stomach contents, and intestine contents), and vaginal and anal swabs have been sent to the FBI Crime Lab in Quantico, Virginia, for toxicology testing. Due to potential National Security concerns, these analyses have been assigned the highest priority and results are expected within 48 hours. Portions of all biological samples have been retained on site at Yellowstone for possible future testing.

CAUSE OF DEATH

The preliminary finding is that the primary cause of death for all four victims was acute cyanide poisoning. The final determination will be made after toxicology analyses have been completed.

Neither of the medical examiners offered any conjectures about possible sources of the cyanide. However, the medical examiner from Jackson Hole who conducted the autopsies on Victims A and B noted that it is highly unlikely that environmental

```
sources of cyanide (e.g., apricot pits,
lima beans, and cassava roots) would
produce cyanide levels sufficient to
result in instantaneous death.
```

TIME OF DEATH
```
Based on the amount of fixed lividity,
the lack of rigor mortis, and temperature
readings taken by medical personnel in the
field, it was estimated that victims A,
B, and C had been dead for approximately
thirty minutes to an hour when discovered.
Due to the amount of rigor mortis present
in Victim D, it was estimated that Victim
D had been dead for approximately three
to four hours when discovered.
```

MANNER OF DEATH
```
Manner of death is presumed to be homicide.
```

"Wow, cyanide poisoning!" Sage exclaimed. "Who would've thought?"

"Seems like we've got ourselves a serial killer," Adam said.

"Maybe," Anaya said. "But did you guys notice the phrase, 'Due to potential National Security concerns' in the toxicology section?"

"Does that mean ... *terrorism*?" Adam asked anxiously.

"The FBI seems to think so."

"I think we ought to get outta here right now!" Adam's panic was palpable.

"And do what?" Sage asked. "Go home and watch all of this unfold on TV? No way. I'm not going anywhere."

Three loud blasts from a siren reverberated throughout the cafeteria, followed by an announcement over the PA system.

```
YOUR ATTENTION PLEASE! AN IMPORTANT
ANNOUNCEMENT WILL BE MADE OVER THE OLD
FAITHFUL EMERGENCY BROADCAST SYSTEM IN
ONE MINUTE. PLEASE GO OUTSIDE IMMEDIATELY.
```

There was a mad rush to exit the cafeteria. Adam, Sage, and Anaya joined a crowd of about a hundred people outside, anxiously turning and looking all around. A second volley of siren blasts emanated from the parking lot behind the Old Faithful Inn, and everyone turned to face the sound.

```
DUE  TO  RECENT  UNUSUAL  ACTIVITY  IN
YELLOWSTONE NATIONAL PARK, THE PARK HAS
BEEN PLACED UNDER TEMPORARY LOCKDOWN BY
ORDER OF THE FBI.

RETURN  TO  YOUR  RESIDENCE,  INN,  LODGE,
CABIN, OR CAMPGROUND IMMEDIATELY. IF YOU
ARE VISITING THE PARK FOR THE DAY, REPORT
TO THE OLD FAITHFUL VISITOR CENTER.

FURTHER INFORMATION WILL BE PROVIDED AT
3 P.M.
```

Even Sage was uneasy now. "So what do we do?"

"We go back to the apartment," Adam said.

"And what if we don't? Will they arrest us?"

"They might. What if they search us and find those secret FBI reports?"

"I'm with Adam," Anaya said. "Let's go back to the apartment."

"Okay, okay," Sage said. "But first I want to see if Penny knows anything about this. You two go on and I'll meet you back there as soon as I can."

"C'mon Adam," Anaya said. "Let's go to the general store and get some supplies in case we're stuck in the apartment for a while."

As Anaya and Adam headed toward the general store on the far side of the Old Faithful Inn, Sage went to the parking lot behind the inn to look for Penny. Even more media representatives were jammed into the cordoned-off enclosure than had been there just an hour earlier. Many of them were shouting and pushing, and a few skirmishes were breaking out. Sage finally spotted Penny, who was almost swallowed by the large throng, and waved to catch her eye. Penny made her way to the front of the crowd.

"Looks like you're having fun," Sage said.

Penny managed a weak smile. "Absolutely. No place I'd rather be."

"So when are they going to—"

Eight large, brightly colored tour buses rumbled by in single file. A few National Guard soldiers were on each bus, but they were empty of other passengers.

"Where are they going?" Sage shouted over the racket.

"I think they're rounding up people in campgrounds and other areas to bring them back here," Penny shouted back.

"Why do they need soldiers on the buses?"

"I heard it was in case violence breaks out. Nobody's going to be happy about the mandatory lockdown."

"What about you? Are you subject to the lockdown?"

"No. In fact, they just told us that all members of the press are being moved to the Jackson Hole Airport in about a half hour. That's what those other buses are for." Penny pointed to two dark gray buses about fifty yards away. "They won't let us take our cars. They won't even let us go back to our cars to get our stuff. All we can take is what we've got with us right now."

"I wish you could stay."

"Me too. I want to get to the bottom of this, and there's no way I can do that from the outside."

Just then a fight broke out between a TV cameraman and a National Guardsman in the far corner of the media enclosure. A half dozen FBI agents and guardsmen rushed over to break it up.

Sage strained to see what was happening, and when she turned back to say goodbye to Penny, she was gone. She scanned the crowd to no avail and reluctantly decided to return to her apartment. After a few steps she felt a quick tap on her shoulder and turned around.

"Penny! How did you—?"

"We reporters are resourceful. Let's get out of here before anyone notices."

* * *

By the time Sage and Penny got back to the apartment, Anaya and Adam had already unloaded their booty from the general store— canned food, pasta, granola bars, bagels, milk, juice, yogurt, five flashlights, and enough batteries to last a year.

"What's with all the flashlights and batteries?" Sage asked.

"You never know," Adam replied.

"Hey, Penny, how'd you get out of that enclosure?" Anaya asked.

"That's a trade secret."

"If it's okay with you two," said Adam. "I'd like to move in here until this is over. You're way more fun than my creepy roommate."

Sage smiled. "I guess that'll be okay."

"Haven't you moved in already?" Anaya said. "You've got half your stuff down here."

"Don't listen to Anaya," Sage said. "It'll be fine."

"Great! I'll run upstairs and get my laptop and some more things." Adam almost sprinted out the door.

"Adam seems awfully anxious to get away from his roommate," Anaya said. "Do you think he knows something about what's going on?"

"Adam or his roommate?"

"Either."

Sage smiled. "Maybe he just wants to spend a little more time with me."

"Who, Adam or his roommate?"

Sage threw a cushion at Anaya but was wide of the mark.

"Sage, have you met Adam's roommate?" Penny asked.

"Only once, a couple of days ago, and he's really weird. He skins dead animals."

"What?"

"He collects dead animals and skins them. That's what Adam says."

"Why would he do that?"

"I have no idea."

"Do you think he could be involved in the killings?"

"How would I know? I certainly hope not since he lives right upstairs."

"I'm curious about something else," Penny said. "What's the deal with you and Adam?"

"There's not much to tell. We just really like each other."

"My reporter's instinct tells me sparks are about to fly."

Anaya smirked. "They already have."

Sage went to grab another cushion but there were none left.

"You know, I'm going to need a place to crash too," Penny said.

"You can stay with us," Sage offered.

"How do we know we can trust you?" Anaya asked, only half-joking.

Penny didn't miss a beat. "How do I know I can trust *you*?"

Anaya laughed. "Well played. So what should we know about you?"

"Let's see. I'm mostly serious but not against having fun once in a while. I like any type of adventure, and I never turn down the opportunity to go exploring. I'm curious by nature, which is probably why I became a reporter." Penny thought for a moment. "And I'm a really heavy sleeper."

"That'll come in handy around here."

Sage shot Anaya a dirty look.

Anaya continued to grill Penny about her job and personal life, asking her more than once about her interest in the killings. Penny assured her it was nothing more than journalistic curiosity. She knew this was going to be a big story, and she wanted to remain in Yellowstone so she could be the one to report it.

"Did I pass?" Penny asked when it appeared Anaya was out of questions.

"You did. Welcome roomie!"

"There is one teeny, tiny problem," Penny said. "I don't have any clothes with me. All I've got is what I'm wearing and a windbreaker in my backpack."

"No worries. Sage and I share stuff all the time. I'm sure we'll manage."

"Thanks, but I'm almost a foot shorter than both of you."

"We'll figure something out," Anaya reassured her.

When Adam returned, he threw his stuff in Sage's bedroom, then opened the windows in the living room so they'd hear the next announcement. But three o'clock came and went in silence.

"Maybe we should go outside to make sure we don't miss anything," Sage suggested.

"I don't think we'd miss an announcement in here," Adam said. "It was loud enough the last time."

Just after four o'clock, two sheets of paper emerged from under the apartment door, gliding silently across the wood floor. Sage grabbed the papers and placed them on the kitchen counter. They all squeezed together as they read the announcement.

THE YELLOWSTONE DIRECTIVE
MAY 29

BY ORDER OF THE DIRECTOR OF THE FBI, YELLOWSTONE NATIONAL PARK HAS BEEN PLACED ON LOCKDOWN EFFECTIVE IMMEDIATELY. THE AREA AFFECTED UNDER THIS ORDER IS BORDERED BY KEPLER CASCADES TO THE SOUTH AND FIREHOLE LAKE DRIVE TO THE NORTH. IT EXTENDS TWO HUNDRED YARDS ON EITHER SIDE OF THE GRAND LOOP ROAD CONNECTING THOSE TWO POINTS AND ALSO INCLUDES THE UPPER GEYSER BASIN AND THE ENTIRE OLD FAITHFUL AREA.

NO ONE MAY LEAVE OR ENTER THE LOCKDOWN AREA FOR ANY REASON.

THE REMAINDER OF THE PARK WILL BE EVACUATED TODAY. EVERYONE WHO IS NOT CURRENTLY IN THE LOCKDOWN AREA MUST LEAVE THE PARK IMMEDIATELY AND MUST BE COMPLETELY OUT OF THE PARK BY 8 P.M.

FOR DETAINEES IN THE LOCKDOWN AREA, THE FOLLOWING RULES AND REGULATIONS ARE EFFECTIVE IMMEDIATELY.

• ALL DETAINEES—INCLUDING PARK VISITORS, PARK EMPLOYEES, OTHER GOVERNMENT EMPLOYEES, CONCESSIONAIRE EMPLOYEES, AND PRIVATE CONTRACTORS—ARE RESTRICTED TO THEIR LODGING OR PLACE OF RESIDENCE UNTIL FURTHER NOTICE.

• DETAINEES WHO ARE CURRENTLY STAYING IN CAMPGROUNDS WITHIN THE LOCKDOWN AREA OR WHO DO NOT HAVE LODGING OR A PLACE OF RESIDENCE WITHIN THE LOCKDOWN AREA MUST REPORT IMMEDIATELY TO THE FBI COMMAND POST IN THE OLD FAITHFUL VISITOR CENTER FOR A HOUSING ASSIGNMENT AND FURTHER INSTRUCTIONS.

- DETAINEES WILL ONLY BE ALLOWED TO LEAVE THEIR PLACE OF RESIDENCE TO EAT OR FOR MEDICAL EMERGENCIES. NO OTHER MOVEMENT WILL BE ALLOWED WITHOUT PERMISSION OF THE FBI.
- ALL PERSONAL ELECTRONICS AND COMMUNICATION DEVICES, INCLUDING, BUT NOT LIMITED TO, LAPTOPS, NOTEBOOKS, SMART PHONES, TABLETS, MUSIC DEVICES, VIDEO DEVICES, GAMING CONSOLES, AND HANDHELD GAMING DEVICES, AS WELL AS ALL ASSOCIATED DEVICES AND ACCESSORIES SUCH AS EARBUDS, HEADPHONES, CHARGING CASES, AND CHARGING CORDS, MUST BE TURNED OVER TO THE FBI. FBI AGENTS WILL COLLECT THESE DEVICES THIS EVENING. ALL ELECTRONIC DEVICES WILL BE LABELED AND HELD IN A SECURE FACILITY UNTIL THE LOCKDOWN IS OVER. AT THAT TIME THEY WILL BE RETURNED TO THEIR OWNERS.
- UPDATES TO THESE RULES AND REGULATIONS WILL BE DISTRIBUTED BEFORE 7 A.M. EACH DAY.

THIS DIRECTIVE WILL REMAIN IN EFFECT UNTIL FURTHER NOTICE. ANY DETAINEE WHO VIOLATES ANY TERMS OF THIS DIRECTIVE WILL BE SUBJECT TO IMMEDIATE DETENTION AND ARREST.

* * *

The seizure of personal electronics in Apartment 1B that evening did not go well.

The FBI agents didn't show up until after ten, and by that time everyone was tired and cranky. The two agents, one male and one female, asked everyone to put their electronics in a pile in the middle of the living room floor. Then they rummaged through every drawer and cabinet in the small apartment. After that, they dealt with the four occupants one by one. Each person had to empty their bags, backpacks, and suitcases onto the floor, and the agents carefully sifted through the clothes and personal belongings looking for any additional electronics.

"I assume you guys have a warrant," Anaya said sharply while they looked through her belongings.

"No, we don't, ma'am. Is that a problem?"

"Well, I just thought that—"

"Why don't you stop thinking and keep your mouth shut so we can get through this as quickly as possible."

"Yes, sir, officer agent, sir!"

With a dramatic wave of his gloved hand, the male agent held up a cell phone. "So what is *this*?" He stared at Anaya. "You thought you could hide this in your cosmetics bag?"

"I don't know *how* that got in there." Anaya didn't bother to hide her sarcastic tone.

"You have any other contraband?"

"My phone is NOT contraband!"

"Thank you for confirming that this *is* your phone," the agent said smugly. "So, I'll ask again—are you hiding anything else?"

"No, sir, officer agent, sir!"

"That's more like it."

When they were done with everyone's belongings, the agents commenced the final phase—individual pat-downs of each resident. The male agent frisked Adam, and the female agent frisked the other three. This was no cursory airport security pat-down. This was a thorough, intimate, tactile inspection from head to toe. Although she didn't have to disrobe, Sage felt naked and exposed throughout the entire experience.

After the agents distributed receipts for the confiscated electronics, they finally left the apartment. Exhausted from the day's events, the residents of 1B put their belongings away and went to bed.

MAY 30

The morning update arrived the same way as the original Yellowstone Directive—on a piece of paper slipped under the apartment door. Other than clarifications about when and where people could move about, there was no additional information about why people were dying, why the FBI had imposed a lockdown, or how long it would last.

"I just want to go home," Adam said.

"I just want to knock somebody for a loop." Anaya swung her fist fiercely through the air.

Adam covered his head and ducked, which elicited a chuckle from Sage.

With no Internet, no phones, no music, and no radio, they were already bored, and it was only nine thirty in the morning.

"I've got to get out of here and find out what's going on," Sage said. "Who wants to come with me?"

"I'm in," Penny said immediately.

"I think I'd rather hang out here," Anaya said. "Will you stay with me, Adam?"

"Sure. You like to play cards?"

"Yeah."

"We'll be back in a while," Sage said. "You two behave yourselves."

Anaya smiled weakly. "We'll do our best."

On their way out of the apartment building, Sage and Penny were met by two young National Guardsmen; they couldn't have been more than twenty-one or twenty-two.

The cuter of the two ordered them to stop. "We need to see your IDs, ladies."

Sage handed him her DOI ID card. The guardsman took a long look and handed it back to Sage.

Then he turned to Penny. "How about you, ma'am? ID please."

"Mine's in my car. We weren't allowed to get our things from our vehicles once the lockdown went into effect."

"Then I'm afraid you'll have to stay inside."

"But we're just going to get something to eat, Officer …"

"Stabler."

"Do you have a first name?"

"Ricky."

Penny smiled. "Ricky, we just want to go to the Lodge Cafeteria to grab a bite to eat. We're starving."

"I guess that'll be okay."

"Thank you, Ricky. You wanna come?"

"I can't. I'm on duty."

"How long have you been out here?"

"All night. We get off at ten."

"You want to join us when you're done?"

"I don't know, ma'am. I've got a lot to do after my shift … paperwork and stuff."

"Well, you know where to find us. Thanks anyway."

Sage and Penny walked off toward Old Faithful Village.

"That was masterful back there," Sage said.

"You never know if he's going to be helpful at some point. Let's try to stay on his good side."

"I'll leave that up to you. Are you hungry?"

"Nope."

"Me neither. Let's go exploring."

"Where?"

"Everywhere. Let's try the Visitor Center first."

The scene in Old Faithful Village was even more frightening than the day before. Several new tents and trailers had joined the burgeoning installation, and a colossal communications tower had sprung up in the middle of it all, festooned with more than a dozen satellite dishes and antennae. Dozens of National Guard soldiers and other officials buzzed about, and two guardsmen were stationed at the entrance of each tent, trailer, and building.

Visible security measures had increased substantially. The police tape that had cordoned off portions of the parking lot the day before had been replaced by concrete barriers and metal barricades. Half a dozen jeeps were lined up near the Visitor Center and an armored personnel carrier was parked at the far end of the ranger station. Security cameras were everywhere; some were fixed while others tracked people's movements as they walked throughout the village.

Sage and Penny avoided eye contact with everyone as they made their way through the encampment toward the Visitor Center. Sage felt a chill run down her back that had nothing to do with the brisk morning air. This wasn't the Yellowstone she had come to know and love over the past three weeks.

When they arrived at the main door to the Visitor Center, they discovered that Penny's ID card ploy didn't work. No matter how hard she tried, she couldn't convince the FBI agent and the two guardsmen to let her in, so she decided to leave Sage to her own devices for a while and meet up with her again an hour later.

"What are you going to do while I'm in the Visitor Center?" Sage asked.

"I'll poke around and see what I can find out—you know, good old-fashioned sleuthing."

Inside the Visitor Center were even more FBI agents. Sage headed straight to the ranger's office without speaking to anyone. The only person in the office was Superintendent Thomas.

"Morning, Sage!" He waved for her to take a seat across the desk from him.

"Good morning, Superintendent."

"I'm glad you're here. I was going to send someone for you, but it seems you've saved me the effort."

"Am I in some sort of trouble, sir?"

"Not at all. On the contrary, I was hoping you'd be willing to work with me during this crisis."

"I'd be honored, sir … but why me?"

"I've examined your personnel file closely—top of your class in high school, college, and graduate school. A Ph.D. from one of the best volcanology programs in the country. A postdoc with the USGS. All very impressive. And you're a scientist like me. I like that. You understand the need to deal in facts instead of conjecture. And from what I understand from your trainer, Kurt Becker, you aren't afraid to speak your mind."

"I'm afraid I don't like Kurt."

"That's exactly what I'm talking about. Nobody likes Kurt, but you're the first seasonal ranger to say that to my face. I need someone who tells it like it is. And there's one more thing."

"What's that, sir?"

"I trust you. I've checked around, and everyone I've talked to has praised your truthfulness and integrity."

Sage wasn't sure what to say. "Thank you for your confidence in me. So, how can I help?"

"I need someone to accompany me to meetings, read reports, help me analyze information—those sorts of things. You can do that, can't you?"

"I'll do my best, sir."

"That's all I ask."

"So why is the FBI holding us in this lockdown? Why don't they just let everyone leave so no one else gets killed?"

Superintendent Thomas stared intently at Sage. "You understand that what I'm about to tell you has to be held in the strictest confidence?"

"Of course, sir."

"They think it's one of us."

"What?"

"The FBI thinks the killer is a Park Service employee."

"But why?"

"I don't know, but I'm going to try to find out."

"What do *you* think, sir?"

"I can't imagine any of our employees would be capable of something so horrible."

"So how many people are dead?"

"Nine that I know of—four discovered on the twenty-seventh and five more on the twenty-eighth. One of the victims was a seasonal ranger."

"I know—Caitlyn Daniels." Sage's voice trembled.

"Were you friends?"

"Sort of. We went through training together a few weeks ago."

"Very sad."

"They're all sad ... I'm sorry, sir. What I meant was ..."

"I know what you meant. They *are* all sad."

"Sir, I've been thinking about the couple in the sleeping bag. Their situation seems a little different to me."

"How do you know about the couple in the sleeping bag? That's classified information. I'm the only one outside the FBI who knows about that."

"I think I heard about it somewhere."

Superintendent Thomas leaned forward in his chair and adjusted his glasses. "I *can* trust you, can't I?"

"Yes, sir. Absolutely."

"So where did you get the information about the couple in the sleeping bag?"

"A friend of mine got it."

"Who?"

Sage swallowed hard. "My roommate. She's a seasonal ranger too."

"Anaya Patel?"

"That's right. Do you know *all* of us, sir?"

"Almost. How did she find out?"

Sage mumbled as she looked down at the table. "She might have taken a classified FBI report when no one was looking."

Superintendent Thomas leaned back, put his enormous hands behind his head, and smiled broadly. "Do you think she could do that sort of thing for us again?"

Sage looked up in surprise. "Maybe. So why are all these people dying?"

"The FBI says cyanide poisoning ... but you already knew that, didn't you?"

"Yes, sir."

"We're going to make a good team, Sage."

"I hope so. I just want to know what's going on."

"As do I." The Superintendent tapped a pencil lightly on the desk.

"Do you know why the FBI took our electronics away, sir?"

"As I understand it, they wanted to block all communications going in or out of Yellowstone."

"It wasn't really a big deal anyway because the Wi-Fi hasn't been working for the last day or so."

"That's not a coincidence. As soon as they got here, the FBI shut down all cellular, Internet, and Wi-Fi services and instituted electronic jamming procedures for good measure."

"So why did they bother taking away our electronics?"

"They told me it provided an extra layer of security to make absolutely certain no one could communicate with the outside world." Superintendent Thomas paused. "But I think there may have been other reasons as well."

"Such as?"

"To prevent anyone—especially the killer—from using electronic devices to hack into the FBI communications network."

"That makes sense."

"Also, I think they used the confiscation process as a pretext to search everyone's belongings."

"What were they looking for?"

"Weapons, drugs, cyanide."

"So that's why they went through every nook and cranny in our apartment. And the pat-downs were incredibly intrusive."

"They patted you down?"

"Yes, and it was *very* invasive."

Superintendent Thomas folded his hands on the desk. "You might find this to be a little paranoid, but I also think they took our electronics away to show us who's in charge."

"As a way of controlling us?"

"Precisely."

Before the Superintendent could say anything else, two FBI agents entered the office without knocking.

"Time for the morning briefing, sir," one of them said. "It's in the usual place, Trailer 2."

"Dr. Maldonado will be coming with me."

"That won't be possible, sir," the agent huffed.

The Superintendent stood up, his six-foot-six frame towering over the young agents. "Oh yes it will!" he thundered. "Dr. Maldonado is the Executive Assistant to the Superintendent and is required to attend all meetings with me."

"Sir, we have to clear this with Special Agent Velasquez."

"Don't bother. I'll call Washington directly myself. What are your full names?"

"Give us a moment please." The agents stepped out of the

room and closed the door behind them. Seconds later, one of them poked his head around the door and indicated that both Superintendent Thomas and Sage were to follow him.

"Thank you for the promotion, sir!" Sage whispered, grinning from ear to ear as they left the room.

"Don't mention it. Are you sure you're up to this?"

"Yes, sir!"

"Please, call me Ben."

Sage grinned. "So, Ben ... does this mean I'll be getting a pay raise?"

"Don't press your luck."

* * *

FBI CLASSIFIED BRIEFING
YELLOWSTONE NATIONAL PARK COMMAND POST
MAY 30 – 10:00 A.M.

Sage and Ben were greeted at the entrance to Trailer 2 by two National Guardsmen holding their rifles diagonally across their chests. The guardsman on the left waved them in; the one on the right held the door open.

Once inside, Sage was amazed at the complete absence of ambient noise. The trailer housed but a single room, with a large maple conference table in the middle surrounded by ten black leather swivel chairs. The overhead lighting was soft and warm, and the room was devoid of windows. At one end was a wall of electronic equipment, including eight large video monitors. All in all, the setup would have been more at home in the Pentagon than in a trailer in the parking lot behind the Old Faithful Inn.

Three men and two women were already at the conference table when Sage and Ben took their seats. Ben was decked out in his superintendent's uniform, and the others were wearing dress pants and dark jackets with "FBI" emblazoned on the front and back in bright yellow letters several inches high. Feeling decidedly underdressed in her jeans and t-shirt, Sage steeled herself for whatever was to come, determined to prove that she belonged at the grown-ups' table.

"It looks like we have a new face today." The woman directly across from Sage spoke in a clear, crisp voice. "State your name."

"Sage Maldonado, seasonal ranger with the National Park Service."

"Who invited you?"

"I did, Special Agent Velasquez," Ben said. "She's my Executive Assistant."

"Who authorized her attendance?" Special Agent Velasquez looked around the room.

"I did," Ben said quickly.

"This is highly unusual, Superintendent."

"This whole situation is highly unusual, ma'am," Sage interjected.

Ben gave Sage a sharp nudge with his elbow.

"Ms. Maldonado, you will not speak in here unless you are spoken to."

"It's *Doctor* Maldonado," Ben declared.

Special Agent Velasquez tilted her head. "*Doctor* Maldonado?"

"Yes, I have a Ph.D. in volcanology from the University of Hawaii."

"Well, *Doctor* Maldonado, do you understand that you will not speak in here unless you are spoken to?"

"Yes, ma'am."

"And do you further understand that these proceedings are classified and completely confidential, which means you are not to discuss them with anyone outside of this room?"

"I do."

"One more thing. You are indeed correct. This *is* very unusual." After a brief pause, Special Agent Velasquez continued. "Let's go through introductions for Dr. Maldonado. I'm Special Agent in Charge Monica Velasquez from the Denver Field Office."

"Special Agent Hank Rosenberg, with the FBI's Critical Incident Response Group, Investigative and Operations Support Section."

"Special Agent Gus Carter, also with the IOSS Section of CIRG."

"Tactical IA Dominick Pagano from the Counter Terrorism Division of the NSB."

"Excuse me?" Sage said tentatively.

Dominick frowned at Sage. "Tactical Intelligence Analyst from the Counterterrorism Division of the National Security Branch of the FBI."

"Public Affairs Specialist Maddie Spurlock from the Denver Field Office."

As members of the FBI's Critical Incident Response Group, Agents Hank Rosenberg and Gus Carter were specially trained to investigate a wide range of crises, with a focus on those involving serial killers, mass murderers, and terrorists, while Intelligence Analyst Dominick Pagano was an expert in all things security related. Public Affairs Specialist Maddie Spurlock had been brought in to control the flow of information into and out of Yellowstone and to deal with all forms of media communications. The group at the table led a contingent of twenty-two FBI agents, investigators, analysts, and specialists who had been dispatched to Yellowstone to investigate the mysterious deaths.

"Those are awfully long titles," Sage said with a bit more confidence. "How should I address each of you?"

"Out here in the field we're a bit less formal," Maddie responded with a smile. "First names will be fine."

"Except for Special Agent in Charge Velasquez," Gus added. "She insists on using titles for everyone."

"Just following Bureau protocol," Special Agent Velasquez said stiffly. "But for simplicity's sake, I've shortened everyone's titles to Agent, Analyst, or Specialist. And you can just address me as Special Agent. The *in Charge* designation is implied."

Monica Velasquez was an army brat growing up. When she was a toddler, her mom and dad divorced because her mom decided that the army life was not for her. From then on, it was just Monica and her dad, and he took her on all his tours around the world. When her father retired from the army, they settled in the D.C. area. After Monica graduated from Georgetown, she joined the FBI, where she had been for the past twenty-two years, rising steadily through the ranks.

Her angular face, framed by jet-black hair that fell just short of her shoulders, seemed well suited for the FBI, and her rigid bearing was buttressed by an air of confidence honed from years of commanding challenging FBI investigations. She was clearly in her element when conducting official FBI meetings.

Special Agent Velasquez opened a black binder bedecked with the FBI seal on its cover. "All right then, let's get down to business. We'll start with an update on the firearm policy. Given that most of the buildings here in Yellowstone do not have secure lockers or other secure storage areas, all agents will be required to keep their firearms on their persons at all times, even indoors. I'll inform you should there be any changes to this policy. Any questions?"

"What about when we take a shower?" Gus asked with a smirk.

"I'll leave that to your discretion, Agent Carter. Does anyone have any *serious* questions?"

Since there were none, Special Agent Velasquez continued. "I've received multiple requests from Homeland Security to be involved in our operations here. Based on my previous experience with field operations like this one, I've decided that we only need the FBI, National Guard, and National Park Service Rangers on site for the time being. We can consult electronically with Homeland Security at any time and bring them on board in the future if need be. All personnel here in Yellowstone will report directly to me—the FBI, the National Guard, even the National Park Service, including Superintendent Thomas. Is that clear?"

Everyone nodded silently.

"Agent Carter, give us an updated body count."

"Eleven total, including two discovered last night."

"Where were the last two?"

"One was just off a spur trail near Biscuit Basin and the other was adjacent to Daisy Geyser. They were discovered by National Guardsmen as they were securing trails within the lockdown area."

"How long had they been there? Did they die before or after the lockdown had gone into effect?"

"Don't know yet. We're waiting on the autopsies."

"When will those be completed?"

"Sometime today."

"Send me those reports as soon as you get them."

"Yes, ma'am."

"Agent Rosenberg, how are the witness interviews going?"

Sage thought that, with his gentle round face, large expressive brown eyes, and broad thin smile, Hank Rosenberg looked more like a genial high school English teacher than a career FBI agent. His round cheeks creased deeply when he smiled, and Sage noticed that he played with his watch as he spoke.

"We've finished interviewing the families and friends of

Victims A through I, and we've just started interviewing people associated with Victims J and K."

"What do you know so far?"

"Nine of the eleven victims were female and all were under the age of twenty-seven. There are plenty of older folks in the park, so it's highly unlikely that the young age of the victims is a coincidence. We've no idea why the killer would be targeting young people, since none of the victims were sexually assaulted and there's no evidence of any sex crimes. Other than the three girls who were part of a church group from Boise, there's nothing connecting the other victims to each other."

"Any witnesses to the killings?"

"None that we know of. And since all the deaths occurred far away from any buildings, there is no security camera footage of any of them."

"Maybe it's time to set up additional surveillance cameras."

"We're on it," interjected Dominick, who was sitting next to Gus. The contrast between the two men was almost comical. Gus Carter was squat, bordering on pudgy, with a round head that was as naked as could be—not a single hair anywhere. The ceiling lights reflected off his shiny pate, giving it a luminous sheen. In contrast, Dominick Pagano's elongated head, which sat atop his tall, reedy frame, seemed to have enough hair for two people, and his bushy eyebrows wiggled when he spoke.

"Analyst Pagano, where are the new cameras?" Special Agent Velasquez asked.

"We've been installing small video cameras in close proximity to where the eleven bodies were found, and we're monitoring those video feeds 24/7 because killers often go back to the scene of their crimes."

"Have you installed cameras in any other locations?"

"We've more than doubled the number of surveillance cameras in Old Faithful Village, both inside the buildings and around the grounds. We've got about ninety percent coverage now and should be at full coverage by tomorrow afternoon. All the video cameras are connected to our central command center, which has advanced facial recognition capabilities."

"Excellent." Special Agent Velasquez reached back to a small table directly behind her and retrieved a large brown accordion folder. She pulled out a sizable stack of papers from the folder and dropped the stack on the conference table with a resounding thud. "These are the preliminary toxicology reports for Victims A through D. I just received them via secure transmission from Quantico about thirty minutes ago. Take a copy as they come around."

When the stack got to Sage, she took one and passed the rest to Ben.

"Dr. Maldonado!" boomed Special Agent Velasquez. "This is a classified report. Put that back immediately."

Sage started to put the report back, but Ben grabbed her hand. "Sage must have access to everything I do."

Special Agent Velasquez narrowed her eyes and glared at Sage. "Dr. Maldonado, do you know what the punishment is for revealing the contents of a classified document?"

"No, ma'am, and I don't want to find out."

"Good. I'm glad we understand each other." Special Agent Velasquez glanced around the table. "Does everyone have the reports now? Take a few moments to read them."

The four reports were extremely technical and hard to understand, even for a scientist like Sage. After an introductory cautionary note that assessing levels of cyanide in postmortem biological samples is fraught with uncertainty due to numerous factors such as the ambient temperature of the body and the amount of decomposition that had occurred prior to autopsy, the reports explained how the FBI crime lab had quantified the amount of cyanide in the blood and tissue samples of the victims. Although Sage got lost in the details, one thing was clear from all four reports—there were massive levels of cyanide in the blood samples, as well as in many of the vital organs, especially the livers and spleens. The concentrations of cyanide in the blood ranged from 27 mg/l to 51 mg/l, all well above the fatal level of 3 mg/l.

Once everyone had finished reading, Special Agent Velasquez continued. "As you can see, the crime lab detected extremely high levels of cyanide in the blood of the first four victims, and we should have the results from Victims E through I soon. I know these delays can be frustrating, so to streamline the testing procedures we're setting up a field lab here in Yellowstone that will enable us to test samples within hours of collection. It will be staffed by specialists from the FBI's Hazardous Evidence Response Team and should be operational later today. In the meantime, let's focus on finding the perpetrator."

"We're working on that," Hank said. "As soon as the interviews with the family and friends of the last two victims have been completed, we're going to begin interviewing the rest of the detainees to look for possible suspects, accomplices, and persons of interest. It'll probably take us two or three days to interview everyone still in Yellowstone. As we conduct the interviews, we'll also collect fingerprints and facial scans."

"Why both?" Ben asked.

"The fingerprints will be used to conduct criminal background checks, and the facial scans will be stored in our on-site security system."

"For what purpose?"

Dominick stepped in. "To control ingress and egress for all buildings and to monitor detainees' whereabouts in the lockdown area."

Sage erupted. "You're going to spy on us?"

"I wouldn't call it that."

"Well, I would!"

Special Agent Velasquez pointed a finger at Sage. "That's enough, Dr. Maldonado!"

I see what Ben was talking about, Sage thought. *They really do think it's one of us.*

Special Agent Velasquez continued. "Now would be a good time to talk about the overall security situation. Can you give us an update, Analyst Pagano?"

"We've already established a secure perimeter around the park, and we have three dozen National Guard soldiers patrolling all known access points, including public and private roads and all marked trails. We have another fifty guardsmen patrolling within the lockdown area. We can increase these staffing levels if the situation warrants. In addition, all five entrances to Yellowstone have been closed and barricaded, and National Guard soldiers have been posted at each entrance. We've put up notices at the entrances and on the National Park Service website to inform the public that Yellowstone is closed due to an ongoing FBI investigation, and we've included a redacted version of the Yellowstone Directive."

"Specialist Spurlock, how are we handling requests from the press?" Special Agent Velasquez asked.

"At the moment, we're referring them to the redacted version of the Yellowstone Directive on the website and telling them that further information will be forthcoming," Maddie Spurlock replied. She tended to mumble, which made it hard for others to make out what she was saying, and she avoided direct eye contact much of the time. Her unkempt ash brown hair, slouched shoulders, and ruffled clothes seemed out of place for an FBI communications specialist.

Sage couldn't contain herself. "But as soon as word gets out that the park is closed, hundreds of journalists will descend on Yellowstone. And what about the families of all the people being held in lockdown? They'll want to know what's happening to their loved ones."

"What do you suggest we do?" Special Agent Velasquez asked.

"I'm a big fan of telling the truth," Sage said.

Special Agent Velasquez glared at Sage. "I was speaking to Specialist Spurlock."

Before Maddie could respond, Gus jumped in. "I think we should provide as little information as possible to the public."

"But that's just going to make the public and the press even more curious about what's going on," Sage said. "They'll demand answers."

The room fell silent while Special Agent Velasquez clicked her pen in and out.

"I think we need to get ahead of this," she said at last. She turned to Maddie, seated immediately to her right, and they had a brief whispered exchange. "Specialist Spurlock will issue internal Daily Updates to be distributed to the detainees here in Yellowstone as well as daily press releases for the media. She will also hold periodic in-person press briefings."

"Since this is happening under my watch, I demand to be present at the press briefings," Ben insisted.

"That won't be necessary," Special Agent Velasquez said. "Let me remind you that the FBI is in charge of this investigation."

"Let me remind *you* that I am still in charge of Yellowstone National Park."

"Your point is duly noted, but your request is denied."

"Can I at least have some input as to what's in the press releases?"

"That's fine with me," Maddie replied weakly. "I can use all the help I can get."

"But *I* will have the final say concerning the content of the press releases and the information provided during any press briefings," Special Agent Velasquez added.

"Where will the briefings be held?" Ben asked. "How about in the Old Faithful Visitor Center?"

"We can't allow people to go in and out of Yellowstone while the lockdown is in effect, so the briefings will have to be held at one of the park entrances. I suggest the South Entrance, since it's closest to Old Faithful. I'll order the National Guard to erect a large media tent there with full AV capabilities."

"And what about notification of the next of kin of the victims?"

"In order to ensure the integrity of our investigation, we'll continue to withhold all information about the victims for the time being. We won't release their identities or any details about their deaths to the press, and we won't notify their families. The autopsies are being conducted in a temporary morgue on the edge of the village, and the bodies will be kept there in case we need to conduct additional forensic examinations on them. Since we won't be releasing the bodies any time soon, there's really no need to notify the next of kin at this point."

"But many park visitors left Yellowstone after people started dying," Sage said. "Surely some of the victims' names will leak out to the public soon, if they haven't already."

Special Agent Velasquez didn't budge. "Specialist Spurlock, let's hold off on identifying the deceased for now, either to the press or to the next of kin. We can buy some time with the explanation that we're dealing with a large crime scene and positive identifications may take a while."

Sage wasn't satisfied. "But when *will* you notify the next of kin?"

"Only when we have to," Special Agent Velasquez responded.

"I have a few more questions."

Special Agent Velasquez sighed. "Why am I not surprised, Dr. Maldonado?"

"Why are you calling everyone in Yellowstone *detainees*?"

"Because that's what they are. We strive to be accurate and factual at the Bureau at all times."

"But it's so impersonal."

"That's the point. Do you have any more questions?"

"You've talked about press releases and press briefings for the outside world, but what are you going to tell the hundreds of people who are being held here against their will?"

"Nothing more than what we've already said."

"But you've got to tell them *something*. About why people are dying. About why they can't leave."

"I agree with Sage," Ben said.

Special Agent Velasquez took a deep breath. "What do you suggest, Dr. Maldonado?"

"I hate to sound like a broken record, but I'm in favor of telling the truth."

"But we don't even know what the truth is. And if we divulge too much information it might compromise our investigation and make it harder to catch the killer. Any other questions, Dr. Maldonado?"

"Yes, but I don't think it'll do any good to ask them."

"Well, that's something you and I can agree on. We're adjourned until four this afternoon."

* * *

Sage got back to the apartment just before noon. Penny rushed up to her as soon as she came through the door.

"Where were you? We were supposed to meet after an hour. What happened? Are you okay?"

Sage flopped down on the couch. "You won't believe the morning I had."

"We're all ears," Anaya said.

"The funny thing is, I can't tell you."

"Why not?"

"I've been sworn to secrecy."

"By who?"

"The FBI."

Anaya scowled. "You're on the other side now?"

"No, no. It's nothing like that. I just went to an FBI briefing with Superintendent Thomas."

"Where? ... This morning?"

"I've already probably said too much."

A sheet of paper came flying under the door. Sage grabbed it, placed it on the kitchen counter and tapped it twice. "This should explain everything."

THE YELLOWSTONE DIRECTIVE
SUPPLEMENTAL UPDATE
MAY 30

THIS UPDATE IS BEING PROVIDED AS A JOINT COMMUNICATION FROM THE FBI AND THE NATIONAL PARK SERVICE.

OVER THE PAST THREE DAYS, ELEVEN PEOPLE HAVE DIED IN YELLOWSTONE NATIONAL PARK. THE FBI HAS BEEN WORKING TO DETERMINE HOW AND WHY THESE PEOPLE DIED AND WHO IS RESPONSIBLE. PRELIMINARY REPORTS INDICATE THAT AT LEAST SOME OF THE VICTIMS DIED OF CYANIDE POISONING.

THE FBI IS IN THE PROCESS OF INTERVIEWING ALL DETAINEES IN THE LOCKDOWN AREA. THESE INTERVIEWS WILL CONTINUE OVER THE NEXT TWO OR THREE DAYS AND WILL INCLUDE PERSONAL QUESTIONS. IT IS IMPERATIVE THAT ALL DETAINEES ANSWER ALL QUESTIONS TRUTHFULLY.

DURING THE COURSE OF THESE INTERVIEWS, THE FBI WILL COLLECT FINGERPRINT EXEMPLARS AND FACIAL SCANS FROM ALL DETAINEES. ALL DETAINEES MUST COOPERATE WITH THE FINGERPRINTING AND FACIAL SCANNING PROCESS.

ANY DETAINEE WHO OBSERVES ANOTHER DETAINEE ACTING SUSPICIOUSLY MUST NOTIFY AN FBI AGENT OR NATIONAL GUARDSMAN IMMEDIATELY. ALSO, ALL DETAINEES MUST NOTIFY AN FBI AGENT IF THEY HAVE ANY INFORMATION THAT MIGHT BE RELEVANT TO THE ONGOING INVESTIGATION.

THE ORIGINAL YELLOWSTONE DIRECTIVE, AS MODIFIED AND CLARIFIED BY ALL SUBSEQUENT UPDATES, INCLUDING THIS ONE, REMAINS IN FULL FORCE. AT PRESENT, THERE IS NO ESTIMATE AS TO HOW LONG THE YELLOWSTONE DIRECTIVE WILL REMAIN IN EFFECT.

ANY DETAINEE WHO VIOLATES ANY TERMS OF THE YELLOWSTONE DIRECTIVE WILL BE SUBJECT TO IMMEDIATE ARREST.

FURTHER UPDATES WILL BE PROVIDED EVERY MORNING AS WELL AS AT OTHER TIMES, AS WARRANTED BY FUTURE DEVELOPMENTS.

Over the next half hour, Adam, Penny, and Anaya peppered Sage with questions about the confidential briefing. True to her promise to Special Agent Velasquez, she told them nothing more than what was already in the Supplemental Update.

Eventually Sage changed the subject. "So what did you all do this morning?"

"Not much," Anaya said. "Adam and I played some rummy, but most of the time we just hung out here and read. Actually, it was kind of nice."

"How about you, Penny?"

"Other than worrying about you? I did a little more investigating and then came back here after I couldn't find you."

After lunch, they chatted about their predicament and speculated wildly about what lay ahead. At 3:30, Sage announced that she had to go.

"Where to? Can I come?" Adam asked.

"Nope, 'fraid not. I'm going to the afternoon briefing."

"There's another one?"

"Yep, there are two every day."

"When will you be back?"

"When the meeting's over."

Sage changed out of her t-shirt and into a standard ranger shirt, kissed Adam on the cheek, and hurried out the door.

* * *

FBI Classified Briefing
Yellowstone National Park Command Post
May 30 – 4:00 p.m.

Special Agent Velasquez called the afternoon briefing to order. "As you can see, we have a new addition to our team. Dr. Arnold, please introduce yourself."

A thin, white-haired man north of sixty spoke with a slightly raspy voice. "My name is Walter Arnold. I have a Ph.D. in forensic psychology, and my specialty is criminal profiling. I'll be creating a psychological profile of the killer. In order to do this I'll need to examine the cause and manner of the eleven deaths, look at where each victim died, and delve into the personal histories of all the victims."

"Welcome, Dr. Arnold. I'm sure everyone will give you their full cooperation."

"Thank you. I'm counting on it."

"Let's begin with Analyst Pagano's report."

"Over the past twenty-four hours there have been two breaches of the park perimeter, both by members of the media. One of the breaches involved a reporter and a cameraman from a Jackson Hole newspaper who were hiking in from the South Entrance. They were apprehended within two miles of the entrance, questioned, and released. The other breach involved a helicopter that landed near Madison, about sixteen miles north of here. In addition to the pilot, there were two reporters and a camerawoman from CNN on board. All four individuals were detained, and the helicopter was impounded."

Special Agent Velasquez grimaced.

Dominick continued. "There's more. This morning we caught three individuals trying to leave the park. A couple in their twenties was apprehended heading south on a hiking trail near Grant Village and a man in his fifties was discovered jogging along the road toward Madison. All three are still in custody and their interrogations are ongoing."

"Interrogations?" Sage asked.

"We still don't know what's going on here, and we can't be too careful," Dominick replied.

Special Agent Velasquez was clearly upset. "These breaches are unacceptable!"

"We've already taken measures to beef up our security," Dominick said. "We've requested additional National Guard soldiers to patrol the park perimeter, and we've brought in three UH-60V Black Hawks from our Tactical Aviation Unit to conduct round-the-clock aerial surveillance of the perimeter, as well as focused aerial surveillance of the lockdown area here in Old Faithful Village."

"Will that be enough to prevent security breaches in the future?"

"It should be."

Special Agent Velasquez glared at Dominick. "It better be."

"I have a report too," Maddie offered softly.

"Go ahead." Special Agent Velasquez was still eyeing Dominick.

"Just after lunch, I issued a brief press release explaining that a lockdown had been instituted in Yellowstone National Park because eleven people had died over the past few days. The release stated that the FBI was working around the clock to identify the person or persons responsible for the deaths and that Yellowstone would remain closed until further notice. Within moments of the release hitting the wires, I received dozens of requests from major news outlets asking for more information."

"What did you tell them?" Ben asked.

"Nothing yet. I've discussed this with Special Agent Velasquez, and we've decided I will hold a press briefing at nine o'clock tomorrow morning at the South Entrance."

"I want to renew my request to be present at the briefing," Ben said. "I have a right to be there."

"Denied," Special Agent Velasquez said firmly. "Agent Rosenberg, has the fingerprinting and facial scanning begun?"

"Yes, we're doing those as we interview everyone in the park."

"And?"

"It's coming along, but the process is very time-consuming."

"Any possible suspects yet?"

"Not yet."

"Your report, Agent Carter?"

"I've received the preliminary toxicology reports for Victims E through I, and the results were the same as for the first four victims. Massive doses of cyanide killed them all. In each case, the levels of cyanide were high enough to be lethal within a matter of seconds."

"It'll be better when we can do these analyses right here in Yellowstone. Has the FBI field crime lab been set up yet?"

"Yes," Gus replied. "We're in a nondescript trailer marked Government Supplies at the back of the parking lot. We'll begin conducting toxicology tests and other forensic analyses later today or first thing tomorrow."

"Excellent. Anything else?"

"The autopsies have been completed for Victims J and K. Both appear to have died from cyanide poisoning like the others, but we need to wait for the toxicology analyses for confirmation."

"Do we have a time of death for those two?

"Yes. The estimated time of death was between seven and nine a.m. on May 29 for Victim J and the between eight and ten a.m. on the same day for Victim K."

"So both of these deaths occurred before the Yellowstone Directive went into effect later that day?"

"That's correct. There have been no new deaths since then, which suggests that the lockdown appears to be working."

"That's one bit of good news," Special Agent Velasquez said. "What might that tell us about the killer?"

"That he left Yellowstone before the lockdown went into effect," Gus suggested.

"Or that he's still here but stuck in his room," Dominick said.

"But maybe the killer is a *she*," Sage countered.

Gus glared at Sage. "Excuse me?"

Sage stood her ground. "How do we know the killer is a he? Maybe it's a she."

"Statistics tell us that over ninety percent of serial killers are male," Walter stated.

Special Agent Velasquez pounded her fist on the table. "I don't give a damn about statistics! I just want to find this killer before he, she, or it kills again."

Sage elevated slightly in her chair. "Special Agent Velasquez may be on to something. Maybe the killer isn't a she *or* a he. Maybe it's not a person at all."

"What do you mean?" Gus asked.

"I'm not sure. I just think we should consider all possibilities."

"So how many murder investigations have *you* been involved in?" Gus asked gruffly.

"This would be my first."

"That's what I thought. Well, this is not *my* first. It's probably my hundredth. I recommend you listen to those of us who know what we're doing."

"Are you suggesting that I don't know what I'm doing?" Sage's voice grew louder.

"I'm not just suggesting it ..."

"That will be enough, Agent Carter," Special Agent Velasquez said. "We'll take your suggestion under consideration, Dr. Maldonado." She looked around the room, making eye contact with everyone. "Anyone else have any ideas about why the killings have stopped?"

Dominick spoke up. "Maybe they haven't stopped completely. Maybe they've just paused."

"Go on."

"I believe we're dealing with a new type of terrorist."

"Terrorism?" Gus slowly rubbed the top of his bare head as if searching for long-lost remnants of hair. "This looks like the work of a serial killer to me. Young victims, almost all women or girls, hiking by themselves out of sight of other people."

"Indeed, it *does* look like a serial killer. But I think this serial killer is a terrorist."

"You mean ISIS?"

"Maybe, maybe not. He could be an international terrorist or he could be homegrown. He might be part of a local cell or even a lone wolf."

"But terrorists usually kill as many people as possible in very public settings," Gus said. "Detonating suicide vests in crowded markets. Driving trucks onto packed sidewalks. Setting off bombs in subway stations. Flying planes into buildings. Those sorts of things."

"That's what most people think of when they hear the word *terrorist*, but I think we might be dealing with a new M.O. here, one designed to instill fear in ordinary Americans. This new form of terrorism could employ a readily available poison such as cyanide to kill random individuals one at a time. What better place to carry out such a horrific scheme than at Yellowstone National Park, an iconic American landmark? There's very little security here, virtually no electronic surveillance, and hundreds of miles of isolated hiking trails. This is the softest of soft targets."

"Agent Rosenberg, has there been any progress in identifying how the cyanide was administered?" Special Agent Velasquez asked.

"Not yet. Cyanide can occur in many different compounds. Some of these are inorganic salts, such as potassium cyanide and sodium cyanide, which can be mixed into food or dissolved in water. Another form is hydrogen cyanide, which can exist in a liquid or gaseous state. In any of these forms, sufficient doses of cyanide can be fatal immediately. Because the autopsy reports of the victims were inconclusive as to whether the cyanide was inhaled or ingested, we don't know which type of cyanide to look for."

"Well, report back to me if you learn anything new." Special Agent Velasquez closed the folder in front of her. "I have one other announcement before we adjourn. The Centers for Disease Control and Prevention is sending some high-level personnel to assist with our investigation."

Gus groaned. "Why is the CDC coming? This isn't a disease we're talking about. This is homicide by poisoning."

"You know as well as I do that the CDC usually gets involved in any type of public health threat. They have some of the best scientists in the country. This order came from the top, the very top, so we must do our best to play nicely with them."

* * *

Just after dinner that evening, the same FBI agents who had confiscated the electronics the day before arrived to interview the residents of Apartment 1B. They ordered everyone to wait out in the living room while they set up shop in Sage's bedroom. After ten minutes, they called Sage in and asked her to shut the door.

Sage sat in the small wooden chair while the female agent perched on the edge of the bed, a laptop open across her knees. The male agent, who remained standing, did all the talking.

"Name?"

"Sage Maldonado."

"Full name, please."

"That's it. Sage Maldonado."

"No middle name?"

"No."

After beginning with routine questions about her date of birth, hometown, education, and current occupation, the agent moved on to more sensitive territory.

"Have you even been arrested?"

"Once."

"What for?"

"Trespassing on the beach."

"What happened?"

"It was when I was in high school. My boyfriend and I were making out on the beach after dark and the cops gave us a citation. I went to court with my dad, and I think we had to pay a hundred-dollar fine."

"Any other arrests?"

"No."

"Have you ever owned any firearms?"

"No."

"Used any illegal drugs?"

"No."

"Have you ever belonged to any groups that advocate the overthrow of the United Sates government?"

Sage chuckled. "Of course not."

The male agent glowered. "You find this whole thing funny?"

"Not at all."

Then the interview gradually morphed into an interrogation. Had Sage known any of the victims? Could she account for her whereabouts during the three days in which the bodies were found? Had she heard anything about who might be responsible for the deaths? Though she had nothing to hide, the questions made her feel surprisingly nervous and she certainly didn't laugh.

When the male agent had completed his list of questions, he turned to his colleague. "All yours, Agent Stringer."

Agent Stringer moved to the small desk where she had set up two biometric scanners—one for fingerprints and the other for faces. After processing all ten fingers in under two minutes, she instructed Sage to look at the gleaming metallic-blue face scanner. Sage dutifully followed the verbal prompts issued by the device, looking up, down, and to both sides.

When she finally left her bedroom, her face was flushed and her palms sweaty.

"That doesn't look like it was much fun," Penny said.

"It wasn't."

Adam was next, then Penny, and finally Anaya.

Anaya's interview took twice as long as the others, and several angry exchanges could be heard out in the living room. Suddenly, the bedroom door flew open. Anaya stormed out and stomped into her own room, slamming the door behind her.

Sage, Penny, and Adam stayed where they were, waiting for the FBI agents to exit Sage's bedroom. When the agents finally appeared, Sage leaped to her feet.

"Is Anaya okay? What happened in there?"

"Ms. Patel is fine," the male agent said. "She refused to cooperate, and we told her she had no choice."

"But we *do* have a choice," Sage insisted.

"Not really."

"Of course we do! None of us have committed any crimes."

The agent paused before responding. "That's for us to determine. Everyone is a possible suspect at this point."

"Then we're all entitled to lawyers. Right?" Sage was almost shouting now.

"I don't know about that, Dr. Maldonado."

"Well, I do. The Constitution of the United States guarantees that each of us is entitled to speak with a lawyer. It's in one of the Amendments—the Fourth or the Sixth. I can't remember which one, but I know it's there. I demand that you appoint a lawyer right now for Ms. Patel—and for the rest of us as well."

"That's not possible."

"Well, then, you better get out of here immediately, or I'll notify Special Agent Velasquez that you should be arrested for trespassing."

"But we didn't get Ms. Patel's fingerprints or facial scan."

"You have a warrant for those?"

"No."

"Then leave immediately!"

"We'll have to come back to finish with Ms. Patel."

"Next time you better have a warrant."

Adam and Penny rose and stood next to Sage as the two agents made their way out of the apartment. When the door closed behind them, Sage exhaled loudly and fell back onto the couch.

Anaya slowly opened her bedroom door and peeked out. "Are they gone?"

"Yes," Sage said.

Anaya came over and gave Sage a big hug. "I heard every word. Thanks for having my back!"

"So what happened in there?"

"Not much. They wanted to print me and ask me lots of questions. I refused."

"How come? You don't have anything to hide do you?"

"Of course not! Don't you trust me?"

Sage blushed. "Of course I do. So why not just cooperate?"

Anaya explained that her father was a graduate student in the United States. When he returned to his family in India after finishing his studies, he told them that he'd been harassed in the U.S. by the police on numerous occasions because he was a foreigner. From that point on, he didn't trust the police or any other American authorities.

"And so I don't trust them either—the police, the FBI, anyone in law enforcement. In fact, every time I go through customs I get really nervous 'cause I'm afraid they might detain me or something."

"I didn't know," Sage said. "I'm sorry I doubted you."

"There was another reason I didn't cooperate with them."

"Which was?"

"I can be pretty difficult sometimes."

Sage smiled. "I hadn't noticed."

MAY 31

FBI Classified Briefing
Yellowstone National Park Command Post
May 31 – 10:00 a.m.

When Sage arrived at the morning briefing, she couldn't wait to complain about the way she and her friends had been treated the night before. But she soon found out there was much bigger news.

"Let's get right to it," Special Agent Velasquez said. "Tell us about the suspect, Agent Rosenberg."

"Early this morning, we determined, based on a fingerprint match, that we have a registered sex offender here in lockdown. His name is Ralph Battle, a thirty-four-year-old male from Tacoma, Washington. He was convicted of sexual assault seven years ago and served four years in state prison. We don't know the exact nature of his previous crime—we're still trying to pull those records. At five a.m. we went to Mr. Battle's room in the Old Faithful Inn and detained him. Two of our best investigators were dispatched to interrogate him. Unfortunately, he asked to speak with a lawyer right away so we had to terminate the questioning.

"We've asked the local bar association in Jackson Hole to provide an attorney for Mr. Battle. My understanding is that she'll be here by noon. In the meantime, we obtained a warrant and searched his room and his rental car. Everything we've recovered is being inventoried and analyzed. So far, there's no evidence of cyanide, other poisons, or weapons, but we're still looking."

"Anything else?" Special Agent Velasquez asked.

"Yes, there is one promising piece of evidence. We found an image of the victim from the Fairy Falls Trail on his camera. She's in a photograph he took of Fairy Falls on the same day she died."

"I thought that trail was closed to the public due to bear activity," Sage said. "Doesn't *anyone* adhere to these warnings?"

"I'm afraid not," Ben said.

"Was she the only one in the picture?" Sage asked.

"Yes."

"Are you sure he was taking a picture of her and not of the falls?"

"It's hard to say," Hank conceded, rolling his watch around his wrist. "The falls were in the center of the frame and the victim was off to the side."

"So maybe he wasn't actually taking a picture of her."

"But it does show he encountered her on the day she died."

"That doesn't mean he killed her. I was on that trail that day too, and I didn't kill her."

Gus opened his mouth to speak, but Sage stared him down. "Don't even think about it!"

Walter pushed his glasses up the bridge of his long nose. "Mr. Battle does fit the typical profile of a serial killer—white male with a previous conviction for sexual assault. Although there's no evidence he's killed before, something might have caused him to snap this time."

"Such as?" Sage asked.

"Could have been anything. Social rejection, substance abuse, a psychotic break. Those sorts of things."

"Is he traveling by himself?" Special Agent Velasquez asked.

"We believe he is, but we're still checking on that," Hank replied.

Ben butted in. "I'm confused. I thought none of the eleven victims were sexually assaulted."

"They weren't," Hank said. "But nine of them were young females, and the males were companions of two of the females. That suggests that a sex crime is a possibility."

"I don't mean to belabor the point, but if there's no evidence of any sexual assaults why do you keep coming back to this serial sex offender theory?"

Walter ran a hand through his shock of white hair. "Maybe this guy gets his kicks by killing young girls. It may be part of a fantasy or fetish in which he equates the act of killing with a sexual act. It's called erotophonophilia, more commonly known as lust murder. For him, murder is much safer than sexual assault because there's no one left to testify against him."

"It still doesn't make sense to me," Ben continued. "Do you have any concrete evidence tying him to any of these deaths?"

"Other than the one photo, not yet," Hank said.

"Well, don't you think it's a mistake to put all your eggs in this one basket?"

"I'm afraid it's the only basket we've got right now."

"Well, maybe you should start looking for other baskets."

That was the opening Dominick had been waiting for, and he launched into another narrative about his bioterrorist theory. This one didn't vary much from the previous version except it was about twice as long.

"Very interesting, Analyst Pagano," Special Agent Velasquez said. "But at this point, Ralph Battle's our only viable suspect. Agent Rosenberg, keep conducting your investigation of him and give us a full report this afternoon. We are adjourned."

* * *

When Sage got back to the apartment, she couldn't keep the big news to herself.

"The FBI thinks they've caught the murderer! It's a guy named Ralph Battle. He's a registered sex offender and he fits the profile of a serial killer."

"Says who?" Anaya asked.

"Walter Arnold, a profiler the FBI brought in yesterday."

"That means we can go home!" Adam exclaimed.

"I'll believe it when I see it," Anaya grumbled.

"Why are you so skeptical?" Penny asked.

Adam grinned. "She doesn't want to leave because that means she won't see me anymore."

"Nice try, Mr. Wonderful. I just don't think they've solved anything. They're locked in on their sex serial killer theory, but I just don't see it. I thought that at first too, but none of the victims were sexually assaulted."

"So who do *you* think the killer is?" Penny asked.

"My money's on some weirdo—like Adam's roommate," Anaya said. "We know he kills small animals. Maybe he's graduated to killing people."

"I didn't say he actually *kills* animals," Adam said. "I think he just collects dead ones he finds on his hikes."

"That's just as weird, in my opinion. I think we ought to report him to the FBI."

Sage agreed. "That's not a bad idea. What do you think, Adam?"

"Now that I've moved out, I'm okay with it. Do you think we can do it anonymously?"

"I'll see what I can do," Sage said.

"What about you, Sage? Who do you think it is?" Penny asked.

"Gus Carter," she said without a moment's hesitation. When she got blank looks all around she added, "One of the FBI agents. He's a pain in the ass."

* * *

FBI Classified Briefing
Yellowstone National Park Command Post
May 31 – 4:00 p.m.

The mood of the afternoon briefing was decidedly less upbeat than it had been in the morning. Despite having ten agents working furiously since before dawn, the FBI had failed to find any direct evidence linking Ralph Battle to any of the eleven deaths, save the lone picture of one of the victims in his camera.

One bright spot was that Mr. Battle had agreed to speak to Hank and another investigator after consulting with the lawyer who had driven up from Jackson Hole. Referring frequently to his notes, Hank summarized the interview for everyone at the briefing.

"Mr. Battle told us he's on vacation by himself and it's his first trip since being released from prison three years ago. The reason he refused to speak to us earlier was because he hadn't

. It would be fitting to end these illustrations with what has been
g on in Iran in the past few years. Iran has been consistently ma-
ed in the Western press, brandished as a pathetic island of doomed
enchment. Thoughtful observers of the area have long known the
mic revolution to hardly merit such facile dismissal. Already at the
ginning, in early 1979, Iranians were freer than hostile reports by their
versaries suggested. In a report recently published in the *Washington*
t, the striking manner in which Iranians have stamped their social
eferences on an officially conformist landscape has finally become
ailable to a wider readership. According to the report, whoever wishes
circumvent the ban on alcohol (an enduring symbol of the reduction
Islam to a number of anachronistic, oppressive, or irrelevant strictures)
akes it at home and brings it to parties in jerricans. Women, though not
rmitted to swim with men, can sunbathe in their bikinis "under guard"
some areas reserved for them. Videotapes circulate as they do in Saudi
rabia. The report adds:

> Two years ago, Iran's film industry began making movies about love
> again. Cinemas, by some fluke, have always escaped the government's
> attempts to segregate the sexes. While men and women—even married
> couples—must take separate cable cars on the ski slopes of the Elburz, they
> are allowed to sit side by side in a darkened movie theatre.
>
> Yes, young men do take their girlfriends to the movies, said Hamid
> Taqavi, an Iranian reporter. "We can't put a policeman for every individual
> in Iran," he said. "But I, as a religious man, I wouldn't take my girlfriend
> to the movies because I think *it* starts with the movies." "It" needed no
> elaboration.
>
> "This is a river—they can't stop it," said an Iranian woman. "You cannot
> separate men and women. They were created together."
>
> Every week, the Islamic censor uses a thick black pen to blot out female
> necks, breasts and arms in the photographs of Newsweek magazine. But
> stores selling Persian handicrafts have shelves full of traditional drawings
> of women with flowing hair, bare arms and breasts—usually locked in an
> erotic embrace with a wild-eyed lover.[20]

Yet it would be hasty to conclude that all free action flows against
strictures supported by the revolution and (increasingly sporadically)
enforced by zealots. In certain respects, the revolution itself has been a
harbinger of freedom. Many women have been liberated from their cultural shackles by the Islamic upsurge.

> "We were just like puppets," before the revolution, said Sakineh Nouri,
> a 33-year-old volunteer at the Bader Health Center in Shahr-e-Rey, a low-
> income neighborhood in southern Tehran. "The most important thing," a
> fellow volunteer, Shahnaz Ghanavati, 30, said, "is the participation of all

simple and direct. The description of the elements of that dynamic, in
which Muslims repeatedly reject some of their scriptural injunctions and
act freely without waiting for their official spokesmen to catch up with
them, can be pieced together by anyone who regularly follows the events
of the Arab Muslim world, and are most visible to those at the scene,
travelers and locals alike. Popular defiance is not restricted to Islamic
strictures, but also regards all sorts of other political, intellectual, and
social prohibitions. The following examples will reflect the multifarious
defiance and display various free actions that circumvent or brush aside
the official unfreedom.

1. The eyes of modernity's leading powers have recently been on
Saudi Arabia, which, after Oman, is the most closed Arab Muslim society
of them all. Films and videotapes are banned in the kingdom. But those
Saudis who can afford it have large screens in their homes for private
viewing. This has been the case for decades. With the advent of video
technology, there is no way to stop salesmen from circulating tapes pur-
chased abroad.

The modern history of Saudi Arabia has been officially rewritten. So
sensitive is the subject that some crucial records are said to have been
destroyed. Nevertheless, a Saudi writer has produced a massive historical
novel that chronicles the kingdom's rise with the house of Saud at the
helm. Whenever the author seems to be on solid ground, fiction barely
disguises fact, often not at all. He otherwise resorts to imaginative specu-
lations that frequently match eyewitness accounts. Abdulrahman Mou-
nif's pentalogy, *The Cities of Salt*, is banned in Saudi Arabia and most
Arab countries. But it can be bought by all Arabs abroad, or in Beirut and
Damascus, and thus reach its intended audience anyway. A bookseller in
London has described it to me as a "best-seller."

As for all the social restrictions that have made Saudi Arabia notorious,
one need only take account of the behavior of Saudis abroad or, again, in
the privacy of their homes, to evaluate their assimilation to official Saudi
life. And here, we are not concerned with compulsive gamblers and their
ilk, but with those for whom Islam means much and yet suffocate under
what legally constitutes Islam in their country. There are many in Saudi
Arabia, some of whose true feelings were made known to a worldwide
audience by the women who drove their cars through the streets of
Riyadh. No one quite knows how many believing Muslims suffer under
what passes for Islam in Saudi Arabia. And many of their excesses can
be excused considering the suffering.

The Saudi authorities, like many unyielding at heart but intelligently
aware of the contemporary situation, act paradoxically. For instance, they
pay for a station for Washington, D.C.'s large and growing Arab community that features talk shows where all sorts of subjects tabooed in the
kingdom are freely discussed: dictatorship, personal problems of a ro-

mantic or psychological nature, women explaining their illnesses (some-times in graphic detail) to a male general practitioner, and so on. Once, the moderator of a weekly review of the major political events broadcast on Sundays signed off by noting what day it was, wished followers of the Roman and other Western churches a happy Easter, a happy Palm Sunday to Orthodox Christians, and a happy Passover to Jews. This is remarkable for a kingdom that is officially severely intolerant toward the other monotheistic faiths.

2. The phenomenon of discussion far freer than allowed by both Is-lamic and secular authorities has spread throughout the Arab Muslim world. Although the wide audiences of magazines and radio shows enjoy greater social and cultural freedom than is officially suggested, limited audiences can extend their leeway even to the political sphere. Thus a forum on freedom and democracy, with some speakers espousing contro-versial and radical views, can take place in Cairo and be sponsored by a prestigious center that has received much money from the Iraqi regime. On the other hand, because the airwaves do not recognize political boundaries, inflammatory poetry and music easily reaches audiences whose governments would prefer otherwise. Nizar Qabbani's later po-etry may not be of the highest literary quality. But it repeatedly breaks political and sexual taboos, relentless in its rousing condemnation of dictators and the plight of women. Qabbani had already written poetry that must have occasionally shocked some people when he made a tour throughout the Arab world and lectured on poetry—with allusions to his deepest concerns that were hardly lost on the audience.[18] Here, we come across a combination of phenomena. Besides the free travel of broadcasts and booklets, poets, singers, and comedians like the Syrian Dorayd Lah-ham can rise to such popularity that few governments would dare refuse them entry. Thus another door to freedom is opened for those who wish to cross the threshold.

3. The ease of travel and the globalization of communications have exposed unprecedented numbers of travelers from the Arab Muslim world to other alternatives. The ideas, habits, attitudes, and trends thus encountered are not necessarily adopted indiscriminately (although they often are). But people from all walks of life meet directly with what they might know indirectly through broadcasts and hearsay. When they return to the Arab Muslim world, if they are unhappy with the official position, they can back up their intuitive cynicism with a concrete picture of what changes they would like to see. The global intersection of cultures is now unavoidable, and people can no longer be expected to accept that their official version is the best. They need to be convinced that it is so. And if they find certain particulars preferable elsewhere, they are bound to clamor for some reform. For instance, people from the Arab Muslim world may take a strong liking to writing letters to the editor in which

one can speak one's heart and mind. This practice has
Islam or traditional culture in the Arab Muslim world
not run contrary to these. It would simply worry thos
phancy. Many other practices, though they may have g
inated in the West, are really part of an emergent univ
add to the means of contemporary self-expression. Th
meant to supplant local traditional frameworks.

4. The worldwide intersection of cultures and the e
also helped transport many among those who would en
est and most far-reaching discussions in the Arab Muslin
where they can pursue their activities more freely. Beirut
before the Lebanese civil war began in 1975 (it contin
widest selection of books among any Arab city). Lon
Washington, D.C., have become major centers of Arab Mu
Participants are stirred to greater extremes by exile and tl
restraint. And the written or broadcast record of their wo
les back to their native lands, flows into an oppositiona
made all the stronger.

5. Whatever people might say about Islam's intolera
mirth and the visual arts (largely based on false impressio
rose groups of revivalists who occasionally impose their
Muslim societies), millions of faithful Muslims enjoy the c
sion comedies, the theater, and festivities of song and danc
the region. Egyptian films are popular throughout the Ara
world (and the cinema is loved throughout the region), Mu
Subcontinent have adopted the great Indian musical traditi
plays freely abuse and condemn the authorities with an allusi
familiar to the audience and sometimes make fun of every
Kulthum's stature hardly needs mention, and love songs are h
where, from revolutionary Iran's clandestine markets to Alg
These are not new upsurges, but are the contemporary form of
siveness that has always been there. And they are joys in whic
who believe in Islam participate in far greater numbers than wo
their sterner religious leadership.

6. The Islamic revolutionaries, for all the nonsense they s
promulgate (say, about music or the cinema being "un-Islamic"
freedom they would curb if in power, are themselves a good ex
free action at the popular mass level. They openly reject politic
ism, and have taken the cause of action against state injustice, co
and impotence into their own hands. Occasionally, they have
heroic confrontations with brutal regimes that destroy entire ne
hoods to quell dissent without blinking. Such heroism is rem
of Ibn Hanbal's brave stand against al-Ma'mun, which has neve
forgotten, and will galvanize those fed up with the present state of

the ladies in whatever [is being done] in the country," and making a woman aware "that she is not just a decoration in society."[21]

Nesta Ramazani has recently written a fascinating article on the various ways in which the Islamic revolution has, not entirely unwittingly, furthered the cause of women in Iran.[22] She argues that the regime's interest in mobilizing women and women's outward acceptance of "Islamic" strictures (notably the *chador*) have combined to place women in a far stronger position than before. They have effectively become integrated into the workforce, gained Islamic sanction for their right to vote, attained a much higher rate of education, and won access to almost every academic field (except banking, accounting, and—for some mysterious reason—archaeology). Family planning is now accepted as consistent with Islamic law, prenuptial agreements are allowed (and often encouraged) in marriage contracts, custody laws have become fairer to women than before, there is more sexual permissiveness (as evidenced in the return of *mut'a* or "pleasure marriages," and current president Rafsanjani's public disapproval of repressed sexual desire), and the chador is frequently replaced with a stylish, colorful tunic called the *roopoosh* (and the black head cover with livelier shawls). Women are generally experiencing a much stronger sense of participation than under the Pahlavi regime. They are learning about Islam and using some of what is said on its behalf— for instance the claim that Islam does not differentiate between men and women—to promote their interests under cover of Islamic "soundness" (which primarily consists in observing a few simple if inconvenient externals). In this spirit, women have founded associations and journals in which their affairs are openly debated.

The reports by Murphy and Ramazani underline what has been articulated in the last section. Just as Islam at the outset dramatically improved the lot of women, so can Islam again be true to itself by freeing women from the culturally entrenched practice of looking upon them as merchandise. The Iranian revolutionaries show de facto recognition that hitherto, Islam had looked the other way as women suffered. Within Islam, the resources for liberation are considerable, but have yet to be adequately tapped by those who cry loudest in its name.

All the foregoing illustrations show various instances of the people expressing their political, intellectual, social, and cultural freedom. This does not mean that all that is thereby done is good. The point here is to emphasize that in the event of conflict between those acts and Islamic strictures, it rarely follows that the agents no longer consider themselves Muslim. After all, it surely is possible for someone who observes Muslim rites with great devotion to feast with family and friends, tell jokes, swim in the company of the other sex, and go to the movies. There is no prohibition on mirth and joy in Islam. Only the joyless and mirthless distort Islam in their image. The Egyptians are an excellent example of a people largely religious and also renowned for their love of life. Egypt is also a good example of the shadow hanging over the enduring and wholesome balance its people have cultivated.

Those who engage in practices at odds with certain Islamic strictures have tacitly or explicitly realized that whether they are Muslims does not depend on their stance toward those strictures. Many reductionisms surround such independent-mindedness. It is falsely associated with modernism. Those who fear modernity thus identify their struggle to save Islam with the attempt to reinforce the abandoned strictures. But at the same time, they promote their own independent ideas, for instance, that women should fight alongside men for the Islamic revolution, which has a liberating effect on those women. Thus the revolutionaries who in some respects fear modernity in others are modernizers.[23] Conversely, those dismissed as simple modernizers for their rejection of some Islamic strictures may be quite conservative and devout. All such distinctions are lost in the vortex of polarization and oversimplifation.

The compatibility of Islam with the practices of independent-minded Muslims thus needs to be emphasized. For the problem is not how to herd the independent-minded back to outworn strictures, or how to overcome an Islam identified therewith, but how to make the Arab Muslim ecology congenial to religiousness *and* free expression, ideally to the benefit of both. We have seen at length the profound reserves of the greatest possible freedom, both communally and personally, in Islam. From these reserves, scholars and Sufis can draw the inspiration to attune Islam further to its contemporary situation without closing off the avenues to the moral and spiritual dimensions of freedom, the core of freedom, that it has so well preserved.

There is a venerable precedent for such attunements within Islam. It is none other than *ijma'*, the consensus of the community. When the community is seen to follow a practice for which there is no official sanction, scholars eventually find a legal basis for it and incorporate it into the shari'a. Thus, Goldziher tells us that a custom that takes hold among Muslim people, even if still rejected by theologians as an illegitimate innovation (bid'a), will in the end be tolerated, then accepted as it gains currency. Once it is formally acknowledged as part of the ijma', it becomes a bid'a to oppose it! The celebration of the Prophet's birthday was originally a bid'a, but it is now widely observed by Muslims.[24] Ottoman jurists universally accepted ijma', and used it skillfully in enabling the various communities within the empire to feel at home. One of the most prominent writers of the Ottoman period, Katip Çelebi, admitted that laws change with time. Ijma' could alter the shari'a.[25] Gilles Kepel, in writing about the current problem with Islamic revolutionaries in Egypt, also asserts that most Muslims "accommodate themselves to the history of Muslim societies" rather than espouse the absurd and unworkable view that history has stopped since the death of the last "rightly guided caliph" in 661 C.E.[26]

The consensus of the community may be too much to ask for in effecting the necessary attunements in Islam. But some kind of serious agreement is essential, for that is one way that Islam can remain dynamic without lapsing into historicism—which in any event is impossible in Islam without a complete loss of identity. The idea is for Islam to move in harmony with history and not to become subservient to it. Islam has originally shaped and moved history and it would be most inappropriate for the relationship to reverse itself (as inappropriate as the phenomenon of human life being moulded by machines originally invented by humans). Islam's continued ability to be constitutive of history seems to depend largely on thoughtful Muslims with the ability to craft the desired equilibrium. We therefore turn next to the likely range of such thought.

The Scholarly Heralds of Freedom

The bedrock of Islam is besieged by the unlikely alliance of Islamic revolutionaries who in their religious-minded zeal have distanced themselves from the moral and spiritual core of their religion, and Muslims whose rejection of several Islamic strictures puts them under pressure to demote Islam to the extent that it remains identified with those strictures. Islam is therefore not only faced with the need to articulate a framework that undercuts the argument of the revolutionaries and reasserts the moral and spiritual core to confirm the sentiment of Muslim individuals that their religion has little to do with the strictures and attitudes that now stand in its way; but the articulation must also retain continuity with the traditions that have assured the unbroken presence of the Medinan paradigm in Islamic life and thus the symbolic unity of Muslims, for which the shari'a has been a chief token. The fulfilment of this complex of requirements would alone assure Islam lasting resonance and vigor in its contemporary situation, while not abandoning the moral and spiritual depth attainable within it. It would assure the embrace of new-found social, cultural, intellectual, and political freedoms without shrinking the range of moral and spiritual freedom for which those new-found freedoms had originally been asserted. The individuals competent to articulate the appropriate framework must therefore be embedded in the central traditions of Islam, yet also be conversant with modernity's best cultural and intellectual offerings and in touch with the mindset of their constituency. Such people will be able to reinterpret key Islamic concepts (such as "innovation" [bid'a]) and key Islamic injunctions (such as that to obey those in authority), reevaluate the status of the reports about the Medinan community, judge how the principles governing the derivation of the shariʿa may shift given recent developments at least as compelling as earlier ones that had justified prior shifts, then have the authority for their rulings to carry weight throughout the Arab Muslim world. They can do so while reaffirming and revitalizing the moral and spiritual core of Islam. And thus, the many-sided ferment, so ominous now for the chaos, divisiveness, and dilution beheld by a badly led community, can be cast into a dynamic stability that offers Muslims freedom without dissolution. Here, we shall examine briefly whether the shariʿa indeed lends itself to the necessary adaptation, and consider the emergent Islamic leadership.

As far as the shariʿa is concerned, we have already seen that the principles governing its derivation have shifted and that the conditions justifying those shifts are certainly not more compelling than the transition, if not to modernity, then to the intersection of modernity with the Arab Muslim world to form a hybrid civilization. But is there any major precedent in which the purpose of the law is adumbrated so that one can clearly see that none of the changes implied or suggested in this book are incompatible therewith? Al-Ghazzali once wrote that "the purpose of the Law for [hu]man [beings] is fivefold: the preservation for them of their religion, soul, intellect, offspring and property." [27]

The reader can be easily satisfied that the conditions of compatibility are met, for nothing positively expressed in this book can harm what al-Ghazzali took it to be the law's purpose to preserve. On the contrary, the idea is to enhance the prospects for preservation. To judge how contemporary Muslim thinkers might view the status of the shariʿa, with respect to what can change and what cannot, it is best to present two points of view that roughly demarcate the boundaries of change, from the more conservative to that which is less so. The lower bound of change may be represented initially by the position developed in Seyyed Hossein Nasr's essay *The Shariʿah and Changing Historical Conditions*.[28] Four points are highlighted.

1. Nasr asserts that Muslim law is "the embodiment of the Divine Will, as a transcendent reality which is eternal and immutable, as a model by which the perfections and shortcomings of human society and the conduct of the individual are judged . . ." [29] For the secular-minded and many religious persons alike (notably Christians), this doctrine is impossible to apprehend. Yet from a Muslim perspective, it is a given, and no one who deals with the Arab Muslim world can expect any reversal. Thus, it is not human reason that judges the status of the law, but the law that directs the use of reason.[30] For reason to be the basis for change in the law, to the extent that the law is believed to be immutable and divinely inspired, is for the ontological order in Islam to be inverted. If the shariʿa guarantees the proper functioning of reason, then how can reason

guarantee the aptness of the shari'a? This is especially problematic when it comes to spatiotemporal developments that appear to make several laws inapplicable, irrelevant, or counterproductive, and may go so far as to question traditional dogma regarding the shari'a's ontological position. It is not the shari'a, however, that ought to conform to the spatiotemporal world, but the spatiotemporal world that ought "to conform to the Divine Law."[31]

2. It thus follows that to ask the shari'a to conform with the times is to weaken the shari'a to the point of "spiritual suicide."[32] For if the times are full of developments that show how far human beings have led themselves spiritually astray—and if this has happened precisely because of the abandonment of guidelines for spiritual (and intellectual) health—then to reform the shari'a accordingly is to make a supposedly divinely inspired legal code reflect that malaise. It would deprive Muslims of the very criteria by which they can judge that things have gone wrong in modern times, if what has happened in modern times is to furnish their new criteria for judgment.[33] What we have before us is the apotheosis of a civilizational conflict. One civilization has been on the ascendant (in spatiotemporal terms). Its ascendancy exerts all sorts of pressures on the other to adopt appropriate reforms. The other sees these reforms not as concessions to a new global outlook, but as changes that carry the gravest implications, so grave that to implement them would institutionalize a malaise and seriously undermine the divine underpinning of the traditional order that ensures protection against just such malaise. The gap between the modern and traditional perception of reforms, when these touch on the heart of the shari'a, cannot be greater.

3. Nevertheless, Nasr is hardly unaware of irreversible and unavoidable changes, and is not going to compromise the sanctity of the shari'a by simply wishing them away. As he puts it, "[n]o Islamic state can avoid owning trains and planes, but Muslims can avoid hanging surrealistic paintings on their walls."[34] The owning of planes and trains does not conflict with anything the shari'a says. However, other necessary changes may conflict with the shari'a. If so, Nasr does not think it proper to conclude that the shari'a is imperfect. Rather, the condition of the world is imperfect, the world to which the shari'a, after all, extends. This condition has fallen sufficiently short of the shari'a as to prevent its full implementation.[35]

4. But to discuss how conditions in the world fall short of those necessary for the shari'a's full implementation is no easy matter. Because the shari'a is believed by Muslims to have issued from God, those who are competent to deal with the extent of its implementation and decide new rulings must enjoy a status analogous to Christian theologians.[36] Discussion of the shari'a is a theological issue. Thus,

[t]o discuss, much less change, Islamic Law cannot be done by anyone except those competent in the Shari'ah, no more than Christian theology could be discussed and doctrines of the Christian church altered by any other than those vested with authority in such matters. It would be as unthinkable from the Islamic point of view to change Muslim personal law through any simply elected legislative body as it would be to change doctrines of the Christian church through a similar body of laymen.[37]

How would Nasr's views measure up to the need, for instance, to reevaluate the injunction to obey those in authority? Let us suppose, with Nasr, that the injunction is divinely ordained and therefore nonnegotiable. We would then have to turn to the third point above to see how this would not lead Muslims to obey despots who in modern times have such power that it is no longer possible to live according to the shari'a itself if one submits to that injunction. To adhere to the shari'a by refusing to rebel against an amoral modern despot is effectively to ensure that it not be respected by government officials, that it may even be defiled. This is how imperfect the condition of the world has become. Those once meant to lead the community, politically or otherwise, have in some cases, on the political plane, evolved into despots. To obey them leads Muslims to substantially curtail their Islamic (not to mention their generally human) aspirations. Thus, if the structure of the contemporary world provides for endemically imperfect (political) leadership, then the injunction to obey them cannot possibly obtain. Nor can anything that, to the shari'a, has become self-undermining given the contemporary situation. Does this mean that all such injunctions and strictures could not be divinely ordained? Not if one supposes the world to be, say, a place where political leaders regularly serve the Islamic community well—or, when politics and community life follow different directions, other leaders emerge who have the good of the community at heart; nor if one supposes that the world ought to be made such a place if it is not. If the world is imperfect, however, the injunction becomes self-contradictory, for it would imply disobedience in order to help the cause of an alternative leadership worthy of obedience. One may deftly rework the injunction to avoid the appearance of such self-contradictoriness. But it seems better to abandon it altogether. Even the Qur'an could not be expected, given the spatiotemporal location of its appearance and the very specific anthropology of those who first responded to it, to spell out the dramatic bifurcation that has occurred in the modern world between the various domains of life, so that politics, for instance, now has a life of its own—a situation entirely alien to the spirit of the Qur'an and the early Medinan community. However, the authority and stature of the Qur'an are not compromised because it fails to precisely predict a global condition alien to its spirit. It can continue to be seen as setting enduring basic standards for communal health and harmony.

In point 4 above, Nasr tacitly admits the need for change in the shariʿa by sketching the quality of those competent to bring it about. But when he openly admits change (as in point 3), he becomes extremely cautious. Such caution is understandable given the stakes. It would certainly endanger Islamic spirituality were reformers given license to liberally define the legitimate object of their reforms. And yet, the question forces itself upon us—is change only a matter of unavoidable gadgetry? And if Muslims can do quite well without surrealistic paintings on their walls, does this imply a stricture against them? If so, how many other similar strictures may be generated? Would there not be an endless list of things that Muslims can arguably do well without? This is not to say that there should be no such list at all. But it is one thing to say that Muslims can do well without movies that graphically depict the slitting of throats, quite another to extend this to what is not harmful, but merely unnecessary. Sufis find most things unnecessary. Imagine how oppressive life might become for the rest of the population if the list of essentials and inessentials were drawn up by austere mystics and somehow legislated. This would run quite contrary to the compassion and generosity traditionally shown by Sufis toward the less spiritually able or advanced. Moreover, it would compromise Islam's historic stature as a popular religion and the shariʿa's as its popular symbol. Change is not only relative to what modernity has introduced into lifestyles all over the world but, as we have seen, it has become unavoidable regarding some of the central political and social doctrines of Islam. And it is not just reason that tells Muslims that they ought no longer obey those in authority (unless they truly represent Muslim aspirations) or that to take measures to ensure that women in no way display any of their charms (literal or metaphorical) to any strangers is to deny them their humanity and distort relations between the sexes so badly as to invite built-in perversion (the obverse of what has been brought on by mindless sexual "liberation" in modernity's chief quarters, which is hardly what Muslims need when freed of their shackles, but to which these shackles are, alas, driving them). The use of reason to express necessary transformations in social and political doctrines is underlaid with sentiments accessible only to the heart and soul. For these reject, among other things, the deplorable contemporary political culture in much of the Arab Muslim world, and the status of women and relations between the sexes.

What the Qurʾan says about women and relations between the sexes was a boon to the humanity of women and to those relations at the time of the revelations. If the traditional interpretation of the same statement now definitely runs contrary to the original effect, is it not far more important to emphasize the humanity of women and sound relations between the sexes than the *letter* of what was necessary for these more than a thousand years ago? Is that emphasis not more in harmony with the Qur'an's intentions? Is this not the reason the Qur'an keeps Muslims on their feet when it comes to specific strictures, occasionally contradict-ing itself to remind them that God knows better and perhaps implying similar contradictions (or abrogations) where the spatiotemporal condi-tions of the revelation made it impossible for the Qur'an to perform them itself without seeming forbiddingly incomprehensible to its first followers and many, many succeeding generations, or without racing destructively ahead of itself?

The problem that arises from the revelation of the eternal and immuta-ble in a temporal and changeable context is compounded in Islam by the extension of the revelation to specific aspects of life. If the Qur'an does not contain specific solutions for this problem for all time, one can assume that it at least furnishes the clues for overcoming that problem in every era and among every people. But even if the problem were shifted to the detection of the clues and the divination of the manner of their use to overcome the problem, its difficulty remains just as enormous. Now the Qur'an's eternity and immutability do not entail the denial of the tempo-rality and changeability of its setting, nor the consequent necessary change in the mode of its reception and application; for the latter para-doxically are eternal and immutable facts about the Qur'an's earthly set-ting. It follows that the Qur'an must contain the clues for the changed way it is to be applied given the inevitable change in the mode of its reception. These changes affect the conditions of the applicability of time- or culture-bound strictures. For the Qur'an to have to go further and spell out the content of specific strictures for a setting far removed in time and culture from its original setting, it would have placed insurmountable barriers in the way of those seeking to understand it—barriers whose transcendence is not contingent upon an exceptional intelligence or pro-fundity, nor even prophecy, but a literal ability to see far into the future as though one has made a journey in a time machine. Thus one can expect to find only hints in the Qur'an that whatever pertains specifically to what is time-and culture-bound must remain consistent with the nature of its context—that is to say, the two change together if the Qur'an is to resonate at that level.

The conclusion is not that the Qur'an is therefore to be neatly divided into what transcends all temporal and cultural change and what does not. For there is the further issue of God's reminders to believers that they need not understand all that they do in the name of faith. It is natural for one to be asked to obey a stricture or injunction whose basis he either rejects or does not understand as a token of reverence for God. Worship ceases to be what it is without the observance of blatantly irratio-nal commands. So besides the radical difference between eternity and time, there is the problem of appreciating what must be left in place for proper worship despite the appearance of irrationality or some other objectionable quality. Thus, though exertion and effort are worthy of prayer, there is no reason one form of effort is better than another. But if one is commanded, to obey the command must first be understood as a token of worship. If something is forbidden, and the obedience to such a stricture in no way compromises one's humanity or something significant about it, for instance, the stricture on alcohol in Islam, then however "irrational and outdated" the stricture may seem, one can nevertheless see it as having nothing to do with what is rational and fashionable, but as simply a token of respect for the authority of God.[38] On the other hand, the foregoing does not apply to the command that women refrain from any imaginable display of their charms to strangers. For to follow this today is to seriously undermine the humanity and freedom of Muslims, and it would be hard for them to believe that that is God's command. All these judgments are not made by reason alone, but can be only the outcome of a sound moral sensibility and healthy spirituality clarifying themselves through rational and imaginative means.

The problem, then, is how an eternal and immutable text is read in a temporal and changeable setting, a problem that is bridged by the dynamism and openness of the Qur'an. And if much learning and subtlety are needed to appreciate these, also much open-mindedness and perhaps courage, then still more subtlety is needed for the reading to retain the sense that the Qur'an, after all, is a book of worship and a vision of lasting standards and ideals, for all the reinterpretation and reevaluation that some of its specific content needs. Such versatility exemplifies in the symbolic language of Islam the ideal of the retention and revitalization of the moral and spiritual core of freedom in an environment of social, political, cultural, and intellectual openness. It would be tragic for the Qur'an to become torn between antagonistic reductionists if the seeds of a remarkable synthesis lay in wait within it for a new generation of Muslims to cultivate them.

We remain near the lower bound of change. Returning specifically to the shari'a, wherein the possibilities of change are a measure of Islam's flexibility and openness, there may be a solution in the careful study of the shari'a's historical makeup. One of Islam's most influential modern thinkers, Zia Gökalp (1876–1924), himself like Nasr a conservative within the Islamic spectrum, recognized that the shari'a has two distinct sources: one is scripture (nass), and the other local practice, mores, custom, or convention ('urf).[39] The legitimacy of 'urf as a source of Islamic law has a distinguished line of support stretching all the way back to the prophet Muhammad himself. Gökalp adduces the hadith: "What the faithful regard as good is good with God."[40] In any given locality, what the faithful regard as good, apart from what the Qur'an and reliable hadith reports specifically mention, is their particular *a'raf* (the plural of 'urf). These a'raf, unless they be in contradiction with the scriptural texts, are then considered good in the eyes of God. It is well known, and has been mentioned here, that the shari'a's sources have indeed been a combination of scriptural texts centered in the Qur'anic revelations and the Prophetic sayings and maxims, as well as local practice. *Thus the shari'a has both a divine and a socio-cultural aspect.* Only the divine aspect is exempt from change and has the other qualities correctly attributed to it by Nasr. Customs and folkways, on the other hand, change over space and time as a matter of course. Gökalp stresses that regarding these, what is good or bad is relative to the society in which an act is performed.[41] He therefore distinguishes between the traditional shari'a, which is eternally valid, and the social shari'a, which far from being eternally valid must change.[42]

The metaphor "tree of life" is often used in Islam. When applied to the shari'a, Gökalp deftly throws it open:

the *raison d'être* of this tree [which has its roots in the heavens] is to live in an earthly environment and atmosphere, and to get its air, heat, and light from the social 'urf to satisfy the civil needs. It cannot be said that this tree, after giving fruits during some centuries, does not need to get its food any more. Those who believe that the Islamic *shari'a* will remain the *shari'a* of every age to the last have to accept the fact that the tree should always be living and fruitful. A law which does not live and give life cannot be the regulator of life. It is evident, therefore, that there must be social fundamentals as well as dogmatic fundamentals of *fikh* [jurisprudence].[43]

The historical evidence strongly supports Gökalp's distinction between the divine and the sociocultural aspects of the shari'a. It is true that without such evidence, one could still observe the obvious time- and culture-bound nature of much that the shari'a contains. But with the help of Gökalp's distinction, one can avoid the dilemma that Nasr's "purer" conservatism poses. Rather than state flatly that the shari'a is wholly a divine law, one distinguishes between what is divine and what is not, in accordance with the shari'a's actual (and, to the best of our knowledge, true) history. Thus, the divine element is not compromised. For anything that strains the imagination when regarded as divine can be considered based on 'urf unless demonstrated to be otherwise (in which case there would really be a dilemma, for Muslims would then be faced with accepting that an injunction that is now harmful to the community is a divine command).

Gökalp's distinction preserves the sanctity of the divine while it also legitimizes the need for change. For in all probability, those injunctions that have run their course originated in customary practice rather than divine command. And to change customary practice, far from violating divine sanctity (with which it has nothing to do), is not only acceptable, but, in the very nature of what is customary, unavoidable.

The problem Muslims are left with is how to circumscribe the domain of the eternal, unchanging elements of the shari'a and that of the elements derived from local mores. Because the historical evidence will never be such that the circumscription can be precisely made, principles are needed that will enable Muslims to separate the divine from the human contributions to the shari'a. These principles, as may be expected, range from those that make the divine domain exceedingly wide to those that make it exceedingly narrow, to the extent of appearing not to acknowledge any divine intervention in Muslim law at all. We have examined a view that maximizes the divine domain. Let us now turn to another that allows more room for human intervention while remaining respectful toward divine fundamentals.

Fazlur Rahman believed that all the foregoing problems could be solved if only Muslims grasped the underlying unity of the Qur'an and hadith reports and allowed that grasp to guide specific judgments and rulings. Such unity eludes the grasp of Muslims for several reasons, among them:

1. The long-standing habit of quoting specific Qur'anic verses or hadith reports out of context to support certain arguments, which caused much of the shari'a to be based on a fragmented reception of its sources.[44] Thus the rules and laws that regulate Muslim life in approximation of the Medinan paradigm are structurally separated from their goal—for the community they uphold is captured in bits and pieces that have drifted from the whole. The most alarming consequence of such severance is that so many Muslims today who seek a return to the paradigm can do no better than affirm damaging and counterproductive strictures that in the eyes of other Muslims and outsiders have for good reason become notorious.[45]

2. A practice as simple and self-evident as direct interaction with the Qur'an has been hampered through the intercession of commentaries and supercommentaries. These, which exist only because of the Qur'an, have replaced the Qur'an as the objects of study and distance worshipers still more from the grasp of its wholeness. Furthermore, the need to understand and master the Qur'an's difficult language to appreciate it has also degenerated into a maze of grammatical and rhetorical pedantry, so that the energies of the Qur'an's students are exhausted by the study of Mudari Arabic. In the process, much hairsplitting occurs to further put the Qur'an's unity out of reach.[46]

On the other hand, a sure grasp of the wholeness of the scriptural sources would enable Muslim scholars to undertake the reinterpretation and reevaluation of some of the Qur'an's specific content in view of the mounting evidence against its applicability—while heeding the permanence of the standards and ideals it sets. The elements of that project are:

1a. Because the Qur'an needs to be seen once more as a series of specific responses to specific situations, then Arabian culture and society at the time of the Qur'anic revelations must be studied as carefully and comprehensively as possible.

1b. Such study would enable scholars to derive eternal moral and social laws from how the Qur'an treated specific cases. The assumption here is that however specific the content of the Qur'an, this must be based on something timeless because the Qur'an itself is timeless. And so the Qur'an transcends space and time to the extent that what lies *behind* its specific commands, strictures, and social and legal injunctions has the same quality. The Qur'an's eternity and immutability are transferred to a level where no spatiotemporal developments may call them seriously into question.

2. A careful and comprehensive assessment of the contemporary situation in the Arab Muslim world, given the eternal moral and social laws derived as in 1b above, will reveal by analogy how those laws bear on specific cases today. Thus, the Qur'an can become as alive for Muslims as it was when the first generation of Muslims were divinely guided over twenty-two years in their specific affairs.[47]

The foregoing provides us with the principles for distinguishing between the eternal and the temporal aspects of Muslim law, but in a way not anticipated at all by Gökalp. For rather than refine the research carried out by social scientists to establish empirically what is temporal and what eternal, Rahman combines historical research with a daring hermeneutical step. Once we know with reasonable assurance what Arabian life was like when the Islamic revelations appeared, we can educe the principles behind the specific injunctions that were divinely commanded. These principles would be the eternal law. But their transposition to specific domains would make them differ over space and time. Rahman sought to educe eternal principles from the Qur'an that in their nature would be worthy of divine sanctity while, returned to the spatiotemporal domain, they would nevertheless be susceptible to change. What is divine is so because it is at an altogether different level from the sociocultural. Once applied to the sociocultural domain, its literal form and spatiotemporal content change. But the change cannot be random or merely follow fashion. It must be based on strict analogy. The relationship between the eternal principles and Arabian life early in the seventh century (C.E.) must be precisely the same as that between the former and the various strands of Muslim life today. Once we educe the divine principles, for instance, those that seek to make individuals good and comunities just, they must be honestly applied in every time and place.

Rahman's project is radical and will undoubtedly meet with stiff resistance. This is why his views represent the upper bound of change. But they remain within the realm of the possible because of Rahman's solid reputation and Muslim credentials, even though his project may give the impression that, for example, moral values can be tampered with. He was strongly averse to such tampering. For he believed that moral values could "not be made or unmade by man at his own whim or convenience and should not be used or abused for the sake of expediency." [48] He clearly spelled out his belief that Muhammad's aim was to constitute "a community for goodness and justice in the world—what I have called an ethically based sociopolitical order 'under God'." [49] One cannot therefore accuse Rahman, having generally described the Qur'an's fundamental principles as aimed toward the creation of good individuals and just communities, of leaving it to human "reason" to define "good" and "just." These must be defined under the sincere aspect of divine guidance.

Thus, though Rahman's interpretation of the Qur'an's eternity and immutablity, which transfers them from the content of the Qur'an's specific commands and strictures to the moral and social laws behind them, represents a decisive break with the traditional Islamic view that the Qur'an is eternal and immutable, period, he passionately upholds the moral and spiritual core of the Qur'an and Islam. He aims at the attainment of a fundamental and sound basis for change, so that in a nutshell Islam becomes attuned to modernity without losing its soul. And Rahman rarely wastes an opportunity to denounce modernity for its soullessness. His project adequately embeds the repulsion of the Arab Muslim world's political, intellectual, social, and cultural unfreedoms in Islam, and thus aspires to promote the core of Islamic freedom.

It speaks something for Islam's internal capacity for revitalization that Rahman's project did not arise in an Islamic vacuum. Rahman owes one of his central doctrines to Muhammad 'Abduh, Egypt's leading modern Islamic thinker. About a century ago, 'Abduh, as witnessed by a student whose notes have survived, urged Muslims to view the Qur'an as a whole and refrain from quoting verses out of context—for that habit, he believed, gave rise to sectarianism, whereas the holistic reading and grasp of the Qur'an would inspire Muslims to transcend their differences (and be generally more tolerant, which was another of 'Abduh's goals). He called upon his brethren to use reason and intelligence in their approach to the Qur'an and to accompany their study with the proper aptitude instead of learning it (and the commentaries) by rote. He preached a return to the spirit of the first century of Islam. He sought agreement on essentials and the omission of details that engender discord. [50]

'Abduh, who eventually was recognized as Egypt's foremost Muslim authority, practiced what he preached without ever having to renounce the slightest detail in the Qur'an. Instead, he emphasized the verses that encouraged the values he thought were paramount: work, justice, and tolerance. As for the remainder of verses, he went around those among them that had legal implications as follows: Wherever there was room for more than one interpretation, he interpreted them in the light of the verses he had already emphasized; where there was not, he subtly modified the "internal equilibrium" of current exegesis to attain the same result.[51] Overall, the Qur'an in his hands exuded a holistic reading centered in transcendent values. Rahman picked up on that, acknowledged his debt to 'Abduh, and produced a more explicit and refined holistic approach. But the example of 'Abduh remains more potent because such an approach was given the chance to be officially put into practice at the highest level in a leading Muslim country by a man whose piety was beyond reproach.

'Abduh's changes in the curricula at al-Azhar were thus an excellent step in the right direction. Let us see whether more was forthcoming.

The prospects for the study of the Qur'an in relation to its past and present contexts as suggested by Rahman can be gleaned by looking at the state of education in Islamic countries. For whether or not Muslims can restore the dynamism and openness of the Qur'an in its contemporary setting depends on whether their education properly attunes them to that setting and its best intellectual possibilities. Rahman thinks of the object of that attunement as nothing less than the systematic fashioning of a modern Islamic worldview: "The crucial question to which we must eventually seek an answer is whether there is an awareness among Muslims . . . that an Islamic world view does need to be worked out today and that this is an immediate imperative; for unless such a system is attempted, there is little that can be ministered through education."[52]

To that end, education in Islamic countries needs radical reform: "Here precisely we come up against the most vicious of all circles in contemporary Islam—that unless necessary and far-reaching adjustments are made in the present system of education, it is not even conceivable that creative minds will arise that will work out the desired systematic interpretation of Islam."[53]

So long as the vicious circle remains unbroken, with Muslims who care most about Islam mostly opposed to the educational reforms that have become essential to the good of Islam, Islam's positive attunement to modernity awaits its heralds: "And yet, strange though it may seem, it is precisely this systematic working-out of Islam for the modern context that has not been forthcoming."[54]

Rahman believes that the condition in the Arab Muslim world is one of "spiritual panic," fed by the clear manner in which Western education and culture (both popular and intellectual) have cast transcendence, spirituality, and traditional morality aside toward the middle of this century. The marginality of critical voices at Western universities who are also unequivocally religious, and the preponderance of orientations inimical to Muslims among most critics of the excesses of positivism, materialism, and rationalism, only augment their fears. Thus their startegy has mainly been to accrue technological benefits and eschew the Western moral-spiritual malaise (roughly Nasr's position because he seems to openly admit change only in the case of unavoidable technologies).[55]

What Muslims therefore generally have is a choice between an education that either slavishly imitates the Western model or perpetuates the colonial system, and a traditional religious education that relative to its contemporary setting has lost its efficacy and resonance. With nonreligious education easily the more prestigious among the two, and with its subservience to the ideal of (material, economic) progress, intelligent and educated Muslims with access to modern methodologies are bound to have a narrow perspective on human affairs and be quite incompetent to handle religion. Meanwhile, those that do go to religious schools graduate with an outlook too ossified to throw Islam open toward its revitalization, and cannot comprehend the world they are in. The strategy of combining technological progress with conservatism in other areas can result only in cultural schizophrenia. The desired Islamic vision thus eludes both sides. The schizophrenia is amplified by the abyss between a small educated modern elite, and uneducated conservative multitudes. The multitudes stand in the way of reforming religious education, while the elite drift further from an unreformed religion. A destructive unspoken compromise is reached: the elites promote material progress and leave the rest untouched.[56]

This situation is clearly unstable. We have seen in the previous section how in many ways the multitudes are not really frozen in a traditionalist time frame, but already express various new attitudes in their lives that they do not believe to be at variance with Islam. On the other hand, the intellectual axes of Islam have all reached a crisis point that demands resolution. In this and the previous chapter, we have seen how some traditional Islamic cultural, social, and political doctrines have now become self-undermining and we have been presented with a preliminary view of how they might be recast toward freedom and revitalization. On the other hand, the undoubted problems with the secular (and especially materialistic) view of development have surfaced so glaringly that only fanatical secularists (among them the materialists) can ignore them. The problematic of Islam and modernity appears ripe for a stable equilibrium to be wrought from the impasse it has reached along every main avenue.

The practical question we are left with is whether the foregoing crises and the openings they create for a stable equilibrium are reflected in developments in the Arab Muslim world, in particular whether Muslims who may fashion that equilibrium are being given the necessary preparation and whether indeed some may have already appeared on the scene.

Rahman thinks that Turkey has offered the most pronounced moves in the right direction. For although Atatürk had outlawed religious education for more than two decades, Islamic sentiment was deep enough to call for its return. And when it did return, it was along new lines: a system of preparatory schools throughout the countryside that taught students about Islam as well; and a small but growing number of higher institutes of Islamic learning, such as the faculty of theology at Ankara University, established in 1949, for Islam to be studied with the benefit of modern intellectual tools. The Islamic character of these institutions was guaranteed by the fact that most were built by the community itself. So the Turks most genuinely interested in Islam can also approach it with a contemporary spirit.[57] The early lack of Islamically competent teachers was soon overcome—for the secular professors of eager students for whom Islam meant much eventually produced graduates able to bring about the envisioned balance:

> [N]ow, after more than two decades and a half, one can meet, among the younger faculty members, people of learning and commitment who hold much promise for the future. Many of them know Arabic adequately, have obtained doctorates from abroad, and are personally and intellectually committed to Islam. Further, they are not only historians, but are concerned with certain central intellectual disciplines of Islam, theology and philosophy, and so on.[58]

Although the study of the Qur'an and the hadith has not yet reached the point where they can be appreciated along the lines urged by Rahman, he believes it is only a matter of time before that can be accomplished. To do so requires a solid grounding in modern philosophy, sociology, and history.[59] Modern philosophy would provide the tools with which the crisis points are clarified, articulated, and turned toward a resolution. The social sciences, on the other hand, will further comprehension of the particular setting of the revelation and allow the separation of specific pronouncements that pertain to the Qur'an's spatiotemporal particularity from the eternal laws or ideals underlying them that compose the Qur'an's true character. Historical developments that have dimmed the perception of the Qur'an's unity and spirit will also be better understood.

Surely Muhammad Arkoun has the intellectual credentials adumbrated by Rahman—and yet we shall be able to reaffirm a crucial balance in briefly examining where Arkoun's work has led him with respect to the Qur'an, hadith, and the shari'a. Beginning with the shari'a, Arkoun acknowledges that it frequently is based in local traditions that predated Islam, and in the reasoned opinion of the early judges who freely exercised their discretionary powers. He reminds us of al-Shafi'i's attempt to

overcome the ensuant chaos, what with different judges initiating different precedents that accumulated in mutually conflicting legal corpora.
Al-Shafi'i's method, as is well known, consisted in either deriving the
law directly from the Qur'an and the sayings and example of the Prophet
or, where this proved impossible, to do so by strict analogy with the
contents of the scriptural sources. Once this practice became institutional-
ized, it gave the shari'a an air of stability and permanence and thus,
Arkoun believes, the illusion of sacredness. This is how Muslims have
confounded the secular with the religious.[60]

The power of the state reinforced the confusion. For the state could
impose the shari'a wherever it held sway. Yet therein lies Arkoun's doubt
as to the eternal validity of the shari'a: it did not touch the lives of
peasants, herdsmen, or nomads in the Middle Ages nearly as much as
Muslims in urban areas. The influence of the shari'a, then, depended on
the power of the central state. This is not the mark of a divine presence.
Furthermore, many of the judges who were instrumental in the shari'a's
imposition were agents of the state whose careers took precedence over
their fidelity to Islam. And it was in the state's interest to give the shari'a
an aspect of holiness to undermine the opposition. Hence philosophers
and other critics of the status quo faced terrible odds.[61]

Why, then, have Muslims been unwilling to face the truth about the
shari'a? Arkoun believes this is because of the continuous threats to Muslim states and communities, beginning with the Crusades and Mongol
invasions and lasting to this day. The shari'a has proved its usefulness
for mobilization, and is enlisted in the cause of nationalism. Muslims
would never be free to explore the facts surrounding the genesis and
accumulation of the shari'a while on the defensive.[62] Muslims have hence
not worried about the distortions, omissions, falsifications, and unwar-
ranted leaps that must have taken place along the shari'a's chain of certi-
fication, which begins with the word of God, passes through the
(unspecified and unclarified) conditions under which authentic revelation occurs, the actual words of the Prophet, the codification of these
words, and the derivation of laws based upon them, and ends with the
interpretation of these laws in current Islamic political practice and the
state that shapes it.[63]

The new elements introduced by Arkoun, besides what we already
know about the sociocultural dimension of the shari'a, are human error,
the limits of knowledge, and how power and politics shape institutional-
ized religion. The shari'a, he thinks, is not only necessarily subject to
change to the extent that it is the product of 'urf; but it also lacks an
eternal quality because of the intervention of rulers and states in need of
legitimization, and because Muslims simply cannot know what words to
which they attribute sacredness were truly revealed by God, and what
words were there because of (unintentional or deliberate) alterations by

humans. So in Arkoun's hands, the shari'a is completely put into question. We cannot be sure about the eternity of any of its parts. If Muslims so desire, they ought to be able to abandon any stricture they no longer find tenable with a clear conscience.

Arkoun's radical position vis-à-vis the shari'a is matched with his trenchant critique of the standard Muslim attitude toward the Qur'an. He again begins with a fact: the Qur'an is a collection made in 656 C.E. of previously writen fragments and oral testimony (Muhammad died in 632 C.E. and the revelations began about 610 C.E.). All caliphs subsequently imposed that collection as the final text. But from here on, Arkoun parts ways with what any Muslim would readily acknowledge. He believes that the sanctity of the extant Qur'an, the certainty that the text first collected in 656 C.E. is the word of God as revealed to Muhammad, became firmly embedded in the "social conscience" of Muslims after four centuries during which the orders of the caliphs were supported by the consensus of Muslim scholars. For anyone to have questioned that orthodoxy was for him to risk the wrath of the whole Muslim *umma* upon himself. The habit of not questioning imperceptibly metamorphosed into the attribution of sacredness.[64]

Just as he argued in the case of the shari'a, Arkoun believes that the (to him) suspicious manner in which the extant Qur'an came to be regarded as sacred is still not up for discussion because of the sense of defensiveness and retrenchment felt by Muslims in confrontation with an ascendant West. Muslim scholars and intellectuals have avoided the subject of Qur'anic critique because they have been loath to undermine Muslim solidarity as the Arab Muslim world struggles for its status and deserts on the international plane.[65]

However, Arkoun insists that a critical reappraisal of the Qur'an is urgently needed. A revision must be made of the standard account of its compilation and the documents on which this account is based. Four different elements are introduced in making such a revision a workable project.

1. In order not to offend Muslim reverence for the Qur'an as the eternal word of God, Arkoun makes the distinction, as Muslims have in the past, between what the Qur'an calls the Book (which is the Book of Heaven), and the partial copy inspired by the Book, which is the Qur'an that is recited.[66] Arkoun is in venerable company when he appeals to this distinction, for it has been made by two of the greatest classic theologians in Islam, al-Ash'ari and Maturidi. Maturidi, still respected as the leading theologian by many Hanafites, especially in the Turkic world, held that only the *meaning* of the Qur'an was God's word, not the letters, words, and sounds that composed it, for these were created, whereas the Book had dwelled eternally with God. The words of the Qur'an were therefore an expression of a (chronologically and ontologically) prior meaning. In

principle, the Qur'an was a creation of God.[67] This would clear the way for a critical reappraisal of the actual Qur'an—for this would not, on a view like Maturidi's, amount to desecration of God's word.

2. There is the claim that dates from the reign of the third caliph, 'Uthman Ibn 'Affan, that the Qur'an was altered at the time of its compilation to the detriment of the spirit of the Prophet and his first two successors. This claim was made by those who survived from among the earliest Islamic consultative body, known as *majlis ash-shura*.[68] Their integrity cannot be questioned.

3. Documents apparently lie under lock and key in India, Syria, Yemen, and Morocco that would shed new light on the portentous events surrounding the compilation of the Qur'an and its immediate aftermath.[69]

4. The legitimacy of the caliphs who legitimized the standard account of the Qur'an's compilation, through which it came to be universally regarded as sacred by Muslims, can itself be disputed. For the Qur'anic concept used to support it, that of *bay'a* (the endorsement of the selected caliph by the community given through its representatives), had a definite historical basis, because the revelation appeared at a decisive moment in the Prophet's military campaigns when he could ill afford dissent. Bay'a has since been made a transcendent concept to lend a divine sheen to the caliph's authority. And here, Arkoun points out, is another instance of confusion between the eternal and the temporal, and of the need to recall to the best of one's ability and scholarship the particular circumstances in which each verse was revealed (which returns us to Rahman's project).[70]

Arkoun's challenge to orthodox Muslims is likely to have the persistence of an unwanted season. Not one of the foregoing four elements is dubious. Together, they form a solid basis for Qur'anic critique, the result of which will be, whenever it comes, that one can differentiate between the eternal and the temporal among the holy book's contents. So far as the shari'a is concerned, whatever is eternally based on the Qur'an will then become manifest, as will its many rulings that cannot be shown to embody the will of God. The shari'a, as Arkoun has demonstrated, has far too much to do with all-too-worldly concerns in how it came about for it to be sustainable as a divine law in its entirety. If applied properly by those who have the community's best interests at heart, Arkoun's daring critique will unburden Muslims from all that obstructs their religious revitalization, all that has become self-undermining or ineluctably self-contradictory in what they have regarded as their sacred scriptures and laws.

However, Arkoun himself does not set the best example when it comes to matters of faith, a privation that will put his whole project in question among Muslim believers. So busy is he in sifting through the historical, sociological, psychological, and political factors that have reinforced orthodoxy and the overall aspect of sacredness ascribed to the texts that he fails to recognize whatever in them is genuinely sacred and therefore merits the reverent response it draws forth from Muslims. Arkoun seems regrettably oblivious to the inner resonance of religious texts, to their unique power to fulfill deep-seated human aspirations, to their contiguity and resonance with what believers commonly experience as the center of their being. Arkoun does not realize that it takes infinitely more than inspired leaders and powerful states to assure the reverberations of inspired, moving words over many centuries and across a staggering variety of cultural boundaries.[71] His silence over the *essence* of religion amid a barrage of externals that can explain only the *politics* of (institutional) religion amounts to a trivialization that threatens to spill over into his otherwise sparkling and erudite critique.

One can hence expect only a ripple effect emanating from Arkoun. An intellectually gifted Muslim more sensitive than he is to the inner dimensions of religion will be able to see in Arkoun's work the means for sharpening the tools needed to undertake a fresh approach to grasping the meaning and eternal significance of the scriptures, an approach akin to that suggested by Rahman. Without that sensitivity, a new reading of the Qur'an and evaluation of the shari'a would leave Islam soulless.

We now have a critical line within Islam that is beginning to assume the shape of a tradition. Beginning with 'Abduh, who fully understood how far Muslims had become distanced from their holiest source and how much of that distance was attributable to a fragmented reading of the Qur'an cluttered with the intercession of layers of antiquated commentaries, and deftly crafted a new reading consistent with his evaluation of Islam's central tenets; continuing with Gökalp, who affirmed the inescapable fact of much of the shari'a's origin in custom and convention, and saw the implications of that for bringing mainstream[72] Islam back to life (albeit limited by his optimistic expectations from nationalism); and ending with Rahman in combination with (a) Arkoun's critical extensions of the work proposed by the former and (b) Nasr's appeal that Islam not lose its soul in the process, with the projected outcome being as firm a foundation as possible for the distinction between the eternal from the temporal within Islam and the fashioning of life in its essential spirit. This tradition holds the middle ground between secularist pressures to uproot Islam from its divine sources and "fundamentalist"-revolutionary pressures to attribute divinity to all the principal sources. Yet the two extremes themselves can serve their purpose well, the one as an unbridled invitation to examine the authenticity of Islam's scriptural sources, the other as a reminder to remain faithful to them.

Both Nasr and Rahman seek the balance that alone can adequately promote freedom in the Arab Muslim world yet firmly root that world's intersection with modernity in Islam. But their respective emphases differ profoundly. Although both affirm the moral and spiritual core of Islam, the core for Nasr is expressed in the vast body of specific rulings and laws that have issued from it, so that the core lives on genuinely in the rulings and laws, and these can be altered only with grave reservations faced with the inevitable changes in the world in which they must be applied. For Rahman, while the intention may have been for the shari'a to embody the core, many of its rulings have strayed from the core to the point of concealment. Specific rulings are therefore no longer binding. Furthermore, they were never meant to be timeless, given their specific context. Only when this is recognized does the core return to view. Far from Nasr's belief that the core lives on in its embodiments, Rahman believes that the core can live on only if it is divorced from its traditional embodiments, which have become a barrier between Muslims and the moral and spiritual core of their religion. Afterward, the core can be embodied anew given its new context. We can roughly delimit the choice of emphasis through the examples of Nasr and Rahman, possibly as modified by Arkoun's intellectual apparatus, and within a tradition that began with figures such as 'Abduh and Gökalp. Whatever the emphasis, Arab Muslim thought will remain firmly embedded in the moral and spiritual core of Islam, and it will also embrace evident changes and acknowledge Islamdom's intersection with modernity. How that core is related to its specific embodiments, from what point of view change is embraced, and whether a firm foundation is provided for the intersection with modernity—all these must remain open for some time to come, to be gradually answered by several types of thoughtful Muslims. And this complex and ongoing process will be decisive for the kind of freedom to be enjoyed in the Arab Muslim world irrespective of the political systems adopted.

The Mystically Inclined Heralds of Freedom

Modernity has masked mysticism. Popular mystical tendencies where modernity has reached its latest stage are themselves a parody of their ancestry. Despite the built-in prejudice, which has carried over into the Arab Muslim world where Sufism has been berated for its general indifference to colonial encroachments and its incompatibility with "progress," on top of its earlier suppression in the name of state-sponsored orthodoxy, the mystical tradition has survived. In some cases, its survival has been in the work of individual thinkers who are not Sufis in the full sense of the word, but have some empathy with mystical experience. In other cases, Sufism persists in orders, such as the Nakshibendi, that have a wide network of affiliates and have become highly influential. The strength of mystical sentiment may be measured by its persistence even in the two countries that have had the longest and most open encounter with modernity, Turkey and Egypt.

What Sufis and those affected by their outlook can contribute to the promotion of freedom in the Arab Muslim world derives from the depth of the freedom they have traditionally attained, of which we have caught some glimpses in this book. Individuals who exercise the highest degree of positive freedom, who feel this inward expansiveness whereby they experience the world as boundless yet full of meaning and purpose, are eminently qualified to seize the opportunity for the fresh expression of that purposeful, meaningful boundlessness. They can absorb and adopt the latest metaphysical ideas. They can accept all that is discovered by modern science, for when it remains within the scientifically admissible, it cannot fail to be consistent with transcendent reality even if the latter is not thereby established or confirmed. They can write more explicitly about freedom, now that freedom has become such a self-consciously central dimension of modernity. And if they are inclined to take up various intellectual disciplines offered by modernity, they can fashion theories of freedom embedded in a novel metaphysical outlook partly inspired by Islamic faith, thought, and mysticism.

Such a synthesis can be found in Mohammad Iqbal's *The Reconstruction of Religious Thought in Islam*. Iqbal's outlook exhibits open-endedness in all fundamental respects. We may contrast it with the common modern attitude, particularly at the apogee of mechanism, that considers the world to be a closed system, limits thought to finite concepts (and hence is itself restricted to the finite), and believes time to be just what we measure and manage with the help of clocks. In contrast, Iqbal considers the world, thought (potentially), and time itself to be suffused with the infinite. The domain of freedom is thereby profoundly altered—for rather than be restricted to an infinity of (mostly quantitative) permutations within a closed system, a boundlessness is imparted to that domain, whereby one's thought and one's own being are experienced as limitless and freedom tends toward the asymptote of the unrestricted. One is not merely free to do this or that within the framework offered by Iqbal, but free to become a human being fully exercising his creativity in its intellectual, moral, and spiritual dimensions. One is free to attain the highest level of humanity of which one is capable, a level where the human meets with, even as it remains essentially different from, the divine. From the vantage point of human beings having lived up to their creation in the image of God and comprehending the world accordingly, freedom, including freedom of action, takes on a completely different meaning. The world itself turns into a larger place, the possibilities within it go deeper, and the sense of one's potency and involvement becomes fuller.

This much may still remain with us from the discussion of Ibn 'Arabi and the references to positive freedom in its individual, personal aspect. And it reminds us of the continuity between his mystico-philosophical theology and Iqbal's metaphysics. However, Iqbal is more explicitly metaphysical than his illustrious predecessor. As we shall see, he has absorbed some of the most brilliant ideas and thought processes offered by his Western contemporaries. We have already seen in the preceding paragraph that much depends on a philosophically adequate treatment of thought as capable of attaining the infinite and time as suffused with it. Only then will the philosophical framework for freedom be up to the latter's boundlessness. It is in this context that Iqbal draws heavily from late-nineteenth and early-twentieth-century European philosophy.

Iqbal's position on the limits (or limitlessness) of thought is expressed through his assessment of al-Ghazzali's work. Although he approves of al-Ghazzali's recognition of mystical experience as necessary for the confirmation of religious *content*, which neither science nor metaphysics can provide,[73] and which is the ultimate anchor for freedom, he criticizes the restrictions that al-Ghazzali imposes on thought (which have been mentioned). He believes the restrictions are based on an erroneous idea about the limitations of thought, in particular that it is necessarily tied to the ordinary sequential flow of time. If thought be limited to the finite and temporal, then the infinite and the eternal, which are most important to the Muslim faith, elude it. Thus thought, in the eyes of al-Ghazzali in his more dogmatic mien, appears ultimately useless—an attitude common among orthodox Muslims. In marked contrast, Iqbal believes that thought can attain to the infinite (and the eternal) because the finite concepts with which it usually works are only moments that surface just as cause/effect relations are abstracted from the world so that reason can order it.[74] In the same way that the world is a vast, continuous whole well beyond any causal scheme used to describe it, so is the mind immeasurably more than the conceptual scheme it works with when rationally ordering its thoughts. The thought compatible with the mind exercising itself as a whole and to its highest ability has the infinite and the eternal within its grasp (a position that goes all the way back to ancient Greek philosophy). If there is some correspondence between finite conceptual ordering and the causal picture of the world, then so do the mind and the world, each taken as a whole, correspond.

But Iqbal is not content to rest with thought alone in facing the infinite. He opens the border between thought and intuition as he sets ordinary time aside, inspired by the philosophy of Bergson. Accordingly, he expands the notion of time itself, so that at one end it is mere ordinary temporality while at the other it dissolves into eternity. Time itself has one face that corresponds with our causal picture of the world and the finite concepts used in fashioning it, and another that corresponds with the world and the mind each taken as a whole. In between are many different levels of temporality. This is where intuition enters the picture: For we need it to recognize these levels.

Iqbal then appeals to intuition to establish the transcendence of the world, time, and thought respectively from the "mechanical" complex of the causal picture of the world set in ordinary time according to reason. The strategy is to undercut the argument of the materialists who regard the world as a closed system subject to ordinary time by showing that they employ only one among the various intellectual modes available to them. Were one to employ all the intellectual gifts that one is given, one would understand that the world is not a closed system and that ordinary time is only one aspect of temporality—and would notice how reductionistic scientific materialism is. So Iqbal wonders, through the voice of Wildon Carr, how a world mechanically abstracted by the intellect can evolve the intellect that performs the abstraction. How is it possible for the intellect to be the product of biological evolution when the world so described is merely a product of the intellect, and in only one of its modes (the analytical) at that?[75] Whatever has evolved the intellect must be something other than what presents itself to the intellect in its *analytical* mode. When the intellect recognizes this, its mode is *appreciative*. The intellect in its appreciative mode is the faculty by which we know the world as a whole and the span of temporality from ordinary (clock-measured and managed) time to eternity. Thus, in one mode, we see the world as a series of causally interrelated events in ordinary time. In another, we transcend our absorption in this external order, apprehend the world as an interrelated whole, and observe that our experiences permeate one another, sometimes to the extent that one experience can permeate the individual's whole temporal domain. The time that marks such experiences likewise becomes more elastic, so that past, present, and future flow freely into one another. When all of time takes on the appearance of a single "now," it becomes "duration,"[76] a concept borrowed from Bergson. Duration is pure time, where the past is not separate from the present, but operates on it, and the future is present as an open possibility, not as a dark unknown yet to be traversed.[77]

The distinction between pure time (akin to eternity) and fragmented time, which allows us to measure discrete temporal segments and easily distinguish between past, present, and future, has important consequences for Islam. It allows us to deal with "predetermination," a concept whose understanding has traditionally hampered Muslims. Iqbal suggests that "predetermination" is an inadequate understanding of "(written) destiny." Instead, destiny should be linked with duration (or with "pure time") and interpreted as time freed from causality, as being before the disclosure of its (causal) possibilities. Predestination is nothing but transcendent time, to live in which is not to submit helplessly to a mechanical sequence of cause and effect, but to creatively overcome it. Duration, time transcending causally defined temporality, does not correspond with a relentless fate working its way from without, but with the inward reach of whatever is immersed in it.[78] Individuals live out their destiny when they live in the fullness of time, which the appreciative mode of their intellect helps set apart from the ticking of the clock.

To interpret Iqbal's singular effort to unshackle Muslims from predetermination, one must first no longer imagine that the Qur'anic notion of "written destiny" alludes to some omniscient palmistry or astrology. What is "written" by God is written in pure time, in eternity, and transcends ordinary time. It is absurd to bring "written destiny" down to the level of precise causal chains that determine every little external in each individual's life. One should rather think in terms of the mystical notion of the interconnectedness of all things in pure time, however fragmented they may appear externally. There is an inner aspect to nature, to the world with which one is in harmony when the mind itself assumes its inner ("appreciative") mode. At the level of such harmony, wherein one is drawn nearer the eternal, one can no longer think in terms of what comes next, or the usual causal chains. It is the "written destiny" of human beings that they should be able to exist, if only momentarily, in pure time, at the level of overall interconnectedness. It is their destiny that, in a way, how much they have lived depends on how far they can transcend externals. That is all that is "predetermined." What goes on in ordinary time is an entirely different matter. Indeed, Muslims ought to creatively direct their lives through ordinary time to transcend it, far from worrying whether the externals of their lives have been predetermined for all time. Iqbal would severely condemn passivity faced with a misconceived fatalism. The true fate of human beings is to transcend the realm wherein fatalists submit to what will be.

One need not agree philosophically with Iqbal to grasp the import of his thrust. He sees a correspondence between the individual mind's ability to transcend causality, duration's transcendence of ordinary time, and the world's transcendence of its causal descriptions. And, like the Sufis who have spelled this out, he sees the summit of such transcendence as an utterly free existence in unbounded time. For freedom depends on the transcendence of causality, and acquires its personal, expansive dimension in a passage of time far less constrictive than that measured with clocks. The spirit of Iqbal's philosophy enables Muslims (and others) to experience the freedom of creative thought in a temporal realm far removed from natural necessity, the freedom of a world viewed as a boundless but meaningful whole, and freedom from the misconceived fatalistic outlook on life.

Iqbal's attempt to interpret modern philosophical ideas by appeal to the metaphysics implied by mystical experience is then turned toward God Himself. Not to be deterred by an austere, inhibitive view of God as utterly immobile (as part of His eternity and immutability), Iqbal boldly suggests that the mechanical notion of immobility is inadequate when it comes to God, for that does not match His infinite creative possibilities and His retention of the wholeness of His being throughout the history of the universe.[79] For God to be continuously in touch with His creation, hard as it is to conceive, His own being must be open-ended. Thus freedom for Iqbal is not only attributable to transcendent individuals who live in transcendent time but is also a reflection of God's own freedom. God, human beings, and the universe all have characteristics that reveal freedom as a fundamental quality.

Finally, to assure individuals of the viability of their transcendent pursuits, and that transcendent meaning is not arbitrarily attached to things but informs them through and through, Iqbal rejects the position that radically separates the world from what transcends it. On a universal scale, he holds, as he believes Muslims generally do, that "it is the mysterious touch of the ideal that animates and sustains the real." What we transcend is permeated with the transcendent. External material reality is permeated with the spirit. And what we are spiritually aware of can effect changes in the material world.[80] Thus, though the intellect has evolved from something other than the world analytically viewed and described, it can nevertheless be regarded as having emerged from what we take to be physical matter. The body is seen as "accumulated action or habit of the soul."[81] Iqbal thinks that Islam is neither dualist nor interactionist, but simply recognizes that body and soul, matter and spirit, though profoundly different, are nevertheless united. This unity facilitates the view that human beings strive purposively; their actions are directed, not as a foreign agency acts upon a passive body, but as an individual furthering the unity of matter and spirit in him, inspired by how the external world is permeated with transcendence. Thus individual human beings are free to transform their inner and outer reality through their purposive acts, and to concretize their transcendence.

The locus of freedom in Iqbal hence comprises the following elements:

1. The individuality of human beings (a point that has not yet been mentioned, but is an obvious requirement for freedom and is noted by Iqbal).

2. The transcendence by individual human beings of causality, all finite concepts, and ordinary time.

3. The direct affirmation that human beings are free.

4. The transcendence by the world of causality and ordinary time.

5. The unity (in the loose sense) of the transcendent and the immanent, which enables human beings to freely transform themselves and their world through purposive action.

6. God as utterly transcendent, with infinite creative possibilities.

We must now see whether any of the foregoing elements has a legitimate basis in Islam. Regarding the fourth and sixth elements, their scriptural admissibility is so much in evidence that it is superfluous to assert it. To support the others, Iqbal produces the following texts (given here with his own translations):

1. To affirm that each individual is unique: "Verily there is none in the Heavens and in the Earth but shall approach the God of Mercy as a servant. He hath taken note of them and remembered them with exact numbering: *and each of them shall come to Him on the day of Resurrection as a single individual.*"[82]

2. To affirm the transcendent aspect of individuals (which enables them to transcend all finite concepts, ordinary time and causality): "Now of fine clay have We created man: There We placed him, a moist germ, in a safe abode; then made we the moist germ a clot of blood: then made the clotted blood into a piece of flesh; then made the piece of flesh into bones: and We clothed the bones with flesh: *then brought forth man of yet another make.*"[83]

3. To affirm individual freedom: "And say: The truth is from your Lord: Let him, then, who will, believe: and let him who will, be an unbeliever."[84]

4. To affirm the unity (in the loose sense) of the transcendent and the immanent (and thus the potential to understand the presence of the transcendent in the immanent and the transformation of the immanent by the transcendent):

> We have not created the Heavens and the earth and whatever is between them in sport: We have not created them but for a serious end: but the greater part of them understand it not.
> Verily in the creation of the Heavens and of the earth, and in the succession of the night and the day, are signs for men of understanding; who, standing and sitting and reclining, bear God in mind and reflect on the creation of the Heavens and of the earth, and say: "Oh, our Lord! Thou hast not created this in vain!"[85]

Iqbal also found support for his views in the Islamic mystical tradition and even in the rites prescribed by the shari'a. For he sees the prescriptions for prayer, for instance, as freeing Muslims from the pull of sleep and their daily business.[86] He also sees the ideal of Sufism as "the possession and enjoyment of the infinite,"[87] which reverberates in his own position that the cumulative outcome of free acts in the life of an individual, if there is real accumulation and not the dispersal of individual freedom, creates situations within the individual more and more able to receive "fresh illuminations from an Infinite Reality."[88]

The philosophical and religious import of the ideas and thought processes that have just been briefly discussed is such that an adequate preliminary exposition would fill a large volume. The reader can therefore be forgiven if he has found the foregoing pages to be dense. It is impossible to do otherwise in a work such as this. But at least it is hoped that some interest is thereby aroused in the possibilities offered by Iqbal's *The Reconstruction of Religious Thought in Islam.* Iqbal too usually confines himself to broad strokes. Nevertheless, one should not lose sight of his project's implications for freedom and the revitalization of Islam, on which a powerful new light is cast. For the most creative thinkers who peaked in Iqbal's lifetime—Bergson, Nietzsche, Whitehead, Einstein, Royce, Alexander, Bradley, and Eddington—have urged him far beyond the mere assertion of freedom, toward a comprehensive exemplification of freedom that runs through every cornerstone of the Islamic totality: God, man, and the world. God's creative freedom, man's freedom of thought (in the fullest sense of the expression, that which pertains to the domain and extent of thought), time's openness to eternity, and the world's suffusion with transcendence together ground a universal freedom relative to which current talk about freedom is empty. Moreover, Iqbal has been able to show that this universal freedom, in all its aspects, is consistent with the teachings of the Qur'an. Here his contribution to Islam is priceless. For he has taught Muslims how to read their most sacred text, without doing violence to it, in the light of contemporary genius. Conversely, he has shown how several verses in their most sacred text resonate and live on and anew in the most daring and imaginative words wrought by the free thought of his day.

The foregoing is not meant to imply that Iqbal fails to offer incisive suggestions as to how traditional Muslim sources and jurisprudential methods may be treated in modern times. He does offer them.[89] Of special interest here is his reference, in discussing the sayings traditionally attributed to the Prophet, to the principle that these sayings must be seen in the context of a prophet's need to address the people among whom he begins his mission in a manner to which they can relate. The sayings of the Prophet, when governed by that need (which is usually the case when they are injunctions), must therefore have a specific character. In that event, what matters is the principle that underlies them. Only such a principle can be eternally valid.[90] Here the reader may recognize one of the central ideas in Rahman's project for Islamic renewal. And if the reader wishes to trace this idea further, he may turn to the thought of yet another Sufi intellectual from the Subcontinent, Shah Vali-ullah (1702–63), who revived the thought of Sirhindi, and about whom Rahman had written nearly thirty years before the publication of *Islam and Modernity*.

This should also remind us just how interconnected the Islamic milieu is for all the separations one has to make in presenting a book that concerns it. For we notice that a Sufi renewer whose work and ideas have more recently inspired a conservative movement that occasionally lapses into fanaticism, Shaikh Ahmad Sirhindi, through a disciple of his, Shah Vali-ullah, influenced two of Islam's brightest and most open-minded twentieth-century innovators, the philosophers Muhammad Iqbal and Fazlur Rahman.

If anything is largely absent from the thought of Iqbal, it is the Muslim community as such. For the Muslim totality of God, man, and world implies a communal order that cannot be overlooked and for which the shari'a, as the reader knows by now, has been a symbol. Novel ideas within a Muslim milieu therefore ought to minimally *imply* a vision of what Muslims would be like as a community. We can begin to satisfy this condition differently from how we have with Nasr, 'Abduh, Gökalp, and Rahman—all of whose ideas about the contemporary treatment of the shari'a have much bearing on Muslim communities—by turning to the work of Bediüzzaman Sa'īd Nursi.

With Nursi, we enter a different world, no less intense than Iqbal's, but more directly conversant with the people whose lives would change because of one man's work. Thus it is suitable for an account of Nursi's achievements to be more biographical than textual. This is what Şerif Mardin has done in his most recent book, *Religion and Social Change in Modern Turkey.*

Nursi himself was not a Sufi, at least not in the traditional sense. But eastern Anatolia, where he grew up, has a long, lively heritage of mystical and saintly lore. Three rather different kinds of mysticism influenced Nursi. One was the mysticism that Nursi directly experienced through his penchant for retreats into contemplation. He claimed to have encountered one of the major figures of Sufism, 'Abd al-Qadir al-Jilani (the founder of the Qadiri order), in a dream.[91] The second was the illuminist school of mysticism, which draws its inspiration from the work of Ibn 'Arabi, and with which "Anatolian mysticism had found an elective affinity."[92] The third was the revivalist version of the mystical movement known as the Nakshibendi, which in contrast to its Central Asian precursor emphasized social and political action. Nursi admired Sirhindi, a major figure in the spread of the renewed Nakshibendi order across India (as we have seen). Sirhindi had preached a return to the spirit of early Islam where high morals and spirituality combined with attention to the social and political plight of Muslims. This doctrine became the spearhead for the fight against European domination.[93] Nursi is said to have believed that his accomplishments were a manifestation of Sirhindi's spiritual power.[94]

Nursi's mystical bent was complemented with intellectual keenness and curiosity. As a young man, he had alternated his contemplative retreats with engaging the local sheikhs and learned men in debates.[95] His reputation took him to a larger town, Van, where he found textbooks on modern science, history, and philosophy.[96] He soon reached the conclusion that the classical refutations of the arguments of unbelievers had become obsolete and that they could regain their vitality only through the study of the modern fields he had become acquainted with.[97] He noticed that when it comes to faith, theology is superseded by appeals to the heart, and connected this with social and political action that would win over estranged Muslims.[98] And he had the courage to declare that the truths of Islam could no longer be asserted, but needed to be argued for, investigated, and expressed with sensitivity to their audience.[99] Meanwhile, he had proven himself in the much more challenging milieu of Istanbul, where he responded to religious and theological queries with originality and intelligence.[100] He had the audacity to suggest that Turkey would not advance in the right way through secularization, but through the introduction of religious education into secular schools and the study of science into religious schools.[101]

Nursi's boldness went further than the foregoing controversial positions. He communicated them openly to the sultan and denounced the sultan's "passivity as caliph and leader of the Muslims." This shows how people with certain religious credentials can cross into terrain that others dare not contemplate. Nursi, however, could stand by his convictions because he also belonged to a people who made a habit of independent-mindedness. When palace officials brought Nursi for interrogation, believing him insane for what he had brazenly pronounced, and to their consternation found him to be quite sane, "[h]e explained that outspokenness was a characteristic of the mountain culture in which he had originated and that the convention of Ottoman politeness current in the capital could not be used to judge his behavior."[102]

Mardin attributes such independence of spirit among rural peoples to lively debate, which is necessary to keep the values and doctrines transmitted through oral traditions alive.[103] This fuses with the competitive spirit prevalent among tribesmen. In Nursi's native circles, exceptional abilities that stood out early were highly acclaimed, so that a talented boy who outargued his peers could flourish.[104] And so, Nursi was natively and amply endowed with the fortitude to act publicly on what he had attained intellectually and spiritually.

Finally, a series of concrete and dramatic events lent special urgency to Nursi's task. For he had witnessed the devastation of his home region in the wake of the Armenian tragedy and war with Russia, then the total collapse of the Ottoman Empire. Once reconstituted as the Turkish republic, he witnessed the strict enforcement of its secular ideology. In many ways, the world as he had known it fell apart, and from that something barely recognizable emerged. Nursi had to find ways to reach those left out or behind by the drastic changes and maintain the continuity, if not the forms, of what had given meaning to their lives—and his.

The people who were most in need of what Nursi could offer tended to have rural backgrounds. However, the individuals who overcame great obstacles to interact with Nursi and his written works, whose stories are movingly told by Mardin, were not the kind who wished to parrot the Qur'an. They rather wished to penetrate its mysteries or develop an integrated cosmology. But they were frustrated by the state through police interrogation and expulsion from school.[105] The state meant to enforce secularism, harshly if need be.[106]

Nursi's first followers, then, were literate, curious, rural people who were deeply dissatisfied with the (dis)information the state had given them on religion. Theological and philosophical issues mattered to them, both intellectually and personally. Fundamental questions about the origins of the world, its meaning and purpose, preoccupied them. So did the search for an internally consistent picture of Islam. These rural seekers were also aware of recent scientific theories that had trickled to the countryside. They wanted to learn more about them and reconcile them with an Islamic worldview. Finally, they felt under assault from the modern Turkish state, whose Kemalist ideology held up the Western model of society and attacked the idea of an Islamic community.[107] In all the foregoing respects, they were hence an ideal audience for Nursi, given what has just been mentioned about Nursi's motives and virtues.

Nursi also found an audience in less-literate circles, cut off from Islamic traditions by the change in the official language and the lack of competent men to address their religious needs. The state simply assumed that people would leave religion behind as their social and economic situation improved and the Turkish nation became stronger and more convincing in its paternalism. Kemalism was afflicted with the positivist notion that religion is not essentially rooted in human nature, but is merely a stage to be substituted by one more "mature." Nevertheless, vast and still accumulating evidence shows that wherever they may be, under whatever circumstances, many human beings are united in their realization that something within them transcends the material world, that the material world indeed transcends itself, and that the enveloping transcendence strongly suggests an *active* transcendent source. They also sense, given their acknowledgment of transcendence, that this somehow is what is really real (not necessarily to the point of denying the reality of immanence, certainly not in Islam). They feel that the transcendent is metaphysically prior to what normally engages them, that indeed it is the ultimate meaning of their daily work and toil. Now, if the language available to them happens to be overwhelmingly tilted in favor of an everyday existence denuded of transcendence, then they do not possess the means for the articulation of their worldview. They relate to transcendence intuitively, but are otherwise inarticulate about it. This can be debilitating at the profoundest level; for those who inhabit a world open to what transcends it would feel, on the one hand, a calling to expand their being into that openness and, on the other, an immediate arrest of the expansion for lack of a medium to shape it (a role that can be played by language when the practice of freely manipulating certain symbols is prevalent). Their selfhood, if one must be fashionably psychoanalytical, is only realized when it expands into realms that they intuitively behold.

But the expression of that yearning is tied down by linguistic incoherence and symbolic voids—for they are told with every official turn that language can be nothing but incoherent, and the symbols nonexistent, when it comes to "fictions" such as transcendence. It is hard to imagine a more substantial denial of freedom, although how substantial the denial is is itself hard to imagine in an age obsessed with consumerism and the institutional guarantees for certain rights including the freedom of choice.

So when an enlightened person comes along, for whom transcendence is much more than the object of a vague awareness and longing, and can thus express it by unshackling secular language and surrounding it with a halo of symbols resurrected from his spiritual ancestry—when such a person comes along, the dimly lit world of those tied down by linguistic incoherence and symbolic voids becomes incandescent. The liberation of the world from the dimness caused by the silencing and inarticulacy of those otherwise sincerely open to its transcendence, and the liberation of the self from similar confines, are momentous. The world, language, and the self are once more oriented toward wider realms. The expansiveness is steeped in resonant metaphors that converge upon the origin of all transcendence. The self grows into its fullness. And the world is experienced as full of purpose and meaning.

One must not rashly retort that Nursi's contribution to the freedom of his followers has been nothing of the sort. Enough such retorts based on comprehensive ignorance of the process at hand have been made. What we ought to consider is whether Nursi had a vision of transcendence in relation to the world, and whether he made it accessible to his followers by expressing it through a language familiar because of both its modernness and Islamic character.

In his evaluations of Nursi's accomplishments, Mardin describes the idiom in which Nursi worked as "concerned with 'spiritual being'" and taking "its force from a basic premise about the existence of God."[108] Mardin asserts that it is unnecessary to know why this is so to appreciate what such an idiom is instrumental in bringing about for those who dwell in it: a relationship of enchantment with the world, the deep expansion of one's personality and realization of one's identity, and a cognitive model of the universe and the world.[109] But if Nursi generally answered the need for the articulation of the transcendent dimension of the world and the self, so that personal experience waxes expansive and full of meaning and the world repeatedly points beyond its surfaces, and if he gave an integrated picture of the cosmos for the more metaphysically inclined among his followers, what did he specifically achieve within an Islamic context?

Besides giving his followers conviction in the meaning of their lives and a better grounded identity, Nursi affirmed the centrality of the community of Muslims. He also envisaged the community as composed of persons who deal with one another as such, rather than see it as a mere aggregate of individuals, which is the predominant modern view. These were crucial in view of the threat that the community had faced from a determined secular government under the spell of positivism.[110] Nursi instead held the state to be there *for* family and community, in contrast with many modernizing Turks who felt burdened by them.[111] He provided an antidote for alienation, by encouraging people to see themselves as involved members of their community, rather than isolated individuals who stand apart from (and analyze) their society.[112]

But Nursi's vision of the community of Muslims was hardly static or a mythical hark back to the past. As has been mentioned, he was conversant with modern thought and realized that modern thinking was necessary to give Islam its modern moorings. One can see this most poignantly in how Nursi handled the Qur'an itself. Having understood the benefits of modern communications, he presented the Qur'an in a language accessible to the audience: Turkish. Rural Turks could thus understand what he said. And they were captivated by the allusive and metaphorical style of Nursi's commentaries even if they could not understand them, for the style called up a folk idiom that had not lost its resonance.[113]

Nursi's innovations regarding how to relate to the Qur'an went beyond style. Given his recognition that religion needed modern arguments in its favor, he shifted emphasis from ritual to meaning, and from ethico-religious commands to the rationale behind them.[114] Muslims ought not attach too much importance to their rituals or commands such as those overemphasized by the Islamic revolutionaries. What matters is what the Qur'an really means and the eternal principles underlying the commands that it mentions or implies. Nursi also encouraged readers of the Qur'an to find in its uncomplicated picture of the created world the encouragement to explore creation as creatively as possible, and interpret the creative power of God as favoring a dynamic universe that invites the constant construction of new cosmic images.[115] He stressed the evocative power and style of the Qur'an to turn Muslims toward an active view of their universe and not just participate passively in the recitation.[116] This turns Muslims away from certain implications of the belief that the Qur'an is uncreated, and therefore eternal and immutable—for rather than uncreatedness leading to an approach so cautious as to have entailed virtual intellectual and spiritual paralysis, Nursi took the Qur'an's timelessness to mean that the seeds of the most dynamic and imaginative relationship with the universe lay in it. He urged that the Qur'an itself be read in that spirit. And so, he liberated his followers from the inhibitive awe with which they had been brought up to regard the Qur'an. The Qur'an would not, he believed, attract people because of its authoritative pronouncements, but because of its richness and humanitarianism.[117] This is how Nursi reconciled reverence for the Qur'an with modernity's aversion to timorousness. More important for our purposes, Nursi's open, humane reading of the Qur'an gives us a clue to how Muslim communities might reconstitute themselves. For when the central text that has welded Muslim communities is unburdened from the unnecessary consequences of its timelessness and authority, the communities themselves are free to gather around rich meanings and eternal humane principles rather than meaningless rituals and brutally enforced commands.

Nursi, as has been mentioned, studied the secular sciences and urged his followers to do the same. But he tried to overcome the sundering of the modern scientific worldview from the religious by grounding science in religious symbols.[118] He tried to use Sufi metaphysics to this end, for he favored the mystical picture of nature as the profounder of the two.[119] We have briefly come across Sufi metaphysics,[120] which recognizes a zone where the immanent and the transcendent intermingle and thus allows for limitless creativity in the visualization of the immanent because of its openness to transcendence. Sufi metaphysics can thus accommodate itself to any new cosmological theory, so long as that theory does not exclude transcendence (which the physical sciences do not have it in their power to do anyway). And because it sees the external world as an enchanted place, a work of love, one is not misled by analytical complexity into deadening the object of study. So Nursi could simultaneously embrace the theories and findings of modern science while trying to keep the scientific worldview embedded in a broader and livelier perspective.

It does not come as a surprise, then, that Nursi sought to keep the outlet afforded by Sufism open.[121] Although he rejected the role of miracle worker and was skeptical about the validity of privileged mystical knowledge, he did accept that the mystical path led to the understanding of religious verities.[122] But most important of all, Nursi believed, was faith,[123] and the unicity and transcendent power of God.[124] His emphasis on these was such that he considered the integral application of the shari'a and the unification of all Muslims goals attainable only in the indefinite future,[125] even though he named these as the duties of the elect. The foremost duty of the elect, the only one realizable in the foreseeable future, is to strengthen their faith.[126]

Nursi set his followers on the way to liberation at many levels. They would regain their freedom as persons composing a community. They were encouraged to participate actively in the Qur'an, and feel free to exercise their creative imagination in interpreting those passages (favored by Nursi) that called for it. They were urged away from the Qur'an's forbidding aspect and the inhibitive awe in which it had traditionally been held, and instead led to its richness and humanitarianism. Their intellectual freedom could gain much from the study of modern history, philosophy, and science, which Nursi held essential. And they could dwell once more in an enchanted world, experienced as a gift from a transcendent God, filled with His presence, its face gradually revealed through scientific theory, imagination, and discovery.

The emphasis Nursi placed on faith and the unity of God, and the relegation of the integral application of the shari'a to an unspecified future date, is at once a clear statement of priorities and a practical and considerate recognition of the freedom of those who wish to pursue other possibilities. In particular, and despite the unsavory impression that Nursi had had of Christian Europe and the ease with which the confrontation allowed local Christians to become (often unfairly) associated with the foreign enemy, his emphasis on faith, transcendence, and unity implies the basis for a healthier relationship between Muslims and non-Muslims. Indirectly, the freedom of non-Muslims is given its room, and perhaps a positive dialogue might follow between Muslims, non-Muslims, and those who have landed in a nonreligious outlook.

The principal negative effect that Nursi and his followers have had on freedom results from their extremely conservative stance toward women. Given all their other positions, it comes as an unpleasant surprise that they prefer, even among Muslims in Europe, to keep women from displaying their charms:

> [W]hile the ideas of positive science have been welcomed by the *nurcus*,[127] some of the symbolic content of Islam has been vigorously reaffirmed. Among the latter, the special place ascribed to women, the underscoring of Islamic sexual ethics and the separation of the sexes have been items on which they have been uncompromising; these ideas have gone against the values promoted by the secular civil code of Turkey.[128]

It seems that in this case, Nursi's followers have succumbed to the temptation to react to government-imposed modern customs rather than confront and overcome the motivation behind the imposition. In their attitude toward women, they have reduced Islam to one of those (by now decidedly self-undermining) symbols that markedly set it apart from other religions instead of, as Nursi usually does, affirm Islam through its inexhaustible communal and spiritual wealth.[129]

      •   •   •

In the work of Iqbal and Nursi, we find an alternative solution to the problem of the attunement of the Qur'an to its modern context. This solution ought not provoke the fear of conservatives, who would see in the abandonment of even the most mundane, specific, and obviously time- and culture-bound verse of the Qur'an a threat to the sanctity of the whole (and would fail to see the weakness inherent in their fear and how it does not measure up to the strength of the book whose sanctity they guard with such zeal). For Iqbal and Nursi aim to interpret the

Qur'an imaginatively because of their faith in its enduring relevance and in the light of their attunement to modernity's highest intellectual accomplishments. Thus, Iqbal finds the Qur'an supportive of individual freedom and creativity and an open-ended, emergent cosmology; and Nursi sets an example of active participation in the Qur'an, reflected by the Qur'an's compatibility with an active view of the universe, and penetrates its ethico-religious commands to their rationale while also emphasizing the meaning of ritual. Nursi does not imply that should the rationale in its present context entail a stricture or mode of conduct different from what the Qur'an specifies, then the relevant Qur'anic verse ought to be questioned. He simply leaves the Qur'an as it is, and tacitly endorses what the rationale entails, whereas Rahman would endorse this explicitly. The difference between the two may be crucial when it comes to entrenched and narrow views about the Qur'an's inviolability. Furthermore, in his attitude toward the Qur'an, Nursi prepares the groundwork for Muslims to worship through its means, to revere it as uncreated and eternal, without being stunned by its authoritativeness and gravity. Once a generation of Muslims can relate to the Qur'an in this way, a different understanding of the implications of its standing may gradually come to light. No one can reasonably expect the Qur'an's standing to ever change among believing Muslims. But the prevalent understanding of what follows from that, much of which must be described as entailing the lack of freedom, is not itself sacrosanct. Nasr, Rahman, Iqbal, and Nursi all find the Qur'an to be deeply conducive to freedom. That the Qur'an stands in the way of such freedom can for them only be a consequence of its misuse, both in how Muslims relate to it and how they then interpret it. Therefore, the thinkers who set different examples for relating to the Qur'an, and who all show that its standing has not thereby been diminished, eventually clear the way for the interpretations that have become necessary for the Qur'an to resonate fully in its present context and become a vehicle for freedom.

The thought of Iqbal and Nursi also provides a solution to a problem Geertz has left us with. Geertz appears to suggest that modernity makes it difficult for people to continue to be religious, for they become distanced from easy access to the rituals and upbringing that inculcate religious sentiments. The unanimity of belief gives way to a mixed environment. Religiousness is then replaced with religious-mindedness. Those who can no longer be religious but very much want to must resort to the evocation of images of what religiousness constitutes, among which the most readily available are externals such as the strictures on pork and alcohol in Islam. Geertz, however, has missed the alternative to the claims that he makes. Nowhere does he suggest that religiousness results from something that lies within human nature, which a certain upbringing and a set of rituals *nourish* rather than *cause to exist*. Given the absence of that possibility, he fails to see that modernity need not result in the erosion of religiousness as such, but of the traditional means of its nourishment. In view of the consistency with which religious sentiment has surfaced throughout human history, and has cut across every conceivable ethnic, cultural, and temporal boundary, and especially in view of the catastrophic failure of recent systematic efforts to expunge religious sentiment from human life, one is advised to assume religious sentiment to be rooted in human nature as we know it rather than tediously spin out implausible but seductively elaborate theories that allege to explain its presence and pervasiveness. All the works and expressions of religious sentiment cannot be simply dismissed as the product of an illusion—and the burden remains overwhelmingly on those who claim that an illusion is indeed involved. All the social sciences appear to share the weakness of having no adequate explanation for religious sentiment, a weakness intrinsic to their assumptions and methodologies.

Nursi and Iqbal affirm that religious sentiment is not reducible to its outer forms, but is an inward reality that belongs essentially to our being. Thus, the problem is not that religious-mindedness has replaced religiousness, but finding adequate contemporary expression for religiousness. Traditional views about the immutability of the scriptural sources in Islam have prevented them from becoming an adequate means of religious expression among Muslims today. In the meantime, some Muslims with limited horizons imagine the problem to be one of the failure to adhere with sufficient force and sincerity to those traditional views. Such Muslims are the religious-minded of which Geertz speaks. But they are prominent only in the absence of the emergence and legitimization of new forms of religious expression (that need not break radically with the old, as we have seen). Thus, Muslim revivalism need not be dominated by revolutionary extremism in the long run, but can turn toward the search for the attunement of (Muslim) religiousness to its present context. The contribution of the likes of Nursi and Iqbal in that regard can hardly be underestimated—for it helps secure that religiousness remain so and is not diverted by the charade of religious-mindedness.

Free spirits touched by the mystical tradition and the intellectual fruits of modernity can therefore complement the work of scholars. Scholars must proceed cautiously and ensure that their work is legitimately grounded in the scriptural sources whose sanctity they feel must not be violated. Free spirits, however, can leap ahead, as their more frankly mystical forebears always have, and rely on their instinctive grounding in Islam to allow them to complement the work of the scholars. Thus, what Rahman anticipated among the new urban Turkish scholars had already taken place in the work of a man from the countryside spurred by the individuality customary among his mountainfolk and a vibrant oral tradition of mystical lore, hagiography, and stories about the Prophet. Thinkers like Nursi and Iqbal keep the intellectual and spiritual field in healthy tumult. Their ilk also quietly lead Muslims away from their political, cultural, and religious oppressors toward greater freedom and lives more fully lived.

Conclusion

Freedom may advance along several fronts in the Arab Muslim world. We have surveyed and reflected upon the following in this final chapter.

1. There is a new awareness by both modernity and Islam, the one of its moral and spiritual failings, the other of the profound need for change. Despite its outward gains in recent years, the humbling of modernity should make it appear less formidable to Islam, while Islam may finally relax the defensive posture that has so distorted its potential and virtues for many generations now. This would create an opportunity for a two-fold extension of freedom: a return to its moral and spiritual roots; and more individual choice in determining the manner of that return now that Muslims hitherto compelled to zealously preserving those roots may soon find themselves faced with a diminished threat.

2. In such a less confrontational atmosphere, if those who feed off civilizational clashes do not have their way, the intellectual possibilities that have clearly come to the fore will be gradually integrated into Islamic life, and later the official articulation of Islam. They will justify the reinterpretation of certain Qur'anic verses and key terms of Islamic political and legal thought. We have seen how some verses, such as those that deal with women or Muslim-Christian relations, have been abused, and how others may never have been intended as eternally valid. We have also seen how the concept of "innovation" (bid'a), the injunction to obey those in authority, and the assertion that Islam is a religion and a state have become harmful to the community and the individuals who compose it. To reinterpret all these more consistently with Islamic vitality and interests will therefore contribute tremendously to the freedom of Muslims and the non-Muslims who have lived among them since the day they first met with Muslim armies, mystics, or merchants.

3. Among ordinary people in the Arab Muslim world, there is a strong sense of indignation over despotism, both political and personal, and an obvious ability to distinguish between outward forms of behavior that are either irrelevant to their faith or concerning which the spokesmen of their faith had been in error, and the Islamic faith itself. Masses of Muslims now feel they can enjoy movies, music, and theater, have a say in whom they shall marry, plan their families, fall in love, and openly agitate against corrupt, inept, or tyrannical rulers without in any way compromising their Islamic faith or, indeed, Islam itself. This is not only a sig-

nificant movement toward freedom, but already involves its expression. In many parts of the Arab Muslim world, people are freer than the actions of their governments and the pronouncements of clerics and Islamic revolutionaries—not to mention the usual chorus of plangent intellectuals—may lead one to believe. Their freedom *as Muslims* will add impetus to the intellectual articulation and subsequent official acceptance of the elements of Islamic vitality just mentioned.

4. Much of Islam's capacity for renewal depends on how the eternal is reconciled with the temporal. For though the Qur'an is regarded by Muslims as an eternally valid work in every respect, it bears on daily life either by suggestion or as detailed, unambiguous injunctions. Many more such injunctions are believed to have been correctly derived from the Qur'an and the sayings of the Prophet, thus themselves acquiring eternal validity. And yet, many among these injunctions can no longer be judged valid. If this be acknowledged, the reverberations seem to threaten the entire edifice of eternity. However, since at least the appearance of Shah Vali-ullah in India in the seventeenth century, Muslim intellectuals have been learning to distinguish between the eternal *principles* of the Qur'an and the specific *injunctions* derived therefrom, most of which are bound to be temporal. In our own century, Iqbal, Nursi, and Rahman, all undeniably faithful to Islam, have tried to reconcile the eternal with the temporal along those lines. Their work contributes to Muslims' assurance about the eternity of their faith while finding an acceptable basis for what must change. It will solidly ground the Muslim sense of freedom in both its positive and negative aspects, as ultimately rooted in the eternal and yet as the idiosyncratic expression of unique individuals and communities.

5. Because Islam is not just doctrines and principles from which various battle lines are drawn over what is or is not Islamic, but *a way of life*, it is important for Muslims to have in their midst individuals who, just by being themselves, embody Islam's greatest virtues and manifest the highest realization of freedom in an Islamic context. Many such individuals have traditionally been Sufis. The mystics of Islam thus still have, and will always have, a central role to play. And it comes as no surprise, given the calm confidence that the mystically inclined enjoy with respect to their fidelity to their faith—far from the fanatic whose frowns and shrieks give away that he more than anyone else needs assurance that he has faith—that they have been able to see Islam in livelier and more imaginative terms than those excessively bound by the legal heritage. Thus someone like Nursi could be freely open to modernity's best offerings, yet preserve Islam's moral and spiritual core in his very being. His disciples could then be free to express and fulfill themselves not only because they had access to ideas they could think through but also because they were directly touched by the freedom that brings such ideas to life in the first place.

The foregoing make up a fivefold path toward freedom in the Arab Muslim world. This path must be seen as a whole, for if freedom, for instance, were exclusively tied with liberation, without any regard for moral and spiritual purposiveness, the liberated would feel betrayed not long after they have reached their objective. With nothing else to be free for, their energies would soon turn narcissistic, devoted to social or political activism for their own sake. This is one of the most serious problems within the leading lands of modernity. The Arab Muslim world has the opportunity to place liberation within the broader framework of the moral and spiritual dimensions of freedom so that an expanse be guaranteed worthy of human beings not condemned to self-absorption. Should Islam attain its best possible state, then freedom for everyone in the Arab Muslim world could itself be exercised to turn human beings toward the realization of what is best in them. From such an outcome, modernity too would have much to gain.

Notes

Bibliography

Index

Notes

Book Epigraphs

1. Jean Baudrillard, *Baudrillard Live*, ed. Mike Gane (London: Routledge, 1993), 48.
2. Unsi al-Hajj, *Khawatem* (Ends)(London: Riad El-Rayyes Books, 1991), 166–68. My translation.
3. Nikolai Berdyaev, *The Destiny of Man*, quoted in *The World Treasury of Modern Religious Thought*, ed. Jaroslav Pelikan (Boston: Little, Brown and Company, 1990), 424.

1. The Assault on Freedom: Orthodoxy, Reform, and Reaction

1. Marijan Molé, *Les mystiques Musulmans* (Paris: Presses Universitaires de France, 1965), 6–9.
2. Şerif Mardin, *The Genesis of Young Ottoman Thought* (Princeton, N.J.: Princeton Univ. Press, 1962), 222–23.
3. Ibid., 137–39.
4. Halil Inalcik, *The Ottoman Empire: The Classical Age 1300–1600* (London: Weidenfeld and Nicholson, 1973), 179.
5. Uriel Heyd, "The Ottoman 'Ulema and Westernization in the Time of Selim III and Mahmud II," in *Scripta Hierosolymitana: Studies in Islamic History and Civilization*, vol. 4, ed. Uriel Heyd (Jerusalem: Hebrew Univ. Press [at the Magnus], 1961), 64–65.
6. Ibid., 65–66.
7. Ibid., 67–68.
8. Ibid., 68–69.
9. Ibid., 71–72.
10. Ibid., 73.
11. Mardin, *Young Ottoman Thought*, 139.
12. See Heyd, 78–87 and 96.
13. The best possible candidates for exceptions are Indonesia and Malaysia. There are also encouraging developments in Turkey, Jordan, and Pakistan. By 'encouraging,' it is not meant, as is often the case, "according to the Western definition of 'modernity'." I simply mean that such developments are encouraging from the standpoint of freedom. As will be argued in the coming chapters, it is not clear that modernity as it is usually thought of is as great a boon to freedom as is commonly supposed.
14. Inalcik, 173.
15. For a more detailed account of this pivotal period in modern Egyptian history, see 'Afaf Lutfi Al-Sayyid Marsot, *A Short History of Modern Egypt* (Cambridge, U.K.: Cambridge Univ. Press, 1985), 47–81.
16. Ira Lapidus, *A History of Islamic Societies* (Cambridge, U.K.: Cambridge Univ. Press, 1988), 620. For al-Afghani's rationalism and his enthusiasm for science, see also Nikki Keddie, *An Islamic Response to Imperialism* (Berkeley: Univ. of California Press, 1983), 14, 110, 121–22, 182–83, and 187.

17. The work of the late Pakistani religious thinker, educator, and scholar Fazlur Rahman, some of whose ideas we shall encounter in the course of this book, is a good illustration of 'Abduh's enduring influence.

18. Lapidus, 621. For a subtle, clear, and superbly researched account of 'Abduh's fresh approach to Islam, see Jacques Jomier, *Le commentaire Coranique du Manar* (Paris: G.-P. Maisonneuve, 1954), 10, 12–19, 69–70, 87–95, 102–5, and 350, among others. I shall say more about 'Abduh in the last chapter.

19. Fazlur Rahman, *Islam and Modernity* (Chicago: Univ. of Chicago Press, 1982), 65–67.

20. Ibid., 101–2.

21. Ibid., 104.

22. Only recently has the Israeli historian Benny Morris argued convincingly that Israel enjoyed a clear military advantage on several counts in 1948 over all the Arab armies put together. The advantage was even *numerical* when only the forces truly available for combat are counted. One conclusion is that there is nothing fantastic about Israel's victory in 1948, nor do the Arabs have good reason to feel ashamed of their defeat. Israel's superiority was in numbers, firepower, organization, mobilization, and preparedness, not in valor. See Benny Morris, *The Birth of the Palestinian Refugee Problem 1947–9* (Cambridge, N.Y.: Cambridge Univ. Press, 1987).

23. Hassan Hanafi, "Al-Judhur at-Tarikhiyya li-'Azmat'il-Hurriyya w'ad-Dimuqratiyya fi Wujdanina al-Mu'asir" (The historical roots of the impasse with regard to freedom and democracy in our collective consciousness), in *ad-Dimuqratiyya wa Huquq al-Insan f'il-Watan al-'Arabi* (Democracy and human rights in the Arab homeland)(Beirut: Markaz ad-Dirasat al-Wihda al-'Arabiyya [Center for Arab Unity Studies], 1983), 188. The translation from the original Arabic is mine. All other such translations are also mine unless otherwise specified.

24. Hanafi, *Freedom*, 189.

25. Ibid, 189.

26. The critical assessment of this theme will return in much more detail, and in the light of all that has gone on before, near the end of the book in chapter 6.

27. Hanafi, *Freedom*, 187.

28. Ibid., 187–88.

29. At the very least, these grounds have to do with human nature (including the question of whether that nature is primarily spiritual or not), values, the emotions, the psychological disposition of individuals, and historical developments that change much of what seems rational from one epoch to the next.

30. This is all preliminary. Much more is to follow in chapters 2 and 3.

31. There will be a general account of the different kinds of freedom and the complexities surrounding its definition in chapter 4.

32. This can be gleaned from a great variety of references, from the speeches of officials to written accounts of symposia on democracy in the Arab Muslim world or the future of that region, including its economic development. (The Center for Arab Unity Studies based in Beirut has put out a number of publications in Arabic to that effect, some of which are being translated into English.) Almost every major newspaper or periodical that originates from the Arab Muslim world or is published abroad on its behalf has numerous articles that directly or indirectly affirm an unquestioned faith in the introduction of democracy (wherever it is relatively free to say so) and the latest technology. Several periodicals dealing with economic or technological affairs maintain an axiomatic stance toward technology's prowess in effecting economic and indeed cultural revitalization.

33. The reference is to the rival "Baathist" regimes of Syria and Iraq.

34. "Fundamentalists" is inaccurate to describe the current generation of Muslim activists. As has often been pointed out, to describe a group of people whose Book is literally held to be the word of God by all members of the faith as "fundamentalists" is at best

redundant. At worst, it evokes the simplemindedness of Christian fundamentalists when it is recalled that Christianity is anything but a religion dependent on texts whose literal meaning must be sacrosanct. "Activists" is inaccurate because it denies the possiblity that other Muslims can also be activist. "Revivalists" does not convey much when it is remembered that the Muslim world has had many generations of revivalists throughout its history, and not just in the past two centuries or so. "Extremists" has automatically negative connotations that are not always deserved. "Islamic revolutionaries" may be better, because those to whom the term refers do seek an Islamic revolution however their program differs from one group to another. That they seek radical action is not suggested by the currently popular expression "Islamists."

35. Şerif Mardin, *Religion and Social Change in Modern Turkey* (Albany: State Univ. of New York Press, 1989).

36. Ibid., 10.

37. Ibid., 119–20.

38. Ibid., 169.

39. Many have moreover asked whether such acceleration, even if possible, is desirable.

40. See Mardin, *Young Ottoman Thought*, 133–55, passim.

41. Mardin, *Religion and Social Change*, 120–21.

42. Ibid., 10–13.

43. See Arunas Sverdiolas and Tomas Sodeika, "Life in the Retort and Soon After," in the collection *Freedom and Choice in a Democracy*, ed. George McLean and Richard Khuri, forthcoming.

44. Mardin borrows the expression from Ernest Gellner. See *Religion and Social Change*, 119.

45. It must either be true or false just as "Chess is played in China" or "Water drains in clockwise fashion in the southern hemisphere" are respectively true and false, or "Sandcastles are built by the shores of underground lakes in Pluto" must either be true or false even though we do not yet know which.

46. Mardin, *Religion and Social Change*, 163.

47. Gravity is gravity whatever its magnitude. Thus laws can be formulated that are universally applicable. It is entirely otherwise with human beings insofar as they are persons. For a powerful statement in that vein, see Arthur Schopenhauer, *The World as Will and Representation*, trans. E. F. J. Payne (New York: Dover, 1958), 1: 131–33. The Persian philosopher Mulla Sadra (1580?-1641) put this fact differently, but to similar effect: The closer one gets to inanimate nature, the more the essence of the thing that one considers stands out. Not much argument is generated over what the essence of helium or water are. On the other hand, the closer one gets to human nature, the less essences matter. Human beings have been described as, say, "rational animals" by Aristotle, but that hardly tells us anything about a particular human being; whereas the essence of helium or water as defined by physical chemistry tells us much, if not everything, about every particular instance of their presence. From that, Mulla Sadra went on to conclude that essence and existence are in inverse proportion: the more a thing can be said to have an essence, the lower it can be located on the rungs of existence. See Fazlur Rahman, *The Philosophy of Mulla Sadra* (Albany: State Univ. of New York Press, 1975), 36.

48. Mardin, *Religion and Social Change*, 163.

49. Ibid., 11–13, 16, and 117–18.

50. See n. 34.

51. Mardin, *Religion and Social Change*, 121–22.

52. Enough has been written about the political and military setbacks and ideological bankruptcy that have given rise to Islamic revolutionism. These are adequately dealt with in any good book on the recent political history of the Arab Muslim world.

53. F. Rahman, *Islam and Modernity*, 136.

54. Ibid., 137.

2. The Future of a New Illusion

1. Jacques Berque, *Cultural Expression in Arab Society Today,* trans. Robert W. Stookey (Austin: Univ. of Texas Press, 1978), 330. For further reflection on the ideas discussed here, readers may also consult Wilfred Cantwell Smith's article, "The Historical Development in Islam of the Concept of Islam as an Historical Development," in *Historians of the Middle East,* ed. Bernard Lewis and P. M. Holt (London: Oxford Univ. Press, 1962), 484–502.

2. Berque, *Cultural Expression,* 330.

3. Ibid.

4. Such distortions and built-in unhappiness will be clarified in various sections of this book.

5. This is not to say that Arab Muslim society is incapable of economic efficiency or technological advance. It is rather that Arab Muslim society, in remaining true to itself, would not accept the price for unbridled technological advance and single-minded attention to economic efficiency.

6. Immanuel Kant, *Critique of Practical Reason,* trans. Lewis White Beck (New York: Macmillan, 1956), 126.

7. See Thomas Powers, *Heisenberg's War: The Secret History of the German Bomb* (New York: Knopf, 1992).

8. Stephen Toulmin, *Cosmopolis* (Chicago: Univ. of Chicago Press, 1990), 180.

9. Ibid., 201.

10. Gerald Holton, *The Advancement of Science and Its Burdens* (Cambridge, U.K.: Cambridge Univ. Press, 1986), 177–78.

11. Or fundamentalists in the United States for that matter.

12. Kant, *Critique of Pure Reason,* trans. Norman Kemp Smith (New York: St. Martin's Press, 1965), 310.

13. Ibid., 311

14. Ibid., 312.

15. Ibid., 313.

16. Ibid., 323–25.

17. Ibid., 315.

18. Ibid., 319.

19. Ibid., 319–20. Some readers may feel that between p. 37 and here, there is a contradiction. On the one hand, I said that Kant was not all that much of a rationalist. On the other, I seem to say here that he was. But there is no such contradiction in fact. What I said above (p. 37) was that there is much more to Kant than mere rationalism. And what I say here shows us just how much more. For though Kant's conception of Reason extends far beyond ours, even Reason cannot find its own direction without immersing itself in three clearly defined ideals. The only rationalism left over in this is Kant's unjustified optimism that Reason would of itself, automatically, follow those ideals. Of course, it does not. But to claim that Kant conceded too much to rationalism is not the same as claiming that he was merely a rationalist. In any case, no scholar of Kant fails to allude, even if he dearly wished it were not there, to Kant's idealism, so unequivocal is its presence in his critical philosophy.

20. Ibid., 629.

21. Ibid.

22. Ibid., 631.

23. Ibid., 632.

24. Ibid.

25. Ibid., 631.

26. Ibid., 637.

27. Ibid., 640.

28. Ibid., 642–43.

29. Gerald Holton, *Thematic Origins of Scientific Thought: Kepler to Einstein* (Cambridge, Mass.: Harvard Univ. Press, 1973), 51.

30. Ibid., 53.

31. Ibid., 50–52.

32. Ibid., 53.

33. Ibid., 127–33.

34. Stephen Hawking, *A Brief History of Time* (London: Bantam Press, 1988), 136–37.

35. Holton, *Thematic Origins*, 116–17.

36. These are not only favored by the impulse to control. One may simply prefer the idea of a detached gaze that coolly analyzes the closed systems before it on aesthetic grounds.

37. They may also favor those who are more comfortable with an intuitive approach and are averse to regarding things with a detached gaze and analyze them coolly.

38. Holton, *Thematic Origins*, 53–60.

39. Ibid., 53.

40. Ibid., 57.

41. Ibid., 59.

42. Paul Davies, *God and the New Physics* (London: Penguin Books [Pelican], 1984), 9.

43. Ibid., 26.

44. Ibid., 28.

45. Ibid., 102–3.

46. Ibid., 107.

47. Ibid., 151–52.

48. Gottfried Wilhelm Freiherr von Leibniz, "Letters to Samuel Clarke," in *Selections*, ed. Wiener (New York: Charles Scribner's Sons, 1951), 223, 235.

49. St. Augustine, *Confessions*, trans. R. S. Pine-Coffin (London: Penguin Classics, 1961), Book 11, chaps. 11–13, pp. 261–63.

50. Davies, 13, 17.

51. Ibid., 14–16.

52. Ibid., 40.

53. Kant, *Critique of Pure Reason*, 113.

54. Davies, 34–35.

55. Ibid., 39, 56.

56. Ibid., 148–49.

57. Ibid., 103–6, 11.

58. Ibid., 60–64.

59. Ibid., 68–69.

60. Ibid., 82–85.

61. Ibid., 108–10.

62. Ibid., 113.

63. Ibid., 30.

64. Hawking, 157–58.

65. Holton, *Thematic Origins*, 55.

66. Holton, *Advancement of Science*, 171.

67. Paul K. Feyerabend, *Farewell to Reason* (London: Verso, 1987), 170.

68. Ibid., 171.

69. An allusion to a well-known work by Popper that is held by those outside the scientific community to exemplify the scientific method.

70. Holton, *Advancement of Science*, 169.

71. Ibid., 170.

72. Mach also explicitly rejected the use of formal and inductive logic by scientists because of the constant fluctuations in the situation under study.

73. Feyerabend, 187–89.

74. Hawking, 121–22.

75. Davies, 179.

76. Ibid., 168–70.

77. Modern physics combines space with time, so that the origin of the universe is a spatiotemporal point to which "nearness" can be attributed in a sense that is deliberately ambiguous with respect to space and time.

78. Hawking, 126–27.

79. Ibid., 127–32.

80. Ibid., 136–37.

81. Note the apparent logical equality of the opposite assumption, namely that God did create the universe and suffuse it with purpose, and the consequent logical equality of the worldview that depends on that assumption. But when we compare the *attitude* of scientists desperate to leave God out of the universe with a religious outlook that accepts all the evidence established by science, then the logical balance appears to tilt in favor of religion (see following note). Such a comparison, in the light of current scientific evidence, shows the unfamiliar sight of scientists espousing fantasies and people open to religion adopting a reasonable outlook.

82. Hawking is not an isolated example of this overt quest to leave God out of the universe when faced with the evidence. Davies puts forward models popular among like-minded scientists that must seem ludicrous to anyone not similarly motivated. For instance, it is suggested that the entire universe divides into two whenever a single electron has a choice between two alternatives, so that our universe becomes an "infinite array of parallel worlds" (see Davies, 172–73). Such are the absurdities compelled by the need to drive out scientifically gathered evidence when the evidence upsets the scientists. Note that the evidence in question, like all scientifically gathered evidence, does not *force* anyone to conclude that God created the universe and suffused it with purpose. Some scientists are led to their theoretical charades because, on the contrary, they seek to establish that God did not create the universe, and therefore do not welcome their own evidence, however firm and substantial, evidence that suggests (but does not prove) the contrary. Apparently, some scientists let the evidence speak for itself only when it suits their purpose.

83. Hawking, 157–65 passim. Such problems naturally arise when the attempt is made to demonstrate unity scientifically. However, they do not bear on the traditional metaphysical or religious conception of an underlying unity in the universe. In religion, for instance, unity is either revealed or mystically experienced. There is never the claim that unity is demonstrated as it would have to be in science. An incongruity always arises when what can only be metaphysical is made the object of physics.

84. Such hostility is evident in the work cited by Paul Davies, for whenever he must face the possiblity of an origin for the universe, he mentions "a feeling of unease" (Davies, 29), presumably within the scientific community; and when Ryle contrasts living with inanimate being, he compares the (theoretically elusive) movement of the living to that of "a species, a disease or an epidemic" (quoted in Davies, 83). The hostility evidently extends to life itself, for it eludes physical laws and philosophical analysis.

3. The Fate of Freedom under the Rule of Reason

1. Kant, *Critique of Practical Reason,* 97–98.

2. Karl Jaspers, *Philosophy,* trans. E. B. Ashton (Chicago: Univ. of Chicago Press, 1970) 2: 159.

3. This change is forcefully expressed by the claim that Hawking's book is nothing less than the attempt to understand the mind of God (see Hawking, 175); for the mind of God, it seems, has been reduced to the single physical law (if it exists) that unites the fundamental forces of nature. That Paul Davies has called his latest book "The Mind of God" is further testimony to the *diminution* of reason.

4. Contrary to what many may think, the rationalist turn in modernity, which began in the seventeenth century, was not accompanied with economic prosperity. The seventeenth century marked hard economic times throughout much of Europe.

5. Logic and mathematics form special abstract fields that can be harmlessly acknowledged, because they have no bearing on the direction of reason and because, in any case, they can be used to further one's theoretical compass of and practical control over the surface of the world.

6. This is what enabled serious thinkers in the eighteenth and nineteenth centuries to see the whole of history in materialistic terms. Marx and Marxism can be retrospectively seen as symptoms of the materialistic slant that modernity had by then taken.

7. By "theoretical terminus," I mean the idea that the materialization and commercialization of culture will be globally realized. Ironically, the collapse of the Soviet empire has accelerated the emergence of a global situation that can be described in modified Marxist terms. The extent of capitalism's triumph is the extent to which there can be a materialistic analysis.

8. The account that follows up to the next quoted passage is based on Berque, *Cultural Expression*, 324–26.

9. This is remarkably like what Holton says of the themata that determine the overall direction of theories in physical science. When atomism fell out of favor, for instance, it was never refuted, but lay dormant for centuries to await its return in modern times. And just when it seemed silly to think of an aethereal medium throughout physical space, new discoveries forced physicists to reconsider. Before one hastens to make history comply with physics as some modernizers seem to wish, one ought to take note that the physical universe itself seems replete with interpretive possibilities (see pp. 49–54).

10. The overview before this section illustrates what has generally been suppressed in the name of material advancement.

11. Berque, *Cultural Expression*, 334–36.

12. One can make a case that the shari'a is somewhat sounder than the U.S. legal system when compared according to whether they exist for their own sake or as embodiments of higher ideals. (Other comparisons may indicate the shari'a's inferiority.)

13. Not everything can be adequately clarified in place, but the persistent reader who has trouble with Berque's ideas as tersely presented so far should understand them better by the time he reaches the end of this book. Some of those ideas should gain in substance over the coming few sections.

14. See Toulmin, 5–137, passim.

15. Jürgen Habermas, *The Philosophical Discourse of Modernity,* trans. F. Lawrence (Cambridge, Mass.: MIT Press, 1990).

16. Habermas, 16–19.

17. Ibid.

18. Ibid., 18.

19. We are again reminded of the original compass of the intellect, reduced by Kant's attempt to give it a rational character, and then further reduced. Hegel represented a decisive reaction against such reduction, but still believed himself to speak the language of reason (see chapter 2, 43–49).

20. Habermas, 21.

21. For it tells us that reason is diverted by an external principle that it cannot support, in this case the principle of subjectivity.

22. Habermas, 31.

23. Ibid., 315–16.

24. Ibid., 55–56.

25. Ibid., 366.

26. Ibid., 338.

27. Hermann Broch, *The Sleepwalkers,* trans. Willa and Edwin Muir (San Francisco: North Point Press, 1985).

28. What follows is a brief elucidation of the ideas in Broch, 414–16.

29. Ibid., 416.

30. Ibid., 422–26.

31. Ibid., 445–48.

32. Ibid., 445–46.

33. Ibid., 448.

34. Ibid.

35. *The Sleepwalkers* is itself divided into romantic, anarchist, and realist viewpoints and works its way through compelling human situations within them—but further discussion of this remarkable book does not belong here.

36. Robert Reich, "The Real Economy," *Atlantic Monthly* 267, no. 2 (February 1991): 37.

37. Ibid., 37.

38. Ibid., 44.

39. Ibid., 40.

40. Robert N. Bellah, "The Triumph of Capitalism—or the Rise of Market Totalitarianism?" *New Oxford Review* 58 (March 1991): 8–14.

41. Note that the atomistic view of individual autonomy does not *necessitate* the definition of human motives in terms of self-interest. Kant, whose moral philosophy starts out with atomized, autonomous individuals, was vehemently opposed to self-interest as a motive for *any moral* action. But Kant's hope that rational beings, even though atomized, would nevertheless aspire to moral actions so commendable as to be universalizable has proved unfounded. One need only look at moral philosophy today and witness the institution of self-interest not only as an acceptable motive for moral action but also as the primary one. In fact, even ideals like Kant's are reduced to what is vaguely termed "interest" in a "higher sense," as though to confirm the prevalence of self-interest to the extent that no moral action, however noble, can in the end be acknowledged to have a motive other than self-interest.

42. What is meant here is that rational beings will choose the more profitable course, with minimal restraint if any. Economists seem to be the last to know about what goes on in physical science, for if they did, and still insisted on wanting their field to be a proper science (a doubtful proposition to begin with), they would relegate "rational choice" to a minor principle used for statistical purposes. "Rational choice" is a poor representation of human beings acting on their freedom, and a token of poor science as well.

43. Bellah, 10.

44. Ibid.

45. Ibid., 10–11. This point hardly needs annotation, for what it mentions is noticeable to anyone who visits the United States and modernity's other forward positions.

46. Ibid., 11.

47. Ibid., 11–12.

48. Ibid., 12.

49. Ibid., 13.

50. Mardin, *Religion and Social Change*, 11–12.

51. Ibid., 166.

52. Ibid., 6.

53. As has been mentioned more than once, the difference between what is due to modernity as such and what is due to the main current flowing through modernity cannot be resolved in this book. And it would be stylistically repugnant to routinely substitute expressions such as "the main current flowing through modernity" or "modernity's most visible tendency" for "modernity." It is intended that the interested reader should give this matter some thought. But there is no escape from *some* attribution of the consequences discussed here to modernity.

54. Mardin, *Religion and Social Change*, 21.

4. The Recovery of Freedom

1. Berque, *Cultural Expression,* 17.

2. Berque seems to be silent about the internal dimensions of political liberation. But as we shall see, he implicitly includes political repression as one of the elements of the "false starts" that are a consequence of the general state of groping that marks the postindependence period.

3. Berque, *Cultural Expression,* 17.

4. Ibid.

5. As if, for instance, the citizens of a country such as the United States were not told in a thousand ways each day—and quite explicitly—how they must live, in everything from food and dress to political action, personal expression, and private life. All that matters is for such intrusiveness to seem unofficial. Apparently, no amount of unofficial intrusiveness and frequently overwhelming peer pressure are worthy of official condemnation as serious limitations on the officially guaranteed liberties.

6. Again, the official position (certified in the semiofficial work of intellectuals) is that individuals should be left to make their choices unmolested. What this really means is that they must not be *officially* molested in their choices. It is then all right to unofficially hound individuals mercilessly into making the narrowest of choices.

7. Isaiah Berlin, *Four Essays on Liberty* (Oxford: Oxford Univ. Press, 1969), 28.

8. Ibid., 29.

9. Ibid., 30.

10. Ibid.

11. Ibid., 33.

12. For a good clarification of the differences between negative and positive freedom, see Berlin, 122–34. Berlin, however, fails to give an adequate account of positive freedom, which causes him to underestimate its value.

13. Charles Taylor, *Philosophy and the Human Sciences (Philosophical Papers 2)* (Cambridge, U.K.: Cambridge Univ. Press, 1985), 213.

14. Ibid., 215.

15. See, for example, Charles Taylor, *Human Agency and Language (Philosophical Papers 1)* (Cambridge, U.K.: Cambridge Univ. Press, 1985), 16–17.

16. See, for example, Taylor, *Human Sciences,* 220.

17. Naturally, the umbrella or the hotel might themselves be good, in the limited objective sense implicit in reliable guidebooks. But this sense of "good" has nothing to do with morality and is therefore irrelevant to the present discussion. Insofar as trivial choices are at all morally relevant, it is with regard to the evaluation of the desire for them. If we introduce no further framework for moral evaluation, then whatever I desire is good simply because I desire it. If I am to make the further step and overrule my desire, for instance, on the ground that its fulfillment will harm someone else, then I have made the transition from weak to strong evaluation already.

18. Taylor, *Human Agency,* 18–19.

19. Ibid., 48 and 61–65.

20. Ibid., 65–68.

21. Taylor, *Human Sciences,* 224.

22. Again, the lack of choice here does not imply external coercion, for one is always free in principle to disembark from any chosen course. Rather, one has less and less choice the more serious the course because of the gravity of the internal (spiritual, psychological, emotional, etc.) consequences for oneself given continuous lack of resolve.

23. It is always worth remembering that the twentieth century's two greatest criminals both tried to destroy whatever *real* communities they could lay their hands on, supposedly to create new "communities" that in reality were figments of bad imaginations.

24. John Macmurray, "Freedom in the Personal Nexus," in *The Problem of Freedom,* ed. Mary T. Clark (New York: Appleton-Century-Crofts, 1973), 197.

25. Ibid., 196.

26. Berque, *Cultural Expression,* 322.

27. Mardin, *Religion and Social Change,* 178–80.

28. This is not to be exploited by those for whom tyranny or economic injustice are most advantageous, for their actions are fairly easy to condemn on solid moral grounds. If a morally reprehensible action has the unintentional result of being for the good of others, this does not diminish from its reprehensibility. One must never excuse tyrants because they accidentally force their subjects to concentrate on deeper freedoms.

29. See William A. Luijpen, "Phenomenology of Freedom," in *The Problem of Freedom,* ed. Mary T. Clark, 155–59.

30. Ludwig Wittgenstein, *The Blue and Brown Books* (New York: Harper Colophon, 1965), 47–48.

31. See William Chittick, *The Sufi Path of Knowledge* (Ibn al-'Arabi's Metaphysics of Imagination)(Albany: State Univ. of New York Press, 1989), 94.

32. We shall never know how far we can trace that distinction, but we do know that Plato and, above all, Plotinus were in the thought of Ibn 'Arabi, even though an unfortunate error of transmission did not enable the greatest Muslim thinkers to acknowledge their debt to Plotinus, believing the *Enneads* to have been Aristotle's *Theology.*

33. The foregoing is partly based on Luijpen, 163–64.

34. "Bizarre and perverse ways" have naturally always existed among human beings and always will. But it becomes a problem when they are no longer even recognized as such. In hypocritical societies, this is not the case, for they at least retain a public sense of what merits disapprobation, to which they mostly remain sensitive. It is one thing to preach one thing and do another, quite another to claim with a straight face that one is now free to *promote* what had been widely condemned. It does not follow that what is worthy of disapprobation ought to be severely and inhumanly punished. There must surely be a happy medium between inhuman punishment and the equally inhuman inability to recognize what is worthy of disapprobation.

35. One must not be carried away by modernity's superficial tolerance either. For modernity, as has been pointed out in chapter 3, has developed quite sophisticated and invisible ways for quelling serious dissent. So interest in how modernity might make Islam more open and tolerant can be legitimately countered with interest in how Islam might make modernity more open and tolerant. Moreover, late modernity cannot make much of its religious tolerance—for if it encourages weak, if any, religious sentiments, it hardly takes much effort for those nominally from one religion to tolerate those nominally from another. The real test of tolerance, let alone acceptance, lies among people who *substantively* follow different religions. There are signs that the intolerance often shown by dominant religions with a substantive following has been replaced with intolerance for those who reject democracy, capitalism, liberalism, or the free market, rejections that are *not* a monopoly of the left or extreme right.

5. The Islamic Transposition of Positive Freedom

1. Kant, *Critique of Pure Reason,* 323–25.

2. Ibid., 631.

3. Ibid., 629.

4. Habermas, 392–93.

5. There is, however, another way to retain the universality of reason that has been excluded from modern discourse. It has to do with the ancient conception of the Active Intellect, a transcendent source of individual rationality believed to ensure rationality's universality and veracity to the extent that it partakes of the Active Intellect. This conception

has remained alive in limited Islamic and Christian circles. But it would take us too far afield to consider this aspect of reason in our discussion, especially because it is virtually impossible to evoke the Active Intellect through the word "reason" in a modern context. It is therefore expedient to use another word to refer to the universal and enduring recognition of transcendence and relate it directly to the soul. Some use "intellect" for the faculty in question.

6. Habermas, 295.

7. John Searle has done much work in this vein. See for example his *Intentionality* (Cambridge, U.K.: Cambridge Univ. Press, 1983), 141–59.

8. Habermas, 298.

9. Ibid.

10. Ibid., 301.

11. Ibid., 314–15.

12. Ibid., 299.

13. This is the great illusion of modernity's rational turn in the eighteenth century: the belief that reason can be entirely context-free and universalized.

14. Berque, *Cultural Expression*, 319–20.

15. Ibid., 324.

16. At the beginning of chapter 2, I have discussed the distortions that result when the Arabs look into a mirror given them by the West. In the light of our improved understanding of the *potential* of modernity and the West, however, it is possible for Arabs who live as though under a Western gaze to transform themselves positively. This may even entail a better grasp and appreciation of their own past. This theme will be developed in the final sections of this book.

17. Berque, *Cultural Expression*, 331.

18. Ibid., 336.

19. Ibid., 250.

20. Ibid., 251.

21. Ibid., 249.

22. Ibid.

23. Ibid., 327–28.

24. This is the opinion given me directly by Yusuf Ibish, a scholar of Islam and the Arabic language and literature who, after a lifetime of teaching and experience, has a remarkable feel for the people and the problems of the entire region. With this in mind, the reader may turn to H. A. R. Gibb, "The Structure of Religious Thought in Islam," in his *Studies on the Civilization of Islam* (Princeton, N.J.: Princeton Univ. Press, 1962/1982), 200–201.

25. Marshall G. S. Hodgson, *The Venture of Islam* (Chicago: Univ. of Chicago Press, 1974), 1: 180–83.

26. This, to remind the modern reader, must not be seen anachronistically. It was a comparative (and substantial) improvement compared to what had gone on before.

27. See Hodgson, 1: 184–85.

28. Ibid., 217–23.

29. Ibid., 247–48.

30. Ibid., 248–49.

31. Ibid., 223–27.

32. Ibid., 280–84.

33. Ibid., 252–55.

34. Ibid., 321–22.

35. Ibid., 323–24.

36. Ibid., 325.

37. Ibid., 328.

38. Ibid., 338–39.

39. Ibid., 337.

40. Ibid., 339–40.

41. Ibid., 341–42.

42. Ibid., 342.

43. Ibid., 343.

44. Habermas, 295.

45. Ibid., 392.

46. For a brief but pithy account, see Gilles Kepel, *The Prophet and Pharaoh*, trans. Jon Rothschild (London: Al Saqi Books, 1985), 44–47.

47. Ignaz Goldziher, *Introduction to Islamic Theology and Law*, trans. Andras and Ruth Hamori (Princeton, N.J.: Princeton Univ. Press, 1981), 230. What Goldziher says is still sometimes true even among Arabs leading outwardly highly Westernized lives.

48. Ibid., 231.

49. Ibid.

50. Ibid., 238–40.

51. Albert H. Hourani, "Culture and Change: The Middle East in the Eighteenth Century," in his *Islam in European Thought* (Cambridge, U.K.: Cambridge Univ. Press, 1991), 159–62.

52. Inalcik, 181–82.

53. See A. Hourani, "Culture and Change," 160–61, and Muhammad Farman's article on Sirhindi in *A History of Muslim Philosophy*, ed. M. M. Sharif (Wiesbaden, Germany: Otto Harrassowitz, 1963), 875.

54. See Kepel, 197–98.

55. Serajul Haque, "Ibn Taymiyya," in Sharif, 796.

56. Ibid., 799–802.

57. Ibid.

58. See Jamil M. Abun-Nasr, *A History of the Maghrib in the Islamic Period* (Cambridge, U.K.: Cambridge Univ. Press, 1987), 60–66.

59. Ibid., 87–90.

60. Inalcik, 182.

61. Ibid., 183.

62. Ibid., 184–85.

63. A. Hourani, "Culture and Change," 160–61.

64. Albert H. Hourani, "Sufism and Modern Islam: Mawlana Khalid and the Naqshbandi Order," in his *Emergence of the Modern Middle East* (Berkeley: Univ. of California Press, 1981), 82–85.

65. Kepel, 45–55.

66. See, for example, Julian Baldick, *Mystical Islam: An Introduction to Sufism* (New York: Columbia Univ. Press), 65–66.

67. Goldziher, 245.

68. H. A. R. Gibb, "An Interpretation of Islamic History," in Gibb, 28.

69. Gibb, "Religious Thought," in Gibb, 207.

70. Inalcik, 165–66.

71. Ibid., 175.

72. Abu Hamid al-Ghazzali, *al-Munqidh min ad-Dalal* (The deliverer from error)(Beirut: Nasser Cultural Institute, 1980), 50.

73. Ibid., 51–52.

74. Literally "lay out his breast in openness," *yashrahu sadrahu*.

75. His gifts, including light.

76. Al-Ghazzali, *Deliverer*, 53–54. My translation.

77. See chapters 2, 3, and 4.

78. See chapter 3, which deals expressly with the inadvertent narrowing of the domain of freedom under the regime of sovereign reason.

79. Al-Ghazzali, *Deliverer*, 55–56.

80. Ibid., 58–61.
81. Ibid., 88.
82. Ibid., 83.
83. Ibid., 82.
84. Ibid., 89.
85. Ibid., 87.
86. Ibid., 92–93.
87. Ibid., 93.
88. Ibid., 106.
89. Ibid., 93.
90. Ibid., 95–96.
91. Ibid., 103–4.
92. Ibid., 106–7.
93. See chapter 4, 134–42.
94. This, however, is understandable. Heads have never rolled because of one's musical statements. Given the authority potentially vested in those who believe they echo God's will, and the potential abuse of that authority (as we have seen in the foregoing section on communal extremism), it makes sense to make the conditions for prophecy or other direct access to divine truth *nearly* impossible to meet. But to turn this into skepticism toward all transcendence is an exaggerated reaction self-defeating for human experience. One can do better than to protect human life by trivializing experiential possibilities through their reduction to immanence. There may come a time when the very life with whose protection modernity is obsessed is diminished almost unto lifelessness.
95. Al-Ghazzali appears to have had a limited idea of what philosophy can accomplish, as evidenced by his emphasis on logic, mathematics, science, independent proof, and whatever is acceptable to reason (not understood in its broadest sense, for instance as "intellect" in Avicenna's philosophy). One must either say that reason in al-Ghazzali could do much less than in Plato, or that al-Ghazzali's view of philosophy's domain is much more restricted than Plato's. On the other hand, al-Ghazzali's view is more in tune with today's. If anything, even less is expected from philosophy.
96. Hodgson, 2: 187. This makes moot the objections raised, for instance, by Julian Baldick (see Baldick, 65–66). His objections depend on whether al-Ghazzali indeed had profound mystical experiences or not. But al-Ghazzali was willing to trust those who could go further than himself. It is sad that modernity has generally lost trust in the claims of the spiritually diligent and endowed, while it places human life more than ever in the hands of experts who, to mention but one group, progressively invade, try to control, and hence narrow down the most personal and private human reserves. Evidently, one ought to trust experts who make one a better producer and consumer, but not those who would make one a better human being.
97. Marcel Proust, *Remembrance of Things Past,* trans. C. K. Scott Moncrieff, Terence Kilmartin, and Andreas Mayor (New York: Vintage Books, 1982), 3: 186.
98. See chapter 4, 138.
99. Proust, 3: 258–60.
100. The reader familiar with the Chinese tradition will notice an analogous identification in Daoism.
101. Nikolai Berdyaev, *Slavery and Freedom,* trans. R. M. French (New York: Charles Scribner's Sons, 1944), 82–83.
102. Karl Rahner, *Grace in Freedom,* trans. Hilda Graef (New York: Herder and Herder, 1969), 196–97.
103. Gilbert Keith Chesterton, *St. Francis of Assisi* (Garden City, N.Y. Image Books [Doubleday], 1957), 76.
104. Fakhruddin 'Iraqi, *Divine Flashes,* trans. William C. Chittick and Peter Lamborn Wilson (New York: Paulist Press, 1982), 74.
105. Ibid.

106. Ibid., 75.

107. From the introduction by Chittick and Wilson in 'Iraqi, 12.

108. Ibid., 13.

109. Ibid., 11.

110. Ibid.

111. Ibid., 13.

112. Seyyed Hossein Nasr, *Islamic Life and Thought* (London: George Allen and Unwin, 1981), 22.

113. Ibn 'Arabi's thought indeed has significance well beyond the boundaries of Islam, for it is intended to be truly universal.

114. Chittick, 205.

115. Ibid., 204–5.

116. "Him" is used by the Sufis to avoid placing any limits on nondelimited Being, such as those implied by "God."

117. Chittick, 126–28.

118. Ibid., 13–14.

119. Ibid., 14.

120. Ibid., 117.

121. Ibid., 123. This is a direct translation of a passage from Ibn 'Arabi's magnum opus, *al-Futuhat al-Makkiyya* (The Meccan openings, Cairo, 1911), vol. 2, 361, l. 5.

122. Chittick, 9–10.

123. Ibid., 17.

124. Ibid., 240–41.

125. Ibid., 231–32.

126. Ibid., 350.

127. Ibid., xv-xvi.

128. This is another way that Ibn 'Arabi refers to the unnameable Being that is before all else, even the divine aspect known as "God."

129. Chittick, 173.

130. Ibid., 27.

131. Ibid., 243.

132. Ibid., 177.

133. Ibid., 207.

134. Ibid., 209.

135. Ibid., 335.

136. Ibid., 97.

137. Ibid., 153.

138. Ibid., 154.

139. Inalcik, 183.

140. Ibid., 199–200.

141. See A. Hourani, "Culture and Change," 158.

142. Hodgson, 1: 359.

143. Ibid., 395.

144. Annemarie Schimmel, *Mystical Dimensions of Islam* (Chapel Hill: Univ. of North Carolina Press, 1978), 24.

145. *The Holy Qur'an* (7: 172–74), trans. A. Yusuf 'Ali (Washington, D.C.: Islamic Center, 1978), 393–94.

146. Chittick, 212. *Samaʿ* literally means "listening" or "audition," but in the mystical setting it is a rather special kind of auditory awareness and experience.

147. Molé, 34.

148. This has become the name of Islam's third holiest site, in Jerusalem.

149. Qur'an 17:1, from Kenneth Cragg, *Readings in the Qur'an* (London: Collins, 1988), 204.

150. Molé, 36–37.

151. Ibid., 33.

152. Ibid., 43.

153. Schimmel, 25, and Molé, 31.

154. Schimmel, 26, and Molé, 28–30.

155. Molé, 37.

156. Schimmel, 30–31.

157. Ibid., 32–33.

158. Gibb, "Religious Thought," in Gibb, 206–7.

159. Schimmel, 35.

160. Molé, 4–5.

161. Ibid., 9.

162. Ibid., 9–12.

163. Molé, 7, and Schimmel, 45.

164. Molé, 12–21.

165. Ibid., 49.

166. Schimmel, 12–22.

167. Ibid., 15.

168. Ibid., 106–7.

169. Not "always," as we have just seen, but in general, and mainly since the Sufis realized the need to distinguish themselves from charlatans.

170. Nasr, 20–21.

171. Hodgson, 2: 209–10.

172. For an extended discussion of these, see Schimmel, 109–48.

173. Ibid., 110–16.

174. Ibid., 121–34.

175. Ibid., 99–100.

6. The Roots of Unfreedom in the Arab Muslim World

1. A. Hourani, "Culture and Change," 156.

2. The Arabic phrase is "yustanzalu al-furqanu w'al-lisanu"; each word has two meanings and Adunis surely intends this: "Yustanzalu" ordinarily refers to something decided, deduced, or settled, but is also related to "inzal," which to all Muslims refers to the revelation of the Qur'an; "yustanzalu" literally means "is made to come down" in the sense that a revelation "comes down" from Heaven. "Firqan" means proof or evidence, but is also a synonym for the Qur'an. And "lisan" means "tongue" as well as "language" ("speech" indicated itself to me as a poetically sound choice). Adunis implies a sense of decisiveness related (or allegedly related) to the Qur'an, but also to the perceived consequence of tongues being tied by the overall decisiveness, and the perceived identity between the Qur'an and what counts as evidence. The passive verb "yustanzalu" further suggests that evidence, proof, and language are made to come down (upon Muslims to bind them), which contrasts with the free descent of the Qur'an from Heaven. In other words, what Muslims have done with the Qur'an is separated from the revelation and the integrity of the Qur'an itself. The misuse of the Qur'an is therefore the object of Adunis's attack.

3. "Al-ghuyub," plural of "al-ghayb," which refers to the supernaturally hidden or invisible, transcendence, or the metaphysical.

4. The Arabic is isra', which normally means nocturnal journey, or sleepwalk, but also refers to the Prophet Muhammad's midnight journey to the seven heavens.

5. Adunis, al-Masrah w'al-Maraya (The theater and the mirrors)(Beirut: Dar al-Adab Publications [new and final edition], 1988), 119–26. My translation.

6. This is not suggested by the selections that I have translated, but is how the long poem concludes.

7. For a neat account of the fall of the 'Abbasid empire, see Lapidus, 126–36.

8. Hodgson, 2: 131–35.

9. Ibid., 146–47.

10. Ibid., 148.

11. Ibid., 149.

12. Ibid., 149–51.

13. Ibid., 108–12.

14. It also went far in protecting individiual Muslims from the excesses of the state, but this point belongs to the next section.

15. Hodgson, 2: 119–25.

16. Ibid., 57.

17. Ibid., 64.

18. Ibid., 66.

19. Ibid., 107.

20. Ibid., 65.

21. Ibid., 95–96.

22. Questions have been raised as to whether those informal associations constituted guilds or not. See S. M. Stern, "The Constitution of the Islamic City," and C. Cahen, "Y-a-til eu des corporations professionnelles dans le monde Musulman classique?" in *The Islamic City*, ed. Albert H. Hourani and S. M. Stern (Oxford: Bruno Cassirer, 1970), 25–63, passim.

23. Hodgson, 2: 213.

24. Ibid., 220–21.

25. Ibid., 220.

26. Ibid., 220–22.

27. Ibid., 229–30.

28. Ibid., 206.

29. Ibid., 204–5.

30. Adunis cannot be accused of critical or historical inaccuracy or wantonness based on his poetry alone. Poetic license entitles him to say whatever he wishes. But positions implied in the poem I have chosen are explicitly and consistently taken up in his critical and historical works, so that the views attributed to Adunis here are far more typical than a single reference suggests.

31. For a review of the positions held by al-Ghazzali, see chapter 5, 174–84.

32. This is not in contradiction with the opening sentence of this section. There, I said that "the freedom generally discussed so far has little to do with the outward conditions in which communities live." Modernity has influenced *access* to the spiritual dimension of freedom. But a person open or otherwise disposed to this dimension can never be stopped, however complex and potent the obstacles in his way. What has changed is simply the *likelihood* that people have that openness or disposition, not what they are capable of in the event that they do have it. As for the community, I have already said that in the extreme, a climate of fear and suspicion can be generated so as to threaten it with disintegration. But the recent collapse of various such efforts in many countries has revealed just what it takes to seriously compromise communal solidarity where it already exists, for instance, in Poland. It is probably a practical impossibility to deliberately and seriously compromise the kind of solidarity typically found in Islamic communities. One can only drive it temporarily underground. As for the grave communal breakdown in places such as the United States of America, it was at least as much willed as imposed—assuming that communal solidarity was properly there to begin with—and it is now much lamented (in the devastation of Native American communities, as well as the diminishing number of other communities, such as can be found in small towns throughout the country).

33. 'Abdul-'Aziz ad-Duri, "ad-Dimuqratiyyah fi Falsafat-il-Hukm-il-'Arabi" (Democracy in the Arab philosophy of government), in *ad-Dimuqratiyya wa Huquq al-Insan fʾil-Watan al-'Arabi* (Conference papers, commentaries, and discussions)(Beirut: Markaz ad-Dirasat al-Wihda al-'Arabiyya, 1983; Cairo: Dar al-Mustaqbal al-'Arabi, 1984), 192–93.

34. Ibid., 193.

35. Ibid., 195.

36. Ibid., 195 and 197.

37. Ibid., 195–96.

38. See Qur'an 4:59.

39. Albert H. Hourani, "The Islamic City in the Light of Recent Research," in Hourani and Stern, 13, 14, and 24.

40. Stern, in Hourani and Stern, 29.

41. Ibid., 31–33 and 36.

42. Yahya Sadowski, "The New Orientalism and the Democracy Debate," *MERIP* 183, vol. 23, no. 4 (July-August 1993), 16–19.

43. Hodgson, 1: 256.

44. Ibid., 260–67.

45. Lapidus, 184.

46. Ad-Duri, 199–202. See also Lapidus, 182–83.

47. Ad-Duri, 203–4. See also Lapidus, 182–83.

48. See M. Ruknuddin Hassan, "Nizam al-Mulk Tusi," in Sharif, 747.

49. Ibid., 764.

50. Ibid., 766.

51. For the remainder of the foregoing account on Nizamulmulk, see ibid. 762–68.

52. Lapidus, 190.

53. Ibid., 191.

54. Hodgson, 1: 292.

55. Ibid., 348–50.

56. Ibid., 356.

57. Hodgson, 2: 51–52.

58. Ibid., 54.

59. Ibid., 55–56.

60. Al-Ma'mun had first attempted to favor Shi'ism, and then decreed Mu'tazilite doctrine—somewhat rationalistic, but not to be conflated with Western rationalism—as a state religion. Once the decree was revoked, religious doctrine and belief returned firmly to the hands of the 'ulama.

61. Hodgson, 2: 119–25.

62. Ibid., 102–5.

63. Ibid., 112–15.

64. Ibid., 227–29.

65. Lapidus, 166, 173–74 and 236–37.

66. See chapter 5, 157–63.

67. Hodgson, 2: 46–49.

68. Muhammad Arkoun, "As-Siyadatul-'Ulya wa's-Sultatus-Siyasiyya fi'l-Islam" (Supreme sovereignty and political authority in Islam), in *Tarikhiyyat'ul-Fikr'il-'Arab'il-Islami* (The historicity of Arabo-Islamic thought)(Beirut: Markaz al-Inma'il-Qawmi, 1986), 171, 176, and 178–79.

69. See Seyyed Vali Reza Nasr, "Students, Islam, and Politics: Islami Jami'at-i Tulaba in Pakistan," *Middle East Journal*, vol. 46, no. 1 (winter 1992), 60–63.

70. Abun-Nasr, 102.

71. Ibid.

72. Hanafi, *Freedom*, 187–88, my translation.

73. George F. Hourani, *Reason and Tradition in Islamic Ethics* (Cambridge, U.K.: Cambridge Univ. Press, 1985), 272.

74. Ibid., 139.

75. Ibid., 141.

76. Ibid., 148–49.

77. S. H. Nasr, 11.

78. See Hodgson, 2: 165.

79. Majid Fakhry, *A History of Islamic Philosophy* (New York: Columbia Univ. Press, 1983), 96–97.

80. Ibid., 101.

81. Ibid., 105.

82. Hodgson, 2: 191–92.

83. Hodgson, 1: 386–89.

84. Ibid., 389–92.

85. Today, Hanbalism is dominant in Saudi Arabia and the Sudan.

86. See Hodgson, 1: 401–3.

87. Hodgson, 2: 203.

88. And who would go on to argue the need for an infallible imam, so al-Ghazzali here is confronting certain strands of Shi'ism.

89. Al-Ghazzali, *Deliverer*, 75, my translation.

90. Hodgson, 2: 195–96.

91. Illuminationist.

92. S. H. Nasr, 159.

93. Keddie, 6–9.

94. Ibid., 114.

95. Ibid., 19.

96. These publications have been authored by Fazlur Rahman, Seyyed Hossain Nasr, and William Chittick, among others, in the English-speaking world.

97. Hodgson, 2: 166.

98. Ibid., 218.

99. Ibid., 220.

100. Al-Ghazzali, *Deliverer*, 65–66.

101. Ibid., 59–60.

102. Ibid., 66–67.

103. Ibid., 66.

104. Ibid., 67.

105. Ibid., 59.

106. Ibid., 61–64.

107. See Muhsin Mahdi, "Ibn Khaldun," in Sharif, 974–76 and 979–80.

108. Ibid., 982.

109. S. H. Nasr, 174.

110. Jomier, 118–22 and 318.

111. Ibid., 130.

112. Ibid., 132.

113. Ibid., 122.

114. Clifford Geertz, *Islam Observed* (Chicago: Univ. of Chicago Press, 1971), 14–15.

115. Ibid., 15.

116. Ibid., 65–70.

117. Ibid., 72.

118. For more details, see Ernest Gellner, *Muslim Society* (Cambridge, U.K.: Cambridge Univ. Press, 1981), 40–41, 120–21, 122–23, 133, 148, 58, and 150–66 in that order, and Abun-Nasr, 254, 271, and 333–36.

119. Muhammad Farman, "Sirhindi," in Sharif, 877–78. The foregoing remarks on Sirhindi can be found in the same source, 873–82.

120. A. Hourani, "Sufism and Modern Islam," 79–81 and 87–88.

121. Inalcik, 181–85.

122. A. Hourani, "Sufism and Modern Islam," 80.

123. Ibid., 88–89.

124. Geertz, 18.

125. Ibid., 61.
126. Ibid.
127. Qur'an 2:256 (Yusuf Ali translation, 103).
128. Qur'an 4:168,9 (Ibid., 233).
129. Qur'an 9:33 (Ibid., 449).
130. Qur'an 2:136 (Ibid., 55). See also Qur'an 5:72.
131. Qur'an 5:85 (Ibid., 268).
132. Qur'an 5:75 (Ibid., 266).
133. Qur'an 5:54 (Ibid., 260).
134. Poll tax.
135. Qur'an 9:29 (Yusuf Ali translation, 447).
136. Qur'an 4:171 (Ibid., 234).
137. See chapter 5, 157–63.
138. Hodgson, 1: 269.
139. See chapter 5, 167–74.
140. Lapidus, 175.
141. Ibid.
142. Ibid., 137–91, passim.
143. Ibid., 351–58.
144. Ibid., 308.
145. Ibid., 308–9.
146. See A. Hourani, "Culture and Change," 136–39.
147. See Kamal Salibi, *Tarikh Lubnan al-Hadith* (The modern history of Lebanon)(Beirut: Dar An-Nahar l'in-Nashr, 1967), 144–45.
148. See Kepel, 231–40.
149. Qur'an 24:30,31 (Yusuf Ali translation, 904–5).
150. Lapidus, 891.
151. Hodgson, 1: 267.
152. Ibid., 342–43.
153. Hodgson, 2: 140–46.
154. Lapidus, 892–93.

7. Toward Greater Freedom in the Contemporary Arab Muslim World

1. See chapter 6, 228–42.
2. See Jean-Claude Vatin, "Popular Puritanism versus State Reformism: Islam in Algeria," in *Islam in the Political Process*, ed. James P. Piscatori (Cambridge U.K.: Cambridge Univ. Press, 1983), 98–121, passim.
3. African and Eastern Christians, for instance, may choose to reject thorough secularization.
4. Hodgson, 2: 186.
5. Hodgson, 1: 159.
6. Berque, 257.
7. Quoted in chapter 6, 272–73.
8. *The Holy Qur'an* (Yusuf Ali translation), 904.
9. Cragg, 313.
10. *The Holy Qur'an* 16:101 (Yusuf Ali translation), 684.
11. Ibid., 2:106, 46–47.
12. See chapter 6, 254–59.
13. Again, by "modernity," it is meant the dominant current within modernity, which reaches the Arab Muslim world in the guise of secular materialism. As stated earlier, it would be tedious to qualify what is meant by "modernity" each time.
14. The exception is the Sudan, where an armed conflict has raged for a long time. But it is not easily defined as an Arab country given its huge non-Arab minority.

15. It is hazardous to venture political predictions in such an explosive situation, but among the countries mentioned Malaysia seems the best candidate for long-term inter-communal harmony.

16. See chapter 5, 157–63.

17. This is also true politically. For instance, as we have seen just a few pages previously, a more considered interpretation of the doctrine "Islam is a state and a religion," especially by focusing on how radically the meaning of "state" has changed from Muhammadan to modern times, will clarify the relationship between Islam and the modern state as follows: "State" in the doctrine will be seen to refer to Muhammadan times, thus making it inadmissible to interpret the doctrine as an unequivocal call for the Islamization of the modern state, certainly not literally. This furthers the Muslim cause of freedom to the extent that the Islamization of the modern state is ultimately inimical to Islamic ideals; and the non-Muslims living in the Arab Muslim world would no longer fear the consequences of the Islamization of the states that govern them. To repeat, this need not follow the Western model of the separation of the state from religion. Rather, a redefinition of the relationship between state and religion is called for, whose practical form is best left alone as new attitudes gradually take effect in various political climates.

18. See Nizar Qabbani, *Ma Huwa ash-Shi'r?* (What is poetry)(Beirut: Manshurat Nizar Qabbani, Beirut, 1981).

19. This goes back to a tradition centuries old, be it the popular Turkish theater where the injustice of rulers was decried and the justice of the ruled celebrated, or the attitudes shown in late 'Abbasid literature.

20. Report by Caryle Murphy on the Iranian revolution, *Washington Post,* 28 April, 1992, A-19.

21. Ibid.

22. Nesta Ramazani, "Women in Iran: The Revolutionary Ebb and Flow," *Middle East Journal,* vol. 47, no. 3 (summer 1993), 409–28.

23. I thank James Piscatori and Şerif Mardin for bringing this to my attention.

24. Goldziher, 232–33.

25. Inalcik, 182–85.

26. Kepel, 227–28.

27. Abu Hamid Al-Ghazzali, *al-Mustasfa min 'Ilm al-Usul* (Cairo, 1937), 1: 144, quoted in G. F. Hourani, 163.

28. S. H. Nasr, 24–30.

29. Ibid., 25.

30. Ibid., 26.

31. Ibid., 25–26.

32. Ibid., 26.

33. Ibid.

34. Ibid., 28.

35. Ibid.

36. Ibid., 25.

37. Ibid.

38. Thus Muslims can understand strictures such as those on pork or alcohol as tokens of worship. But to enforce these or, worse, identify them with being religious in the Islamic manner, would be a disservice to Islam and its reduction to a trivial level.

39. Niyazi Berkes, *Turkish Nationalism and Western Civilization: Selected Essays of Zia Gökalp* (London: George Allen and Unwin, 1959), 194.

40. Ibid.

41. Ibid., 195.

42. Ibid., 196.

43. Ibid., 198.

44. Rahman, *Islam and Modernity,* 23.

45. Ibid., 31.
46. Ibid., 36–37.
47. Ibid., 5–8.
48. Ibid., 15.
49. Ibid.
50. Jomier, 15–17.
51. Ibid., 351.
52. Rahman, *Islam and Modernity*, 86.
53. Ibid.
54. Ibid., 85.
55. Ibid., 86.
56. Ibid., 90–91.
57. Ibid., 92–94.
58. Ibid., 95.
59. Ibid., 96–97.
60. Arkoun, "Al-Islam w'al-'Almana" (Islam and secularization), in *Historicity*, 297–98.
61. Ibid.
62. Ibid.
63. Ibid., 288.
64. Ibid., 288–89.
65. Ibid., 289.
66. Arkoun, "Supreme Sovereignty," in *Historicity*, 172. See also n. 13 on p. 194.
67. A. K. M. Ayyub Ali, "Maturidism," in Sharif, 271.
68. Arkoun, "Supreme Sovereignty," 176.
69. Arkoun, "Islam and Secularization," 291.
70. Arkoun, "Supreme Sovereignty," 177.
71. See for example Arkoun, "Islam and Secularization," 299.
72. Mystical Islam and the concentric circles of its reach throughout much of the community had not meanwhile slumbered, despite severe repression in the Ottoman Empire in the sixteenth and again in the nineteenth century.
73. Muhammad Iqbal, *The Reconstruction of Religious Thought in Islam* (New Delhi: Kitab Bhavan, 1974), 5.
74. Ibid., 5–6 and 108.
75. Ibid., 44–45.
76. Ibid., 48.
77. Ibid., 49. St. Augustine, Kierkegaard, Bergson, Proust, Wittgenstein, and Heidegger all have made profound contributions to the discussion of time, in particular the notion of "the eternal present," a term used to refer to the moment that stretches far beyond its temporal boundaries as measured by clocks and noted by calendars. This cannot be pursued further here. I have expounded upon some of their ideas and in that setting developed some of my own in my doctoral dissertation, "The Artist-Philosopher's Struggle to Save Appearances" (Univ. of California at Berkeley, 1986)(Ann Arbor, Mich.: Universal Microfilms International, 1986), 70–147, passim.
78. Iqbal, 50.
79. Ibid., 60.
80. Ibid., 9.
81. Ibid., 106.
82. Ibid., 117. Verses quoted from the Qur'an are 19:95–96 (Iqbal's italics).
83. Ibid., 104. Verses quoted from the Qur'an are 23:12–14 (Iqbal's italics).
84. Ibid., 109. Verse quoted from the Qur'an is 18:28.
85. Ibid., 10. Verses quoted from the Qur'an are 44:38 and 3:188.
86. Ibid., 109.
87. Ibid., 132.

88. Ibid., 123.

89. See ibid., 168–78.

90. See ibid., 171–72.

91. Mardin, *Religion and Social Change,* 72.

92. Ibid., 70.

93. Ibid., 54–59.

94. Ibid., 59.

95. Ibid., 72.

96. Ibid., 75–76.

97. Ibid., 76–77.

98. Ibid., 77.

99. Ibid., 81–82.

100. Ibid., 80–81.

101. Ibid., 81.

102. Ibid., 81.

103. Ibid., 67.

104. Ibid., 66.

105. Ibid., 198–99.

106. The Turkish state eventually realized the futility of rigorous secularization, but the consequences of its early harshness have not faded.

107. Mardin, *Religion and Social Change,* 156–60.

108. Ibid., 217.

109. Ibid.

110. Ibid., 161–63.

111. Ibid., 169.

112. Ibid., 170–71. Nursi also saw knowledge in participatory and interactive terms rather than possessively. We partake of what we know, but we do not possess it.

113. Ibid., 36–37 and 5–6.

114. Ibid., 173 and 224. This again reminds us of the position originally developed by Shah Vali-ullah and adopted by Iqbal and Rahman.

115. This is consistent with Ibn 'Arabi's view that God creates the universe anew at every moment, so the symbols that can be used to depict it are inexhaustible. The universe is hence compatible with any scientifically rigorous picture of it, for there is far more to it than any one picture can portray.

116. Mardin, *Religion and Social Change,* 206–7.

117. Ibid., 231–32 and 225–26.

118. Ibid., 205.

119. Ibid., 212, 214–15 and 216.

120. See chapter 5, 191–206.

121. Mardin, *Religion and Social Change,* 176–77.

122. Ibid., 186–88.

123. Ibid., 176.

124. Ibid., 188–89.

125. Ibid., 100.

126. Ibid., 99.

127. "Nurcus" refers to the followers of Nursi's movement.

128. Mardin, *Religion and Social Change,* 40.

129. Alas, some of Nursi's followers (in the branch headed by Fethullah Hoca) have also recently succumbed to the institutional logic that seems to get the better of any enduring movement. So keen have they become on good organization that they have lost sight of the transcendence that illuminated Nursi's life and graced his work. Instead of openness to fluid interaction between science and metaphysics, for instance, we now see emphasis on "hard science," i.e., the old caricature for which Turkish positivists had fallen hook, line, and sinker.

Bibliography

'Abduh, Muhammad. *Al-Imam Muhammad 'Abduh*. Anthology edited by Adunis and Khalida Sa'id. Beirut: Dar al-'Ilm l'il-Malayin, 1983.

Abun-Nasr, Jamil M. *A History of the Maghrib in the Islamic Period*. Cambridge, U.K.: Cambridge Univ. Press, 1987.

Adunis ('Ali Ahmad Sa'id). *Al-Masrah w'al-Maraya* (The theater and the mirrors). Beirut: Dar al-Adab Publications, 1988 (new and final edition).

Ali, A. K. M. Ayyub. "Maturidism." In *A History of Muslim Philosophy*, edited by M. M. Sharif, 259–73. Wiesbaden, Germany: Otto Harrassowitz, 1963.

Arkoun, Muhammad. "As-Siyadatul-'Ulya wa's-Sultatus-Siyasiyya fi'l-Islam" (Supreme sovereignty and political authority in Islam). In *Tarikhiyyat'ul-Fikr'il-'Arabi'l-Islami* (The historicity of Arabo-Islamic thought), 165–96. Beirut: Markaz al-Inma' al-Qawmi, 1986.

———. "Al-Islam w'al-'Almana" (Islam and secularization). In *Tarikhiyyat'ul-Fikr'il-'Arabi'l-Islami* (The historicity of Arabo-Islamic thought), 275–300. Beirut: Markaz al-Inma' al-Qawmi, 1986.

Arkoun, Muhammad, et al. "At-Turath: Muhtawahu wa Hawiyyatuhu—Ijabiyyatuhu wa Salbiyyatuhu" (Tradition: its content and identity—its pros and cons). In *at-Turath wa Tahaddiyat al-'Asr f il-Watan al-'Arabi* (Tradition and Contemporary Challenges in the Arab Homeland)(Conference papers, commentaries, and discussions), 155–212. Beirut: Markaz ad-Dirasat al-Wihda al-'Arabiyya, 1985.

Augustine, St. *Confessions*. Translated by R. S. Pine-Coffin. London: Penguin Classics, 1961.

Baldick, Julian. *Mystical Islam: An Introduction to Sufism*. New York: Columbia Univ. Press, 1990.

Bellah, Robert N. "The Triumph of Capitalism—or the Rise of Market Totalitarianism?" *New Oxford Review* 58 (March 1991): 8–15.

Berdyaev, Nikolai. *Slavery and Freedom*. Translated by R. M. French. New York: Charles Scribner's Sons, 1944.

Berkes, Niyazi. *Turkish Nationalism and Western Civilization: Selected Essays of Zia Gökalp*. London: George Allen and Unwin, 1959.

Berlin, Isaiah. *Four Essays on Liberty*. Oxford and N.Y.: Oxford Univ. Press, 1969.

Berque, Jacques. *Cultural Expression in Arab Society Today*. Translated by Robert W. Stookey. Austin: Univ. of Texas Press, 1978.

———. "The Expression of Historicity in the Koran." Translated by Khalil Semaan and Charles Butterworth. In *Arab Civilization: Challenges and Responses (Studies in Honor of Constantine K. Zurayk)*, edited by George N. Atiyeh and Ibrahim M. Oweiss, 74–81. Albany: State Univ. of New York Press, 1988.

———. "Nahwa Hiwarin Andalusiyyi'l-Ab'ad" (Toward a dialogue with Andalusian dimensions). Translated by Abu Bakr Binnur. *Mawaqif*, no. 58 (spring 1989): 29–45.

Broch, Hermann. *The Sleepwalkers.* Translated by Willa and Edwin Muir. San Francisco: North Point Press, 1985.

Cahen, C. "Y-a-til eu des corporations professionnelles dans le monde Musulman classique?" In *The Islamic City*, edited by Albert H. Hourani and S. M. Stern, 51–63. Oxford, U.K.: Bruno Cassirer, 1970.

Chesterton, Gilbert Keith. *St. Francis of Assisi.* Garden City, N.Y.: Image Books (Doubleday), 1957.

Chittick, William C. *The Sufi Path of Knowledge (Ibn al-'Arabi's Metaphysics of Imagination).* Albany: State Univ. of New York Press, 1989.

Cragg, Kenneth. *Readings in the Qur'an.* London: Collins, 1988.

Davies, Paul. *God and the New Physics.* London: Penguin Books (Pelican), 1984.

ad-Duri, 'Abdul-'Aziz. "Ad-Dimuqratiyya fi Falsafati'l-Hukmi'l-'Arabi" (Democracy in the Arab philosophy of government). In *ad-Dimuqratiyya wa Huquq al-Insan fil-Watan al-'Arabi* (Democracy and human rights in the Arab homeland)(Conference papers, commentaries, and discussions), 191–212. Beirut: Markaz ad-Dirasat al-Wihda al-'Arabiyya, 1983; Cairo: Dar al-Mustaqbal al-'Arabi, 1984.

Fakhry, Majid. *A History of Islamic Philosophy.* New York: Columbia Univ. Press, 1983.

Farman, Muhammad. "Shaiikh Ahmad Sirhindi." In A *History of Muslim Philosophy*, edited by M. M. Sharif, 873–82. Wiesbaden, Germany: Otto Harrassowitz, 1963.

Feyerabend, Paul K. *Farewell to Reason.* London, New York: Verso, 1987.

Gane, Mike, ed. *Baudrillard Live.* London: Routledge, 1993.

Geertz, Clifford. *Islam Observed.* Chicago: Univ. of Chicago Press, 1971.

Gellner, Ernest. *Muslim Society.* Cambridge, U.K.: Cambridge Univ. Press, 1981.

al-Ghazzali, Abu Hamid. *Al-Mustasfa min 'Ilm al-Usul.* Cairo: Al-Matba'a at-Tijariyya, 1937.

———. *Al-Munqidh min ad-Dalal.* Beirut: Nasser Cultural Institute, 1980.

Gibb, Hamilton Alexander Rosskeen. "An Interpretation of Islamic History." In *Studies on the Civilization of Islam*, 3–33. Princeton, N.J.: Princeton Univ. Press, 1962/1982.

———. "The Structure of Religious Thought in Islam." In *Studies on the Civilization of Islam.* 176–218. Princeton, N.J.: Princeton Univ. Press, 1962/1982.

Goldziher, Ignaz. *Introduction to Islamic Theology and Law.* Translated by Andras and Ruth Hamori. Princeton, N.J.: Princeton Univ. Press, 1981.

Habermas, Jürgen. *The Philosophical Discourse of Modernity.* Translated by Frederick G. Lawrence. Cambridge, Mass.: MIT Press, 1990.

al-Hajj, Usni. *Khawatem* (Ends). London: Riad El-Rayyes Books, 1991.

Hanafi, Hassan. "Al-Judhur at-Tarikhiyya li-'Azmat'il-Hurriyya w'ad-Dimuqratiyya fi Wujdanina al-Mu'asir" (The historical roots of the impasse with regard to freedom and democracy in our collective consciousness). In *ad-Dimuqratiyya wa Huquq al-Insan fil-Watan al-'Arabi* (Democracy and human rights in the Arab homeland)(Conference papers, commentaries, and discussions), 175–89. Beirut: Markaz ad-Dirasat al-Wihda al-'Arabiyya, 1983; Cairo: Dar al-Mustaqbal al-'Arabi, 1984.

———. "Mawqifuna al-Hadari" (our civilizational stand). In *Al-Falsafa f'il-Watan al-'Arabi al-Mu'asir* (Philosophy in the contemporary Arab homeland). (Conference papers, commentaries, and discussions), 13–42. Beirut: Markaz ad-Dirasat al-Wihda al-'Arabiyya, 1985.

Haque, Serajul. "Ibn Taymiyya." In *A History of Muslim Philosophy*, edited by M. M. Sharif, 796–819. Wiesbaden, Germany: Otto Harrasowitz, 1963.

Hassan, M. Ruknuddin. "Nizam al-Mulk Tusi." In *A History of Muslim Philosophy*, edited by M. M. Sharif, 747–73. Wiesbaden, Germany: Otto Harrassowitz, 1963.

Hawking, Stephen. *A Brief History of Time: From the Big Bang to Black Holes*. London: Bantam Press, 1988.

Heyd, Uriel. "The Ottoman 'Ulema and Westernization in the Time of Selim III and Mahmud II." In *Scripta Hierosolymitana: Studies in Islamic History and Civilization*, vol. 9, edited by Uriel Heyd, 63–96. Jerusalem: Hebrew Univ. Press (At the Magnes Press), 1961.

Hodgson, Marshall G. S. *The Venture of Islam: Conscience and History in a World Civilization (vol. 1: The Classical Age of Islam)*. Chicago: Univ. of Chicago Press, 1974.

———. *The Venture of Islam: Conscience and History in a World Civilization (vol. 2: The Expansion of Islam in the Middle Periods)*. Chicago: Univ. of Chicago Press, 1974.

Holton, Gerald. *Thematic Origins of Scientific Thought: Kepler to Einstein*. Cambridge, Mass.: Harvard Univ. Press, 1973.

———. *The Advancement of Science and Its Burdens: The Jefferson Lecture and Other Essays*. Cambridge, UK: Cambridge Univ. Press, 1986.

Hourani, Albert H. "The Islamic City in the Light of Recent Research." In *The Islamic City*, edited by Albert H. Hourani and S. M. Stern, 9–24. Oxford: Bruno Cassirer, 1970.

———. "Sufism and Modern Islam: Mawlana Khalid and the Naqshbandi Order." In *The Emergence of the Modern Middle East*, by Albert H. Hourani, 75–89. Berkeley: Univ. of California Press, 1981.

———. "Culture and Change: The Middle East in the Eighteenth Century." In *Islam in European Thought*, by Albert H. Hourani, 136–63. Cambridge, U.K.: Cambridge Univ. Press, 1991.

Hourani, Albert H., and Stern, S. M., eds. *The Islamic City*. Oxford: Bruno Cassirer, 1970.

Hourani, George F. *Reason and Tradition in Islamic Ethics*. Cambridge, U.K.: Cambridge Univ. Press, 1985.

Inalcik, Halil. *The Ottoman Empire: The Classical Age 1300–1600*. Translated by Norman Itzkowitz and Colin Imber. London: Weidenfeld and Nicolson, 1973.

Iqbal, Muhammad. *The Reconstruction of Religious Thought in Islam*. New Delhi: Kitab Bhavan, 1974.

'Iraqi, Fakhruddin. *Divine Flashes*. Translated by William C. Chittick and Peter Lamborn Wilson. New York: Paulist Press, 1982.

al-Jabiri, Muhammad 'Abed, et al. "Ishkaliyyatu'l-'Asala w'al-Mu'asara f'il-Fikri'l-'Arabi'l-Hadith w'al-Mu'asir: Sira' Tabaqi am Mashkal Thaqafi?" (The problematic of authenticity and contemporaneity in modern and contemporary Arab thought). In *at-Turath wa Tahaddiyat al-ʿAsr fil-Watan al-ʿArabi* (Tradition and contemporary challenges in the Arab homeland)(Conference papers, commentaries, and discussions), 29–83. Beirut: Markaz ad-Dirasat al-Wihda al-ʿArabiyya, 1985.

Jaspers, Karl. *Philosophy* (3 vols). Translated by E. B. Ashton. Chicago: Univ. of Chicago Press, 1970.

Jomier, Jacques. *Le commentaire Coranique du Manar.* Paris: G.-P. Maisonneuve, 1954.

Kant, Immanuel. *Critique of Practical Reason.* Translated by Lewis White Beck. New York: Macmillan/Library of Liberal Arts, 1956.

———. *Foundations of the Metaphysics of Morals.* Translated by Lewis White Beck. Indianapolis: Bobbs-Merrill Company/Library of Liberal Arts, 1959.

———. *Critique of Pure Reason.* Translated by Norman Kemp Smith. New York: St. Martin's Press, 1965.

Keddie, Nikki R. *An Islamic Response to Imperialism (Political and Religious Writings of Sayyid Jamal ad-Din "al-Alghani").* Berkeley: Univ. of California Press, 1968, 1983.

Kepel, Gilles. *The Prophet and Pharaoh (Muslim Extremism in Egypt).* Translated by Jon Rothschild. London: Al Saqi Books, 1985.

Khouri, Mounah A. "Criticism and Heritage: Adonis as an Advocate of a New Arab Culture." In *Arab Civilization: Challenges and Responses (Studies in Honor of Constantine K. Zurayk),* edited by George N. Atiyeh and Ibrahim Oweiss, 183–207. Albany: State Univ. of New York Press, 1988.

Khuri, Richard K. "The Artist-Philosopher's Struggle to Save Appearances" (Ph.D. diss., Univ. of California at Berkeley, 1986). Ann Arbor, Mich.: University Microfilms International, 1986.

———. "A Critique of Hassan Hanafi Concerning His Reflections on the Scarcity of Freedom in the Arab Muslim World." In *Cultural Transitions in the Middle East,* edited by Şerif Mardin, 86–115. Leiden: E. J. Brill, 1994.

Lapidus, Ira M. *A History of Islamic Societies.* Cambridge, U.K.: Cambridge Univ. Press, 1988.

Leibniz, Gottfried Wilhelm Freiherr von. "Letters to Samuel Clarke." In *Selections,* edited by Philip P. Wiener, 216–80. New York: Charles Scribner's Sons, 1951.

Luijpen, William A. "Phenomenology of Freedom." In *The Problem of Freedom,* edited by Mary T. Clark, 154–66. New York: Appleton-Century-Crofts, 1973.

Macmurray, John. "Freedom in the Personal Nexus." In *The Problem of Freedom,* edited by Mary T. Clark, 186–99. New York: Appleton-Century-Crofts, 1973.

Mahdi, Muhsin. "Ibn Khaldun." In *A History of Muslim Philosophy,* edited by M. M. Sharif, 888–903 and 961–84. Wiesbaden, Germany: Otto Harrassowitz, 1963.

Mardin, Şerif. *The Genesis of Young Ottoman Thought (A Study in the Modernization of Turkish Political Ideas).* Princeton, N.J.: Princeton Univ. Press, 1962.

———. *Religion and Social Change in Modern Turkey.* Albany: State Univ. of New York Press, 1989.

———. "The Just and the Unjust." *Daedalus* 120, no. 3 (summer 1991): 113–29.

———. "Culture Change and the Intellectual: A Study of the Effects of Secularization in Modern Turkey." In *Cultural Transitions in the Middle East,* edited by Şerif Mardin, 189–213. Leiden: E. J. Brill, 1994.

Mitchell, Timothy. *Colonizing Egypt.* Berkeley: Univ. of California Press, 1991.

Molé, Marijan. *Les mystiques Musulmans.* Paris: Presses Universitaires de France, 1965.

Morris, Benny. *The Birth of the Palestinian Refugee Problem, 1947–9.* Cambridge, U.K.: Cambridge Univ. Press, 1987.

Nasr, Seyyed Hossein. *Islamic Life and Thought.* London: George Allen and Unwin, 1981.

Nasr, Seyyed Vali Reza. "Students, Islam, and Politics: Islami Jami'at-i Tulaba in Pakistan." *Middle East Journal* 46, no. 1 (winter 1992): 59–76.

Pelikan, Jaroslav, ed. *The World Treasury of Modern Religious Thought.* Boston: Little, Brown and Company, 1990.

Powers, Thomas. *Heisenberg's War: The Secret History of the German Bomb.* New York: Alfred A. Knopf, 1992.

Proust, Marcel. *Remembrance of Things Past* (3 vols). Translated by C. K. Scott Moncrieff, Terence Kilmartin, and Andreas Mayor. New York: Vintage Books, 1982.

Qabbani, Nizar. *Ma Huwa ash-Shi'r?* (What is poetry?). Beirut: Manshurat Nizar Qabbani, 1981.

The Holy Qur'an. Translated by A. Yusuf Ali. Washington, D.C.: The Islamic Center, 1978.

Rahman, Fazlur. *The Philosophy of Mulla Sadra.* Albany: State Univ. of New York Press, 1975.

———. *Islam and Modernity.* Chicago: Univ. of Chicago Press, 1982.

Rahner, Karl. *Grace in Freedom.* Translated by Hilda Graef. New York: Herder and Herder; London: Burns and Oats, 1969.

Ramazani, Nesta. "Women in Iran: The Revolutionary Ebb and Flow." *Middle East Journal* 47, no. 3 (summer 1993): 409–28.

Reich, Robert. "The Real Economy." *Atlantic Monthly* 267, no. 2 (February 1991): 35–52.

Sadowski, Yahya. "The New Orientalism and the Democracy Debate." *MERIP* 183, vol. 23, no. 4 (July-August 1993): 14–21 and 40.

Salibi, Kamal. *Tarikh Lubnan al-Hadith* (The modern history of Lebanon). Beirut: Dar An-Nahar li'n-Nashr, 1967.

al-Sayyid Marsot, Afaf Lutfi. *A Short History of Modern Egypt.* Cambridge, U.K.: Cambridge Univ. Press, 1985.

Schimmel, Annemarie. *Mystical Dimensions of Islam.* Chapel Hill: Univ. of North Carolina Press, 1978.

Schopenhauer, Arthur. *The World as Will and Representation* (2 vols). Translated by E. F. J. Payne. New York: Dover Publications, 1958.

Searle, John. *Intentionality (An Essay in the Philosophy of Mind).* Cambridge, U.K.: Cambridge Univ. Press, 1983.

Sharif, M. M., ed. *A History of Muslim Philosophy.* Wiesbaden, Germany: Otto Harrassowitz, 1963.

Smith, Wilfred Cantwell. "The Historical Development in Islam of the Concept of Islam as an Historical Development." In *Historians of the Middle East,* edited by Bernard Lewis and P. M. Holt, 484–502. London: Oxford Univ. Press, 1962.

Stern, S. M. "The Constitution of the Islamic City." In *The Islamic City*, edited by Albert H. Hourani and S. M. Stern, 25–50. Oxford: Bruno Cassirer, 1970.

Sverdiolas, Arunas, and Sodeika, Tomas. "Life in the Retort and Soon After." In *Freedom and Choice in a Democracy*, edited by George F. McLean and Richard K. Khuri. Forthcoming from Paideia Press.

Taylor, Charles. *Human Agency and Language (Philosophical Papers 1)*. Cambridge, U.K.: Cambridge Univ. Press, 1985.

——. *Philosophy and the Human Sciences (Philosophical Papers 2)*. Cambridge, U.K.: Cambridge Univ. Press, 1985.

Toulmin, Stephen. *Cosmopolis*. Chicago: Univ. of Chicago Press, 1990.

Vatin, Jean-Claude. "Popular Puritanism versus State Reformism: Islam in Algeria." In *Islam in the Political Process*, edited by James P. Piscatori, 98–121. Cambridge, U.K.: Cambridge Univ. Press, 1983.

Washington Post. 28 April 1992, sec. A.

Wendell, Charles. *The Evolution of the Egyptian National Image: From its Origins to Ahmad Lutfi Al-Sayyid*. Berkeley: Univ. of California Press, 1972.

Wittgenstein, Ludwig. *The Blue and Brown Books*. New York: Harper Colophon, 1965.

Index

'Abbasid caliphate: al-Amin, 219; decline of, 219–21; Harun al-Rashid, 219, 233; al-Ma'mun, 219, 234, 247, 357n. 60; and Sassanian tradition of monarchic rule, 229
'Abd al-Mu'min Ibn 'Ali, 169
'Abd al-Qadir, 169
'Abduh, Muhammad: al-Azhar reformed by, 10–11, 312; and balance of freedom and Islam, 319; on *ijtihad*, 10; intellectual limitations of, 253–54; on the Qur'an, 311–12, 318; Rahman as influenced by, 311, 342n. 17; on rationality of Muslim faith, 16
absolute space and time, 57
Abu-l-'Ala' al-Ma'arri, 245
Abu Madi, Iliya, xxxix
Abun-Nasr, Jamil N., 239
Abu Shabakeh, Ilyas, xxxix
Active Intellect, 350n. 5
Adunis: al-Ghazzali attacked by, xxxiii, 215–19, 253; poetic license of, 218, 356n. 30
al-Afghani, Jamal al-Din, 10, 250–51
Afghanistan, 109, 110, 273
'Aflaq, Michel, 156
agnosticism, applied science engendering, 27
ahl al-hadith, 247–48
Ahmed III (Ottoman sultan), 3, 4
Akbar (Moghal emperor), 169, 258
'Alawis, 218
alcohol, prohibition on, 307, 334, 360n. 38
Alfarabi, xxxviii, 7
Algeria, 109, 175, 238, 257, 280
'Ali, 229
Ali, Yusuf, 287
alienation, 93, 94
'alim. See 'ulama
allegorical interpretation (*at-ta'wil*), 14
almsgiving, 222

al-Amin, 219
Ankara University, 314
antimatter, 56–57
Antun, Farah, xxxix
apologetics, 15
Al-Aqsa mosque, 207–8
Arabic language: and the Qur'an, xxxvi, 309; and traditional worldview, 28
Arab Muslim world: authoritarianism as gravest problem of, 18; awareness of gap with the West, 26; certainties of, 28–29; Christians in, xxxiv, 262–71, 276, 289–94; Crusades, 1, 169, 248, 253, 270; democracy and technology in, 18, 342n. 32; educational reform in, 312–14; and efficiency, 344n. 5; Europe of early Renaissance compared with, 111–12; fivefold path for freedom in, 336–38; freedom as desired by, xvii, 17; when heterodoxy gets out of hand, 169; intellectual limitations in, 253; mechanism as inconsistent with, 19; modernity as advancing in, 110–12; modernization in, xviii–xx, xxviii; Mongol invasions of, 1, 2, 169; national liberation in, 115–16; and observer's intentions, 71–72; reason and its context in, 152–57; relation to God in, 154–56; religious minorities in, 262–71, 289–94; religiousness shifting to religious-mindedness in, 259–60, 334–35; Renaissance (an-Nahdah) of, xxxix; scholars and jurists as influential in, xxiii; science in, 17; shrinkage of freedom resisted in, 121–22; shrinkage of freedom's domain in, 109–12; social relations as personalized in, 24, 25–26, 73; spiritual panic in, 312; state-supported modernizers and Muslims in, 5–6; transcendent regularities, 89–90;

369

quietism (*continued*)
al-Ghazzali, 228; Qur'an enjoining
obedience to authority, xxiv, xxxiii,
229–30, 238, 241–42, 280, 304
Qunawi, Sadruddin, 194, 205
Qur'an: 'Abduh on, 311–12, 318;
al-Afghani on, 250; alleged alteration
of, 317; and Arabic language, xxxvi,
309; Arkoun on, 316–17; broad and
flexible framework implicit in, 172;
changing context of application of,
306–7; on Christianity, 264–67, 292; on
Christian-Muslim relations, xxxiv; in
code of Muslim community, 160, 161,
282; commentaries on, 15, 309; debates
over status of, 2; difficult language of,
309; al-Ghazzali on, 177; hadith folk
on, 247; Ibn 'Arabi on, 200, 201; Ibn
Taymiyya on, 170; on inquiry into the
world, 7; Iqbal on, 326, 333–34; modern study of, 314; on
non-Muslims, 291, 292–93; Nursi on,
331–32, 333–34; obedience to
authority enjoined by, xxiv, xxxiii,
229–30, 238, 241–42, 280, 304;
principles versus injunctions of, 337;
quoting out of context, 309, 311;
Rahman on, 309–11; recitation of, 208,
210; sacred and profane juxtaposed in,
158; Shi'ite interpretation of, 250;
standardization of, 159, 316; in Sufi
origin and methods, 207–8; theoretical
science in potential conflict with, 27;
on tolerance, 264, 292; on women,
xxxiv, 272–73, 287–89, 294, 305, 307;
written destiny notion of, 323
qutb, 235
Qutb, Sayyid, 168, 169, 174, 267

Rahman, Fazlur, 309–12; 'Abduh's
influence on, 311, 342n. 17; on classical
modernists, 31; and Iqbal, 326; Nasr
contrasted with, 318–19; Nursi
compared with, 334; on the Qur'an,
309–11; on religious education in
Turkey, 314; on the *shari'a*, 310, 319;
spirit of work of, 15; on spiritual panic
in Arab Muslim world, 312; on vicious
circle of reductionism and
counterreductionism, 31; works on
Persianate mystical philosophy, 358n.
96

Rahner, Karl, 183, 190–91, 192
Ramadan, 222
Ramazani, Nesta, 299
Ras Beirut, 20
rational choice theory, 106, 348n. 42
rationality. *See* reason
al-Razi, Abu Bakr, 245–46
reason (rationality): and the Active
Intellect, 350n. 5; as always guided by
something else, xxix; and apologetics,
15; in Arab Muslim world, 152–57;
broad interpretation of, xix, 76; as
calculation, 49, 84; communicative
reason, 152; from external to internal
constraints on, 41–43; in German
idealism, 44, 48; al-Ghazzali on, 176–
77, 243; Habermas on, xxxii, 76, 113–
14, 147–48, 149–52, 153; ideals as
directing for Kant, 43–49, 148–49,
344n. 19; and intellect of ancient and
medieval philosophy, 44; and Islam,
xxxii, 244–45; Kant on, xxxii, 111, 147,
285–86; Kant's rationalism, 36, 344n.
19; life world as ground of, 152, 153;
link between modernity, science, and,
36–41; modernity associated with, xix;
and Muslim paradigm, 164–66; in
natural sciences, 49–54; physics and
ideal of rational worldview, 65–68;
reevaluation of reason and its context,
148–52; and revelation, 7, 14, 286; role
in Muslim community, 285–87; in
science, xix, xxix, 8, 41–42, 75; secular
rationalism, 11–12, 244; and synthesis
of modernity and tradition, 74–75;
theoretical untenability of rationalism,
82; understanding distinguished from
by Kant, 43–44. *See also* sovereign
reason
reductionism: freedom limited by, 6–7;
giving way to holism in physics, 59–
60; in Islamic revolutionaries, 26–32;
and Kant, 36; Muslim fundamentalism
as effect of, 8. *See also* reductionist
modernism
reductionist modernism: and Egyptian
attack on traditional Islam, 8–17;
freedom restricted by, xxvi; as
gateway to fundamentalism, 17–26;
modernity associated with
reductionism, xix, xxvi, xxvii, xxix,
xxxvii, 75, 77; in Ottoman Turkey, 20–
26

received permission from his parole officer to travel out of state. He explained that the sexual assault charge that landed him in prison was the result of a messy romantic affair involving the younger sister of one of his co-workers at his old job. After their relationship turned sour, she had accused him of physical and sexual abuse. He pled guilty to third degree sexual assault to avoid the possibility of a longer sentence. He lost everything as a result of that case—his job, his wife, custody of his two children—but since he got out of prison he's been doing his best to build a new life. He now has a steady construction job and lives by himself."

"How old was the victim?" Special Agent Velasquez asked.

"Eighteen. Mr. Battle was twenty-seven at the time."

"You've been very quiet this afternoon, Dr. Arnold," Special Agent Velasquez said. "What do you think?"

"Everything is fitting together rather nicely. Rejected by at least two women—his mistress and his wife. Served time in prison for sexual assault, lost his job, lives alone. Despite the lack of direct evidence tying him to the deaths, I'm convinced this is our guy."

Hank then detailed Ralph Battle's whereabouts during the three days in which the eleven bodies had been found.

"Mr. Battle said that most of the time he had been hiking by himself. He claims to have been on two ranger-led hikes, one to Lake Overlook in the West Thumb area, which is about seventeen miles south of here, and one to Mystic Falls, which is a trail where two of the bodies were found. He also says he rented a fishing boat with a captain on Yellowstone Lake on the twenty-eighth."

"Have you confirmed his claims?" Special Agent Velasquez asked.

"Not yet, but we're working on it. Of course, even if the ranger hikes and the fishing boat stories check out, the vast majority of the time he was hiking alone." Hank added that the suspect had made a disconcerting comment right at the end of the two-hour interrogation. Looking down at his notes, he recounted the suspect's exact words: "I haven't been in any relationships since I got out of prison. Women are nothing but trouble. They're what sent me to prison in the first place, and I got no use for 'em. Like I said, nothing but trouble."

Hank opened another folder. "Our agents interviewed numerous people who've interacted with Mr. Battle while he's been here at Yellowstone—other guests, park rangers, waiters and waitresses, gift shop clerks, and front desk staff. Many of them described him as a loner, but only one—"

Walter cut in. "Many people who are loners have chosen that path. They simply prefer to be by themselves. However, some loners have been forced into that lifestyle because of repeated failures establishing friendships or romantic relationships. In my opinion, people in the latter group are more likely to have pathological tendencies."

Hank frowned at Walter. "As I was saying before I was interrupted, only one person noticed any red flags. Our agents showed a picture of Mr. Battle to guests in the Old Faithful Inn, and they found a college-age woman who had had a drink or two with him on the night of May 26, the day before the killings started. She said they chatted for a while, and then he touched her leg. She pushed his hand away, and he got angry and called her a bitch. She immediately left the bar and went back to her room. She didn't remember seeing him after that."

Walter removed his glasses and placed them on the table. "So what we have here is a registered sex offender who's a loner and was rejected by a young woman the night before the killings started. If only all my cases were this easy."

Ben scratched his broad chin slowly. "So, doc, you're saying this guy killed eleven people because he got rejected by a young lady in a bar? I don't buy it."

Before Walter could respond, Special Agent Velasquez changed the subject. "Agent Carter, where are we on the DNA evidence?"

"Our previous analyses had identified foreign DNA from dozens of different individuals on the clothing and personal effects of the eleven victims. We used CODIS to compare all the foreign DNA samples with NDIS and there were no hits."

"CODIS? NDIS? Can you translate for the lay people here?" Sage asked.

"That would only be you," Gus taunted.

"Actually, I'd like an explanation too," Ben said.

"CODIS is the Combined DNA Index System, which is the FBI's support system for criminal justice DNA databases. NDIS is the National DNA Index System, a component of CODIS. You *do* know what DNA is, don't you?"

Sage didn't bother to reply.

"As I was saying, although we didn't get any hits, NDIS doesn't capture all state-level convictions. So we took a DNA sample from Mr. Battle and are comparing it directly with the foreign DNA collected from the victims' clothing and personal effects. We should have the results by late tonight or early tomorrow morning."

"Let's follow up on Mr. Battle's alibis and see if we can find anyone else who's interacted with him while he's been here," Special Agent Velasquez said. "Is his lawyer asking for a bail hearing?"

"Not yet."

"Good. I'd like to keep him in custody as long as we can. See if you can contact his parole officer and get a parole hold placed on him."

"Will do."

"Let's move on to Specialist Spurlock's report about the press briefing this morning."

Maddie estimated that there were at least seventy-five reporters and twenty cameras at the briefing, and she complained that the proceedings quickly devolved into chaos, with dozens of reporters shouting questions over one another.

Ben spun his chair toward Maddie. "What did they ask you?"

"Most of the questions concerned the identity of the eleven victims, the causes of death, whether there are any suspects—those sorts of things."

"And what did you tell them?"

"I explained that the investigation is still ongoing and there was nothing new to report."

"Did you say anything about Ralph Battle?"

"I didn't know about him before I left for the briefing this morning."

"I think you should hold another briefing tomorrow at nine a.m.," Special Agent Velasquez said.

"Once again, I would like to renew my request—"

"And once again, your request is denied, Superintendent."

Ben persisted. "Can you at least tell me whether the FBI is looking for other suspects in case Ralph Battle isn't the killer?"

"You have a valid point, Superintendent. Agent Rosenberg, how is the search for other suspects going?"

"We've temporarily halted interviews of the detainees because we've been directing all our resources into investigating Mr. Battle. I think I can spare a few agents to start those interviews back up."

"I really don't see the point," Walter said.

"Well, I do," Special Agent Velasquez responded. "One thing I've learned in my twenty-two years at the FBI is to always keep an open mind."

JUNE 1

The next morning, Sage and Penny woke up early and waited for the Daily Update to arrive. At the first sound of footsteps in the hallway, Sage poked her head out the door.

"Ricky?"

"Yes, ma'am."

"Please—call me Sage. You have time to come in?"

"Afraid not, ma'am. We're really busy."

Penny stepped past Sage into the hall. "Hi, Ricky."

Ricky smiled. "Hey, Penny! Maybe you and I could have coffee later—if you're not busy, that is. I'm off at ten."

"That would nice. Can you come back then?"

"Sure."

"Will I need my ID?"

"No, ma'am. I can identify you on sight." He gave Penny a playful grin and handed her the Daily Update.

Back inside the apartment, Sage poked Penny on the shoulder. "Look at you! You like guys in uniform?"

Penny laughed. "Maybe. I just want to see if I can find out anything."

Anaya emerged from her bedroom. "Find out what?"

"Don't know yet."

Adam called from Sage's bedroom with a gravelly morning

voice. "Hey, Sage, come back to bed. It's way too early!"

Anaya and Penny looked at Sage, who shrugged her shoulders. "What? Can't a girl have some fun?"

Anaya shuffled over to the coffee maker. "Sure. I just don't want you to get hurt, girlfriend."

"Thanks, but I can handle myself."

Things are *moving really quickly*, Sage thought. *But he's so darn cute! And what better place for a summer romance than Yellowstone?*

"Let's take a look at today's update," Sage said quickly.

The three women huddled around the single sheet of paper.

THE YELLOWSTONE DIRECTIVE
DAILY UPDATE
JUNE 1

THERE HAVE BEEN NO NEW FATALITIES DURING THE PAST 24 HOURS.

THE ORIGINAL YELLOWSTONE DIRECTIVE, AS MODIFIED AND CLARIFIED BY ALL SUBSEQUENT UPDATES INCLUDING THIS ONE, REMAINS IN FULL FORCE. AT PRESENT, THERE IS NO ESTIMATE AS TO HOW LONG THE YELLOWSTONE DIRECTIVE WILL REMAIN IN EFFECT.

ANY DETAINEE WHO VIOLATES ANY TERMS OF THE YELLOWSTONE DIRECTIVE WILL BE SUBJECT TO IMMEDIATE ARREST.

FURTHER UPDATES WILL BE PROVIDED EVERY MORNING AS WELL AS AT OTHER TIMES, AS WARRANTED BY FUTURE DEVELOPMENTS.

Penny tossed the update on the counter. "That's it?"

"There's got to be more," Sage said. "I'll find out at the briefing this morning."

"But you won't be able to tell us, will you," Anaya grumbled. "Or maybe you won't *want* to tell us."

"C'mon, Anaya, I'm in a tough spot here."

"I still don't understand exactly how you got in this tough spot. Can you explain that again?"

"If it makes you feel any better, Ben thinks you might be able to help too."

"Who?"

"Superintendent Thomas."

"How nice of him."

"No, really. That's what he told me. He especially likes how you stole the confidential FBI reports."

"You told him about that?" Anaya's voice rose. "I could get in real trouble for that!"

"Calm down. Everything's good. He sort of sees the FBI as an enemy. No, that's not quite it. Maybe more like an adversary. Anyway, he's looking for any information he can get his hands on."

"So how about you bring me along to your super-secret meetings?"

"I don't think I can."

"Why not? Can't you at least ask?"

"Well, I'm not sure that would be—"

"If you're going to be that way about it, then fine. I'll just hang out here with Adam. We had plenty of fun yesterday." Anaya sidled up to Adam, who had taken a seat at the kitchen table.

Sage glowered at Adam and he jumped up from the table. "Hey, leave me out of this, you two."

After breakfast, Sage went off for a shower and got dressed. At 9:30 she announced it was time to go.

"When will you be back?" Adam asked.

"I don't know." She kissed him on the cheek and left.

* * *

FBI CLASSIFIED BRIEFING
YELLOWSTONE NATIONAL PARK COMMAND POST
JUNE 1 – 10:00 A.M.

"To summarize, then, we still have no direct evidence tying Mr. Battle to any of the eleven fatalities. No witnesses can place him near any of the victims at the times of their deaths, except for that one photo by Fairy Falls, and we haven't found any cyanide or weapons in his room or his car. According to the preliminary analyses, his DNA does not match any of the foreign DNA on the victims' clothing or personal effects. And finally, his alibis have generally checked out, although we're still completing our investigation of those." Hank paused before continuing. "I don't think he's the killer."

"What do you recommend we do with him?" Special Agent Velasquez asked.

"I think we should ship him back to the state of Washington for a parole violation hearing."

"I strongly disagree," Walter protested. "His profile matches perfectly with that of a serial sex predator. I think we should keep him here in lockup as long as we can and interrogate him until he cracks. All serial killers eventually want to claim credit for their crimes. He won't be any different."

"We can't keep him forever without any evidence," Special Agent Velasquez said. "At some point his lawyer will ask for a bail hearing."

"She already has," Hank said. "It's set for eleven tomorrow morning via a video link."

"Let's keep him in custody until his bail hearing. If we don't have any more evidence by then we'll release him to his parole officer."

Ben picked up where he'd left off the day before. "Hank, what about the search for other suspects?"

"Since yesterday afternoon we've made considerable progress interviewing and fingerprinting the detainees. We hope to complete all interviews by this evening or tomorrow."

"Any promising leads?" Special Agent Velasquez asked.

"Not really." Hank looked down at his notes. "We've found a few people with criminal records—two with prior weapons charges and a half dozen with a variety of drug offenses, mostly possession of marijuana or cocaine. And two others have convictions for domestic violence."

"Are any of these people possible suspects?"

"We've just started interviewing them for a second time, but I have a feeling none of them is our killer."

Special Agent Velasquez's sigh was barely perceptible. "Let's move on. Analyst Pagano, can you tell us about the two aerial incidents?"

"Two days ago we instituted round-the-clock airspace surveillance of the park. Yesterday, two UAVs were spotted over the lockdown area. One was flying toward Old Faithful Village from the west and the other was approaching the village from the southeast."

Sage looked at Dominick quizzically. "UAV?"

"Unmanned aerial vehicle. A drone," he said impatiently. "Both UAVs were quickly neutralized."

"And what does *that* mean?" Sage asked.

"They were shot down."

"Were they retrieved?" Special Agent Velasquez asked.

"Yes."

"What type were they?"

"Medium-sized commercially available UAVs like those typically used by law enforcement agencies. Both had high-resolution cameras but no other payloads."

Sage shook her head. "I'm telling you, until we release more information to the public, this sort of thing is going to keep happening."

"Our public information protocol is just fine as is," Special Agent Velasquez said brusquely. She then introduced a new member to the group. The CDC had sent three of their brightest scientists to Yellowstone, and Dr. Whitney Hughes—a tall, lanky biochemist in a white lab coat—was going to be representing them at the twice-daily briefings. A squabble broke out almost immediately between the FBI and Dr. Hughes. The usual rules of decorum were forgotten, and Special Agent Velasquez quickly lost control.

Gus wanted to continue focusing their efforts on finding the serial killer while Dominick kept pushing his *nouveau* terrorist theory. But Whitney thought the best approach was to identify the source of the cyanide and determine how it entered the bodies of the victims. This, she believed, would lead them to the killer.

"And I must add that there's another possibility worth considering," she said, looking around the table.

"What's that?" Gus asked.

"That the deaths are due to an environmental source of cyanide."

"But the autopsy and toxicology reports indicate that the high levels of cyanide and the sudden nature of the deaths were inconsistent with an environmental source."

"I've read those reports, and it's clear that the pathologists were thinking about typical environmental sources such as apricot pits, lima beans, or other flora that contain very low levels of cyanide. When I say environmental, I'm speaking in the broadest terms. For example, it could include water or food that has somehow been contaminated with cyanide—maybe from an unknown natural source or via accidental exposure to industrial chemicals."

"But the victims didn't ingest any contaminated food or drink."

"We don't know that," Whitney replied. "The autopsy reports didn't rule out food or drink as a source. They simply said the test results were inconclusive."

"Even if you're right, the food or drink could have been intentionally contaminated by a serial killer," Gus said.

"Or a terrorist," Dominick added.

"Possibly, but it also could have been accidental. First we need to find the source of the cyanide and then we can work on determining how it got into the victims."

"I think you're making this way more complicated than it needs to be," Gus said. "I know where the cyanide is. It's in the hands of a killer."

After another couple of rounds of sparring, Special Agent Velasquez stopped the bickering. "Agent Rosenberg, can you give us a breakdown of how many people are in the lockdown area and where everyone is located?"

"I don't have those numbers with me."

"Well, get them."

"Okay. I'll report on them at the briefing this afternoon."

"No, get them right now. We can wait."

While Hank hurried out of the trailer to retrieve the figures, Whitney provided an update on the CDC's field operations. They had been assigned to a small tent next to the trailer that housed the FBI crime lab, and she complained that the setup was completely unsatisfactory. The tent was not airtight, and it couldn't be secured at night. There were only two electrical outlets and no running water. Most of their supplies had not arrived, and the few instruments and materials that had been delivered hadn't been set up.

"I don't mean to be rude, but it's almost as if our efforts are being sabotaged."

"I can assure you that's not the case, Dr. Hughes," Special Agent Velasquez said. "We'll do everything in our power to accommodate you. Agent Carter, can the CDC work with you in the FBI crime lab trailer for now?"

"Well, it's really crowded in there, and I'm not sure—"

Just then, Hank returned with the figures, red cheeked and out of breath. "There's a total of two hundred and thirty-three people in the Old Faithful Inn, the Old Faithful Snow Lodge and Cabins, and the Old Faithful Lodge Cabins. All of them are park guests. Most were already staying in the inn or lodges when the lockdown went into effect. The others were relocated from campgrounds in the lockdown area. In addition, there are seventy-five employees, which includes people who work for the National Park Service, concessionaires, private contractors, and medical staff. The employees are mostly housed in dorms and apartments, with a few of them in their own trailers.

"Does that number include personnel from the FBI, National Guard, and CDC?" Special Agent Velasquez asked.

"No."

"Do you have those numbers with you?"

"I think so. Let me take a look."

After shuffling through a few folders, Hank looked up. "We just brought in eight more FBI agents, so we now have thirty FBI personnel, one hundred twenty-two National Guard soldiers, and three scientists from the CDC, for a total of one hundred fifty-five, all housed in the temporary barracks set up by the National Guard."

Special Agent Velasquez scribbled the numbers on her note pad. "That comes to—"

"Four hundred sixty-three," Sage said smugly.

Special Agent Velasquez shot Sage a look and then turned toward Hank. "Agent Rosenberg, how are we doing on food?"

"At the moment we're fine. But we'll need to bring in additional food and other supplies if the lockdown continues for another three or four days."

"That seems likely, so let's get ahead of—"

Maddie burst into the conference room clutching a stack of

papers to her chest. Breathing heavily, she dropped them on the table and several sheets fluttered to the floor.

"I thought you were going to give us your update on the press briefing this afternoon," Special Agent Velasquez said.

"So did I, but it couldn't wait."

"Why not?"

"I think we may have underestimated the amount of public interest in what's happening here. It was even worse than yesterday."

Sage couldn't resist. "What a surprise! The most famous National Park in the country—probably in the whole world—is closed. Eleven people are dead, and hundreds more are trapped here for God knows how long. Of course people are interested!"

"So how many members of the press were at the briefing?" Special Agent Velasquez asked.

"Probably double yesterday. Maybe a hundred and fifty. I'm not sure." Maddie was visibly shaking as she recalled the briefing. "This is all so new to me," she admitted. "I'm usually just writing press releases, not standing in front of a throng of reporters."

"What did you tell them?"

"Same as yesterday—because of the ongoing investigation we can't release any new details."

"That doesn't sound too bad."

"It gets worse," Maddie said haltingly. "Among the attendees at the press conference were relatives of nine people still here in the park—spouses, siblings, and three sets of parents. They were demanding to know what has happened to their loved ones."

"And what did you say?"

"I just kept repeating what I've been saying all along—the investigation is ongoing and we can't release any additional information at this time. I had a guardsman get their names, phone numbers, and e-mail addresses, along with the name of the family member they were concerned about. I told them I would see what I could find out."

"That seems reasonable."

"But there's a problem. On the ride back here I went through the files on my laptop to look up the nine detainees."

"And?"

"Two of them are dead."

Over the next half hour, a lively discussion ensued about

whether to notify the families of the victims. Finally, Special Agent Velasquez announced she had made her decision.

"I don't think we have any choice at this point. I'm going to order that we notify the next of kin of the eleven decedents."

"How do you plan to do that?" Ben asked.

"In the usual way—an agent from the Victim Services Division of the FBI will visit the homes of the next of kin to deliver the news and offer counseling and other forms of support. All notifications will occur tomorrow morning. After the final notification has been made, we'll release the names of the deceased to the press."

"What about the bodies?"

"We'll keep them here for the time being in case we need to conduct additional forensic analyses. Any other updates?"

"I've got something," Dominick said. "It seems that many of the detainees are becoming increasingly frustrated and even angry, which is creating some serious security challenges."

"I'm afraid there's nothing we can do about that," Special Agent Velasquez said.

Sage jumped in. "But there is. We can try to make life a little more bearable for everyone."

"And just what do you suggest, Dr. Maldonado?"

"For starters, how about holding a daily public briefing in the auditorium of the Visitor Center? People could come and ask questions about what's going on. We're holding daily briefings for the press—why not do the same for everyone who's stuck here?"

"Your request is denied."

"Well, then, let's make the Daily Updates more informative— maybe include a summary of the information presented during these FBI briefings."

"The Daily Updates are fine as is."

Sage pushed on. "Well … how about we loosen the restrictions on people's movements in the village? Let everyone walk about more freely without having to show their identification every couple of feet. Maybe even allow them to walk around the geyser basin. Something to get their minds off the lockdown."

"But what if someone tries to escape again?" Gus asked. "Remember, we had three escape attempts two days ago."

"What do you mean *escape*? We aren't prisoners!" Sage exclaimed.

Special Agent Velasquez glared at Sage. "Is that all, Dr. Maldonado?"

"Can't we at least give everyone their personal electronics back?"

"Those are still being processed."

"What does *that* mean?" Ben demanded. "I thought they were just being stored."

Sage's voice rose even more. "What the Special Agent is trying to tell us is that the FBI is using our electronic devices to spy on us."

"That's enough out of you, Dr. Maldonado!" Special Agent Velasquez looked slowly around the packed conference table. "I think it's become too crowded in here. Too many people."

"Don't you mean too many *opinions*?" Sage said defiantly.

"There's only one person in here who's not essential to our investigation. Dr. Maldonado, I'm going to excuse you from attending all future briefings."

"But I don't mind attending. In fact, I want to be here."

"Perhaps I wasn't clear enough. I'm forbidding you from attending these briefings."

"But why?"

"We're adjourned until four p.m. I'll see all of you back here at that time—except for Dr. Maldonado."

Sage pushed back abruptly from the conference table, almost knocking Hank out of his chair, and stormed out the door. She was brought to an abrupt halt by the bright June sun. After donning her sunglasses, she headed back toward her apartment.

I can't believe I got kicked out of the damn briefings! All I did was speak my mind, just like my mom taught me. What's wrong with that?

"Dr. Maldonado?"

"What?" Sage kept walking, her eyes fixed on the ground.

"That took a lot of guts in there."

Sage stopped and turned round.

"I'm Whitney Hughes from the CDC. I'm afraid I don't know your first name." Whitney spoke with a pronounced Southern drawl. She towered over Sage, her gangly arms protruding awkwardly from the too-short sleeves of her bright white lab coat. Her golden blond hair fell just below her shoulders and her pale skin was lightly sprinkled with freckles.

"Sage ... Sage Maldonado."

"As I was saying, you showed a lot of courage in there. Not many people would stand up to an FBI agent like that."

"I probably shouldn't have said anything, but I was just so damn mad. I should have just kept my cool like you did, Dr. Hughes."

"No, your response was spot on. And please ... call me Whitney."

"I don't like it when some know-it-all big shot tries to tell me what I can and cannot do."

"I wish I had your courage."

"It's not that hard really. All it requires is a bit of obstinance and a dash of rudeness."

Whitney laughed. "You weren't rude. You were just standing up for what you thought was right."

"I was right, wasn't I?"

"Of course you were."

"So why'd I get kicked out of the meeting?"

"The Special Agent's probably used to everyone following her orders without question. I'm guessing she doesn't like being challenged."

"But my parents raised me to challenge authority when the authority is wrong."

"That's really admirable, but keep in mind that Special Agent Velasquez has probably had to fight many of the same battles we have."

"You mean as a woman in a profession dominated by men?"

"Exactly."

"I hadn't thought about it that way."

Whitney drew out each word as she spoke. "My mama used to tell me that life is a team sport. I didn't really listen at first, but as I grew older I realized she was on to something. Maybe you should try thinking of the Special Agent as an ally instead of an adversary. After all, we're all trying to figure out what's going on here."

"I guess you're right. Do *you* think of her as an ally?"

"Are you kidding? Of course not! I don't trust the FBI one bit."

They both laughed heartily, releasing some of the tension still lingering from the contentious briefing.

"Where are you headed?" Whitney asked.

"Back to my apartment."

"I have a few minutes. Can I walk with you?"

"Sure."

They walked together, Sage barely keeping up with Whitney's loping gait.

"I'd like to know what you think is going on," Whitney asked.

"I don't know. Maybe there really is a serial killer or even a terrorist here in Yellowstone. Dominick's ideas about a new type of terrorism are pretty convincing."

"And pretty scary."

"What do you think?"

"I'm not sure yet, but I like to consider all possible options."

"You don't think there's a killer here, do you?"

"That's not what I said. I just want to consider everything before I come to any conclusions. That's the way we approach things at the CDC."

"Is there anything I can do to help?"

"Actually there is. I was thinking that maybe you could be our eyes and ears out here. You never know what you might come across."

"I'll try. And can you do something for me in return?"

"Like what?"

"Fill me in on what happens during the FBI briefings."

"That might be a little risky since the meetings are classified."

"Well, if you don't think you can …"

"I'm sure we can work something out."

"Maybe we could meet after each briefing."

"Where?"

"Probably the safest place is my apartment. We're almost there now."

Within a couple of minutes they reached the front door of Sage's building. Sage greeted Ricky at the entrance. "I thought you got off at ten."

"I did, but they needed me to cover for another guardsman, so I'm back here again."

"Did you and Penny have a good time this morning?"

"We did. We couldn't do much—just got a soda and walked around for a while. We took a leisurely stroll through the geysers and hot springs over by Old Faithful. We must have spent about an hour just walking on the boardwalk. It was kind of like being a tourist, except we had the place all to ourselves because no one else has permission to be out there. Then I had to get back to work. Say hi to her for me, will you?"

"Of course. By the way, this is Dr. Whitney Hughes from the CDC. We're working together, and she'll need to visit me from time to time. Will that be okay?"

"I'm not sure. We're under strict orders not to allow any visitors. I should probably run this by my supervisor."

"But Dr. Hughes has already been approved by Superintendent Thomas."

"In that case I guess it'll be okay."

Once inside the apartment, Sage introduced Whitney to Anaya, Penny, and Adam. They chatted for a few minutes, and then Whitney announced she had to leave.

"I don't think I'll be able to get back here this afternoon," she said on the way out. "We're still setting up our lab. I'll try to come by after the morning briefing tomorrow."

After Whitney left, Sage filled everyone in on what had happened during the briefing and how she'd been banned from all future briefings because she'd stood up to Special Agent Velasquez.

"Way to kick butt!" Adam gave Sage a big hug.

Sage smiled at Penny. "Ricky tells me you guys had a good time this morning."

Penny grinned. "He seems like a nice guy."

"Does he know much about what's going on?"

"I don't think so—actually, I forgot to ask." Penny laughed. "But he might be helpful in the future. You never know. I think I'll try to get to know him better."

* * *

After lunch, Sage took a shower while Adam, Anaya, and Penny relaxed in the cramped living room.

While Sage was still in the shower, two FBI agents arrived to obtain Anaya's fingerprints and facial scan. This time she complied without a fuss and they were done in less than five minutes.

After the agents left, Adam asked Anaya why she hadn't caused a ruckus.

"It's not worth it. They'd probably just keep coming back until I gave them what they wanted."

"I can't believe we've been stuck in this apartment for four days," Adam said.

"Is that all? Seems more like four weeks. The days are all starting to run together."

Sage emerged from the bathroom in her robe, her voluminous hair barely corralled by a large white towel wrapped loosely around her head. "Who used the last of the shampoo?"

"That would be you. Yesterday," Anaya snapped.

"I don't think so," Sage shot back.

"I know so."

Penny looked up from her crossword puzzle. "C'mon guys, cut it out."

"Ever since Sage got to go to her fancy meetings she's been unbearable," Anaya said.

"You're just jealous," Sage replied sharply. "Anyway, I can't go anymore. You happy now?"

"Ecstatic."

Penny threw the puzzle book on the table. "I just want to go home. I've been wearing other people's clothes, eating other people's food, and sleeping in other people's beds for too long."

Suddenly the windows rattled and the dishes in the sink clattered. There was no major jolt this time, just a continuous rolling motion punctuated by a few shudders.

"Not another one!" Adam shouted. "I can't stand all these aftershocks! I want to go home too!"

"We all do," Sage said.

JUNE 2

The oppressive fog of fear and anxiety that had hung over Yellowstone since the start of the lockdown gradually began to dissipate. In its place, boredom and frustration settled in. The denizens of Apartment 1B spent their days reading, chatting, and playing games. Now that Sage couldn't attend the FBI briefings, she was stuck in the apartment with everyone else. In the cramped quarters tempers flared occasionally, especially between Sage and Anaya, who argued over the most mundane aspects of their circumscribed existence.

Since they were only allowed to leave their apartment for meals, they took full advantage of those brief moments of freedom. Although National Guard soldiers posted along the way ensured that no one deviated from their route to and from the Lodge Cafeteria, it was still nice to breathe the fresh air, smell the lodgepole pines, and view the occasional geyser eruption from afar.

After dinner that night, they settled into what had quickly become an evening routine—Sage, Adam, and Penny talked and played cards in the living room while Anaya retreated into her bedroom. But that evening she didn't stay there long. After a few minutes, she emerged and casually tossed two newspapers on the table.

"What are those?" Sage asked.

"They're newspapers!" Penny exclaimed. "The *Los Angeles Times* and the *Chicago Tribune!*"

Sage could barely speak. "Where did you get them?"

Anaya smiled. "You never know what you might find in the Visitor Center."

"But you were with us all day."

"Not quite. Remember the bathroom break I took while we were eating dinner in the cafeteria?"

"You *were* gone for an awfully long time."

"Well, I made a quick trip to the Visitor Center."

"But how did you get past security?"

"Just showed them my DOI ID card and walked right in."

"How were you able to take the newspapers without being seen? And how did you get out?"

"Just like with the FBI reports—I grabbed them from the counter near the front of the Visitor Center and just walked out the door."

"Why didn't you tell us at dinner?"

"I didn't want anyone else to see them."

While Sage marveled at Anaya's ingenuity, Penny and Adam started reading the papers.

"Yellowstone Hostage Situation Intensifies," Penny read aloud from the *L.A. Times.*

" 'No End in Sight for Yellowstone Drama,' says the *Tribune,*" Adam announced.

The four of them devoured every single article about their plight. Several mentioned that the President was considering closing all National Parks and Monuments as a precaution until the mystery at Yellowstone was solved.

"This really *is* looking more and more like a terrorist attack," Anaya declared.

"I'm still not so sure about that," Sage said.

Most of the accounts stuck to the facts, but a few veered off into hyperbole and unfounded speculation as they described tales of starving park visitors, prison-like conditions, and frequent fights among those still in the park.

Virtually every story mentioned the word "hostage" at least once.

"We really *are* hostages, aren't we?" Sage said.

"Damn right we are!" Anaya responded. "Not hostages of terrorists, but hostages of the government of the good ol' U. S. of A."

Around eight, Whitney stopped by to give them an update. "Sorry I didn't come by after the morning briefing, but it's been really hectic getting our lab set up."

"How's that going?" Sage asked.

"It's taken much longer than it should have because we had to wait for a lot of the equipment to get here. Yellowstone is a long way from everywhere."

"That's the reason I like it here," Anaya said. "Or at least it's why I *used* to like it."

"Anyway, the lab's up and running now. We moved from that minuscule tent next to the FBI crime lab trailer to a much larger space in the Old Faithful Snow Lodge. It's not perfect, but it'll do. We've created a Biosafety Level 2 lab that we can use to test for cyanide and other poisons."

"Other poisons?" Sage asked. "I thought the toxicology reports only found cyanide."

"They did, but I like to be ready for all possibilities just in case."

"So have you found anything yet?"

"Nope. We started by testing the clothing and personal effects of all the victims and so far we've come up empty—no cyanide or other common poisons on any of them. Tomorrow we're moving on to the water supply and the food in the kitchens. After that we'll look for cyanide out on the trails where the bodies were found."

"So what have I missed in the FBI briefings?"

"Not much. Just the usual bickering between Gus, Dominick, and yours truly. I really want to get along with them, but they make it so difficult. They're so full of themselves, and they're hardheaded, stubborn, and mean-spirited to boot."

"I hadn't noticed." Sage grinned. "Anything else?"

"Yeah, the notifications of the next of kin occurred this morning as planned, and a press release was issued this afternoon listing the names of the deceased. Maddie said that led to a media frenzy." Whitney paused. "I'm starting to worry about her."

"How come?"

"I'm not sure she can handle the pressure of being the FBI press liaison. She's clearly not comfortable holding live press briefings, and every day she seems more and more unnerved by the intensity of the media interest."

"You think maybe she's so stressed because the FBI is hiding something?"

Whitney stared out the window. "I don't know."

JUNE 3

"It's hard to believe it's only been a week since we found that girl's body on the Fairy Falls Trail," Sage said, rinsing out their coffee cups. The four friends were spending yet another afternoon cooped up in the apartment.

"The last couple of days have been especially brutal," Adam said. "Nothing new in the Daily Updates, no news from anyone, and no new food in the cafeteria. I just wish this was over."

"Me too," Anaya and Penny said in unison.

There was a knock at the door.

"Who is it?" Sage called out.

"It's Ricky."

"C'mon in Ricky, the door's unlocked," Penny said brightly. She got up and greeted him with a hug. "It's so sweet of you to come by to see me."

"Actually, I'm here on official business," he said, blushing. "I have a message for Sage. You've been invited to the afternoon briefing at four."

"That's in fifteen minutes! Who invited me?"

"FBI Agent Hank Rosenberg."

* * *

FBI Classified Briefing
Yellowstone National Park Command Post
June 3 – 4:00 p.m.

"Dr. Maldonado, I thought you understood that you are no longer welcome at these briefings!" Special Agent Velasquez's tone was even sharper than usual.

"But I was invited to this one."

"By whom?"

"By me," Hank said with authority.

"May I ask why?"

"We've been here for almost six days and we're no closer to solving this than when we first arrived. I thought we could use some help. Sage is the only one of us who can spend time with the detainees without raising any suspicion. You never know what she might see or hear that could help our investigation."

"We can use her help too," Whitney said. "She has more knowledge about the Yellowstone ecosystem than any of us in the CDC."

"I need her as well," Ben added. "She has scientific insight and acumen that can help us all."

"It seems there's a groundswell of support for you, Dr. Maldonado." Special Agent Velasquez eyed Sage intently. "But let me make one thing perfectly clear—if you disrupt these proceedings again, you will be banished for good. Do you understand?"

"I do. A colleague recently reminded me that we're all on the same team here." Sage smiled at Whitney across the table. "I'll do my best to be a better team player from now on."

"That's more like it."

Sage took a seat next to Ben.

"Welcome back," he whispered.

"Let's begin with an update on the interviews, fingerprints, background checks, and facial scans of all the detainees. Agent Rosenberg, how are those going?"

"We had to go back a second time for some of the detainees, but they're all completed now, and the facial scans have been stored in our database. Other than a few people with surly attitudes, there's nothing new to report. No detainees have criminal records other than the ones I reported previously, and none of them are on no-fly lists or terrorist watch lists. Dominick has communicated with numerous foreign governments, and none of our detainees are on their radar."

"Of course, several countries did not cooperate," Dominick added, "so we can't be absolutely certain that we don't have any international terrorists here."

"I'll take that under advisement," Special Agent Velasquez said. "Dr. Hughes, what is the status of your investigation?"

"We don't have anything new to report either. We've tested dozens of food and water samples from all around Old Faithful Village, and no cyanide or other poisons have been detected in any of them. We've begun to look for other environmental sources of cyanide such as plants or soil. That hasn't turned up anything either, although our investigation is still ongoing."

Special Agent Velasquez looked around the table. "So where are we, people? These deaths started seven days ago and we don't have a single viable suspect. There haven't been any new fatalities in the last four days, and I'm starting to think we should just send everyone home."

"Are you crazy?" Dominick shouted, raising his bushy eyebrows in disbelief.

"Excuse me?"

"I don't mean to be disrespectful, but we can't just let everyone go home!"

"And why not?"

"What if the terrorist is still here? We'd be letting him slip through our fingers."

"Give me one credible piece of evidence that this has been an act of terrorism," Special Agent Velasquez said.

Dominick paused.

"That's what I thought."

"I'm with Dominick," Gus said. "I don't think we should send everyone home just yet."

Special Agent Velasquez leaned forward. "And how long do you propose we keep everyone here? A week? A month? A year?"

"Until ..."

"Until what?"

"Until we catch the killer."

"What do you think, Dr. Hughes?"

"There are a variety of factors to consider, including whether or not—"

"Just tell us what you think, Dr. Hughes. Should we send everybody home?" Special Agent Velasquez tapped her fingers on the table.

"I do. As I've said from the beginning, I think there's a good chance that the killer is not a human but rather some sort of environmental source of cyanide. The longer we hold people here, the greater the chance more people will die. I don't want to keep hundreds of people at risk here while we figure this out."

For almost an hour the discussion continued, often raucous and occasionally bordering on hostile. As the debate dragged on, it became clear that Gus and Dominick were the only ones who opposed letting everyone go home.

Finally Special Agent Velasquez held up her hand and asked for silence. "I've heard enough and I've made my decision."

"Don't we get to vote?" Gus asked.

"There'll be no voting. I've listened carefully to all your arguments, and I believe it's time to send everyone home. Therefore, I'm going to order an evacuation of the park to commence at ten a.m. on June 5th, two days from now. A small cohort from the FBI, National Guard, and CDC, as well as a few support personnel from the Park Service, will stay and continue to work until we figure out who or what has killed all these people. Everyone else will be evacuated."

"What about the victims' bodies?" Sage asked.

"We'll send them home as part of the evacuation. The bodies will be flown home early in the morning of the fifth. Specialist Spurlock, prepare a press release regarding the evacuation to be distributed to the media tomorrow afternoon."

"Don't you think the press release should be followed by a press briefing?" Sage asked. "I imagine the evacuation news will generate a fair bit of excitement."

"Let me think about that. If we decide to hold a press briefing I suppose you'll want to attend, Superintendent Thomas?"

"Of course."

"I think that's everything. I'll instruct the FBI and the National Guard to work together to formulate an evacuation procedure.

The evacuation will be announced to the detainees in tomorrow morning's Daily Update. Until that time, no one—*and I mean no one*—is to discuss this matter outside of this room. Is that clear?" Special Agent Velasquez didn't bother to wait for a response. "We're adjourned."

JUNE 4

"Anyone wanna look at the Daily Update?" Adam asked. "It's over by the door."

"Why bother?" Anaya whined. "It says the same thing every day. There have been no new deaths, blah, blah, blah. The Yellowstone Directive will remain in full effect for another ten years, blah, blah, blah. All detainees must follow the rules or they will be decapitated, blah, blah, blah."

Penny retrieved the update from the floor; her hands shook as she held it. "Hey, guys, you better take a look at this."

"Has there been a new death?" Adam asked.

"No, something much more exciting!"

"They're going to host an all-night movie marathon at the Visitor Center?" Sage offered with a quick laugh.

"No!"

"Then just read it to us," Anaya said.

Which Penny did.

THE YELLOWSTONE DIRECTIVE
DAILY UPDATE
JUNE 4

THE FBI HAS COMPLETED ITS INVESTIGATION
OF ALL DETAINEES SUBJECT TO THE LOCKDOWN.

THIS INVESTIGATION HAS NOT RESULTED IN ANY CHARGES BEING BROUGHT AGAINST ANY DETAINEES FOR THE DEATHS THAT HAVE OCCURRED IN YELLOWSTONE NATIONAL PARK.

THEREFORE, IN CONSULTATION WITH THE CENTERS FOR DISEASE CONTROL AND PREVENTION, THE FBI HAS DECIDED TO COMMENCE AN ORDERLY EVACUATION OF YELLOWSTONE NATIONAL PARK BEGINNING AT 10:00 AM ON JUNE 5.

THE EVACUATION WILL PROCEED IN THE FOLLOWING ORDER:
• GROUP 1: PARK GUESTS AND VISITORS
• GROUP 2: EMPLOYEES OF THE NATIONAL PARK SERVICE, CONCESSIONAIRES, AND PRIVATE CONTRACTORS
• GROUP 3: EMPLOYEES OF THE FBI, NATIONAL GUARD, AND CDC

A CORE GROUP OF FBI AGENTS, INVESTIGATORS AND ANALYSTS, CDC SCIENTISTS, NATIONAL GUARD SOLDIERS, AND NATIONAL PARK SERVICE EMPLOYEES WILL REMAIN IN THE PARK AFTER THE EVACUATION IS COMPLETE.

ALL EVACUEES WILL BE TRANSPORTED TO THE JACKSON HOLE AIRPORT ON BUSES SUPPLIED BY THE NATIONAL GUARD. EVACUEES WILL BE FLOWN VIA CHARTER FLIGHTS TO DENVER INTERNATIONAL AIRPORT WHERE THEY WILL BE MET BY FEDERAL MARSHALLS WHO WILL FACILITATE TRAVEL ARRANGEMENTS TO THEIR FINAL DESTINATIONS.

PERSONAL ELECTRONICS THAT WERE CONFISCATED BY THE FBI WILL BE RETURNED TO THEIR OWNERS AT DENVER INTERNATIONAL AIRPORT.

EACH EVACUEE WILL BE ALLOWED TO TAKE TWO SUITCASES AND ONE PERSONAL CARRY-ON ITEM SUCH AS A BACKPACK, PURSE, OR BRIEFCASE. EVACUEES SHOULD PACK ALL ESSENTIAL

ITEMS SUCH AS PASSPORTS, ALL FORMS OF
IDENTIFICATION, MONEY, AND MEDICATIONS IN
THEIR PERSONAL CARRY-ON ITEM.

IF AN EVACUEE DOES NOT HAVE ENOUGH SPACE IN
THE ALLOTTED BAGS FOR ALL THEIR CLOTHES AND
PERSONAL EFFECTS, THE EXCESS ITEMS MUST BE
LEFT IN THE EVACUEE'S ROOM. THESE ITEMS WILL
BE RETURNED TO THEIR OWNERS AT A FUTURE DATE.

ALL PERSONAL VEHICLES, INCLUDING CARS,
TRUCKS, MOTOR HOMES, MOTORCYCLES, AND
BICYCLES, MUST BE LEFT BEHIND AT YELLOWSTONE.
THESE WILL BE RETURNED TO THEIR OWNERS AT A
FUTURE DATE.

FURTHER UPDATES CONCERNING ADDITIONAL
DETAILS ABOUT THE EVACUATION PROCESS WILL BE
PROVIDED THROUGHOUT THE DAY.

Everyone was momentarily stunned. Then Apartment 1B erupted into a paroxysm of screaming, shouting, and hugging.

"We're going home!"

"Finally!"

Adam looked at Sage. "You already knew about this, didn't you?"

Sage smiled coyly. "My mom always told me I was pretty good at keeping secrets."

"I can't believe you didn't tell us," Anaya snapped. "I thought we were friends."

"Even your crummy attitude isn't going to bring me down today," Sage said.

"At this point I don't care what you think," Anaya retorted. "I'm just happy we're finally getting out of this hell hole."

"You don't really mean that, do you?"

"I meant every word."

"The part about not caring or the part about the hell hole?"

"Both."

"I still want to know why all those people died," Sage said. "Don't you want to know what happened to Caitlyn?"

"I'm really sad for her and all, but she's already gone. I just want to leave before something happens to me." Anaya retreated to her room.

Adam frowned at Sage. "Wait a sec! Are you staying?"

"Whitney did ask me to stay and help out, but I decided it was time for me to leave and let the professionals take it from here."

"I'm really glad you're not staying." Adam hugged Sage tightly.

"I don't know about the rest of you, but I'm going to start packing," Penny said. "It's probably going to take me a couple of hours to gather all my stuff."

"But you don't have any stuff," Adam said.

Penny smiled. "Duh!"

While Sage, Adam, and Penny talked excitedly about what they were going to do when they got home, Anaya was off by herself organizing her clothes and packing her bags.

Sage had almost filled her two largest suitcases and was contemplating which of her remaining clothes to leave behind. She held up a dark blue dress for Adam's scrutiny.

"What d'ya think? Take it or leave it?"

"What were you thinking when you brought that to Yellowstone? Did you think we'd be having dinner parties out here?"

"You never know. My dad taught me to be ready for anything."

"Well, I think it's cute, so bring it."

By ten, everyone was done packing. There wasn't much left to do except sit around and wait. Another update appeared under the door around three thirty. It contained general procedures for the evacuation and lists of what could and could not be brought onto the evacuation buses and it repeated the information that evacuees' personal electronics would be returned to them at Denver International Airport.

At 5:30 p.m., two National Guard soldiers knocked on the door and announced they were there to transport Sage to the press briefing at the South Entrance at 7:00 p.m.

"Really?"

"Yes. Superintendent Thomas insisted on it."

"Can you give me a few minutes to get ready?"

"No. We leave immediately."

Still dressed in her sweats, Sage joined Ben and Maddie, who were already seated in a military transport vehicle. On the way to the briefing, Maddie reminded Sage and Ben that they were attending only as observers and that they were not to say anything at all during the briefing.

* * *

The press briefing was even larger and more chaotic than Sage had anticipated. Three tents—one monstrous pavilion and two smaller ones on either side—had been erected to accommodate the ever-increasing throng of journalists. Surrounding the press tents was a small village of temporary structures, including several trailers from FEMA and the Red Cross, both ready to offer assistance to the hundreds of people trapped in Yellowstone.

At the front of the largest press tent, Maddie took her place behind a raised podium adorned with the official seal of the FBI, flanked by Sage and Ben. A dark blue curtain behind them fluttered in the stiff breeze. The collar on Maddie's FBI jacket was turned up on one side and her hair blew around her face as she spoke. Her soft voice trembled as she opened the briefing. When she finished speaking, the first question was directed at Sage.

"Dr. Maldonado, can you comment on what it's been like to be a hostage for seven days?"

Sage couldn't see which journalist had asked the question. There were hundreds of them. She leaned in toward the microphone on the podium. "I'm only at this briefing as an observer. Please direct your questions to Specialist Spurlock."

"So what have the conditions been like, Dr. Maldonado?" another reporter shouted.

Sage couldn't help herself. She moved behind the podium and stood shoulder to shoulder with Maddie. "It hasn't been too bad, really."

"So what *has been* bad about it?"

"Mostly the boredom. And not knowing if ... I mean *when* ... we'd go home."

"How's the food?"

"Do you have to sleep outside?"

"Have you been interrogated?"

"How many fights have there been?"

"Did you know any of the victims?"

"Do you have any idea who the killer is?"

"Is the killer still in Yellowstone?"

Despite Maddie's frequent interruptions, Sage answered each and every question. Finally, Maddie announced they had to leave and she guided Sage clumsily off the platform.

As they headed back to Old Faithful Village in the transport vehicle, Sage was buoyant. "I thought that went pretty well. In fact, it was actually kind of fun!"

"I'm going to be fired for sure," Maddie muttered.

JUNE 5

By 6:15 the next morning, Penny, Adam, and Sage had showered and dressed. No one, not even Anaya, who was the last to get up, complained about the lack of shampoo.

At seven, everyone was ready. Their bags were lined up by the door, and the things they had to leave behind were laid out neatly on their beds. Adam made eggs and bagels but no one was very hungry. Their excitement was tempered by nervousness as the day ahead seemed filled with uncertainty.

"We're in the second evacuation group," Adam said. "What time do you think they'll get to us?"

"We're not *all* in the second group," Penny said. "I'm a park visitor, so I get to go home first."

"I'd forgotten about that. You seem like you're one of us."

"I *am* one of us, but I'm still going to keep my place at the head of the line if you don't mind."

Even though the evacuation wasn't scheduled to begin until ten, the final update the evening before had instructed all evacuees to be in the large parking lot behind the Old Faithful Inn no later than nine. The four occupants of Apartment 1B headed out with their belongings at 7:45 hoping to get an early start. As they approached the main road separating their apartment building from the center of the village, they had to stop while a convoy of hearses passed by.

Adam's panic was palpable. "Look! More victims!"

"No, those are the original eleven," Sage said quietly. "They're finally going home."

They all bowed their heads until the last hearse had disappeared down the road toward the South Entrance and then they walked the remainder of the way in silence. As they joined the throng of people waiting to be processed for the evacuation, Adam remarked that the scene looked like a jam-packed airport.

"Looks more like a refugee camp to me," Anaya said.

Six evacuation buses were lined up nose to tail at the curb immediately behind the Visitor Center. They were gray with no discernable markings; the colorful tour buses that had rounded up park guests during the first day of the lockdown were nowhere to be seen.

About twenty feet away from the first bus was a security setup worthy of an international airport. An x-ray machine, complete with conveyor belt and standard gray bins, was attended by several National Guard soldiers conducting practice runs with their own shoes and bags. Two large walkthrough metal detectors flanked the x-ray machine, ready to screen evacuees entering the embarkation area. Three FBI agents stood off to the side with explosive-sniffing dogs at the ready.

The parking lot was divided into two enclosures, one much bigger than the other, each ringed by metal barricades. The smaller enclosure was adjacent to the security station, and the larger one took up the remainder of the parking lot. Every twenty feet or so around the perimeter of the two enclosures was a National Guard soldier, a weapon slung over their shoulder. A handful of people were scattered in the larger enclosure, but the smaller one was completely empty.

Sage and her friends joined a line that snaked along the edge of the parking lot and doubled back in the other direction. The line led to a check-in area in front of the larger enclosure.

"No wonder they wanted us here at nine. This line is even slower than the DMV," Adam quipped.

"Quit joking around, Adam," Anaya said. "It looks like they mean business."

"C'mon Anaya, lighten up. We're all going home."

"Please keep your eyes to the front and refrain from talking," one of the National Guard soldiers barked.

Duly chastised, they waited in silence as the line inched forward. After forty-five minutes, they finally reached a staging area in front of three check-in counters that were staffed by FBI agents. The single line split into three, one for each counter. Adam and Anaya were directed to the counter in the middle while Penny and Sage proceeded to the one on the left.

"Name and status, please."

"Penny Phillips, park visitor."

"Destination?"

"Jackson Hole."

"I mean your final destination."

"That is my final destination. I live there."

"Where are your bags?"

"All I've got is my backpack."

"What about suitcases?"

"I don't have any ... it's a long story. Let me get my driver's license." Penny started to reach into her pack.

"You don't need it, ma'am. Just look directly into the face recognition interface."

Penny stared at the rectangular black and silver instrument on the counter. The agent squinted at his computer screen and then looked up at Penny.

"You're all set to go, Ms. Phillips. You're on Bus 4 in Group 1. Here's your evacuation pass. Do you have your receipt for your personal electronic devices?"

"Yes."

"Keep your receipt with you. Your personal electronics have already been loaded onto your bus, and you'll need the receipt to claim your devices. Please proceed into the large holding area directly behind me."

Penny took the blue cardboard evacuation pass and headed into the holding area.

"Next. Name and destination, please."

"Sage Maldonado. Not sure."

"Not sure about what?"

"About where I'm headed. I had hoped to become a full-time

ranger and stay here at Yellowstone."

"I need to input a final destination to process you."

"Put down my parents' address. They live in Honolulu."

"Number of bags?"

"Two suitcases and my backpack."

After checking her bags with the agent, Sage completed the facial recognition process and received her luggage claim check and a bright orange evacuation pass.

"You're on Bus 1 in Group 2, Dr. Maldonado."

"When do you think we'll be leaving?"

"No telling. Probably sometime this afternoon."

"What do we do until then?"

"Now that you've been processed, you have to wait in the large holding area with everyone else. You'll find vending machines and Porta Potties on the far side."

"You mean we're stuck in there until we leave?"

"That's right."

"So when do we get our laptops and phones back?"

"They're already on your bus. You'll get them when you reach Denver."

"That's a bummer."

The FBI agent allowed himself a small chuckle. "I haven't heard that expression in a while."

"I'm glad I made your day."

Adam and Anaya were already with Penny in the holding area when Sage joined them. They staked out a small grassy spot at the edge of the parking lot where they could sit and wait their turn. Adam tried to start a game of hearts but no one wanted to play.

"What bus are you on, Penny?" he asked.

"Group 1, Bus 4. How about you?"

"Anaya and I are on Bus 2 in Group 2. What about you, Sage?"

"Group 2, Bus 1."

"Bummer," Adam said.

Sage grinned.

"What's so funny?" he asked.

Before Sage could explain, two quick blasts of a siren preceded an announcement broadcast over the loudspeakers.

```
ATTENTION  GROUP  1.  PLEASE  BEGIN  THE
BOARDING PROCESS.

PROCEED  IMMEDIATELY  TO  THE  SMALLER
HOLDING  AREA  ADJACENT  TO  THE  SECURITY
SCREENING  STATION.  TAKE  YOUR  CARRY-ON
ITEM  WITH  YOU.  AFTER  YOU  HAVE  COMPLETED
THE  SECURITY  SCREENING  PROCESS,  LINE  UP
IN FRONT OF YOUR DESIGNATED BUS.

FAMILIES  WITH  CHILDREN  UNDER  THE  AGE  OF
TEN  WILL  BE  GIVEN  PRIORITY  IN  BOARDING
THE BUSES.
```

Penny scrambled to her feet. "I guess this is it. I know it's been rough the past few days, but I'm really going to miss you guys," she said with tears in her eyes.

"So what are you going to do when you get home?" Sage asked.

"Apart from eating pizza? Work on this story—it's far from over. How about you?"

"I don't know yet. I'm sure there are other volcanoes out there somewhere waiting for me."

Sage gave Penny a long hug. Penny started to walk away, but after a few steps she spun around and waved. "Bye, everyone!"

"You be safe, girl!" Sage yelled.

They all watched as Penny and the other evacuees in Group 1 were directed by National Guard soldiers to enter the smaller holding area next to the Security Screening Station.

"It's really happening, isn't it?" Adam said. "It doesn't seem real yet."

Anaya shrugged. "Something will undoubtedly go wrong."

Adam and Anaya sat back down, but Sage remained standing to keep Penny in view while she waited to board her bus.

"It looks like the security screening process is going incredibly slowly," Sage said. "We're going to be here all day."

An hour and a quarter passed before Bus 4 was finally ready for boarding. Just before getting on the bus, Penny waved to Sage one more time. Sage waved back and then joined Adam and Anaya on the ground.

After a while, a cluster of teenage girls near the end of the line in the smaller holding area began singing "Amazing Grace." The crowd fell silent, mesmerized by the beautiful melody.

Sage studied the girls. "Do you think?"

"I do," Adam replied.

"Who are they?" Anaya asked.

"The church group that three of the dead girls belonged to."

As Sage had predicted, the pace of the evacuation was slow—excruciatingly slow. It took over two hours to process everyone in Group 1 and load the six buses. Two armed National Guard soldiers stood at the entrance of each bus during the boarding process, and when the last evacuee had boarded, the soldiers joined the evacuees on the bus for the ride to the airport.

As the last of the Group 1 buses rumbled slowly out of the parking lot, two more buses arrived to take their place while the announcement for Group 2 blared out over the loudspeakers.

"It's our turn!" Adam exclaimed. "We're finally going home!"

"I'll believe it when we're on the bus," Anaya said.

As they headed into the smaller holding area for the security screening, Adam and Sage held hands. They talked quietly about what the future might hold for them.

Adam shuffled his feet and stared at the ground. "After I'm done with school, I think maybe I'd like to see some volcanoes up close and personal."

"Really?"

"Really."

Sage pulled Adam close and they kissed tenderly, ignoring the mass of people surrounding them.

"Get a room!" Anaya snapped.

"Sorry," Adam said sheepishly.

"I'm not!" Sage pressed her body tightly against Adam and kissed him again, even more passionately than before.

For the next forty-five minutes, the line in the smaller holding area didn't budge.

"Now can I say I told you so?" Anaya complained.

Sage and Adam just ignored her.

After another fifteen minutes, Sage decided to go find out how much longer it was going to take. "You two stay here and keep each other company."

She headed back toward the check-in area. Twice she tried to approach the counters only to be rebuffed each time by a National

Guardsman, so she resorted to shouting in the direction of the FBI agents.

"Does anyone know how long this is going to take?"

No one replied, so she gave it another go, this time even louder.

"DOES ANYONE KNOW WHEN WE'RE GOING HOME?"

Just then, she spied a familiar figure striding quickly toward her. It was Hank Rosenberg.

"Hi Sage," Hank said with a smile.

"Why is this taking so long?"

"I'm not sure what the hold-up is. I think there might be some sort of issue with the x-ray machine. This whole evacuation thing is outside our area of expertise, and it's been going much slower than we anticipated. But we'll get it done, even if it takes all day."

Three piercing siren blasts reverberated throughout the village, followed by screeching feedback from the PA system.

YOUR ATTENTION PLEASE!

Sage recognized the voice immediately. It was Special Agent Velasquez.

AN INCIDENT HAS OCCURRED DURING THE EVACUATION. ALL EVACUATION ACTIVITIES WILL CEASE IMMEDIATELY.

THE EVACUEES ON BUS 1 IN GROUP 1 HAVE ALREADY DEPARTED ON THEIR CHARTER FLIGHT TO DENVER AND THEY WILL NOT BE RECALLED. HOWEVER, ALL OTHER BUSES HAVE BEEN ORDERED TO RETURN TO THE EVACUATION PROCESSING AREA IN OLD FAITHFUL VILLAGE. ALL SECURITY PERSONNEL ARE INSTRUCTED TO REMAIN IN THE EVACUATION AREA IN ORDER TO PROCESS THE EVACUEES WHEN THEY RETURN.

RETURNING EVACUEES WILL RE-ENTER THE VILLAGE THROUGH THE SECURITY SCREENING AREA. SOME EVACUEES WILL BE HOUSED ON A SECURE MEDICAL FLOOR IN THE OLD FAITHFUL INN. ALL OTHER RETURNING EVACUEES WILL BE DIRECTED BACK TO THEIR PLACE OF RESIDENCE.

ALL EVACUEES STILL IN THE HOLDING AREAS
MUST RETURN TO THEIR PLACE OF RESIDENCE
IMMEDIATELY AND REMAIN THERE UNTIL FURTHER
NOTICE.

LUGGAGE WILL BE RETURNED TO EVACUEES AS
TIME PERMITS.

FURTHER INFORMATION WILL BE DISTRIBUTED
VIA SUPPLEMENTAL UPDATES.

THE YELLOWSTONE DIRECTIVE CONTINUES TO BE
IN EFFECT.

Sage looked at Hank. "You have any idea what this is about?"

"No." He rolled his watch methodically around his wrist, occasionally changing direction.

"What do we do now?"

"You should do what the announcement said—return to your residence."

"Then what?"

"Wait for further instructions, I guess."

"I don't like this one bit."

"Me neither."

* * *

Sage had been back at the apartment for only a couple of minutes when Adam and Anaya came barreling in.

"*Now* I'm going to say I told you so." Anaya stormed off to her room.

Adam looked like he was about to erupt. "What the hell is going on? I just want to get out of here!"

"Something must have gone wrong with the evacuation— something really bad," Sage said.

"Like what?"

"I've no idea. Maybe a fight broke out on one of the buses. Or maybe somebody got sick … or worse."

"You mean somebody died?"

"I don't know."

"Maybe the FBI got some new information about the killer,"

Adam said. "Maybe the killer was on one of the buses and they wanted to bring him back here and arrest him before he escapes."

"Or *she* escapes."

"What makes you think the killer is a woman?"

"Nothing, but how do you know for sure it's a man?"

"I guess I just assumed."

"Apology accepted."

"But I didn't really apologize."

"I know." Sage smiled.

Anaya rejoined Sage and Adam in the living room. "I don't think there was an incident on one of the buses. I think it's all just a ruse so the FBI could halt the evacuation."

"Why on earth would they do that?" Sage asked.

"You tell me," Anaya snapped. "You're the one who's all cozy with them."

"So what do we do now?" Adam asked.

Anaya exhaled loudly. "We just wait here like caged rats. Do this, do that. Press the bar, get some food. I'm starting to think they're doing some sort of psychological experiment on us."

"I still don't get why they won't let us have our laptops, tablets, and phones," Adam said. "If we could listen to music or watch a movie it would help pass the time."

"It's all about control," Anaya responded. "They're the Feds. They want to control our movements, whom we can talk to, and all our information. They've probably got hidden cameras everywhere— maybe even in here." Anaya looked slowly around the apartment.

"You sound like one of those conspiracy theorists," Sage said.

"Maybe I am."

Sage tried to sound upbeat. "C'mon guys, we're all tired and upset, and it's been a really long day. Let's just try to relax."

"Why don't we eat," Adam suggested.

Sage smiled. "Is that all you ever think about?"

"Don't you think we should wait for Penny?" Anaya asked.

"No, let's go ahead and eat," Sage said. "You saw how long the security screening took when people were leaving. It'll probably take twice as long when they return. Penny can eat when she gets back."

Adam opened the fridge. "So what do we have?"

"Not much," Sage said. "We've run out of almost everything, but I'll see what I can do."

She cobbled together some noodles, scrambled eggs, and spinach, and they ate in complete silence. Adam and Anaya cleaned their plates, but Sage barely touched her food. After dinner, Sage and Adam cuddled on the couch while they waited for Penny; Anaya went to her room.

"I wonder when we'll get our luggage back," Sage said.

"Hopefully tonight," Adam responded.

"Probably never!" Anaya shouted from her room.

The knock on the door at nine thirty was so soft they barely heard it.

"Penny?" Sage called out. "Come on in—it's unlocked."

Ricky poked his head around the door. His face was ashen. "I thought you should know about this." He handed Sage two pieces of paper, folded sloppily in half. "Please don't tell anyone I gave this to you. I could get in big trouble."

"What is it? What's wrong?"

"Just read it. I've got to get back before anyone misses me."

As Ricky disappeared down the hallway, Sage unfolded the papers and stared at them for a long time. Then she let out a piercing howl and burst into tears.

Anaya and Adam rushed to Sage's side. She threw the papers at them and ran into her room, slamming the door behind her. Adam grabbed the papers and read them with Anaya.

FEDERAL BUREAU OF INVESTIGATION
YELLOWSTONE NATIONAL PARK COMMAND POST
CLASSIFIED REPORT

REPORT NUMBER: YNP.6.5-4

APPROVED BY: Special Agent in Charge Monica Y. Velasquez

TITLE: Evacuation Fatalities

SYNOPSIS: Three fatalities occurred during the evacuation from Yellowstone National Park.

=======================================

INCIDENT LOCATION
Group 1, Evacuation Bus 4

INCIDENT DATE
June 5

INCIDENT SUMMARY
During the course of the evacuation from Yellowstone National Park, three evacuees died suddenly on Bus 4 in Evacuation Group 1. All three victims started gasping for air and then went into full-body convulsions for approximately 15 to 30 seconds, after which they were unconscious and unresponsive. One victim started convulsing 45 minutes after the evacuation bus left the Old Faithful area, and the other two victims succumbed approximately 15 minutes after that. The two guardsmen on the bus administered a cyanide antidote via a Cyanokit to the first victim as per established protocol, but it was too late to be effective. As there was only one Cyanokit on the bus, no antidotes were administered to the other two victims. All efforts to revive the victims were unsuccessful.

The victims were transported by ambulance back to Old Faithful Village for autopsy and further processing by the FBI. The results of the autopsies are pending.

Due to the three deaths, the evacuation was halted and all buses except Bus 1 in Group 1 returned to Old Faithful Village. The 45 evacuees on Bus 1 had already boarded their charter plane headed to Denver International Airport. Those evacuees underwent a thorough medical examination when they arrived in Denver. All were cleared medically and allowed to board flights to their final destinations.

FBI investigators will follow up with the

evacuees from Bus 1 in one-week intervals
over the next month. At the time of this
report, none of the evacuees from Bus 1,
or any evacuees from any other buses,
including the surviving evacuees from Bus
4, have exhibited any signs of cyanide
poisoning or other illness.

DECEDENTS' NAMES, AGES, AND HOMETOWNS
- Michael Lowe, 19, Chicago, Illinois
- Charlotte McAllister, 24, Virginia Beach, Virginia
- Penny Phillips, 26, Jackson Hole, Wyoming

---

* * *

No one felt like going to sleep, so Sage, Adam, and Anaya held an all-night vigil for Penny.

It was Sage's idea to light candles—they had plenty on hand since they were prepared for the power outages that occasionally plagued Yellowstone—and the apartment was transformed into a spectacle of dancing lights, accompanied by the delicate scents of lilac, jasmine, and vanilla. Anaya placed all their pillows in a circle in the middle of the living room floor, and Adam made some ginseng tea. Sage thought it looked a bit like a séance.

Even though they had known Penny for only a week, they all had favorite memories about their departed friend, which they shared in between sobs and sniffles. Sage spoke about Penny's dream of winning a Pulitzer Prize, and Anaya described some of the conversations she and Penny had late at night, including the time Penny had confided that she was quite lonely and had been so excited to find three new friends, even under such unfortunate circumstances.

Suddenly Sage had an unsettling thought. "Maybe Penny knew more than she'd let on. Maybe she was about to crack the case wide open and had been murdered to silence her permanently."

"But why would she be killed on a crowded bus?" Anaya wondered.

"Maybe it was the last chance the killer had to eliminate her before she left Yellowstone," Sage hypothesized.

"And what about the other two people who died on the bus?"

"Maybe they were killed to throw everyone off track. You know, to disguise the real purpose of Penny's murder."

"I don't know," Anaya said. "Now you're the one sounding like a conspiracy theorist."

"You're right," Sage said glumly. "I'm just trying to make sense of something that makes no sense at all."

By four in the morning, everyone was physically and emotionally spent. Anaya and Adam each took a pillow and retreated to their respective bedrooms, but Sage wanted to be by herself for a while, so she sat on the remaining pillows in the living room as the candles burned out one by one until she was alone in the darkness.

I know you would have won that Pulitzer Prize. You were a great reporter and a good friend. I'm really going to miss you.

When the sun finally peeked over the mountains to the east of Yellowstone, Sage crawled into bed and cuddled up next to Adam.

"I didn't really know her, but I did," Sage said. "It's amazing how close you can become to someone in such a short amount of time."

"I know." Adam kissed Sage softly as she fell asleep.

JUNE 6

Adam woke Sage a few minutes after the Daily Update arrived, almost two hours later than usual. He and Anaya had just finished reading it.

"Sage, the Daily Update's here. Wanna see it?"

"Mmmmph."

"You want to see it?"

"No."

"I think you ought to take a look."

"Not now."

"I'll just leave it on the kitchen counter for you."

Sage finally pulled herself out of bed and stumbled into the kitchen. The update was waiting for her.

THE YELLOWSTONE DIRECTIVE
DAILY UPDATE
JUNE 6

YESTERDAY AFTERNOON THREE EVACUEES PERISHED DURING THE EVACUATION PROCESS. THESE NEW DEATHS APPEAR TO HAVE BEEN CAUSED BY CYANIDE POISONING, ALTHOUGH FINAL

TOXICOLOGY RESULTS WILL NOT BE AVAILABLE FOR ANOTHER 24 HOURS. THE FBI AND THE CDC WILL PROVIDE FURTHER INFORMATION ON THESE FATALITIES AS SOON AS IT BECOMES AVAILABLE.

THERE HAS BEEN NO PROGRESS IN IDENTIFYING THE KILLER OR KILLERS, AND THE FBI AND CDC ARE CONTINUING TO WORK DILIGENTLY TO EXAMINE ALL POSSIBILITIES.

BECAUSE OF THE NEW FATALITIES, THE CDC HAS DETERMINED THAT ALL DETAINEES WILL BE HOUSED IN THE OLD FAITHFUL INN UNTIL FURTHER NOTICE. MOVING ALL DETAINEES TO A CENTRAL LOCATION WILL ALLOW FOR ENHANCED SECURITY MEASURES AND INCREASED SAFETY.

THE FOLLOWING ENHANCED LOCKDOWN REGULATIONS WILL APPLY:

- ALL DETAINEES, INCLUDING PARK GUESTS AND VISITORS, EMPLOYEES OF THE NATIONAL PARK SERVICE, CONCESSIONAIRES, PRIVATE CONTRACTORS, EMPLOYEES OF THE CDC, AND ALL MEDICAL PERSONNEL, WILL BE MOVED INTO THE OLD FAITHFUL INN TODAY.
- FBI AND NATIONAL GUARD PERSONNEL WILL CONTINUE TO BE HOUSED IN THE TEMPORARY BARRACKS IN OLD FAITHFUL VILLAGE.
- ALL DETAINEES ARE TO REPORT TO THE OLD FAITHFUL INN BETWEEN 1 P.M. AND 4 P.M. TODAY FOR ROOM ASSIGNMENTS. DETAINEES MAY BRING WHATEVER THEY CAN CARRY WITH THEM. NO RETURN TRIPS WILL BE ALLOWED TO CURRENT RESIDENCES.
- ALL LUGGAGE THAT WAS CHECKED DURING THE EVACUATION PROCESS WILL BE AVAILABLE IN THE LOBBY OF THE OLD FAITHFUL INN SOMETIME AFTER 6 P.M. DETAINEES MUST BRING THEIR LUGGAGE CLAIM CHECKS TO RETRIEVE THEIR BAGS.
- DETAINEES WILL NOT BE ALLOWED TO LEAVE THE OLD FAITHFUL INN WITHOUT EXPRESS PERMISSION FROM THE FBI.

- ALL MEALS WILL BE SERVED CAFETERIA-STYLE IN THE MAIN DINING ROOM OF THE OLD FAITHFUL INN. THE HOURS OF OPERATION OF THE DINING ROOM WILL BE POSTED LATER TODAY.
- NATIONAL GUARD SOLDIERS WILL CONDUCT ROOM CHECKS EVERY EVENING. ANY DETAINEE FOUND TO HAVE LEFT THE OLD FAITHFUL INN WITHOUT PERMISSION WILL BE ARRESTED AS SOON AS THEY ARE LOCATED.
- ANY DETAINEE WHO VIOLATES ANY TERMS OF THESE ENHANCED REGULATIONS WILL BE SUBJECT TO IMMEDIATE ARREST.
- ADDITIONAL MEDICAL PERSONNEL, INCLUDING FOUR MORE DOCTORS AND TEN MORE NURSES, WILL BE ARRIVING LATER TODAY. SHOULD ANY DETAINEE FEEL ILL AT ANY TIME, THEY SHOULD CONTACT EITHER THE NATIONAL GUARD OR A MEMBER OF THE MEDICAL STAFF.
- AT THE PRESENT TIME THERE IS NO ESTIMATE AS TO HOW LONG THE ENHANCED REGULATIONS WILL BE IN EFFECT.
- FURTHER UPDATES WILL BE PROVIDED EVERY MORNING, AS WELL AS AT OTHER TIMES AS WARRANTED BY FUTURE DEVELOPMENTS.

"What's going on?" Adam's voice quivered.

"I don't know," Sage replied. "They must have held a briefing without me yesterday after we all went back to our rooms. Hopefully I'll find out more at this morning's briefing. This time I'll tell you everything. I promise."

* * *

FBI CLASSIFIED BRIEFING
YELLOWSTONE NATIONAL PARK COMMAND POST
JUNE 6 – 10:00 A.M.

Special Agent Velasquez called the briefing to order.

"I'll begin by summarizing what happened yesterday so we're all on the same page. At first, the evacuation proceeded without any complications. However, after the three deaths on Bus 4 in Group 1, the evacuation was halted immediately. By that time, the forty-five evacuees on Bus 1 had already boarded their charter plane for Denver. They were met in Denver by a team of doctors who gave each of them a thorough medical examination, and all forty-five were cleared to continue on to their final destinations. Those evacuees will be monitored in the weeks ahead for signs of cyanide poisoning. In one bit of good news, the bodies of the first eleven victims were returned to their families."

Maddie went next. "Because the evacuation was aborted, media interest has intensified dramatically since yesterday afternoon. Several news outlets have published first-person accounts from some of the park visitors who were successfully evacuated, and two evacuees appeared on the *Today Show* this morning." She paused, visibly upset. "To put it bluntly, these accounts have not put the FBI in a good light. We've already issued a lengthy press release this morning in an attempt to stem the negative publicity."

"Who the hell cares about negative publicity!" Sage shouted. "We're in a full-blown crisis here! We need to tell the world what's going on."

"Maddie, what reason did you give for the evacuation being halted?" Ben asked.

"We explained that there were some technical problems that mandated that the evacuation be stopped."

Sage was furious. "Did the press release mention anything about the three deaths on Bus 4? Or the fact that only forty-five people were evacuated? Or that over four hundred people are still left in the park?"

"No, it did not."

"So you lied!"

"I wouldn't call it that. We just didn't include everything in the press release."

"Don't you think our families will be worried about us?"

"We explained that everything is okay and we expect the evacuation to resume shortly."

"But everything is NOT okay!"

"There's no reason to have families and friends on the outside worrying unnecessarily. Everyone will be going home soon."

Sage glared at Maddie. "You don't really believe that, do you?"

Before Maddie could respond, Special Agent Velasquez stepped in. "Let's move on. Analyst Pagano?"

It took Dominick a half hour to describe all the security breaches that had occurred since the failed evacuation. Within minutes of the final bus returning to Yellowstone, two news helicopters had appeared on the horizon over the lodgepole pines that surrounded Old Faithful Village. Initially they ignored commands from the FBI to leave the area, but both eventually relented and returned to the Jackson Hole Airport, escorted by two FBI Black Hawks. Federal Marshals who had been deployed to the airport to assist with the processing of the evacuees immediately arrested the occupants of both helicopters. There were also three new drone incursions into the park, and Dominick admitted there were probably others that had gone undetected because the FBI's resources had been stretched beyond capacity in the past few days.

"Two of the recent UAVs were highly sophisticated military-grade prototypes similar to the Fulmar X and RQ-7 Shadow."

"Who sent them?" Special Agent Velasquez asked.

Dominick shifted awkwardly in his chair. "We're working on it."

"Well, *keep* working on it and report back to me as soon as you know."

"Yes, ma'am."

Most concerning to Special Agent Velasquez were the eight people who had tried to flee on foot—one group of three, one couple, and three individuals. They had headed in various directions, but all had been apprehended within a mile or so of the village.

The Special Agent slammed her open palm on the table. "We can't have anyone getting out of here, no matter what! Is that clear?"

Dominick waited a few moments before continuing. "So far, everyone has heeded our commands to stop, and they've all surrendered peacefully. But what if someone resists? What type of force are we authorized to use?"

"Batons, rubber bullets, tasers, whatever it takes."

"Lethal?"

"No. That's not warranted at this time."

Sage exploded. "What do you mean *at this time*?"

"Exactly what it sounds like, Dr. Maldonado." Special Agent Velasquez seemed unfazed by Sage's outburst. "Agent Carter, what is the status of the autopsies on the three new victims?"

"The last one was completed about an hour ago. The findings are consistent with the previous victims. All indications are that the new deaths were due to cyanide poisoning, but the toxicology testing is still being conducted." Gus turned and looked at Whitney. "Hey, Dr. Hughes, wasn't the evacuation your idea? If I remember correctly, you told us the evacuation would be completely safe. How'd that turn out?"

Before Whitney could respond, Special Agent Velasquez jumped in. "That's enough, Agent Carter. I was the one who ordered the evacuation and I accept full responsibility. How are the survivor interviews going, Agent Rosenberg?"

"We've completed the initial interviews of all forty-five survivors from Bus 4, which includes the driver, two National Guard soldiers, and forty-two passengers. They all basically said the same thing. The first victim, Ms. McAllister, fell out of her seat into the aisle. At first, several people around her thought she was having a seizure. Her body twisted and writhed, and she gasped for air, holding her chest. Then she went completely still. The entire event took less than forty seconds. The two guardsmen on the bus used a Cyanokit to administer a cyanide antidote to Ms. McAllister. Unfortunately, it was too late to have any effect."

"What's a Cyanokit?" Ben asked.

Whitney jumped in. "It's a cyanide antidote that's administered intravenously. It utilizes hydroxocobalamin, which binds with cyanide to form cyanocobalamin, a nontoxic compound that can be eliminated by the kidneys."

Hank looked down at his notes before continuing. "While they were working on Ms. McAllister, the other two victims, Mr. Lowe and Ms. Phillips, also became ill. Mr. Lowe fell into the aisle and Ms. Phillips slumped against the window. There was only one Cyanokit on the bus, so no antidotes could be administered to them. Despite the heroic efforts of the guardsmen and other passengers on the bus, none of the three victims could be revived."

"Thank you for identifying the victims by name," Sage said. "I always detested the letters assigned to them in previous briefings."

"Was there any unusual activity among the passengers before the victims died?" Special Agent Velasquez asked.

"No one noticed anything out of the ordinary. No one was moving about, there were no arguments or disagreements, and no one noticed any weird smells or sounds."

"Where were the victims seated?"

Hank scanned the papers in front of him. "Ms. McAllister was in an aisle seat in Row 5, Mr. Lowe was in an aisle seat in Row 3, and Ms. Phillips was in a window seat in Row 12, near the back of the bus."

"Is that it?"

"That's all I have for now, but we're going to speak with all the witnesses again. The forty-five survivors from Bus 4, including the driver and the two soldiers, are currently being housed on the top floor of the West Wing in the Old Faithful Inn. Pursuant to advice from the CDC, that floor has been completely sealed off from the rest of the inn. The survivors are not being allowed to leave the floor for any reason. Food is being delivered to their rooms, and they're being closely monitored by on-site medical staff. So far, none of them have shown any signs of cyanide poisoning or any other illness."

"Why do you keep calling them survivors?" Sage asked.

"In a sense, we're all survivors." Hank's usually sanguine demeanor was decidedly gloomy.

"Dr. Hughes, what progress have you made in your investigation of the buses?" Special Agent Velasquez asked.

"We've sealed all the buses that returned when the evacuation was halted, and we've isolated them in a secure area away from the village. We've taken biological samples from all surfaces in Bus 4 and collected air samples from throughout its interior. In addition, we're in possession of the personal effects and clothing of the three deceased passengers. Those items are being thoroughly examined, and biological samples have been taken from them as well."

"And?"

"At this point we haven't found any cyanide or other poisons, contaminants, or biologics that might have contributed to the deaths of the three people on the bus."

"How about your search for possible sources of cyanide? Any progress on that front?"

"No, we haven't identified the source of the cyanide yet. But we're continuing to look."

Gus jabbed Whitney again. "That environmental source hypothesis isn't looking so good about now, is it?"

"Thank you for your report, Dr. Hughes," Special Agent Velasquez said.

"Actually, I'm not done. I share everyone's frustration about the lack of progress, so I've been doing my best to speed up the CDC's investigation. For starters, I've instituted an extended work schedule in the lab, which is now being staffed sixteen hours a day. I've also requested the assistance of a world-renowned forensic toxicologist from Johns Hopkins. He should be here later today.

"Due to all the unknowns we're dealing with, a few days ago I ordered the construction of a Biosafety Level 4 lab, the highest level of safety utilized by the CDC. That's the kind of lab we use for lethal infectious diseases such as Ebola and Marburg. Since I'm now more familiar with the logistics of getting equipment and supplies to Yellowstone, this has progressed much more quickly than when we set up the Biosafety Level 2 lab, and the new BSL-4 lab was completed last night."

"Very impressive," Special Agent Velasquez said. "So what do you think is really going on here?"

"I believe there's a chance this might be a more complex problem than we initially thought," Whitney replied.

"In what way?"

"So far we've been looking for environmental sources of cyanide, but that approach may be too narrow. I'm starting to lean toward the theory that these deaths were caused by a living organism that produces cyanide, and the most likely candidates are bacteria and viruses. A few species of bacteria in the *Pseudomonas* and *Chromobacterium* genera are known to produce cyanide, and there are probably other cyanide-producing species we don't know about yet. It's less likely that a virus could make cyanide, but it's conceivable a virus could program a host cell to do that."

Gus let out a nervous laugh. "Come on! How could microscopic bugs produce enough cyanide to kill a person?"

"It actually doesn't take much cyanide to kill. A lethal dose for humans is only about two hundred milligrams of powdered potassium cyanide or liquid cyanide solution. Of course, the higher the amount, the quicker it kills."

"But what's more likely—that a human killer would possess a lethal dose of cyanide or that a teeny, tiny microbe thing would produce it?"

"They're both possible, and it's difficult to say which is more likely," Whitney replied, drawing out her words carefully. "That's why I recommended during our emergency briefing last night that we move everyone into the Old Faithful Inn in order to limit their exposure to all possible sources of cyanide—whether human, animal, environmental, or microbial."

"You were spot on with your recommendation for a safe evacuation," Gus snipped. "Can we expect similar results from your new experiment?"

* * *

Sage raced back to the apartment after the morning briefing to find Adam and Anaya all packed and ready to head over to the Old Faithful Inn. They each had only one small suitcase left, so they stuffed the rest of their belongings into large trash bags.

"I've got a lot to tell you guys, and it's not good," Sage said.

"Can it wait?" Anaya asked. "I think we should get over to the Old Faithful Inn as soon as possible. Remember how long the lines were during the evacuation check-in yesterday?"

"Yeah. I want to get a room with a view of Old Faithful," Adam added.

Sage noticed that Adam and Anaya were wearing their ranger uniforms, which they'd left behind in the apartment when they'd packed their bags to go home the day before.

"Why are you wearing your uniforms?"

"You never know when they might come in handy," Adam replied.

Sage followed suit and changed into her uniform, then threw the rest of her belongings into her suitcase and a couple of trash bags. Before leaving, they made a final check of the apartment.

"Goodbye 1B," Sage said. "I'm going to miss you."

"I'm not," Anaya muttered.

As they walked to the Old Faithful Inn, slowed by their

unwieldy retinue of suitcases and trash bags, Sage explained what she had learned during the morning briefing.

"So let me get this straight," Adam said. "They're moving everyone into the inn because they don't know where the cyanide is coming from?"

"That's basically it," Sage replied. "They think we'll be safer there."

"And what about those weird bacteria and viruses Whitney mentioned in the briefing?" Anaya asked.

"It's just a theory at this point," Sage replied. "She doesn't even know if they exist."

They arrived at the Old Faithful Inn at 11:45, more than an hour before check-in was due to begin, but the line was already several dozen people long. After securing their place in the queue, they took turns dashing into the dining room to wolf down some lunch. The line finally started moving at 1:15.

The venerable Old Faithful Inn—the world's largest log cabin— was Sage's favorite building on the entire planet, and she was excited to spend the night there, even if it was under such horrible circumstances. Rough-hewn timbers cut from local lodgepole pines supported the massive structure from within; the grand lobby was six stories high, with interior balconies on the second and third floors. The focal point of the lobby was an enormous stone fireplace rising up from the ground floor. The steeply sloped roof, designed to prevent heavy winter snows from accumulating, added an extra element of drama both inside and out.

Although the East and West Wings offered deluxe accommodations with private baths, Sage hoped they'd be assigned a room in the Old House, the oldest part of the inn. The inconvenience of sharing a common bathroom down the hall would be more than compensated by the rustic charm of the log-lined rooms.

The inn's staff had been replaced by FBI agents and National Guard soldiers, so the check-in process was painfully slow, not unlike during the aborted evacuation the day before. If the situation hadn't been so dire, the sight of FBI agents awkwardly trying to navigate the front desk area might have been quite amusing. But there was nothing funny about what was happening.

They finally got to the front of the line, where their faces were scanned one by one.

"You don't want our names?" Adam asked.

"Don't need them anymore," one of the agents replied. "You've all been assigned to Room 231 on the third floor in the Old House. The bathrooms are just down the hall from your room."

They headed up the creaky wooden staircase next to the massive stone fireplace.

"I wanted a room in one of the newer wings so we'd have a private bathroom," Anaya complained.

"This will be much better," Sage assured her. "It'll give us an opportunity to mingle with other people in the inn. Who knows what we'll learn from them. Besides, I've always wanted to spend a night in the Old House."

When they opened the door to Room 231, Adam made a beeline for the bed closest to the window. "Okay ladies, who wants to be my bedmate?"

"Not me."

"Not me."

Sage and Anaya laughed and sat down on the other bed. "Now that's the Anaya I know," Sage said.

Room 231 wasn't tiny, but it wasn't exactly spacious either. Typical of rooms in the Old House, there was a small counter with a sink on the wall opposite the two beds. Below the sink were four large bath towels and a few smaller towels and wash cloths; a single small soap in the shape of a bear stood next to the sink. There was no closet; only a small armoire with two drawers at the bottom and just enough room to hang a few articles of clothing. The beds were squeaky and the mattresses old, but the linens and comforters looked new. Two fluffy cotton robes hung on pegs near the door.

They lined up their suitcases and trash bags under the window and placed their backpacks on the floor by the counter that housed the small sink.

Adam peered out the window. "Hey! I think we can see Beehive Geyser, way over there across the parking lot. If you look just to the left of that large tree you can sort of see it."

Sage joined Adam, slipping an arm around his waist. "If you say so. All I see is a bunch of lodgepole pines."

"You lovebirds want some privacy?" Anaya asked.

"No, thanks—we're good," Sage replied. "I think I'll go check out the women's bathroom. Anyone want to come?"

"I do!" Adam grinned.

The women's bathroom was just down the hall. When Sage went in, she found Whitney splashing water on her face.

"Hey, Whitney! Looks like we're hall mates. I didn't expect to see you here."

"They moved us here from the temporary barracks. Although we get to leave the inn when we're doing lab work, the rest of the time we're stuck in here just like you."

"You have a roommate?"

"Two of them. Gayle and Robin—the other two CDC scientists."

"How about we go over to the afternoon briefing together?"

"Sounds good. I'm in Room 240. Come get me at a quarter to four and we'll walk over together."

When Sage got back to her room, Adam was still staring out the window waiting for Beehive's next eruption. She explained that he could be waiting a long time, as Beehive was highly irregular and often went days or even months between eruptions.

"Guess who I ran into in the bathroom?"

"Brad Pitt?" Anaya guessed.

"Very funny. No, it was Whitney Hughes from the CDC."

"What did she have to say?"

"Not much. We're going to the afternoon briefing together."

* * *

Sage arrived at Room 240 at 3:45.

Whitney greeted her at the door. "Hey, Sage. Let me grab my lab coat."

"Don't you have a laptop?"

"I do, but they make me leave it in the lab at all times. I can't take it anywhere."

"Who are *they*? The CDC?"

"No, the FBI."

"Why do they care?"

"I guess they're really paranoid."

Whitney looked over at her roommates. "Gayle, Robin—this is Sage, the park ranger I was telling you about."

"Nice to meet you."

Gayle could have passed for Whitney's younger sister—same slim build, same freckled face, same color hair, just a few inches shorter. Though she didn't have Whitney's Southern drawl, her voice was gentle and full of kindness. Robin was about the same height as Gayle, and her powerful arms and legs hinted at an athletic background. She moved quickly toward Sage and gave her a firm handshake.

Whitney and Sage headed down the stairs toward the doorway between the Old House and the East Wing where they were met by two National Guardsmen.

"Hello gentlemen," Whitney said. "We're going to the afternoon briefing."

"This exit is closed."

"Why?"

"From now on, everyone entering or leaving the inn must do so through the main entrance in the lobby."

When Sage and Whitney arrived at the main entrance, they found the same security setup that had been used during the evacuation the day before: an x-ray machine, a large walk-through metal detector, and a facial recognition system.

It took fifteen minutes to clear security—Sage's ranger uniform kept setting off the metal detector. Finally, she was asked to submit to a pat-down.

"What if I refuse?"

"Then you can't leave the inn."

Figuring this was a battle not worth fighting, Sage reluctantly agreed, but not without exacting her own form of revenge: Every time the female security officer touched her, Sage let out a high-pitched shriek.

"Ma'am, will you stop making those noises?"

"Only if you stop touching me."

Sage was fuming by the time they finally left the inn, and Whitney did her best to calm her down during the three-minute walk to Trailer 2. When they entered the conference room, the briefing was already underway.

* * *

FBI CLASSIFIED BRIEFING
YELLOWSTONE NATIONAL PARK COMMAND POST
JUNE 6 – 4:00 P.M.

"You're late, ladies," Special Agent Velasquez said.

"We had no idea we'd have to go through security just to leave the inn. It took us forever," Sage explained.

"Don't let it happen again."

Sage and Whitney quickly slipped into two seats near the door.

Special Agent Velasquez continued. "Let's move on to the security briefing. Analyst Pagano?"

"Despite Dr. Hughes's fanciful microbe hypothesis, we still believe we have a killer on our hands. Whether it's a terrorist or a serial killer, we need to do everything we can to catch him."

Dominick walked over to the wall of electronics at the end of the room and leaned over a computer console. With a single click of the keyboard, the eight video monitors came to life, each displaying a high-resolution color image of various locations throughout the Old Faithful Inn, including hallways, lobbies, the dining room, doors, and entryways.

Sage jumped to her feet. "What the hell is this? Are you spying on us?"

"Dr. Maldonado!" Special Agent Velasquez shouted. "Sit down!"

After pulling Sage down into her seat, Ben came to her defense. "I share Sage's concern. What *is* going on?"

"May I explain?" Dominick asked.

"Please do," Special Agent Velasquez said.

Dominick typed a few commands into the console and five different images cycled on each video monitor, each image lasting five seconds.

"As you can see, we have installed forty security cameras throughout the interior and exterior of the Old Faithful Inn. Let me show you how this works with a recording from about an hour ago."

On the first monitor in the top row, the camera zoomed in on a bathroom door.

"That's our bathroom!" Sage yelled. "Why the hell are you monitoring our bathroom?"

"We need to observe who's going in and out. We want to see who's associating with whom."

"But why?"

"We still don't know what we're dealing with here, and we want to make sure we cover all the bases."

As they were talking, a figure exited the bathroom on the monitor.

Sage gestured wildly. "That's me!"

"It gets even better." Dominick tried not to smile, but his dancing eyebrows divulged his glee. "Watch this."

A matrix of red lines and dots materialized, superimposed over Sage's face. After a few seconds, several lines of text appeared at the bottom of the monitor.

Name: Sage Maldonado
Age: 30
Hometown: Honolulu, Hawaii
Status: NPS Seasonal Ranger
Old Faithful Inn Room Number: 231

"You really *are* spying on us! I insist this stop immediately!"

"I'm afraid I can't do that."

"Do you have any cameras outside *your* bathroom?"

"All FBI personnel are being housed in the temporary barracks constructed by the National Guard. There are no security cameras in our barracks."

"Why not?"

"None of us are suspects."

"And the rest of us ARE?"

"Those are your words, not mine."

Special Agent Velasquez stepped in. "Thank you for that update, Analyst Pagano. Your report, Agent Rosenberg?"

"We're interviewing the survivors from Bus 4 again to make sure we didn't miss anything the first time around. We should have the new interviews completed by tomorrow morning."

"Can you give us an update on your investigation, Dr. Hughes?"

"There's not much to report since this morning. The good news is that none of the survivors from Bus 4 have shown any signs of cyanide poisoning."

"Is there bad news?"

"Yes. We're still no closer to identifying the source of the cyanide."

"Does anyone have any questions for Dr. Hughes?"

"I do," Gus said. "Let's assume your microbe theory is correct. Where could this thing be coming from?"

"The most common source of a new virus or bacteria is another animal species."

"Such as?"

"Almost any animal—bats, rats, birds, insects, even primates. Viruses and bacteria jump species all the time. In fact, a problematic example of cross-species transmission of bacteria has been occurring right here in Yellowstone. It involves Brucellosis, a febrile disease than can lead to a lifetime of muscular pain and neurological disorders in humans. A species of *Brucella* bacteria can be transmitted from wild elk and bison to domestic cattle. Humans then contract this bacterial disease by eating raw or undercooked meat or drinking unpasteurized milk from the infected cattle."

"Could a human intentionally infect other people with a bacteria or virus?" Gus asked.

"Yes, that's possible. For example, someone could contaminate food or a water supply."

"So we *could* be dealing with a human killer here—maybe a serial killer or even a terrorist."

"I suppose so."

Gus looked directly at Sage. "Now do you see why we've instituted such a high level of security?"

Sage didn't reply.

Whitney continued. "But I think the serial killer scenario you just described is less likely than transmission of a bacterium or virus from an animal host to humans. The Yellowstone ecosystem is incredibly rich, with a diverse range of fauna. Most people picture bears, wolves, elk, and bison when they think of Yellowstone, but there are also countless smaller mammals, reptiles, and insects, any of which could be the source of a bacterium or virus that we've never identified before."

"So what is your plan going forward, Dr. Hughes?" Special Agent Velasquez asked.

"We're going to keep looking for cyanide in the environment, but our main focus will be on detecting and identifying possible species of bacteria or viruses that might be causing these deaths."

"How long will that take?"

"I have no idea. Days. Weeks. Maybe even months."

"You know we don't have that kind of time."

"I know."

* * *

Whitney and Sage took a seat on one of the long benches facing Old Faithful before heading back to the inn.

"So what now?" Sage asked.

Whitney's Southern drawl sounded more at home outdoors than in the restrained formality of the FBI briefings, and her words rolled slowly out of her mouth. "I think we need to start looking for commonalities among all fourteen victims. Where did they go before they died? Did they interact with any animals? What did they eat? What did they drink? Who did they have contact with? Those sorts of things. That might help us identify the source of the lethal microbe."

"Why didn't you say that in the briefing?"

"I don't want the FBI telling us what to do. This is the kind of stuff the CDC is good at. Of course, we could use some help." She looked at Sage.

"My help?"

"Yes. And maybe your friends too if we can trust them."

"You can trust them. So what can we do?"

Before Whitney could answer, a National Guardsman approached them.

"What are you two ladies doing out here?"

"We just came out of the afternoon FBI briefing and we're discussing the use of polymerase chain reaction and gel electrophoresis to identify and sequence new species of microbes," Whitney replied.

The guardsman grimaced. "Can't you do that inside?"

"I suppose so, but it's so much nicer out here."

Just then Old Faithful started to erupt, exploding exuberantly into the brilliant sky. The steam cloud was especially large on this windless day, and it hung above Old Faithful, obscuring the column of water rushing up to the heavens.

"See what I mean?"

"It *is* pretty nice," the guardsman said.

Sage beamed. "Pretty nice? This is one of the world's finest examples of a cone geyser that erupts from a mound of siliceous sinter."

They watched Old Faithful's always-dazzling performance, and it didn't disappoint. But as soon as the eruption subsided, the guardsman ushered them back to the inn.

On the way back, Whitney whispered to Sage, "Can we talk later?"

"Sure. How about in the bathroom?"

"Too icky. Besides, it might be bugged. Come to my room sometime this evening—and bring your friends."

* * *

Additional tables had been brought into the main dining room of the Old Faithful Inn to accommodate the large contingent of diners. Huge buffet tables had been set up on either side of the dining room and the customary fancy glasses and dinnerware had been replaced by paper plates and plastic cups. Although the fare was palatable, there was no prime rib, no venison chops, no orecchiette with broccoli rabe. In their place were penne with two kinds of sauce, salad, rolls, and cookies. National Guard soldiers were positioned throughout the dining hall; their main function seemed to be to monitor the conversations among the detainees.

Sage, Adam, and Anaya chose a table near the entrance so they could do a little monitoring of their own. Eating as slowly as possible, they watched the diners come and go. Sage saw Whitney, Gayle, and Robin; Adam waved hello to Ben Thomas and Kurt Becker.

"That's odd," Sage said. "I don't see any FBI agents anywhere."

"Maybe they've got their own dining area," Adam suggested.

"Or maybe they're aliens and don't need any food or water," Anaya sneered.

A little boy, probably no more than five or six, caught Sage's eye from a few tables away. He made faces at Sage throughout dinner, despite his mother's repeated attempts to get him to turn around and eat his food.

On his way out of the dining room, the boy ran toward Sage and gave her a high five.

"What's your name, young man?"

"I'm Calvin. Who are you?"

"Nice to meet you, Calvin. My name is Sage. How old are you?"

"Almost six. My birthday is in twelve days!"

"What are you going to do on your birthday?" Sage regretted asking the question the moment it came out of her mouth.

"Mommy said we're going to the beach! We live in *Sam* Diego."

Sage did her best to be enthusiastic. "I'm sure that'll be lots of fun."

"Will you be here tomorrow?"

"Definitely," Sage replied. "Stop by and say hi again."

Calvin's mom tugged at his sleeve. "C'mon, Calvin. Stop bothering the nice lady."

Sage smiled broadly. "He's not bothering me at all."

Calvin beamed. "See you later, alligator!"

"In a while, crocodile!"

Calvin ran off, his mom in hot pursuit.

"I feel really bad for the families with young children who didn't get out during the evacuation," Adam said. "How many families are left?"

"About four or five, I think," Sage replied.

After dinner, they had a contest to see who could spot the most security cameras. Anaya was especially adept at locating cameras in the most obscure places. She even spotted one in the center of the large clock that adorned the massive stone chimney in the lobby.

As they walked back to their room, they took turns pointing out cameras in the hallway.

"Anaya, did you just flip off that camera?" Sage asked.

"Maybe I did, maybe I didn't."

Adam laughed. "Good for you!"

They even checked the bathrooms for cameras. When they reconvened in the hallway outside their room, Sage asked Adam if he had found any cameras in the men's bathroom.

"Nope. How about you?"

"None that we could see. But we did find a camera in the hallway facing the bathroom door. Anaya took care of that one."

"How?"

"With a gob of wet toilet paper. Covered the whole thing and made quite a mess of it."

"Whatever it takes," Anaya said smugly.

Adam removed a notice taped to the door of their room. "We're getting our luggage back at eight tonight!"

"It's about time," Anaya said.

When they got inside, Anaya plopped face down on the bed and mumbled into the blanket. "I'm so bored of all of this. There's absolutely nothing to do."

"On the contrary, we might be quite busy," Sage said.

Anaya immediately sat up. "I like the sound of that."

"Whitney's asked us to help her figure out what's going on."

"But we don't know anything about bacteria or viruses," Adam said.

"Maybe not, but we're all scientists."

"And we know a heck of a lot more about Yellowstone than she does," Anaya added.

"So what are we going to be doing?" Adam asked.

"I'm not sure yet. Whitney wants us to come to her room this evening to talk about it. Why don't we go after we get our luggage back?"

Adam looked at his watch. "Speaking of luggage, it's seven thirty. Let's go down to the lobby so we can be at the front of the line."

But by the time they arrived, the massive lobby was already filled to capacity. At a little past eight, an FBI agent addressed the crowd with a bullhorn from the base of the colossal stone fireplace.

"In a few minutes, buses carrying your luggage will arrive at the front of the inn. All the bags will be brought in through the front door and placed in the area near the lobby gift shop. Please wait until your group is called before moving toward the luggage area and be sure to have your baggage claim checks ready."

"What about our phones and laptops?" Anaya shouted.

"Those will be returned to you when leave Yellowstone."

"Why not now?"

"For security reasons."

To no one's surprise, the baggage claim process took forever. In addition to collecting the claim checks, the FBI agents scanned everyone's faces to verify their identity. It was almost ten thirty by the time Sage, Adam, and Anaya dragged their bags up to their room.

Adam stared at the mountain of suitcases. "Where the heck are we going to put all our stuff?"

As they opened their bags to unpack, Sage let out a yelp. "What the ...? They went through our bags! I'm the neatest packer in the world, and now everything is a jumble. This is outrageous!"

"My bags were searched too!" Anaya shouted.

Adam looked through his suitcase. "It's hard to tell if they went through mine—it looked just like this when I packed it."

He did his best to placate Sage and Anaya, but it was no use. Eventually he gave up and just let them vent while they swore and threw their clothes all over the room. By the time they were done, it looked like a tornado had ripped through a clothing store.

Exhausted and out of breath, Anaya sat on the bed and covered her face with her hands. "I want to go home!" she screamed.

"Look, at least we're all still alive," Adam said.

Sage and Anaya glared at Adam, who immediately realized his mistake.

"I'm so sorry. I didn't mean anything by it."

"I know you didn't," Sage said sadly. "We all miss Penny."

* * *

Sage, Anaya, and Adam arrived at Whitney's room just after eleven.

As soon as Sage finished taking care of introductions, the beds rattled and the floorboards creaked. The overhead light flickered several times and a tiny bear-shaped soap toppled from the counter into the sink.

"*Another* aftershock?" Robin's voice quivered noticeably. "Aren't they *ever* going to stop?"

"Welcome to our slice of heaven," Anaya remarked.

"So how can we help you?" Sage asked Whitney.

"We need help looking for commonalities among all the victims. That's how we investigate cases of food poisoning—we examine epidemiological data and employ traceback analyses to determine who ate what, where, and when. We use similar techniques to identify the source of outbreaks of infectious diseases like Ebola."

"So what *exactly* will we be doing?" Anaya asked.

"You're going to be examining the FBI files for each of the fourteen victims."

"In other words, we're going to be helping the FBI?"

"Sort of, I guess, but you'll also be helping the CDC."

"You can count me out."

Sage looked at Anaya. "Why won't you help?"

"You know I can't stand the FBI. Besides, it won't do any good."

"Of course it will. And it might even be kind of fun."

"No, thanks. I'm still out."

"Well, I'm definitely in," Sage said.

"Me too," Adam added. "When do we start?"

"Hopefully tomorrow. But we have one tiny hurdle."

"What's that?" Sage asked.

"We need to get access to the FBI files. As you can imagine, they guard them pretty carefully."

"Ahhh, now you're getting into Anaya's area of expertise," Sage said with a laugh.

Whitney cocked her head. "I don't understand."

"Sorry, inside joke."

"One more thing," Whitney said. "Sage, I'd like you to come see what we're doing in the lab. Are you interested?"

Sage beamed. "Of course! Why wouldn't I be?"

Anaya's shoulders drooped. "One more fun thing Sage gets to do."

"I'm sorry," Whitney said. "If you want to—"

"I'm not interested anyway." Anaya folded her arms and stared out the window.

"Sage, I'll see if I can get you a security clearance tomorrow," Whitney continued. "You'll need it if you're going to come into the lab with me, and it might even help us get access to the FBI files. Is there anything in your background I should know about before I put in the request?"

"I got a citation once in high school for trespassing on the beach. Other than that, I've been a good girl."

JUNE 7

The Daily Update arrived under the door just after six thirty. Sage stumbled out of bed, put on her glasses, and took a look.

THE YELLOWSTONE DIRECTIVE
DAILY UPDATE
JUNE 7

THERE HAVE BEEN NO NEW FATALITIES DURING THE PAST 24 HOURS.

THE ENHANCED LOCKDOWN REGULATIONS REMAIN IN FULL EFFECT. THERE IS NO ESTIMATE AS TO HOW LONG THEY WILL LAST.

THE SURVIVORS FROM BUS 4 WILL CONTINUE TO BE CONFINED TO THEIR ROOMS IN THE ISOLATION WARD IN THE OLD FAITHFUL INN UNTIL FURTHER NOTICE.

THE YELLOWSTONE DIRECTIVE, AS MODIFIED AND CLARIFIED BY ALL SUBSEQUENT UPDATES, INCLUDING THIS ONE, REMAINS IN FULL FORCE.

ANY DETAINEE WHO VIOLATES ANY TERMS OF THE YELLOWSTONE DIRECTIVE WILL BE SUBJECT TO IMMEDIATE ARREST.

FURTHER UPDATES WILL BE PROVIDED EVERY MORNING, AS WELL AS AT OTHER TIMES, AS WARRANTED BY FUTURE DEVELOPMENTS.

Sage knocked on Whitney's door at nine thirty so they could head over to the morning briefing together. Wanting to avoid another hassle with the security screening, Sage wore jeans and a sweatshirt instead of her uniform, and they arrived at the morning briefing fifteen minutes early. When they walked in, Special Agent Velasquez was the only one there.

"That's more like it, ladies."

"Special Agent Velasquez, can I ask you a question?" Sage said.

"Of course."

"Would you be willing to use first names in these meetings? It might help change the tenor of the conversations and possibly even lead to more cooperation."

"Your suggestion is noted but denied."

FBI Classified Briefing
Yellowstone National Park Command Post
June 7 – 10:00 a.m.

Once everyone else had arrived, Special Agent Velasquez called the meeting to order. There wasn't much to report—no new deaths, no progress in the search for the cause of the deaths, and no internal breaches in security, save for a young couple who ran outside after midnight and streaked naked around the Old Faithful Inn before being apprehended by the National Guard.

After the briefing was over, Whitney approached Special Agent Velasquez with Sage by her side. "I have a request."

"What is it, Dr. Hughes?"

"I'd like Sage to be granted a security clearance so she can assist me in my investigation."

"That would be highly irregular. The work in your lab is classified."

"I know, but we need a fresh pair of eyes. Sage's scientific background and her knowledge of the Yellowstone ecosystem could prove invaluable."

"Dr. Maldonado, do you understand that if I allow this, you must maintain the strictest levels of confidence, security, and professionalism?"

"I do."

"Very well. I'll submit an expedited request for your security clearance. We should hear back within seventy-two hours."

"That won't do," Whitney said. "I need her clearance now."

"I'll see what I can do. I'll let you know this afternoon."

Whitney continued. "I'm not making myself clear. We need her clearance immediately. Right now."

Special Agent Velasquez stared at Whitney. Whitney stared back.

"Wait here, ladies. Let me make a call."

She disappeared out the door, and Sage and Whitney took a seat. Fifteen minutes later, Special Agent Velasquez returned and flashed a tight, thin smile. "You're all set. I went out on a very long limb for you, Dr. Maldonado. Don't disappoint me."

* * *

"Welcome to our lab!" Whitney stood in front of a nondescript wooden door. There were no CDC signs, no biohazard warnings. To the left of the door was a large round lens protruding from a polished black metal plate covered with dozens of tiny holes.

Whitney positioned herself directly in front of the lens until a long, low electronic tone sounded, followed by a friendly male voice that had a touch of a Scottish accent: "Good morning. Please verify your identity."

"Dr. Whitney Hughes from the CDC."

"Access granted."

A loud metallic clunk signaled that the door had unlocked.

"Face or voice recognition?" Sage asked.

"Both. We wanted two layers of security. Now we need to get you registered in our system. Sean, please lock the door."

Sage was confused. "Sean?"

Whitney smiled. "Sean Connery." She motioned for Sage to stand in front of the lens.

"But I've already been scanned by the FBI."

"To enter the CDC lab, you need to be registered in our own proprietary security system—which is even more sophisticated than the FBI's, I might add. Plus, we got to choose the computer voice."

Sage moved in front of the lens and stood on her tiptoes, making herself as tall as possible.

"Just relax," Whitney chuckled.

Sage looked into the lens and followed Sean's verbal instructions.

"Facial scan stored successfully," Sean announced. "Verification of identity requested."

"I am presenting Dr. Sage Maldonado from the National Park Service for initial authorization," Whitney declared.

Sean took over from there. "Dr. Maldonado, state your name."

"Sage Maldonado."

"Again, but this time use this exact format: Dr. Sage Maldonado from the National Park Service."

Sage did as instructed.

"One more time, please."

"Dr. Sage Maldonado from the National Park Service."

"Very good. Dr. Maldonado, your identity has been stored in our system. You and Dr. Hughes may enter."

After the door unlocked again, Whitney pulled it open. Once inside, they entered a cramped room no bigger than a child's bedroom. A row of wooden pegs lined one side. Two of the pegs held coats, shirts, and pants, and there were two pairs of shoes on the floor below. Whitney removed her clothes down to her underwear and reached into a small portable closet next to the pegs. She retrieved light green surgical scrubs, a scrub cap, and black slip-on shoes. She instructed Sage to do the same. After they were both properly attired, Whitney opened the door on the other side of the changing area and walked into a large, brightly lit room.

"This is our Biosafety Level 2 lab. Our home away from home," she said.

Sage looked around. The lab was surprisingly empty. The gleaming metal counters and large rectangular lab table were bereft of equipment, save for two computer terminals and a lone microscope. Eight stools were scattered about the lab, and two refrigerators bookended a wall full of cabinets and drawers. But that was it.

"There's hardly any equipment in here," Sage said.

"It used to be full, but yesterday we moved almost all the equipment into the BSL-4 lab."

"So what do you have in there?"

"Only the most advanced biochemistry lab this side of Atlanta. Given what may be at stake here, the CDC gave me carte blanche to set this lab up. We've got two light microscopes, a scanning electron microscope, a cutting-edge gas chromatograph-mass spectrometry system, two automatic genetic sequencers, a pipetting robot system, a centrifuge, two fume hoods, two biosafety cabinets, two autoclaves, a refrigerator, a freezer, and lots of other instruments and supplies."

"Wow! That's quite an operation. I can't believe you set up the entire lab in just a couple of days."

"To be honest, neither can I."

"So where is this BSL-4 lab?"

Whitney pointed at an imposing gray metal door at the back of the lab. Next to the door was the same security setup that controlled access to the BSL-2 lab.

"Can we go in?"

"Not right now. We restrict entry to those who are currently performing analyses. Gayle and Joe just started their shift an hour ago."

"Who's Joe?"

"Joe Fairchild. He's the forensic toxicologist from Johns Hopkins who flew in to help us."

"Where's Robin?"

"She's resting in our room at the Old Faithful Inn. This is highly demanding, taxing work, where even the smallest mistake can spell disaster, so we usually limit each shift to six hours. We recently extended the shifts to eight hours, but that's our absolute limit. We work in pairs. Gayle and Joe are one pair, Robin and I are the other."

"Can't we just take a peek? I'm dying to see what's back there."

"Afraid not."

"So what's the decontamination process like?"

"When you go through that metal door, you enter an airlock with negative air pressure that's designed to prevent any air from getting out of the lab. After the airlock is the changing area where we undress completely. Then we move to the first shower area. In many BSL-4 labs, you only shower when you leave, but here we also shower going in. Next is the suit room where we put on our air-supplied positive-pressure body suits. I won't bore you with all the details, but it involves lots of checks and double checks to make absolutely sure the suits don't leak. The fifth and final chamber is the chemical shower area. We don't use that on the way in, but that's where we decontaminate our pressurized body suits when we leave the lab. After all of that, we're finally ready to enter the BSL-4 lab."

"Wow! How long does all of that take?"

"About a week."

"No, really."

"About a half hour each way, more or less. It's not the safest BSL-4 lab in the world, but we did the best we could on such short notice. The main point of a BSL-4 lab is to make sure that whatever we're dealing with in the lab doesn't infect our scientists and, even more importantly, doesn't escape from the lab into the outside world. On both counts, I think we've succeeded."

"What are Gayle and Joe doing in there now?"

"They're processing tissues, blood, other bodily fluids, clothing, and personal effects from the three victims who died on Bus 4, searching for any foreign bacteria or viruses."

"Are they using cultures?"

"No. Culturing isn't an optimal process when we don't know what we're looking for. There are many possible culture media, as well as numerous ambient factors such as temperature and light, which means we might have to try dozens of different combinations. Besides, it can take days to grow a culture of bacteria or virus-hosting cells and we're under immense time pressure here."

"So what *are* they doing?"

"Genetic sequencing. It's the most effective approach when we're searching for unknown microbes. And the newest automatic genetic sequencers have speeded up the process dramatically—we can now sequence a sample in a fraction of the time it used to take."

"Has there been any progress?"

"Not really. Hundreds of species of bacteria and viruses occur naturally in the human body, so identifying a single species that doesn't belong is exceedingly difficult. But we're giving it our best shot."

"Any luck in getting the FBI files on the victims?"

"Not yet. I knew it wouldn't be easy, but I'm still trying."

"Thanks for the tour. I'm going to head back to the inn to grab something to eat and put my feet up. I'll see you at the afternoon briefing."

* * *

After gulping down a quick lunch, Sage had been back in her room for no more than five minutes when Adam burst in, dressed only in a robe, his hair dripping wet.

"He's dead! He's dead!" Adam was gasping for air.

"Who's dead?"

"A guy in the men's bathroom! He's hanging in one of the showers! I think it's Steve!"

"Your ex-roommate?"

"I think so."

Anaya ran to the front desk to report the incident while Sage stayed with Adam and tried to calm him down. Anaya returned in a matter of minutes accompanied by two FBI agents. The stocky agent with rectangular, black-rimmed glasses did all the talking.

"We're here to speak with you about what just happened in the men's bathroom, Mr. Neyman." The agent turned to Sage and Anaya. "Ladies, this interview might get a bit graphic. Why don't you head out to the lobby for a half hour or so."

"We'd prefer to stay," Anaya insisted.

Adam nodded his approval.

The two agents looked at each other.

"Fine with us," the stocky one said. "My name is Agent Tarver and my partner is Agent Jackson. You understand that you have the right to remain silent. You also have the right to have an attorney present during questioning and—"

Sage couldn't believe what she was hearing. "You're reading him his Miranda rights? He's not a suspect! He didn't do anything!"

"Just standard procedure, ma'am. Are you sure you don't want to take a walk?"

"I'm fine right here, thank you."

"You don't need to read me my rights," Adam said. "I'll answer all your questions."

The interview took almost an hour. The agents asked Adam to walk through the entire incident. Twice. Both times he told them the exact same story. He had gone into the bathroom to take a shower. Someone was already using one of the two shower stalls, so Adam used the other one. When he was done, he dried off, put on his robe, and went to one of the sinks opposite the showers to comb his hair and brush his teeth. In the mirror above the sink, he could see something tied to a pipe above the shower stall next to the one he had been in. He asked if anyone was in there and got no response. He called out again and still there was no response. The shower was going full blast and the bathroom was filling with steam. He thought something might be wrong, so he called out one more time. When he got no response for the third time, he pulled the shower curtain aside and discovered the naked body of a large man hanging from the overhead pipe, a belt tied around his neck. Underneath him was a small stool that had toppled onto its side. Adam bolted out of the bathroom and ran back to his room. He had looked at the body for only a second or two but was pretty sure it was Steve Musk, his roommate from the apartment building.

When he finished his story the second time, one of the FBI agents asked Adam to spit into a plastic cup.

Sage moved to Adam's side. "What's that for?"

"It's a DNA sample, ma'am. Standard procedure."

"You don't have to do this, Adam. They don't have a warrant."

"It's fine. I've got nothing to hide." Adam spat in the cup twice, wiping off his chin when he was done. "Here you go, officers."

"That will be all, Mr. Neyman. We'll be in contact if we have any further questions."

After the FBI agents left, Adam turned to Sage. "You don't think I had anything to do with this, do you?"

"Of course not."

* * *

FBI CLASSIFIED BRIEFING
YELLOWSTONE NATIONAL PARK COMMAND POST
JUNE 7 – 4:00 P.M.

The afternoon briefing was almost ready to wrap up when Special Agent Velasquez opened a blue folder and glanced down at the contents.

"As many of you know, we had a death in the Old Faithful Inn today. His name was Steve Musk, a seasonal maintenance employee of the Park Service. Our agents are still conducting their investigation, but all indications are that he committed suicide. His body was discovered by Adam Neyman, a seasonal ranger. Dr. Maldonado, it says here that Mr. Neyman is your roommate in the inn."

"That's correct," Sage replied.

"Do you have anything to add about Mr. Musk?"

"Steve was Adam's roommate in the employee apartment complex before we were relocated to the Old Faithful Inn. We all thought he was kind of weird."

"In what way?"

"For one thing, he collected dead animals."

"We're aware of that. Anything else?"

"He just seemed kind of off. I can't really describe it any better than that."

"Very scientific!" Gus taunted.

Special Agent Velasquez continued. "Mr. Musk was under investigation by the FBI. We received an anonymous tip about a week ago that he might be involved in the deaths here at Yellowstone, so we interrogated him twice and searched his apartment and his room in the Old Faithful Inn. We were just about to begin interviewing his acquaintances when he turned up dead. My understanding is that we haven't found any evidence linking Mr. Musk to any of the killings. Is that correct, Agent Rosenberg?"

"That is correct."

"Dr. Maldonado, do you think Mr. Musk could have been involved in the killings?"

"It's certainly possible."

"We are keeping this investigation open, so let us know if you think of any additional information that might assist us."

"I will," Sage replied. "To be honest, though, I'm surprised we haven't had more suicides. It's just horrible being locked up 24/7 with no way to communicate with family or friends, not knowing when, or even if, we'll ever go home or whether today might be our last day on earth. Our faces are scanned everywhere we go, we're watched by cameras all the time, we have no privacy whatsoever, and hardly anyone gets to leave the Old Faithful Inn. You have no idea what this relentless, intense scrutiny feels like."

"I understand how hard this is on everyone," Special Agent Velasquez replied.

"With all due respect, no you don't. You should try spending some time with us in the dining room, or being stuck in our tiny room all day, or using our bathrooms knowing that cameras are trained on the door. Then you'd get a taste of what it's really like."

Special Agent Velasquez didn't respond. She simply closed her folder and stood up.

"This meeting is adjourned."

JUNE 8

Whitney and Sage had agreed to meet at the lab prior to the morning briefing. Sage arrived at nine and completed the face and voice identification procedures without a hitch. After changing into her scrubs, she entered the BSL-2 lab and joined Whitney, who announced she had big news.

"We can all go home today?" Sage said wryly.

"Not that great, I'm afraid. I finally got the FBI files for the victims."

"How'd you do it? I didn't think you'd be able to pull it off."

"I just kept asking until someone said yes."

"And who was that?"

"Hank Rosenberg. At first he said no like all the others, but when I mentioned you were assisting me, he changed his mind."

"How about that," Sage said with a little smile.

"He said we can have them for forty-eight hours, seventy-two tops. He checked them out under his name, so there'll be hell to pay if we don't get them back to him by then."

There were two dozen files in all, each enclosed in a plain brown accordion folder secured by an elastic band. Fourteen of the folders were labeled with the names and letters of the victims; the others contained additional information about the investigation.

"Why is the FBI putting all of this on paper? Haven't they gone digital yet?"

"I wondered that too," Whitney said. "When Hank brought the files to the lab last night, he told me Special Agent Velasquez likes to keep everything on paper. She seems to think paper is more secure than digital in a field operation like this."

The accordion folders filled two large plastic containers that Whitney had labeled "Biological Samples" so no one would ask her to open them. The ruse worked, as they were able to carry the containers all the way back to Sage's room without being stopped once. There was no one there when they arrived.

"I suggest you keep these under the bed when you're not working on them. I don't think Hank got approval to give these to us, so his neck is on the line."

"Don't worry, we won't let anyone see them."

Just then, Anaya and Adam burst through the door, laughing heartily.

"What's so funny?" Sage asked.

"Anaya's been messing with the security cameras again," Adam replied.

"What'd she do this time?"

"You don't want to know."

Anaya nodded toward Whitney. "What's *she* doing here?"

"*She* finally got the FBI files for us. We can't let anyone see these files or we could all get in big trouble." Sage slid the two containers under the bed closest to the window and threw some clothes on top of them for good measure. "Whitney and I have to go to the morning briefing. We can start working on these when I get back."

"Helping the FBI?" Anaya mocked. "Yeah, right."

* * *

When Sage and Whitney returned to the room after the morning briefing, a half dozen accordion folders were scattered on one of the beds, their contents spilling out onto the bedspread.

"What the hell is going on?" Sage demanded.

Adam's face flushed. "I thought I'd get started. The sooner we figure this out the sooner we can all go home."

"I want to go home too. But we've got to be super careful. Where's Anaya?"

"In the lobby, I think. I couldn't get her to help."

"I'm afraid she doesn't want to have anything to do with the FBI," Sage said.

"Maybe. But I think she's just given up."

"Well, I'm not giving up."

"Me neither."

"So what have you done so far?"

"I'm trying to categorize the victims to see what they have in common. So far I've tried age, race, gender, hometown, those sorts of things."

"And?"

"We've got a bunch of young white females from the United States."

"Nobody from other countries?"

Adam smiled. "Does Canada count?"

"I've got a feeling it has nothing to do with demographics," Whitney said. "Let's see if we can find out what each person did since arriving in Yellowstone. Maybe they all ate the same food. Maybe they all hiked the same trail. Maybe they all fed the same animal. Maybe they all met the same people. Those sorts of things."

"That's not going to be easy," Adam replied.

"Of course not. That's why I need your help."

Sage and Adam worked all afternoon and well into the evening searching for things the victims had in common. Sage even skipped the afternoon briefing. While they worked, Anaya wandered in and out of the room a couple of times, but she spent most of the afternoon reading somewhere down in the lobby. After dinner, she collapsed on her bed and closed her eyes.

According to the autopsy reports, each of the first eleven victims had died alone—or, at least, they were alone when they had been found—while the last three victims had perished on a crowded bus. The first eleven all had phones or cameras with them when they died, and the FBI had combed through thousands of pictures on the devices looking for clues. Virtually all the photos were typical for a Yellowstone tourist or employee—mostly shots of animals, geysers, and other thermal features. None of the images yielded any clues as to how the victims might have died.

Sage and Adam started to wade through the multitude of interviews with friends and families of the victims, as well as with park employees who had encountered the victims during their time at the park. It was a slow, tedious process.

Whitney checked in about ten, and Sage admitted they hadn't made much headway. Whitney encouraged them to try again the next morning.

After Whitney left, Sage pleaded with Anaya one more time to help out.

Anaya looked at Sage disparagingly. "I already told you, I am *not* going to help the FBI. Plus, it's not like it's going to do any good anyway. Nothing's going to do any good."

JUNE 9 AND 10

The lack of progress over the next two days wore everyone down. Relations between the CDC and the FBI grew even more contentious, each blaming the other for failing to get to the bottom of the deaths.

Both the morning and afternoon briefings on the ninth degenerated into shouting matches, the main antagonist being Gus Carter. He challenged every report, every conclusion, every opinion. Special Agent Velasquez did her best to rein him in, with little success. At the end of the afternoon briefing, she decided to cancel both briefings on the tenth, reasoning that the time off would give everyone an opportunity to recharge.

The CDC team was also showing signs of stress. Whitney grew more frustrated with each passing day and no resolution in sight. Usually calm under pressure, she displayed a few flashes of anger, something almost unheard of for her. Everyone was irritable and tired. Joe Fairchild threatened to quit twice, but both times Gayle talked him out of it.

Things were going no better for Sage and Adam as they continued to slog through the hundreds of FBI documents— witness interviews, autopsy reports, toxicology results, and forensic analyses—as well as thousands of photographs. Some victims had even kept travel journals or had scribbled notes on maps or park brochures. From all this information, they were able to piece together fairly detailed accounts of what each victim had done during their time in Yellowstone.

Except for Caitlyn, the seasonal ranger who died while jogging, the first eleven victims had all arrived at Yellowstone between May 20 and May 26. The two people who died on Bus 4 along with Penny were seasonal employees of a construction firm that had a contract to repair damaged boardwalks around thermal features. They had been working in Black Sand Basin and on Geyser Hill for almost two weeks.

All fourteen victims had been staying in lodges, inns, cabins, campgrounds, or employee housing in the Old Faithful, Grant Village, or Madison areas. They had all eaten at least once in Old Faithful Village—either in the dining room at the Old Faithful Inn, the Lodge Cafeteria, the Geyser Grill, or the Bear Paw Deli— and many had eaten in the village multiple times.

All the victims had watched Old Faithful erupt at least once and had spent time walking among the dozens of thermal features in the Upper Geyser Basin. There was nothing unusual about that since those were favorite activities of virtually all Yellowstone visitors and employees. All but two of the victims had visited Grand Prismatic Spring, and all but four had walked the Fountain Paint Pot trail. All had been in the Old Faithful Visitor Center at some point.

The three girls from the church group had seen a grizzly bear while hiking on the Pelican Creek trail, but the bear got no closer than about seventy-five yards. Almost all the victims had seen at least one bison, and there had been countless small animal encounters. Some had violated park rules by feeding animals such as squirrels, birds, chipmunks, and even a couple of marmots. As far as Sage and Adam could tell, none of the victims had been bitten or scratched by any of the animals, except for the young couple in the sleeping bag, but the medical examiner had concluded that their wounds were postmortem.

The more Sage and Adam looked, the more similarities they found among the victims. They had gone to many of the same places, eaten much of the same food, and been in many of the same buildings. Sage and Adam made charts and tables and lists, but those yielded nothing useful because there were far too many similarities. They knew they must be missing something but didn't know what. On the afternoon of the tenth, they conceded defeat and put all the folders back in the plastic containers and ceremoniously concealed them under the bed. Hank had agreed to let them keep the files a while longer, but it didn't seem there was anything else they could do.

Eleven people had died completely alone outdoors over a three-day period, and a week later three more had died on a crowded bus within fifteen minutes of each other. It just didn't make sense.

Tensions continued to rise throughout the Old Faithful Inn. There were frequent disagreements in the dining hall, and Sage witnessed an especially animated argument over a dinner roll one evening. There was still plenty of food—no one was starving—but the availability of choice items such as fresh fruit was dwindling. The National Guard soldiers became more proactive, trying to intervene in disputes before they escalated.

Even the bathrooms were not immune to repeated skirmishes. On the evening of the ninth, Sage was pushed aside by a middle-aged woman just as she was about to claim the most desirable shower, the one that always seemed to have the hottest water.

The frequency of room checks increased from once a day to three or even four times a day. Previously, room checks had been predictable and non-intrusive. Sometime between dinner and 10 p.m., a pair of National Guard soldiers would knock on the door to each room and wait for an answer. If no one came to the door, they would note the lack of response in their logbook and move on to the next room. If someone did open the door, they would stand in the doorway and ask the names of everyone inside. Ricky was often assigned to room check duty, and he would chat with Sage for a few minutes during her room check, leaving only when his partner pulled him away to the next room.

But the new room checks were nothing like that. They occurred randomly throughout the day, sometimes even after midnight. After knocking, the soldiers would enter almost immediately, not waiting for a response. *The Gestapo*, as they came to be called, had been given master keys, and they used them, no matter the time of day. Once inside the rooms, they identified the occupants with handheld face scanners and occasionally demanded that suitcases and drawers be opened. If no one was present, they searched the room thoroughly, even turning back bed sheets.

Sage wondered what they were looking for. Were they just checking to see if people were in their rooms, or was it something else? Maybe it was stress-induced paranoia, but she was beginning to feel more like a criminal suspect than a park ranger.

Sage and Anaya argued incessantly while Adam did his best to act as peacekeeper and mediator. When they first moved into the Old Faithful Inn, they had all agreed that Sage and Anaya would share one bed and Adam would have the other bed all to himself. But every night Sage and Anaya fought over the blanket and jostled for position in a bed that was much too small for two adults. Their disagreements soon spilled over into the mornings as they competed for space in their tiny room that was overflowing with luggage, backpacks, and assorted personal items. After breakfast one morning Sage couldn't find her hairbrush, so she used Anaya's— which sent Anaya through the roof.

"What's with you, Anaya?" Sage complained. "Sometimes you're so difficult!"

"I'm sick and tired of all of this. This whole situation stinks, and there's nothing we can do about it."

"But I miss the old Anaya, the one who laughed at my jokes, borrowed my clothes, and made fun of all the Kardashians. Where's that Anaya?"

"She left a while ago," Anaya replied glumly.

On the morning of the 10th, people arriving for breakfast in the dining hall were greeted by a huge banner hanging from the second-story railing in the lobby. Fashioned from two bed sheets crudely tied together, it read: "Free the Yellowstone ~~Detainees~~ Prisoners." When she saw it, Sage wasn't sure whether to laugh or cry.

As she had predicted a few days earlier, there was another suicide attempt. This time, an elderly member of the housecleaning staff broke into one of the storage areas in the Old Faithful Inn and downed some sort of cleaning fluid. Fortunately, it made her vomit violently, which caught the attention of a couple walking by in the hallway, and they called for help. After her stomach had been pumped, the woman was sedated and held overnight in the Old Faithful Clinic for observation.

During the evening of the ninth and into the early morning of the tenth, a swarm of aftershocks ranging in magnitude from 3.9 to 4.6 shook Old Faithful Village. Though none were large enough to cause any substantial physical damage, the psychological damage was very real. Already on edge, everyone's nerves were rattled by each additional aftershock. Even Sage no longer found these seismic events interesting.

The FBI continued to focus their investigation on Steve Musk, Adam's former roommate who had hung himself in the shower, primarily because they had no other suspects. They interviewed everyone at Yellowstone who had worked with him or knew him, including Adam, Sage, and Anaya, and they went through his background with a fine-tooth comb. They examined all his clothing and personal effects in their field lab at Yellowstone and then sent the items to Quantico to undergo additional forensic testing. But it appeared he had no connection to any of the deaths.

Amidst all this was one bit of good news—no one had perished since the three deaths on the evacuation bus. As Sage learned in the briefings on the ninth, the FBI took this as evidence of one of three possibilities: The killer had left Yellowstone, the killer had stopped killing out of fear of detection, or the killer had died.

But Sage and Whitney were not convinced that the deaths were the work of a human killer, and they took advantage of the hiatus from the briefings on the tenth to spend much of the day holed up in the BSL-2 lab bandying about theories concerning what was going on. First, they carefully considered and rejected the FBI's two favorite theories—either a bioterrorist or a serial killer was responsible for the horrific events of the past two weeks. Then they turned to many other possible sources of cyanide, no matter how far-fetched—food, water, soil, rocks, trees, plants, animals, clouds, rain, even aliens. Nothing was off limits. At the end of the day, Whitney still believed that a new species of bacteria or virus was responsible for producing the lethal doses of cyanide.

Sage shuddered. "All this talk of killers and terrorists and deadly viruses creeps me out. Does any of this stuff ever scare you?"

"Me? Scared? Never!"

"No, seriously."

Whitney rocked slowly back and forth on the tall stool. "I'm scared all the time. I'm scared I'm going to make a mistake in the lab. I'm scared I'm not a good enough scientist. I'm scared we're never going to find out why all these people died. I'm scared we're not going to get out of here alive."

"If it makes you feel any better, I'm scared too."

* * *

Mealtime in the Old Faithful Inn had become a dreary, monotonous affair. Under the watchful gaze of the National Guard soldiers, most everyone sat at the same tables each meal. The food was pretty much identical every day—eggs, toast, yogurt, and fruit for breakfast; make-your-own sandwiches for lunch; pasta, salad, and rolls for dinner. Sometimes there was soup for lunch and occasionally there was chicken for dinner.

Almost every meal, little Calvin stopped by to say hi to Sage. Sometimes they chatted for a few minutes, other times they just exchanged high fives. They talked about the beach and what he was going to do for his birthday. No matter how brief their encounter, it always ended the same way.

"See you later, alligator!"

"In a while, crocodile!"

On the night of the tenth, Sage, Anaya, and Adam were eating in silence at their usual table when Sage spotted a new face in the dining hall.

"Hey, guys, that's Special Agent Velasquez. She's in charge of the FBI operations here."

"The one who's a bitch?" Anaya asked.

"The very one."

They watched the Special Agent as she got her food from the buffet table on the far side of the room. After loading up her plate, she headed in their direction. Everyone looked down at their food to avoid making eye contact.

"I see you have an empty chair. Mind if I join you?"

Sage didn't have to look up; she knew the Special Agent's voice all too well.

"Of course, have a seat," Sage said and introduced her friends.

"Nice to meet you. My name is Monica."

JUNE 11

Monica called the morning briefing to order.

The difference in her appearance was striking. Her FBI jacket was draped across the back of her chair and she sported a casual red and green checkered shirt. Her straight black hair was pulled back on one side and held in place by two dark green barrettes.

"You'll notice our group has grown a bit smaller," she said. "I've excused Maddie and Walter from our briefings for the time being so they can focus on their work. Also, I thought a smaller group might lead to a more open exchange of ideas. Gus, why don't you give us an update on the incident that happened early this morning."

Gus looked stunned. "Pardon me?"

"Please give us on update on the vehicle incident."

"Uh… yes, ma'am."

"You can call me Monica. Dr. Maldonado—Sage—believes it will help us work better together if we start using first names."

Sage smiled.

Gus began his report. "As some of you know, early this morning four Yellowstone employees—two from food services and two from maintenance—attempted to steal a vehicle in order

165

to escape. Before they could get the car started, three National Guard soldiers intervened and foiled their getaway. Unfortunately, two of the employees suffered minor injuries in a scuffle with the National Guard as they were being detained."

"How minor?" Ben asked.

"One suffered a concussion and the other has a broken leg."

"I'm curious. Whose car were they trying to steal?"

"One of their own."

"They were trying to take *their own car*? How is that *stealing*?"

"Technically, all vehicles currently in Yellowstone belong to the Federal Government until the Yellowstone Directive has been terminated and the lockdown has been lifted."

"Says who?" Ben was almost shouting. "My car doesn't belong to the Federal Government!"

"When we're done here, your vehicle will be returned to you. But for now, it belongs to us."

"Like hell it does!" Ben jumped out of his chair and took several steps toward Gus, who stood up, feet spread apart, fists clenched tightly at his sides.

"Gentleman, sit down immediately!" Monica ordered. "We have to do our best to work together. Ben, I apologize for Gus's overzealous declaration. You know how much pressure we're all under here. Don't worry, your car is still your car."

"Can I make an observation?" Sage asked.

"Go ahead, Dr. Maldo—I mean Sage. It seems that old habits die hard."

"In my opinion we're at a tipping point here. Over the past few days there have been an increasing number of arguments, disagreements, and fights in the Old Faithful Inn. We've already had one suicide and another attempted one. This morning's vehicle incident demonstrates just how desperate everyone is to get out of here. If we don't do something immediately, it'll surely get much worse. The violence will continue to escalate and there'll be many more attempts to leave. Next time, someone might get hurt really badly. Or worse. We need to do something and we need to do it fast."

"What do you suggest?"

"We could relax some of the conditions of the lockdown. We haven't had any deaths for six days. I think we should give everyone a bit of a break."

"Can you be more specific?"

"Two things might help. First, let's allow everyone to leave the Old Faithful Inn for a couple of hours each day to get some fresh air. That would really lift people's spirits."

"And your other suggestion?"

"Give everyone their personal electronics back. Let us have our phones, tablets, and laptops. Then we can contact our families and tell them we're okay, and we can listen to music and watch movies. Everyone's going stir crazy here."

"What do you think, Whitney?" Monica asked.

"There's certainly no problem with giving people their electronics back."

"What about letting the detainees go outside? Aren't you worried they might be exposed to the killer bacteria or virus you've been telling us about?"

"I must admit that suggestion is a bit more problematic, but I still support it as long as we restrict everyone to Old Faithful Village and the adjacent portion of the Upper Geyser Basin. After all, everyone in this room has been outside on a daily basis and none of us have died. To be extra cautious, though, we should probably warn people not to touch any plants or animals."

Monica closed the folder in front of her. "I'll take both of Sage's suggestions under advisement and announce my decision in the afternoon briefing."

"Can't we vote on them as a group?" Sage asked.

"You may be calling me Monica now, but this is still a special operation of the Federal Bureau of Investigation and I'm still in charge. I'll give you my verdict this afternoon. We're adjourned."

* * *

FBI Classified Briefing
Yellowstone National Park Command Post
June 11 – 4:00 p.m.

Monica began the meeting with an announcement. "I've made my decision about Sage's two requests. I'm inclined to grant one of them."

Sage beamed. "Thank you!"

"Hear me out. I said *one* of them. As to the first request, I agree that we all need to get outside from time to time. We're in one of the most beautiful locations in the world and we might as well take advantage of it. Since our morning briefing, I've had further discussions with Whitney about this, and there seems to be no substantial danger in letting people walk around for a bit. Therefore, I've decided that all detainees will be allowed to leave the Old Faithful Inn twice a day—between nine and eleven in the morning and between two and four in the afternoon."

"Do you really have to keep calling everyone detainees?" Sage inquired.

"What would you suggest instead?"

"Resident? Person? Human being? Anything but detainee."

"I think I can live with *resident*," Monica replied. "All *residents* will be restricted to the Old Faithful area of the Upper Geyser Basin."

"The Old Faithful area won't be big enough to accommodate everyone," Sage said. "How about we expand the permitted area to three adjoining groups of thermal features in the Upper Geyser Basin—the Old Faithful area, Geyser Hill, and the Castle-Grand area. They're the three areas closest to the Old Faithful Inn."

"That should work," Monica agreed. "No one will be given access to any other areas, to their previous accommodations, or to any other buildings in the village. If anyone tries to enter a restricted building or leave the immediate area, they'll be detained. Does anyone have any questions?"

"Will we still have to go through security to leave and re-enter the Old Faithful Inn?" Sage asked.

"Yes."

"But there are over two hundred and fifty people staying in the inn. If we all try to leave at once, it'll take forever to go through security."

"I'm way ahead of you. We're in the process of setting up three security stations at the front of the inn. That should speed things up considerably. All three stations will be equipped to process residents leaving and re-entering the inn, and they should be fully operational by tomorrow morning."

"Thank you."

"As to your second request to return personal electronics, I'm going to deny that."

"But why?"

"Security reasons."

"Won't you reconsider?" Sage pleaded. "It would really help boost morale."

"No, my decision is final. The new rules will go into effect tomorrow morning and everyone will be notified via tomorrow's Daily Update. Until that time, this must remain strictly confidential. None of this leaves this room. You can't tell your friends, your colleagues, or your roommates."

Monica looked directly at Sage. "Is that absolutely clear, everyone?"

JUNE 12

"You knew about this yesterday, didn't you?" Adam shouted as he waved the Daily Update in the air.

Sage was barely able to hide her grin. "Knew about what?"

"The new rules! We can finally go outside!"

THE YELLOWSTONE DIRECTIVE
DAILY UPDATE
JUNE 12

THERE HAVE BEEN NO NEW FATALITIES DURING THE PAST 24 HOURS.

THE CDC SCIENTISTS HERE AT YELLOWSTONE HAVE DETERMINED THAT BEING OUTSIDE IN THE OLD FAITHFUL AREA DOES NOT POSE A SUBSTANTIAL RISK OF HARM. THEREFORE, ALL RESIDENTS WILL BE ALLOWED TO LEAVE THE OLD FAITHFUL INN TWICE A DAY, BETWEEN 9:00 AND 11:00 IN THE MORNING AND BETWEEN 2:00 AND 4:00 IN THE AFTERNOON. ALL RESIDENTS WILL BE RESTRICTED TO THREE ADJACENT AREAS OF THE UPPER GEYSER BASIN:

THE AREA AROUND OLD FAITHFUL, THE AREA DOWN TO CASTLE AND GRAND GEYSERS, AND GEYSER HILL. RESIDENTS WILL NOT BE GIVEN ACCESS TO THEIR PREVIOUS ACCOMMODATIONS OR TO ANY OTHER BUILDINGS.

ALL RESIDENTS ARE ADMONISHED TO REMAIN ON THE BOARDWALK AND ESTABLISHED PATHS, AND TO REFRAIN FROM TOUCHING ANY PLANTS OR ANIMALS.

EXIT OUT OF, AND ENTRY BACK INTO, THE OLD FAITHFUL INN WILL BE THROUGH THREE SECURITY STATIONS AT THE FRONT DOOR OF THE INN. IN ORDER TO EXPEDITE THE SECURITY SCREENING PROCESS, RESIDENTS WILL NOT BE ALLOWED TO TAKE BAGS, PURSES, BACKPACKS, OR ANY OTHER ITEMS OUTSIDE THE INN. ONLY CLOTHING THAT IS DEEMED WEATHER-APPROPRIATE WILL BE ALLOWED.

THE FBI AGENTS OPERATING THE SECURITY STATIONS WILL HAVE THE AUTHORITY TO DENY PERMISSION TO EXIT THE INN FOR ANY REASON.

IF ANY RESIDENT ATTEMPTS TO ENTER A RESTRICTED BUILDING OR LEAVE THE OLD FAITHFUL AREA, THEY WILL BE DETAINED IMMEDIATELY AND QUESTIONED.

THE YELLOWSTONE DIRECTIVE, AS MODIFIED AND CLARIFIED BY ALL SUBSEQUENT UPDATES, INCLUDING THIS ONE, REMAINS IN FULL FORCE.

ANY RESIDENT WHO VIOLATES ANY TERMS OF THE YELLOWSTONE DIRECTIVE WILL BE SUBJECT TO IMMEDIATE ARREST.

"I can't believe you didn't tell us," Anaya grumbled.

"I had to swear on my mother's grave I wouldn't tell anyone, not even you guys. By the way, did you notice we've been promoted?"

"What?"

"We're now *residents* instead of *detainees*."

Even Anaya smiled. "Well, I'll be ..."

* * *

At breakfast, the dining room was livelier than it had been in a long time. There was chatter everywhere, and occasional peals of laughter could be heard above the din. Even the National Guard soldiers seemed more relaxed.

"What do you want to do when we get outside?" Adam asked.

"We can't do much—just walk around parts of the Upper Geyser Basin," Sage replied.

"It may not seem like a big deal to you—you've been going outside every day for your fancy meetings," Anaya snapped.

"I'm sorry, you're right. But actually it *is* a big deal for me too. It'll be so nice to walk among the geysers and hot springs again. I haven't done that in forever."

"I'm not even sure I want to go outside," Anaya said. "They've probably got cameras everywhere outside too. Besides, what's the point?"

"It'll make you feel better," Adam said.

"I doubt it."

Sage finished her muffin and glanced at her watch. "It's almost eight thirty. Let's go get in line. I want to be the first one through security."

"You guys go ahead," Anaya said. "I'm going back to the room. It'll be nice to have it all to myself for a while."

"Okay, but if you change your mind, you know where we'll be." Adam grabbed Sage's hand and they headed to the front entrance. The security screening was surprisingly easy, and they were outside shortly after nine.

"Where to?" Adam asked.

"Anywhere! Why don't we start down near Castle, loop around by Sawmill, and then head toward Beehive?"

The weathered wooden sign in front of Castle Geyser had a space for park rangers to write the expected time of the next eruption. Castle usually erupted in roughly fourteen-hour intervals, with a prediction window of about two hours. The last entry on the sign was for 12:15 p.m. on May 27, the day the deaths started.

Castle Geyser was one of Sage's favorites because of its majestic cone shape and its especially long eruptions. The water would shoot up in a narrow stream seventy-five feet into the air for twenty minutes or so, followed by a noisy steam phase that often lasted another thirty or forty minutes.

There was no way to know when Castle would erupt next, but Sage convinced Adam to sit with her on one of the spectator benches on the off chance that an eruption was imminent. She regaled him with a description of the plumbing deep beneath Castle and an explanation of why Castle Geyser's cone was so large and distinct. After twenty minutes they moved on, Sage glancing back every ten steps or so to make sure an eruption wasn't about to start.

Next stop was Sawmill Geyser, which was almost constantly in motion. Not as spectacular as many of its more famous cousins, Sawmill was mischievous, playfully spitting out bursts of water every few minutes. While Adam scurried past Sawmill to avoid getting wet, Sage positioned herself on the boardwalk so the sinter-laced spray rained down on her.

As she was wiping her glasses clean, she heard a commotion in the direction of Grand Geyser. She squinted but couldn't quite make out what was happening. "What's going on?"

"Bison jam on the boardwalk!" Adam shouted.

Sage hastily put her glasses on and spotted a solitary bison about a hundred yards away ambling down the boardwalk toward Grand Geyser. Most of the people in the vicinity were retreating quickly, but a few foolhardy souls held their ground to get a closer look at the wondrous animal. Sage and Adam walked slowly toward the commotion.

"Shouldn't we go down there and help?" Adam asked.

"Probably, but it'll be a lot more fun watching those two National Guard soldiers give it a go."

As the crowd parted in the face of the advancing bison, the two guardsmen emerged to confront the animal.

"Shoo!" one of them yelled. "Shoo!"

"Really?" Sage laughed. "Shoo?"

The other guardsmen made a thrusting motion with his rifle and Sage knew instantly it was a mistake. It was over in a matter of seconds. The bison tossed the offending guardsman off the boardwalk while the other guardsman turned and ran in the opposite direction. Then the bison stepped slowly off the boardwalk and headed toward a small patch of grass, apparently satisfied he had scared off the intruders.

Sage and Adam rushed toward the thrown guardsman.

"You okay?" Sage asked, slightly out of breath.

"Yeah, I'm fine." He stood up slowly, dusted himself off, and checked for injuries. Fortunately only his pride seemed to have been hurt.

Sage shouted loudly enough for the assembled throng to hear. "Thank you for distracting that bison to keep him away from the rest of us! We all appreciate your bravery!"

As the crowd began to disperse, the guardsman whispered to Sage. "Thanks. You didn't need to do that."

"No worries."

"Next time I think we'll leave the bison to the park rangers. Are there any close by?"

"You're looking at two right here."

"I think I'll just keep my mouth shut. I've been embarrassed enough for one day."

"That's okay, we're all having a tough time." Sage stuck out her hand. "My name's Sage and my boyfriend's name is Adam."

"I'm Eric. I think I'll go find my partner so we can fill out the paperwork."

"You have to file a report on this?"

"We have to file a report on everything. Thanks again for coming over and making me look good. Let me know if I can do anything for you."

"I may just take you up on that at some point."

Sage and Adam hopped back on the boardwalk and walked cautiously past the bison, which seemed oblivious to their presence.

"Did I hear you right? Boyfriend?" Adam's voice was almost a squeak. "That's the first time I've heard you call me that."

"It just sort of slipped out. Sorry."

"You didn't mean it?"

Sage's face turned crimson. "Now I think I'll keep *my* mouth shut."

Adam grabbed her hand and they walked back toward the inn. They wandered by Liberty Pool, the Lion Group, and Heart Spring.

"I love the names of all these features," Sage said. "They evoke such beautiful images." As they strolled slowly past the thermal pools and geysers, she saw many familiar faces on the boardwalk—Gus Carter, Dominick Pagano, Ben Thomas, even Monica Velasquez—all out getting some fresh air.

Appearing out of nowhere, Calvin jumped up and gave Sage a high five. "These geysers are pretty neat, huh?"

"I'll say," Sage replied. "Which one is your favorite?"

"All of them!"

Sage could hear Calvin's mom far down the boardwalk. "Calvin, stop running!"

"Your mom is right, Calvin. It's dangerous to run on the boardwalk. Please slow down. I don't want you to get hurt."

"Okay!" Calvin's voice trailed off as he barreled down the boardwalk back toward his mom. "See you later, alligator!"

"In a while, crocodile!" Sage shouted after him.

Just as Sage and Adam got to a slight bend in the boardwalk between Heart Spring and Beehive Geyser, Old Faithful started to erupt. Sage pulled Adam close, and they leaned against the wooden railing while they gazed at the majestic fountain of water. A fine mist rose from a vigorously bubbling hot spring next to the boardwalk, enveloping them in a warm embrace as they stood together, arms around each other.

Sage nuzzled Adam's neck. "This is what I came to Yellowstone for."

"Me too."

Oblivious to the others who had gathered to watch Old Faithful, they shared a passionate kiss.

* * *

"It's almost two o'clock!" Sage exclaimed. "I can't wait to go outside again! Why don't you come with us, Anaya? It'll be fun."

"No, thanks. I kind of enjoyed being by myself this morning. It's awfully crowded with the three of us in this tiny room."

"Just come outside for a little bit," Sage pleaded. "You don't have to walk around with us. You can just wander off by yourself."

"You guys won't give up, will you?"

"Nope."

"Okay, but I'm going to do my own thing."

Once again, security was a breeze and the three of them headed off toward Old Faithful. The wind had picked up from the morning, and heavy clouds were rolling in over the Gallatin Range.

"Great!" Anaya said sarcastically. "It looks like it's going to pour any minute."

"Why don't you sit on the benches by Old Faithful so you can run back inside when the first raindrop falls. Adam and I are going to look for bison."

"What?"

"Never mind. We'll see you back in the room."

Sage and Adam headed off eagerly, walking counterclockwise on the path around Old Faithful.

"Let's go up to Observation Point!" Sage suggested.

"Great idea! There'll probably be no one up there."

They walked across the wooden bridge spanning the Firehole River behind Old Faithful and headed up the slight incline leading to the trail. As they approached the Observation Point trailhead they could see a National Guardsman positioned directly in front of the trail.

"Sorry, the trail's off limits," he said.

"Why?" Sage asked.

"I don't know. It just is. Those are my orders."

"I think we can let these two go up. They look trustworthy to me."

Sage turned around. It was Eric.

"But our orders are to not allow anyone on this trail."

"I'll take responsibility for this, Armando."

"Thanks so much, Eric!" Sage said.

"We *can* trust you, right?"

Sage and Adam were already ten paces up the trail. "Of course!"

Sage could barely keep up with Adam as he bounded up the trail, and she marveled at his exuberance as he easily navigated the rocky path with his long runner's stride.

The climb to Observation Point was steep but short. At each bend of the winding trail, Sage paused to catch her breath and take in the shrinking geyser basin below. She was panting heavily by the time she reached the summit.

"I knew there wouldn't be anyone up here," Adam said, without a hitch in his voice.

Sage threw her arms around Adam's waist and held on tightly, using him as a windbreak against the stiffening breeze. The view was spectacular.

Taking center stage was Old Faithful, with the eponymous inn directly behind it. Dozens of other geysers dotted the landscape below. Sawmill and Daisy were erupting, while tendrils of steam rose from many others in the cool afternoon air. Countless runoff channels crisscrossed the Upper Geyser Basin, carrying water from geysers and bubbling hot springs into hidden crevices and down to the Firehole River. Despite the geothermal turmoil hidden just below the surface, the Upper Geyser Basin looked serene from this vantage point six hundred feet above.

The rain started slowly but intensified quickly into a downpour. They could see people on the boardwalks far below scrambling for cover, most of them heading back toward the Old Faithful Inn. After a rain-soaked kiss and a few more moments looking out over the Upper Geyser Basin, they headed back down the trail, laughing each time one of them slipped. They didn't completely lose their footing until they reached the bottom, when Adam fell and pulled Sage down with him as she tried to hold him up. They sat in the mud, laughing and kissing, the rain pouring down around them. There was no point rushing back to the inn; they couldn't get any wetter.

When they finally reached their room, they quickly stripped down to their underwear.

"Can't you two wait until I'm out of the room?" Anaya complained.

"We're soaked!" Sage said.

"Whatever. Just hurry up and get dressed."

"C'mon, Anaya, try to see the bright side of things every once in a while."

"What bright side? We're stuck here in this hellhole until who knows when. If we're lucky, we'll get to go home at some point. If we're not ..."

Still dripping wet, Sage sat on the bed next to Anaya. "You're really scared, aren't you?"

A single tear rolled slowly down Anaya's cheek. "Aren't you?"

"Of course. I'm just trying to make the best of a horrible situation."

"That's easy for you. You've got a new boyfriend, and you get to go to your meetings every day. I've got nothing."

Sage fell silent for a few moments. "That's not true. You've got us." She tried to hug Anaya, but Anaya slid further away on the bed.

Sage and Adam put on some dry clothes and sat on the other bed, talking quietly to each other.

After a few minutes, Anaya interrupted. "Thanks for trying."

Given that small opening, Sage and Adam told Anaya all about the bison jam in the morning and their hike up to Observation Point in the afternoon.

"You really did have fun, didn't you?"

"We did," Adam said. "Maybe you can walk with us tomorrow."

"Maybe I will."

* * *

Dinner was even more raucous than breakfast and lunch had been. Some of the residents sat with friends and colleagues they hadn't spoken to in weeks, while others made new friends.

"It really worked," Sage said.

"What worked?" Anaya asked.

"Letting people go outside. Look how relaxed everyone is."

"Can I join you?"

Sage looked up and saw Whitney towering over her. "Of course! Any progress today?"

"Not really," Whitney said. "We've done everything we can with the tissue and fluid samples from the victims, and we've completed the analyses of all the items from the evacuation buses. We've analyzed food and water here in the inn, and we've analyzed dozens of water and soil samples from the locations where the first eleven victims were found. But we keep running into dead ends. No novel bacteria, no novel viruses, no nothing. How about you guys? Any luck with the FBI files?"

"We gave up on those two days ago. They're just sitting under our bed. You want them back?"

"Not yet. Hank said we can keep them for the time being. He'll let us know if he needs them."

"Did you go outside today?"

"No, I worked in the lab all day and took a quick nap before dinner."

"Why don't you join us outside tomorrow? Adam and I had a lot of fun today."

"I'll think about it, but right now all I want to do is sleep. I'm going to head back to my room."

"Time for us to go back too," Anaya said.

"You guys go on ahead," Sage said. "I think I'll hang out in the lobby for a while."

Adam took Sage's hand. "Me too."

While Anaya and Whitney went back to their rooms, Sage and Adam wandered into the gift shop adjacent to the lobby. The FBI had allowed the shop to remain open as a minuscule concession to normality. Hand in hand, they walked through the store among the racks of sweatshirts, mugs, and key chains, many adorned with iconic Yellowstone images—geysers, thermal springs, grizzly bears, and bison. As they stopped to look at a book about Old Faithful, Sage thought back to the kiss they had shared while watching the real thing earlier that morning.

They scoured the store for any food to take back to their room, but the clerk told them that all the trail mix, granola, and candy bars had sold out the first day of the lockdown. There were a few jugs of Huckleberry Syrup left, but that didn't seem too appealing as a late night snack.

Mounted on the wall next to the cashier's counter was a flat-screen monitor playing *The Wonders of Yellowstone* on a continuous loop. While Adam continued to wander through the store, Sage stopped to watch. The wildlife in the video was fascinating—a mother grizzly fishing for trout with her cubs, two bull elk butting antlers during rutting season, a lone eagle soaring over Yellowstone Lake—but what truly stirred her soul were the thermal features. Geysers, fumaroles, mud pots, and hot springs—they all had their own charms. Though the spectacular geysers garnered the most attention from the crowds that packed Yellowstone every summer, Sage was partial to the infinite variety of thermal pools with their stunning colors. Some were small and unassuming; others were ostentatious and grandiose. Her favorite was Grand Prismatic Spring, with its magical rainbow of colors spilling over the scalloped terraces that fell away from the central pool.

Sage recalled her first day in Yellowstone, when she had ventured up the short trail to the top of the hill behind Grand Prismatic Spring to take in the magnificent sight. She had headed out just after dawn to beat the crowds and had the overlook all to herself. The dense steam partially obscuring the large oval spring was painted with a multitude of colors. Occasionally a breeze parted the foggy veil and Sage was able to gaze upon Grand Prismatic in all its glory. As the sun continued to rise, the steam dissipated until finally all that was left was the array of blues, reds, oranges, greens, and yellows for which Grand Prismatic was so famous.

While the spring evoked the brightly colored paintings of Matisse, Sage also marveled at the biological processes that produced such vibrant colors. Mats of algae, along with scores of species of heat-loving microbes, including common bacteria and rare, ancient archaea, fashioned this otherworldly palette.

Sage knew many of these thermophiles well, as they were similar to those nurtured by the underwater volcanoes and thermal vents she had studied during her postdoc at the USGS. Like many of her colleagues, Sage believed that life on earth had started around obscure cauldrons deep beneath the ocean's surface and that the earliest forms of life were precursors to the ancient archaea that evolved billions of years ago.

As she watched the colorful thermal features on the monitor—Morning Glory Pool, Silex Spring, and finally Grand Prismatic Spring—she was transfixed by their splendor and otherworldly beauty.

Suddenly, she gasped.

Then she exploded. "ARCHAEA! Maybe it's archaea!"

Adam rushed to her side. "What's wrong? Are you okay?"

Two National Guardsmen arrived a split second later.

"It might be archaea!" she yelled.

"Ar-what?" Adam asked.

Sage's words spilled out uncontrollably. "Archaea! One of the oldest life forms on earth! They're like bacteria but they're not. They're sort of like viruses but they're different. And they were discovered right here in Yellowstone!"

"Ma'am, you're going to have to come with us." One of the guardsmen reached for Sage's left elbow, but she yanked it away.

Adam spoke firmly. "Everything's fine, officer. She's just exhausted. I'll take her back to our room."

"If she causes another disturbance we're going to have to detain her."

"It won't happen again, I promise." Adam turned to Sage. "Let's head back to the room and get some rest."

Adam put his arm around her waist and guided her out of the store, across the lobby, and into the hallway.

Sage erupted again when they were halfway down the hall. "Adam, you don't understand. This might be it! I've got to find Whitney. We've got lots of work to do!"

Sage broke free of Adam's grasp, bounded up the stairs, and sprinted to Whitney's room. By the time Adam caught up with her, she was already banging on Whitney's door.

"Whitney, it's Sage! It's an emergency! We need to go to the lab."

Whitney opened the door in flannel pajamas, rubbing her eyes. "I just got into bed. Can't this wait until morning?"

"No! Get dressed and let's head to the lab. I'll explain on the way."

"Okay, okay! Give me a couple of minutes."

While Whitney was getting ready, Sage placed her hands on Adam's shoulders and looked him straight in the eye. "I may have just figured out what's killing everyone!"

"I don't understand."

"There are these really, really old microscopic organisms called archaea. They've been around for billions of years, and they've been found in numerous thermal features right here in Yellowstone. At first scientists thought they were just another form of bacteria, but now most experts agree that they are actually in a separate domain. They haven't been studied nearly as much as viruses and bacteria so we don't know much about them."

"How could they kill people?"

"Lots of bacteria and viruses are lethal to humans. Why not archaea?"

Whitney emerged from her room and closed her door quietly. "Robin's asleep."

"You all set?"

"Yep."

"Okay, let's go." Sage turned to Adam. "I'm probably going to be really late, so don't wait up."

"How late?"

"Maybe all night."

* * *

As they strode briskly to the lab, Sage shared her revelation about archaea with Whitney.

"So what do you think?" Sage had trouble catching her breath, due in equal parts to exertion and excitement.

"I don't know. I've never heard of archaea being lethal to humans, so we haven't been looking for them."

"But do you think a species of archaea *could* produce cyanide?"

"I don't know of any that can."

"But do you think it's *possible*?"

"I suppose."

"That's all I needed to hear!" Sage sputtered, still out of breath.

"Did you know that several species of archaea are quite common in the human gut?" Whitney asked.

"No."

"Most people don't. It shouldn't be too much of a problem, though, because we'll be looking for archaea species that aren't usually found in humans. But I don't know how archaea could produce cyanide. I guess they could interact somehow with the chemicals in the human body. After all, the right building blocks for cyanide are there in abundance—carbon and nitrogen. Still, I don't know what the chemical process would look like."

"Me neither, but let's take this one step at a time. If we can find foreign archaea somewhere in those dead bodies I think we'll be on our way."

After they quickly changed into their scrubs, Whitney directed Sean to activate the intercom.

"Intercom activated."

Whitney called back to the BSL-4 lab. "Hey, guys, this is Whitney. How's it going in there?"

"What are you doing here?" Gayle asked. "I thought you went back to the inn to get some sleep."

"There's been a change of plan. Sage is here with me and she thinks we should look for archaea in the samples from the bodies."

"Really? Why?"

Sage jumped in. "With all its thermal features, Yellowstone is a hot bed for exotic thermophiles like archaea. Who knows, maybe archaea are somehow related to all these deaths."

"But I've never heard of a lethal species of archaea," Gayle said.

"Me neither," Whitney agreed. "But we're going to give it a shot."

"So what do you want us to do?"

"Nothing. Sage and I are going to take it from here. I told her she could assist me since it was her idea."

"Has she been trained in a BSL-4 lab?"

Sage frowned and shook her head.

"Yep, she's all set." Whitney winked at Sage.

"Are you sure Joe and I can't help?"

"You know the rules, Gayle—no more than two of us in there at a time."

"But you always get to have all the fun."

"That's 'cause I'm the boss. How long will it take you and Joe to clean up?"

"About a half hour. We just finished extracting biological samples from some clothing. We can store them and test them later."

"Sage and I are going to go through decon. We'll probably finish about the time you're ready to leave."

Before speaking to Sage, Whitney made sure the intercom was off, but she whispered anyway. "You know I'm breaking about a dozen CDC rules by letting you into the lab? You're not a CDC employee or contractor, you don't have the proper training to work in a BSL-4 lab—"

"I know, I know. I really appreciate it."

"Are you sure you're up for this?"

"I'm sure."

"You understand the possible dangers?"

"Like if my suit rips?"

"Yes, there's that. Lots of other things can go wrong too."

"Let's just go in before I change my mind."

"Or before I change mine."

After completing the face and voice security screening for the BSL-4 lab, Whitney pulled open the bulky metal door and motioned for Sage to follow. As the door closed automatically behind them, Sage felt a brisk breeze generated by the air-handling system in the airlock. The circulation fans were so loud she could barely hear Whitney.

Confronted with the complex decontamination process ahead, Sage finally grasped the danger of working in a BSL-4 lab. Suddenly unable to move, she leaned against the wall to steady herself.

"You okay?" Whitney shouted. "You don't look so good."

"I'm fine. I just need a moment."

"We can turn back. It's not too late."

Sage stood still for a bit while Whitney held her arm.

"I'm okay now. Let's keep going."

"You sure?"

Sage nodded.

Whitney opened the door to the changing area and guided Sage in ahead of her. After the door closed behind them, the noise level dropped dramatically.

"Here's where we get undressed. Take everything off. Throw your scrubs in the bin and put your underwear, socks, and anything else you're wearing, including your watch and any jewelry, in Locker 5."

"Can I keep my glasses on?"

"Yes, but that's it. Everything else must come off."

After they stripped down and stuffed their belongings into the small lockers, Whitney visually scanned Sage from top to bottom. "What about your pendant?"

Sage glanced down at the tiny gold heart. "But I never take this off. Ever. It was a gift from my mom and dad."

"Sorry, but you have to remove everything. You can put it back on when we leave the BSL-4 lab."

Sage reluctantly removed her pendant and kissed it gently before placing it carefully in the locker.

Whitney nodded approvingly. "Now it's time to get clean."

They moved into the shower area. Whitney closed the door behind them and double-checked to make sure the seal was tight all around. "These doors are super secure. They have a pressurized bladder that seals the door when it's closed. But since we set the lab up so quickly, I always check to make sure each door seals completely."

The shower area was dominated by two oversized showerheads descending from metal pipes that traversed the top of the enclosure; the floor was slightly concave, allowing water to flow toward the large drain in the center of the chamber. Over a dozen large white towels hung on a freestanding rack in one corner.

"I forgot why we're showering on our way *into* the lab," Sage said.

"It is a little unusual, but we want to make sure we don't bring in any microbes that could potentially contaminate our analyses."

"What are these decontamination chambers made of?"

"Hard, clear acrylic panels sealed with a high-grade epoxy. We improvised quite a bit and had to cobble everything together based on what we could get our hands on quickly."

"So why are all the decontamination chambers completely transparent?"

"A couple of reasons. Mostly so we can always see each other, in case anyone gets in trouble. Also, clear acrylic is easy to seal. So far it's held up nicely—no leaks or cracks."

Sage rapped on one of the clear panels. "Are you *sure* this stuff is impermeable?"

"Absolutely."

As Whitney pointed out the controls for the two showerheads, Sage heard a voice. But it wasn't Whitney's.

"Is everything okay?"

Sage turned and saw two people clad in blue body suits standing in the BSL-4 lab on the other side of the acrylic panels. She hadn't noticed them before.

One of the body suits spoke. "I said, are you okay?"

"We're fine, Joe," Whitney replied. "Sage was just testing the integrity of our acrylic walls."

Sage had been so focused on the daunting decontamination process that she had forgotten she was stark naked as she faced Joe and Gayle, separated only by a clear piece of acrylic. Suddenly realizing her predicament, she spun around and tried to cover herself with her hands but quickly realized it was no use. Dropping her hands to her side, she turned back around.

"All in the name of science," she muttered to herself.

"What was that?" Whitney asked.

"Nothing. How am I able to hear Joe so well?"

"Each of the pressurized suits has a wireless communication system built right into the hood so we can talk to each other in the BSL-4 lab. The system's also connected to the intercom so we can speak to anyone who's in the decon chambers or out in the BSL-2 lab. For safety reasons, it's important that we're able to communicate with each other at all times."

"That does make me feel a bit safer, I guess." Sage moved underneath one of the showerheads and turned it on.

"Remember to clean everywhere," Whitney said.

Sage did as she was told, scrubbing vigorously from head to toe, side to side, and front to back with some sort of abrasive material that masqueraded as a shower sponge. It was surprisingly tiring, and she was out of breath when she finally finished.

After drying off, Whitney and Sage deposited their towels in a large red biohazard bin.

"Follow me." Whitney exited the shower area through a door into the suit room.

Sage looked around. "Why is this area different than the others? It looks like we're in a giant bubble."

"Actually, that's what it's called. It's a BioBubble Containment Enclosure. We need a lot more space in the suit room, so it was easier to use a BioBubble instead of dozens of acrylic panels. Also, the walls of the BioBubble are more flexible, which allowed us to configure the connections between these chambers exactly as we wanted."

"But is it really secure? The walls look so flimsy."

"Absolutely. BioBubbles have been used all over the world and there have never been any problems."

Inside the BioBubble was a large gleaming metal rack holding two powder-blue pressurized body suits. Opposite the metal rack was a long, low white bench that housed four drawers; at each end of the bench were red biohazard containers. Four neon-orange coils descended from a network of thin pipes that crisscrossed the ceiling of the bubble.

Whitney pointed at the orange coils. "Those are our air hoses, our lifelines. Not only do they provide us with oxygen to breathe, they also keep our body suits pressurized so nothing can get in if we spring a leak. They stretch to about twelve feet so you can move about the lab while you're hooked up. When you can't stretch an air-supply hose any further, you simply disconnect it and reconnect to another one. You'll see twelve air hoses spread out in the BSL-4 lab."

Sage laughed. "They look like giant orange Slinkys."

Whitney took one of the body suits from the rack and hung it from a large metal hook connected to the overhead piping. "The first thing we do in here is test our suits for leaks."

She placed duct tape over two exhaust valves on the back of the suit and connected it to one of the orange air hoses. The suit slowly inflated, and she unhooked the supply hose when the suit was about the firmness of a pool float. She walked all around it, looking, listening, and feeling for leaks.

"This one's good," she declared. "Let's test the other one." She repeated the testing for the second suit. "All good with this one too." She removed the duct tape from both suits.

"What happens if there's a leak?" Sage asked.

"We've got four spare suits in case one develops a leak. Now let me show you how to get into your suit. I'll go first, and then I'll help you get into yours. It's pretty tricky at first, but you'll get the hang of it eventually."

Sage watched intently as Whitney retrieved scrubs, socks, gloves, and more duct tape from the drawers beneath the bench.

First Whitney put on a full set of olive green scrubs. Next were white socks, which she taped securely to the legs of her scrubs. After that, she pulled on purple nitrile gloves and used duct tape to secure them to the arms of the scrubs. Then she put on another set of gloves.

"I'm exhausted just watching you," Sage said, "and you don't even have your pressurized body suit on yet."

"It becomes routine after a while. Just part of the job."

Finally, she donned her positive-pressure suit, which included a full hood and clear face shield. She zipped up the suit, adjusted the hood, and made sure the outer gloves were secure in the O-rings that connected them to the body of the suit. Then she coupled one of the orange Slinkys to her body suit; it slowly inflated until she looked like a big blue marshmallow.

"You're wearing three sets of gloves!" Sage shouted.

"You don't need to shout. I can hear you loud and clear through the wireless communication system."

"Sorry. But why are you wearing three sets of gloves?"

"Gloves are the weak link in the pressurized-suit system. They're the part most likely to cut or rip when we're handling lab equipment."

Whitney pulled out more supplies from the drawers beneath the bench. "Your turn."

A frown crossed Sage's face. "I don't think all my hair is going to fit inside that hood."

Whitney chuckled. "There's plenty of room, even for that mop of yours. You're not looking for an excuse to back out, are you?"

"Of course not."

Sage tried to do everything herself, but Whitney had to help with some of the taping. Once Sage's scrubs, socks, and gloves were in place, Whitney retrieved the other body suit. "It may feel a little claustrophobic at first, but you'll get used to it."

Sage stepped into the legs of the suit one at a time and almost lost her balance. Whitney steadied her while she pulled the suit all the way up and over her head. She had a little trouble with the zipper but finally got it closed. Whitney hooked up Sage's air hose and the suit started to inflate.

"You doing okay?" The clarity of Whitney's voice surprised Sage.

"It sounds like you're right here in the suit with me."

"These speakers are something, aren't they?"

Whitney circled Sage.

"What are you doing?"

"Just double checking everything for leaks. You can't be too careful in this business. Now detach your air supply."

"Why?"

"I want to make sure you can do it."

Sage decoupled the air-supply hose from her suit.

"Okay, now reconnect the hose."

Sage struggled a bit with the hose but got it connected on the second try.

"Very good. Now do it again."

Sage disconnected the air hose and this time was able to reconnect it on the first try.

"And again."

"Really?"

"Yes, really."

After the third practice run, Whitney nodded approvingly. "You're ready."

They disconnected their air hoses and proceeded into the final decontamination chamber, which was another shower room. Once they re-connected to the orange air-supply lines, Whitney checked the door behind them to make sure it was completely sealed.

"This is the chemical shower area. We don't need to do anything in here right now, but we'll use it to decontaminate our pressurized suits when we leave the lab."

"You mean there's an extra step when we head out?"

"Afraid so. We have to stand under the chemical shower in our body suits and scrub them carefully with large, soft brushes. I'll clean your suit and you'll clean mine."

"Now I see why you do everything in pairs in here."

"Are you ready to head into the lab?"

"As ready as I'll ever be."

As they stepped into the BSL-4 lab, Gayle and Joe greeted them and helped them connect to the air-supply lines.

Sage smiled at Joe. "Enjoy the show back there?"

"Listen, I've seen everyone naked and they've all seen me. It's no big deal. You're welcome to watch when it's my turn."

"No, thanks—I'm good," Sage said coolly.

Gayle and Joe headed into the chemical shower area to begin their long journey out of the lab.

Whitney gave Sage a final caution before they got to work. "Bear in mind that it takes at least twice as long to do even the simplest tasks here in the BSL-4 lab than in a regular lab. We need to conduct all our work carefully and deliberately to avoid any mistakes."

"Got it," Sage replied. "By the way, what happens if I get hungry?"

"You wait."

"And what if I need to go to the bathroom?"

"You hold it."

Whitney moved to the computer terminal near one end of a long counter. "I've got to log in and record the details of our entry into the lab. Why don't you look around while you're waiting for me."

Sage found moving in the pressurized suit to be rather awkward, and she was terrified she might accidently tear it, so she proceeded very slowly through the lab.

The first time she needed to change air-supply lines, it didn't go well. Everything was more challenging in the BSL-4 lab than it had been during practice back in the suit room. Though she was able to decouple the supply line without any difficulty, she struggled to connect the new air hose to her suit. The body suit was uncomfortably hot, and sweat dripped into her eyes. With no way to wipe her brow, she tried shaking her head back and forth, but that only made her dizzy in the absence of a new supply of oxygen. She was just about to yell for help when she finally connected the air hose. The cool rush of oxygen relaxed her, and she inhaled deeply.

"How are you doing?" Whitney asked.

"Fine. Just looking around."

Despite being set up in just a couple of days, the BSL-4 lab looked like it was straight out of Hollywood. But this was no movie set. Full of gleaming chrome and white ceramic, it housed the most technologically advanced scientific instruments available anywhere in the world.

Sage was at a loss for words. All she could utter was a meek "Wow."

"I told you the CDC spared no expense," Whitney said. "This is the first time they've deployed many of these instruments in a field lab."

The five decontamination chambers formed one side of the enormous rectangular lab. Along the end wall nearest the exit of the decontamination area were two fume hoods, each accompanied by an array of beakers, test tubes, and other containers, as well as two sinks and assorted nozzles. In one corner of that wall was a clear box the size of a small refrigerator that contained a complicated-looking mechanism on a track over a series of well plates. Sage asked Whitney what it was.

"Our new pipetting robot. It can be a little finicky at times, but when it's working right it's a sight to behold."

Along the long wall opposite the decontamination area was an impressive collection of scientific instruments. Sage was immediately drawn to a piece of equipment in the middle of a long counter.

"Is this a triple quad mass spectrometer?"

Whitney looked up from the computer. "The most advanced one available."

Sage ventured down the extensive counter, examining other instruments along the way. Among them were two biosafety cabinets with integral HEPA filters, two light microscopes, and a centrifuge. Finally, she came to a table at the end of the counter. "Now this is one instrument I know all about."

"You've used a scanning electron microscope before?"

"I have—to examine crystal patterns in quartz and other minerals. But this looks like a newer model than I'm used to."

"It is. We have only the best and newest stuff at the CDC. It's your tax dollars at work. In fact, most of what you see here isn't even commercially available yet."

Sage turned and caught sight of Joe and Gayle in the suit room in the decon area on the opposite side of the lab. They had already removed their pressurized body suits, which were hanging on the metal rack. Gayle still had her scrubs on, but Joe had just finished stripping his off to get ready for his shower.

As Sage stared, Joe caught her eye and flashed a big smile. She felt herself blush under her hood and quickly turned away. After a few moments, she took another quick peek at the suit room. All in the name of science.

Sage noticed a large red button on the table in the middle of the lab. "What's this?"

"An emergency alarm."

"What's it for?"

"Any type of emergency—a broken flask, a severe medical event, a ripped body suit. There are four alarm buttons in the BSL-4 lab, two in the decon area, and one in the BSL-2 lab."

"What happens if we push it?"

"Alarms sound, lights flash."

"What if no one else is here?"

"It sets off an alarm unit back in our room in the Old Faithful Inn. Also, we all wear portable alarms on our belts that emit a siren if any of the emergency buttons are pushed. It's quite loud."

"Can I get one of those portable alarms?"

"I'm afraid we don't have any more. We gave the last one to Joe."

Finally Sage approached two identical machines that filled the far end of the lab. They were massive—much larger than anything else in the lab. Each was almost ten feet long and consisted of numerous modules and components. The other instruments in the lab paled in significance beside these beasts.

"Are these the automatic genetic sequencers?"

"They are. Be very careful around them. Each one costs more than four million dollars, and they are *very* temperamental."

Sage took a few steps back.

Whitney gave her an abbreviated tutorial on genetic sequencers. "Automatic genetic sequencers have only been around since the 1980s, and it's amazing how much they've improved since then. These two are prototypes of next-generation models not available anywhere else in the world. They've automated virtually every step of the process. Depending on the complexity of the biological sample, they can usually give us results in less than an hour. Not too long ago that would have taken days."

"How do they work?"

"Within each machine are multiple chambers, centrifuges, and thermal cyclers. I don't know all the technical details, but it's almost as if there's an army of tiny robots hidden inside. There are basically four steps for analyzing each sample: DNA extraction, DNA amplification, nucleic acid sequencing, and virtual DNA assembly. It used to take several machines and instruments to do all of this, and each step was very labor-intensive and time-consuming. But now these babies do everything for us.

"First, DNA is extracted from a sample of material. Then PCR amplification generates multiple copies of each DNA strand. Next, the genetic code of each strand is sequenced. And finally, the internal processors virtually assemble longer strands of DNA from thousands of small strands in a trial-and-error process. Basically, an algorithm looks for overlapping pieces of genetic code, which indicates that two pieces of DNA fit together to make a longer piece. That algorithm is used to construct longer and longer sequences of code. Although we don't end up with complete DNA molecules, some of the assembled sequences can be quite long.

"When we're dealing with biological samples that contain DNA from multiple organisms, this last step is incredibly complex and requires a level of computing power we could only dream about a few years ago. In samples of body tissue and fluids, the DNA could come from the human host as well as hundreds of other organisms, mostly microbes such as bacteria and viruses."

"Or archaea," Sage said quietly.

"Or archaea." Whitney paused before continuing. "After the sequencer has done its thing, the final step is to determine whether the genetic sequences match sequences of known organisms."

"How do you do that?"

"We use an online system called BLAST to compare our sequences with databases at the NCBI."

"But we don't have Internet access."

"*You* don't. But here in the lab we've got a secure military-grade Internet connection to the CDC, NCBI, FBI, Homeland Security, and a few other government agencies. Even the White House."

"The White House?"

"Yes. They've been watching the developments here very closely. After all, the FBI thinks we're dealing with a serial killer or terrorist."

"I don't like being watched. Especially by the government."

"Me neither, but there's nothing we can do about it. Anyway, we upload the DNA sequences generated by the sequencer, and the BLAST software looks for matches in the databases at the NCBI. Basically it searches for homologous species—that is, organisms that have sequences identical to, or very similar to, the sequences we upload. The matching process is very quick—it usually takes less than a minute. Then we can follow up any promising leads with good old-fashioned microbiology detective work."

"There's one thing I don't understand," Sage said. "Why haven't you been looking for all types of organisms, including archaea?"

Whitney's face tightened into a grimace. "To be honest, I didn't think it was necessary. Because our samples can contain DNA from many different microbes, we often end up with hundreds of sequences to upload to BLAST. To simplify the search and avoid getting bogged down with massive amounts of irrelevant data, I've only been searching for matches with bacteria and viruses. There's never been a known case of a pathogenic archaea species, so I haven't been looking for them. In retrospect, it wouldn't have been that much more time-consuming to include archaea in our

BLAST searches." She paused a second before continuing. "I won't make that mistake again."

"I didn't mean to imply…"

"I know you didn't. But it really *was* careless." Whitney took a deep breath. "Anyway, all I have to do is put the raw material into the sample receptacle of the sequencer, push a few buttons, and wait. Let's start with a sample from one of the evacuation bus victims and I'll show you how it works."

"Why don't you just use the results from the previous sequencing runs and re-submit them to BLAST to look for matches with archaea?" Sage asked.

"I *am* going to do that, but first I'd like to run the sequencing for each sample again. With such complex biological samples, we may end up with a slightly different set of DNA sequences than the first time. This way, we'll have two sets of data for each sample that we can run through BLAST. I'm not going to cut any corners this time around."

Whitney retrieved a small vial from one of the cold storage units.

"This is a sample of liver tissue from Victim P.P."

Sage gasped. "That's my friend Penny—Penny Phillips."

Whitney put the vial down. "I'm sorry. Why don't I choose a different sample."

"No, it's okay. We can use this one."

"Are you sure?"

"I'm sure."

Whitney moved over to one of the fume hoods, removed about a gram of Penny's liver tissue and placed it in a clear sterile container about the size of two postage stamps. After returning the rest of the material to the cold storage unit, she carefully placed the tiny payload into a receptacle at the end of one of the genetic sequencers, entered a few commands on the touch screen, and then turned toward Sage. "We should have our results in less than an hour. In the meantime, I'm going to put the other sequencer to work."

Once she had loaded a sample of Penny's blood into the second sequencer, Whitney joined Sage on the stools at the end of the counter where they did their best to sit down in their pressurized body suits.

After waiting quietly for a few minutes, Sage broke the silence. "This is all so fascinating, but I'd envisioned we'd be peering into microscopes looking for squiggly microbes."

Whitney sighed. "We don't do that very much anymore. Truth is, I miss those days. I used to feel like a real biochemist. Now I'm basically a glorified computer programmer."

"So how did you get into the disease business anyway?"

"I've always liked biology since I was a little kid—you know, looking at pond water through a microscope at home, watching the amoebas and tiny arthropods swim about. I did my undergrad work in biology at Georgia Tech and got my M.D. and Ph.D. in biochemistry at Emory. After a postdoc at Emory, I took a job at the CDC, partly because their headquarters are in Atlanta. I was born and raised there, and I wanted to stay close to family and friends. Little did I know that I'd hardly spend any time in Atlanta while working for the CDC."

"Where have you been?"

"The CDC has sent me all over. I can't tell you about all of them, but I've been to Florida, Maine, Texas, and California, mostly on investigations into infectious diseases like Zika, meningitis, and giardiasis. During the last ten years, I've spent more time away from Atlanta than in it. In fact, I think I may have lost my Southern accent."

Sage smiled. "Not quite."

"Anyway, my husband didn't like all the traveling, so we went our separate ways a couple of years ago."

"I'm sorry."

"Don't be. I'm married to my work anyway. Maybe someday I'll settle down, but right now I'm having too much fun chasing bugs and diseases all around the country. How about you? Do you have anybody special in your life?"

"People say I'm married to my work too. That's probably why my relationships never seem to work out."

"You didn't answer my question. Is there anybody special?"

"Actually, there is. Adam."

"I figured as much. How long have you known him?"

"We met here at Yellowstone a little over a month ago and hit it off right away."

"He seems nice."

"He is."

"I can tell he really likes you."

"You think so?"

Whitney smiled. "I know so."

The first few hours in the lab were a flurry of activity as Whitney worked the two genetic sequencers in a highly choreographed dance. While one sequencer was analyzing a sample, she loaded a different sample into the other one. She moved back and forth between the instruments in a steady rhythm.

One after another, the two sequencers divulged their results. After each batch of genetic code was generated, Whitney uploaded it to the BLAST system to check for matches. Then she uploaded the sequences from the first time she'd processed each sample, when she'd only been looking for viruses and bacteria. The initial results were from Penny's liver. There were no archaea in either batch.

Next was Penny's blood. Once again, no archaea. Sample after sample was analyzed—over a dozen in all. There were no archaea in any of them except for the sample from her intestines, which yielded several common species of archaea known to inhabit human digestive systems, including *Methanobrevibacter smithii*. But no foreign archaea.

"Let's move on to the next victim," Whitney said.

Sage's eyes grew moist. "It seems weird to keep referring to Penny as a victim."

"You want to talk about it?"

"Actually, I do."

For the next twenty minutes, Sage filled the sterile lab with raw emotions, alternating between grief for Penny's death and embarrassment over feeling so emotional about someone she had known for only a week. Sage did almost all the talking, and Whitney proved to be a good listener.

"Can I make an observation?" Whitney asked.

"Of course."

"I think you cherish personal relationships far more than you're willing to admit."

"Maybe so. That's probably why I've fallen for Adam so quickly. But at least I've known *him* for a whole six weeks!" Sage smiled. "Thanks for listening."

"That's what friends are for."

"We are friends, aren't we?"

"Indeed we are. You okay now?"

"I am. Let's get back to work."

Sage hung back, staying out of Whitney's way as she sequenced samples from the other two Bus 4 victims. Each time, the results were the same. No foreign archaea.

JUNE 13

Just after midnight, the intercom buzzed.

"It's Gayle, Robin, and Joe. We're here to give you guys a break."

"Thanks," Whitney replied, "but Sage and I are going to see this through tonight. Enjoy the time off and get some sleep."

At 1 a.m., Whitney announced it was time for a bathroom break and a snack.

The first stop on the way out through the decontamination area was the chemical shower room.

Whitney grabbed a long-handled brush. "Here's where we decontaminate our body suits. Since there's only one showerhead in here, we have to take turns. First you stand under the shower for about forty-five seconds while your suit is completely covered with chemical disinfectant. Then I'll scrub your entire suit with this super soft brush. After that, you go back under the shower for the water-rinse phase, which takes another forty-five seconds. Then we switch places. After we're both done, we dry our suits with the towels. We don't decouple our air hoses until we're ready to head into the suit changing room. Got it?"

"I think so."

After Sage positioned herself under the shower and gave a quick thumbs-up, a soaking rain of disinfectant quickly engulfed her. Whitney motioned for her to spin around slowly, and Sage obliged, feeling a bit like she was on a rotisserie. When the disinfectant shower stopped, Whitney asked her to stand still with her arms outstretched while she scrubbed her suit. After the scrubbing, Whitney turned the water shower on and again motioned for Sage to spin around slowly. Then they switched places.

Sage copied everything Whitney had done, being especially careful as she scrubbed Whitney's suit. After Whitney was finished with the final rinse phase, they stood in the shower room for a minute or so, letting the excess water drip off their suits. Finally, they toweled themselves off.

After unhooking their air hoses, they moved into the suit room and unzipped each other's suits. Sage pulled her suit all the way down and stepped awkwardly out of both legs.

"I'm soaking wet! My suit must have leaked in the shower!" Sage started to hyperventilate.

"Calm down—your suit didn't leak. It's really hot in these suits and we all sweat a ton. Look at me."

Sage could see that Whitney was just as wet as she was. "Are you sure?"

"Yes, you're fine."

They peeled off their scrubs, gloves, and socks and tossed them in the biohazard bin. Sage shivered as she waited for Whitney to open the door to the final shower area.

After finishing their showers, scrubbing with the same bristly sponge as before, they dried off and entered the changing area where they donned a new set of green scrubs. Sage kissed her gold pendant as she put it back on. After going through the airlock and finally emerging into the BSL-2 lab, Sage immediately sprinted to the bathroom. She re-appeared a few minutes later, relief etched across her face.

"Whew, I didn't think I would make it. How do you do it?"

"You learn to hold it longer than you ever thought possible."

Sage plopped down on a cot in the corner of the lab. "I'm exhausted!"

"I told you working in a CDC lab is hard work."

"So what do you have to eat around here?"

Whitney unlocked a double cabinet at the end of the counter. Inside were all manner of snacks, including nuts, pretzels, dried fruit, cereal, protein bars, even Moon Pies and Twinkies.

"Where on earth …?"

Whitney smiled. "Can't say. It's highly classified information."

"You have anything to drink?"

"Over here." Whitney opened the smaller of two refrigerators to reveal a cache of juice, sodas, and flavored waters.

"You don't keep blood or urine samples in there, do you?"

"Not usually."

They pulled stools up to the large table in the middle of the lab and dove into their snack buffet. Sage preferred nuts and pretzels while Whitney clearly had a sweet tooth. After about twenty minutes, they got ready to head back into the BSL-4 lab.

"This is like looking for a needle in a haystack," Sage said.

"Actually, it's much worse," Whitney countered.

"How come?"

"We don't even know what the needle looks like."

* * *

By 4 a.m., Whitney and Sage got a second wind, and it was clear they were going to be up all night.

"I haven't pulled an all-nighter since grad school," Sage said. "How about you?"

"I was up all night a couple of months ago."

"What were you working on?"

"Can't tell you."

"There's a lot you can't tell me, huh?"

"I can't really say."

They both laughed.

When Sage reached into the cold storage unit for a tissue sample, she noticed something wasn't right.

"The right arm of my suit doesn't seem full anymore. It's sort of flat." She stuck out her arm. "See what I mean?"

Whitney's bulging eyes were clearly visible, even through her face shield. "You have a leak! Go to decon immediately!"

Whitney mashed the red alarm button at the entrance to the decontamination area, and the lab filled with a pulsating red light accompanied by a shrill alarm that sounded every few seconds.

Sweat stinging her eyes, Sage stumbled clumsily toward the chemical shower area. After yanking the door handle down, she felt Whitney guide her firmly through the entrance. Once inside, she bolted straight through the shower chamber, heading for the suit room so she could rip off her damaged pressure suit.

Whitney grabbed her around the waist from behind. "No, no! We have to go through every step of the decontamination process."

Sage tried to break free from Whitney's grasp. "I want to get out of here!"

"Calm down, everything's going to be fine. Get under the shower."

Everything seemed to move in slow motion. Though the chemical shower took the same amount of time as it had before, it felt like an eternity to Sage. When they switched places, she did her best to scrub Whitney's suit, but she fumbled the brush and dropped it twice. Both times Whitney retrieved it for her.

They dried off as quickly as they could with towels that Whitney grabbed from the storage bench, but when Sage reached down to dry the legs of her suit, the blood rushed to her head and she crumpled to the ground. She lay on the wet floor in a fetal position, frozen in panic, enveloped by the throbbing red light and the screeching alarm .

Whitney kneeled down next to her and shouted, "Are you okay?"

"Smmmmbh"

"Breathe. Remember to breathe."

All Sage could do was lie there, marshaling every bit of her energy just to remain conscious. With each passing second, Whitney's voice faded further into the distance. Finally, everything went blank.

* * *

"Are you all right?"

Sage could barely make out Whitney kneeling next to her. It was eerily quiet as the alarm was no longer blaring.

"Sage, are you all right?"

"What happened? How long have I been lying here?"

"About ten minutes. At first I thought you had just fainted, but then I started to worry it was something worse, so I called for the medics. They're out in the BSL-2 lab waiting for my instructions. How are you feeling?"

"I've been better, but I think I'm okay. You can let the medics go."

After Whitney told the paramedics they could leave, she turned her attention back to Sage. "Let's get you into the suit room and get these damn suits off."

Whitney helped Sage into a sitting position where she remained for a minute or so before attempting to stand up. After finally getting back on her feet she almost fell again, but Whitney held her arm as they disconnected their air hoses and walked through the door to the suit room.

Once they were out of their suits they looked for the leak in Sage's suit. Whitney found it first.

"See the tiny tear on the outside of the right elbow?"

Sage couldn't see it, but she nodded anyway.

"I know it doesn't look like much, but it's big enough to let in millions of microbes. Fortunately the positive-pressure suit operated exactly as it should, so nothing got in."

"How did I rip it?"

"No telling. Maybe you rubbed up against a sharp edge somewhere, or maybe the suit was defective. We'll probably never know."

Gayle's voice came over the intercom. "What's wrong? Is everybody okay? Robin and I got here as fast as we could, but it took us forever to get through security at the inn because of the early hour."

"Sage's suit had a tear, so I hit the alarm. She's doing fine now, and everything's under control. The paramedics were here, but I let them go. We're going to come out and take a break."

"We'll wait for you out here."

Sage's heart was still racing when she and Whitney finally emerged into the BSL-2 lab.

"You okay?" Gayle asked.

"I think so. Just shaken up a bit." Sage took a deep breath. "Whitney, I *will* be fine, won't I?"

"Of course you will."

"But what if I've been exposed to something?" Sage nervously rolled her precious pendant back and forth in her fingers.

"You weren't exposed to anything. Like I said back in decon, the positive-pressure suit worked perfectly and prevented anything from getting in through the tear."

"What if I'm infected with something and I die tomorrow?"

"I told you, you're not infected."

"Whitney's right," Gayle said. "Nothing's going to happen to you."

Sage sat down and put her head on the table. "I'm exhausted. Let's call it a night and get a fresh start tomorrow."

Whitney glanced at her watch. "It already *is* tomorrow—6:05 to be exact. You head on back to the inn. I want to keep going."

"I'll go back into the lab with you."

"Oh no you won't. Go get some rest and come back later."

"But that'll be breaking protocol. There's supposed to be two people in there at all times."

"We've broken plenty of rules already. One more won't hurt."

"I'll go into the BSL-4 lab with you," Gayle offered.

"Thanks, but I'll be fine. You and Robin take Sage back to the inn and make sure she's okay. I'll grab a snack and rest for a half hour or so, then head back into the BSL-4 lab."

Sage was still a bit unsteady as she walked slowly to the front of the lab. Just before entering the door to the changing area, she turned around to thank Whitney, but she had already disappeared back into decon.

* * *

Sage opened the door to her room as quietly as she could, but Adam and Anaya were already up.

"I've been worried sick about you," Adam said. "Did you stay up all night?"

"I did."

"You must be exhausted."

Sage slumped down next to Adam. "I am. But I'm also hungry."

"So what'd you find out?"

"Can I tell you over breakfast? I really should get something to eat."

After they made their way down to the dining hall, Sage did her best to eat, but she could barely keep her eyes open, her head bobbing down repeatedly, almost landing in her food more than once. As she poked at her eggs and toast, she offered a quick if somewhat garbled account of what had happened in the lab overnight. In her description of the elaborate decontamination process she conveniently omitted the part about being completely naked in front of Joe. She also didn't mention the tear in her pressurized body suit.

"So have you found the ... *ar-key* yet?" Adam asked.

"They're called archaea. No, not yet."

"You will. Just keep trying."

"But what if I'm wrong? What if archaea are not the culprit?"

"There's no way you're wrong. You're the smartest person I know."

Sage swiped at Adam's hand as he tried to stroke her hair. "Don't patronize me," she snapped. After a few more minutes playing with her food, she pushed her plate away and stood up. "I'm going up for a shower."

"We'll be up soon," Adam said quietly.

Half an hour later, Sage entered their room in her robe, a large white towel wound around her hair, her glasses completely fogged over. A relaxed smile spread across her face. "That was my umpteenth shower since yesterday, but this one was soooo much nicer than the others. I could have stayed in there for hours."

"I'm glad you didn't," Adam said. "It's almost time to go outside."

"I can't. I've got to get back to the lab."

"I thought you wanted to walk among the geysers again. We had so much fun yesterday."

"I'd really like to, but it'll have to wait. I've got to get back to the lab."

"C'mon outside. It'll do you good."

"I can't, Adam. Whitney needs my help."

Adam turned toward Anaya. "Will you come outside with me?"

"Sure, why not."

Adam tried Sage one more time. "Are you sure you won't come with us?"

"I'm sure. I'm just going to lie down for a second before I head back to the lab."

Sage climbed onto the bed and lay on her back, her head sinking slowly into the billowing pillow. She smiled softly at Adam as he headed out the door.

When Adam and Anaya returned to the room around eleven, invigorated by their brisk walk around the Upper Geyser Basin, they found Sage lying on top of the bed in her robe just as they had left her two hours earlier, the terry cloth towel still loosely wrapped around her hair. Even her glasses were still in place.

Adam put his finger to his lips. "Shhhh. She's asleep. Let's not wake her."

"I don't think there's any danger of that."

"Let's go to lunch early and hang out in the lobby so she can get some more rest."

* * *

When they returned to the room shortly after 2 p.m., Sage was still on the bed.

"She hasn't moved a bit," Anaya said. "She must be really exhausted."

"You think we should wake her up?" Adam whispered. "She said she has a lot of important work to do in the lab."

Without waiting for Anaya to reply, Adam gave Sage a little nudge. "Time to wake up, Sage."

She didn't move.

Adam shook her more forcefully. "Rise and shine!"

Still she didn't respond.

"I think something's wrong!" He shook her again even harder. "Sage, get up! Get up!"

Sage didn't budge.

"What do we do?" Adam gasped for air.

Anaya shouted at the top of her lungs, "Hey, roomie! Time to get up!"

Frozen with fear, Adam and Anaya stared at Sage, waiting for a response.

Still nothing.

"Do you think something happened in the lab?" Adam shrieked. "Maybe something happened!"

"See if she's breathing!"

Adam put his ear to Sage's mouth. "I can't tell! I can't tell! What do we do?"

"You start CPR, and I'll go get help!" Anaya bolted for the door.

Adam's hands were shaking as he placed them on Sage's chest. Just as he was about to start pumping ... she finally stirred.

"Okay, okay. I'm awake." Sage sat up slowly, the towel unwinding under the weight of her hair and falling across her face, dragging her glasses down onto the bed.

Adam pulled the towel away and gave her a big hug. "You really scared us! We thought something was wrong. Are you okay?"

"I'm fine. A bit groggy, but fine. What time is it?"

"Almost two fifteen."

"What? Why didn't you wake me earlier?" Sage swung her feet to the floor. "I've got to get back to the lab. I should have been there hours ago."

* * *

Sage emerged from decon into the BSL-4 lab just after three. "Hey, Whitney! Have you been here all day?"

"Almost. I went to the inn to grab some lunch and came straight back. Did you get any sleep?"

"I did, but I slept much longer than I meant to. When are *you* going to get some sleep?"

"Maybe tonight. How are you feeling?"

"Fine—I guess I wasn't infected after all."

"I knew you weren't. How'd you go through decon all by yourself?"

"I'm a fast learner. Did you go to the morning briefing?"

"And listen to the blowhards from the FBI? No thank you. I'd rather be here in the lab."

"So how's it going?"

"Same as yesterday. Lots more *Methanobrevibacter smithii* as well as some *Methanosphaera stadtmanae* in some of the intestine samples, but nothing we wouldn't expect in the human gut. And no archaea of any type anywhere else."

"You said this was going to be difficult, so we just need to keep trying."

"I know, but I'm growing more pessimistic by the hour. If there were any foreign archaea in these victims I'm pretty sure we would have found them by now."

"What if we're looking in the wrong place?" Sage asked.

"We've tested blood, urine, saliva, stomach contents, intestine contents, liver tissue, spleen tissue, heart tissue, and lung tissue. Where else could we possibly look?"

"In thermal features. After all, that's where archaea were first discovered decades ago. Maybe a previously unknown species of archaea is producing cyanide in one of the hot springs or geysers."

"How would that happen, chemically?"

"I've no idea. But maybe one of the thermal features is spitting out hydrogen cyanide as we speak."

"If that's true, why hasn't anyone died over the past few days after walking around the Upper Geyser Basin?"

"Maybe it's not one of the thermal features around here."

"But all the victims died from acute cyanide poisoning in a matter of seconds, right? So why didn't they die right next to the murderous hot spring or geyser instead of on hiking trails, in campgrounds, or on an evacuation bus thirty miles away?"

"It does sound rather absurd when you put it that way."

"Still, you may be on to something," Whitney conceded. "Maybe the archaea *are* originating in a geyser, hot spring, or other thermal feature, and then they're transported somehow into people's bodies where they produce the cyanide."

"But we still haven't found any foreign archaea in any of the bodies," Sage said.

"But if we can find a novel species of archaea in a hot spring or geyser, that could help simplify our search for that same species in the victims' bodies. One of the main problems we've encountered is that the genetic database for archaea is rather small so we're not even sure what we're looking for. Either way, I think you're right. It's time to start looking in thermal features. Let's go to the afternoon briefing and tell Monica about this so we can get some help collecting the samples."

"What time is it?" Sage asked.

"Three fifteen."

"Think we can make it?"

Whitney was already heading to decon.

* * *

FBI Classified Briefing
Yellowstone National Park Command Post
June 13 – 4:00 p.m.

As everyone was taking their usual spots around the conference table for the afternoon briefing, Whitney and Sage burst into the room, completely out of breath from their dash to Trailer 2.

"Hello ladies. Out for an afternoon jog?" Monica asked, a smile playing around her lips.

"We wish," Whitney replied. "If it's all right with you, we'd like to give our update first."

"Have you made a breakthrough?" Monica's voice rose with excitement.

"Sort of ... well, not really ... but maybe. Can I explain?"

"Go ahead."

"Yesterday evening, Sage came to me with a fascinating insight. She hypothesized that these deaths might have been caused by exposure to a new species of archaea."

"What the hell are archaea?" Gus grumbled. "Never heard of 'em."

Whitney launched into a brief primer on archaea and explained that they could, in theory, produce cyanide.

"Are any species of archaea known to produce cyanide?" Hank asked.

"None that I'm aware of," Whitney replied.

"But you think it's possible?"

"I do. As I mentioned during one of our briefings a while back, several bacteria species in the *Pseudomonas* and *Chromobacterium* genera can produce cyanide. Since archaea are similar to bacteria, I don't see why they can't produce cyanide as well."

Whitney described what she and Sage had been doing to look for foreign archaea in the victims' bodies, and she explained that a few species of archaea are common in humans, especially in the digestive track, which had complicated their search. While she was going over some of the technical details of the genetic sequencing, she could see more than one pair of eyes starting to glaze over, so she cut her explanation short and summed up.

"Keep in mind that this is all conjecture at this point. We haven't actually found any new species of archaea in any of the bodies yet, and we don't even know for sure whether any archaea can produce cyanide. But in my opinion, it's worth it to keep looking."

"Where would these archaea be coming from?" Hank asked.

"I was just about to get to that," Whitney replied. "But I think I'll let Sage take over."

Sage stood up and walked to the end of the conference room.

"Archaea are some of the oldest organisms on our planet. They've been around for about three and a half billion years. When they were first discovered a few decades ago, some scientists thought they were eukaryotes, while others thought they were more closely related to prokaryotes such as bacteria. Now, most scientists believe that archaea should be placed in their own domain."

"That's all very interesting, but that's not what I meant," Hank said. "What's the specific source of the archaea that might be responsible for all the deaths here in Yellowstone?"

"Bear with me, I'm getting to that. Archaea were first identified and described in the 1970s right here in Yellowstone. There are many different species of archaea. Some are thermophiles while others are extremophiles, and many of the thermal features in Yellowstone provide perfect environmental niches for both types of organisms. If our archaea theory is correct, the deadly microbes are most likely coming from one or more thermal features here in the park. Therefore, we believe it would be prudent to look in thermal features for previously unknown species of archaea that could possibly produce cyanide."

"Which thermal features are you talking about?"

"It could be any of them."

"How can you find out?" Monica asked.

"Actually, it's pretty simple," Whitney said. "We just need to collect water samples from the features and sequence them, just like we've been doing with the fluid and tissue samples from the victims. I suggest we start with the thermal features in the Old Faithful, Geyser Hill, and Castle-Grand groups of the Upper Geyser Basin because we know all the victims visited at least one of those areas at some point before they died. Then we move northwest though the Upper Geyser Basin. Eventually we can work our way out to other geyser basins if need be."

"Do you need any help collecting the samples?"

"We do. I can spare Robin Johnston from our lab, but it would speed things up considerably if we had a few others working with her."

"I'll assign two National Guard soldiers. Will that be enough?"

"Yes, that'll be perfect."

"When do you need them?"

"Right after this meeting."

"Done. Do you need any additional assistance in the lab? I'm sure we can bring in more experts."

"At this point more scientists wouldn't really help. Our lab is cramped enough as it is."

"Too many cooks. I understand." Monica looked around the table. "Does anyone have any questions for Whitney or Sage?"

Gus shot his hand in the air. "Have we been exposed to these things?"

Whitney paused. "I'm not sure how to answer that."

Gus raised his voice. "It's a simple yes or no question! Have we been exposed?"

"I don't know."

"But is it possible?"

"Yes."

"So what do we do now?" Ben asked.

"I think we should cancel all outdoor privileges for the time being," Sage said.

"But going outside was *your* idea," Gus said.

"I know, I know. But things have changed. It's probably safest to keep everyone inside for a while."

"Do you agree, Whitney?" Monica asked.

"I do. Besides, it'll be easier for us to collect samples from the thermal features in the Upper Geyser Basin without a bunch of people milling about."

"All right. I'll ask Maddie to draft language suspending outdoor privileges to be included in tomorrow's Daily Update."

* * *

Sage and Whitney joined the other members of the CDC team in the lab immediately after the briefing.

"So here's the plan. Sage and I are going to keep looking for archaea in tissue samples while the three of you collect and test samples from thermal features in the Upper Geyser Basin. Robin is going to collect the samples with help from a couple of National Guard soldiers. They'll bring the samples back here, and Gayle and Joe will use one of the sequencers to test them for archaea."

There was a loud knock on the outer lab door.

"Who is it?" Whitney yelled.

"National Guard soldiers reporting for specimen collection duties."

"Excellent! Let me get the door for you."

Once the two guardsmen were inside the changing area, Whitney explained the procedures for changing before entering the lab.

"What do we do with our rifles?"

"I don't know. We've never had any firearms in here before. Are they loaded?"

"Yes, ma'am."

"Why don't you unload them and put the bullets ... or magazines ... or whatever they're called ... in the drawers at the bottom of the closet. Then just lean your rifles up against the wall next to the clothes. Will that work?"

"That'll be fine as long as the outer door is locked at all times."

"It is."

When the guardsmen entered the BSL-2 lab, Sage did a double take. "Ricky! How are you?"

"Okay, I guess. I still can't believe Penny's gone."

"Me neither."

Ricky introduced Eric, the other guardsman.

Sage squinted at Eric. "Eric from the bison jam?"

"I was afraid you'd bring that up," he said sheepishly.

"What bison jam?" Ricky asked.

"I'll fill you in later," Eric said out of the corner of his mouth.

"Sage, you know both of these men?" Whitney remarked. "What a coincidence."

"Not really," Eric said. "We volunteered."

"Were you informed this could be dangerous?"

"Yes, ma'am. But yesterday I told Sage I'd return a favor she'd done for me, so here I am."

"And I'm doing this for Penny," Ricky added.

"Well, thank you. We appreciate your help."

Whitney outlined the water-collection procedures and pulled out a large USGS map of the Upper Geyser Basin that showed every thermal feature in the area. She told Robin, Ricky and Eric to start at Old Faithful and work their way northwest through the geyser basin, taking water samples from the eighty largest features in the Old Faithful, Geyser Hill, and Castle-Grand groups, including geysers, pools, and hot springs. She gave them twenty sterile vials and instructed them to return to the lab when they had collected the initial set of samples so Gayle and Joe could start analyzing them. Then they would go back out to collect the next twenty samples and keep going until they were done.

"How long will all this take?" Ricky asked.

"I'm not sure," Whitney replied. "My best guess is that you can probably get about three or four samples an hour. Just work until it's dark and then start again at first light in the morning and keep going until you're finished."

"Are we going to get sick if we stick our hands in the water?" Eric asked tentatively.

"Nobody's hands are going anywhere near any water. Many thermal features have water that's over seventy degrees Celsius, not to mention that the water might be teeming with microorganisms. You'll be using a mechanical arm to collect the samples."

Whitney went to a locked closet at the far end of the lab and pulled out a large silver and black arm-like apparatus.

"It looks a lot heavier than it really is," she said. "It's mostly aluminum and high impact plastic. This model has been used to retrieve magma samples from lava flows, so it should work very nicely here. It's a little awkward to operate, but it'll get the job done."

Whitney stuck her right hand and forearm into the plastic sleeve at the proximal end of the mechanical arm. After securing the unit to her arm, she used the controls imbedded in the sleeve to slowly move the arm up and down. Then she extended it straight out to about ten feet. At the distal end was a complex grasping device that looked a bit like a human hand with eight fingers.

"Very impressive," Ricky said. "But that won't be long enough to get samples from many of the features."

"I'm not done." All of a sudden the mechanical arm telescoped out to fifteen feet. Whitney swung the arm around, almost knocking Sage on the head. Then she backed slowly into the corner of the lab and extended the arm one more time to a full twenty-five feet. To top off the impressive display, she demonstrated how the joint connecting the last two sections of the arm could rotate 270 degrees.

"This should do the trick for most of the thermal features," Whitney said, grinning.

"But Old Faithful is at least a hundred feet from the boardwalk, maybe more," Ricky said.

"For Old Faithful and a few others you'll have to leave the boardwalk and approach them carefully. For now, it's probably good enough if you can get a sample of water from a runoff channel. If you're unsure about a particular feature, don't try to get too close. We can figure something out later."

"Be extra careful when leaving the boardwalk," Sage warned. "The fragile crust around many of the thermal features is very thin in places, and superheated water may be lurking just below the surface. You definitely don't want to fall through."

"So how do we collect the samples?" Eric asked.

"Let me show you." Whitney retracted the arm until it was about eight feet long. She rotated the grasping mechanism at the end and swiveled it downward, directly over a beaker on the counter. She grabbed the beaker and moved the arm toward Ricky. Just before he reached out to grab the beaker, the mechanical arm lost its grip and the beaker went crashing to the floor.

"Well, you get the idea," Whitney said. "I'm sure you'll get the hang of it with a little practice."

"I've got a lot of video game experience," Ricky chuckled. "This should be a breeze."

"Do we need to wear any safety gear?" Robin asked.

"All you'll need are goggles and heavy-duty gloves in case any of the water splashes up while you're collecting the samples. We've all been walking around the Upper Geyser Basin for the past few days and none of us have gotten sick or died, so you should be fine. Any other questions?"

"What exactly is this thing we're looking for?" Ricky asked. "Does it have a name?"

"No," Whitney replied. "First we have to find it."

"Who gets to name it?"

"Anyone who discovers a new species gets the scientific naming rights."

"That's all the motivation I need," Ricky said. "Let's go!"

As the three-person collection team headed outside, Sage and Whitney made their way into decon, followed by Joe and Gayle a few minutes later. While Sage was changing into her pressurized body suit, she could hear the showers in the chamber behind her. This time she didn't turn around to look.

Since the BSL-4 lab was designed for only two scientists, it was much more cramped than usual, and changing air-supply lines was a challenge in the tight quarters. Gayle suggested they work in pairs, hooking and unhooking the supply lines as they moved about the lab. With a little practice, the arrangement seemed to work well.

A little before 9 p.m., the intercom sprang to life. It was Robin, Ricky, and Eric back with the first set of samples.

"Great!" Gayle said. "Twenty samples should keep us busy for a while."

"Actually, we only got seventeen."

"What happened to the other three?"

"Ricky dropped one of the vials into Silver Spring," Robin said.

"It wasn't my fault," Ricky said in a low voice. "You bumped me while I was operating the magic arm."

"No, I didn't. You're just really clumsy."

"Magic arm?" Gayle asked.

"That's what we've been calling the mechanical arm," Robin replied. "The other two samples fell on the boardwalk while we were manipulating the magic arm."

"No worries. Seventeen will give us plenty to work with."

"Shall we go back out and get more samples?" Ricky asked.

"Sunset's in just a few minutes, so why don't you get some sleep and start back again in the morning," Gayle said.

"We're fine with that. What shall we do with these samples?"

"Just leave them on the table in the middle of the BSL-2 lab. I'll come out and get them."

"Okay. See you tomorrow."

It took Gayle almost an hour to go through decon, grab the samples, and return through decon. Back in the BSL-4 lab, she placed the samples carefully on the counter. Each vial had been marked with either the popular name of the thermal feature or the USGS numerical designation.

"Where shall we start?" Joe asked.

Gayle and Joe looked at each other and spoke in unison, "Old Faithful!"

"What if it *is* Old Faithful? What would that mean for the future of Yellowstone National Park?" Joe asked. "Would the park have to close?"

"We can't worry about that now. Let's just find the culprit, no matter which one it is."

Whitney looked over at Gayle and Joe. "We're still not finding anything in these tissue samples, so why don't you give us some of your thermal feature samples. Then we can go twice as fast. We should also test each sample for cyanide. Joe, can you do the cyanide tests for us?"

"Of course."

The next forty-five minutes went by in almost total silence as everyone focused on the task at hand.

Then Gayle announced the first sequencing results. "There's no archaea in the Old Faithful sample."

"No cyanide either," Joe added.

"I know it sounds weird, but I'm kind of glad it wasn't Old Faithful," Gayle said.

"Me too," Sage agreed from across the lab.

The next three vials were from the thermal features closest to Old Faithful—Split Cone, Teapot Geyser, and Blue Star Spring. Whitney and Sage worked on the samples from Split Cone and Blue Star Spring while Gayle worked on the one from Teapot Geyser. Joe continued to run cyanide tests for all the samples.

The Split Cone and Teapot Geyser samples were negative for both archaea and cyanide.

Finally they struck pay dirt—the sample from Blue Star Spring contained archaea. Unfortunately, it turned out to be *Sulfolobus acidocaldarius*, the most common species of archaea in Yellowstone.

"Joe, what about the cyanide test for Blue Star?" Whitney asked.

"Just finished. It's negative."

"So, does anybody think this is our killer?"

No one did.

When Gayle began to prepare the fifth sample—from Chinese Spring—she fumbled the vial, almost dropping it to the floor. "Whoaa, that was close!"

"What was close?" Whitney didn't bother to look up from her own work.

"It's not important," Joe said.

"Actually, it *is* important," Gayle admitted. "I almost dropped a vial."

Whitney's head shot up. "What if it was a sample that contained a lethal species of archaea? You could have contaminated the entire lab!"

"I'm really tired," Gayle said. "I'll slow down and be more careful from now on."

"I'm tired too," Whitney said. "How about we close up shop and get a good night's sleep?"

No one objected.

JUNE 14

Adam had already been up for a couple of hours when he decided to wake Sage. He sat on the bed and shook her gently. This time she responded right away, pulling the pillow over her head.

"You okay?"

Sage rolled halfway across the bed but kept the pillow over her face.

"Wanna get some breakfast?"

Sage pushed the pillow away. "What time is it?"

"Almost nine."

"I don't remember getting into bed. I don't even remember walking back from the lab."

"You conked out as soon as you got back last night. You must have been exhausted."

Sage slowly kicked the covers off. "I'm still in my clothes!"

"Like I said, you were exhausted."

"And now I'm really hungry. Have you guys eaten already?"

"No, I waited for you," Adam replied.

"I didn't." Anaya was on the other bed reading *The Andromeda Strain.*

"How are you guys feeling?" Sage asked.

"About as good as hostages can be," Anaya snipped.

"I'm feeling fine," Adam said. "Why do you ask?"

"No reason. I just want to make sure you're okay."

Adam gave Sage a hug. "I really missed you last evening."

"Me too. But I was really busy with lab work and couldn't get away."

"That's what I figured. You'll have plenty of time to do your lab work today since we can't go outside anymore."

"The Daily Update came?"

"Yeah, it was already here when I woke up. Wanna see it?"

THE YELLOWSTONE DIRECTIVE
DAILY UPDATE
JUNE 14

THERE HAVE BEEN NO NEW FATALITIES DURING THE PAST 24 HOURS.

DUE TO SOME TECHNICAL PROBLEMS WITH THE SECURITY SCANNERS IN THE OLD FAITHFUL INN, OUTDOOR PRIVILEGES WILL BE SUSPENDED UNTIL FURTHER NOTICE. THERE IS NO ESTIMATE AS TO HOW LONG IT WILL TAKE TO IMPLEMENT THE NECESSARY REPAIRS.

ANY RESIDENT WHO VIOLATES ANY TERMS OF THE YELLOWSTONE DIRECTIVE WILL BE SUBJECT TO IMMEDIATE ARREST.

"They lied!" Sage exclaimed.

"Who lied?" Anaya asked.

"The FBI. The security scanners are fine. That's not why we can't go outside."

"So what's the real reason?"

"Actually, it was my idea."

"Surprise, surprise," Anaya said glumly. "You managed to take away the only fun thing around here."

"Hear me out. We haven't had any luck finding archaea in the victims' bodies so we decided to change tactics and look for them at their source."

"Geysers and hot springs?" Adam asked.

"Exactly. The sample collection process is a little tricky, so we thought it'd be best if everyone stayed inside while we collected the samples."

"How long will that take?" Anaya asked.

"We should be done by today or tomorrow."

"And then can we go outside again?"

"I guess so—unless we find something."

"You mean archaea?"

"Yes."

"If you do find archaea, then what?"

"We'll see if we can find the same species in the victims' bodies."

"Are you saying that we've *all* been exposed to these things?" Anaya's voice rose.

"That's not what I'm saying."

"But it's possible?"

"Anything's possible."

"You should have been an attorney," Anaya snapped.

* * *

The mood in the dining hall at breakfast was surly, even belligerent. The happy, lighthearted chatter of the past two days had been replaced by dejection and pessimism.

Anaya's sour demeanor fit right in. "You know when your mother finally lets you stay out past midnight for the first time, and then the next weekend she decides to move your curfew back to eleven?"

"Uh, not really," Sage said.

"Well, that's what this is like, only much worse. We had a tiny taste of freedom and now it's been ripped away from us. And all because of you."

"Don't you want to get out of here?"

"Of course I do!"

"Well, they're not going to let us leave until they figure out what's going on. So we might as well do everything we can to help them."

"And what if they never figure it out?"

* * *

When Sage arrived at the lab at ten, Gayle and Joe were already hard at work.

"Sorry I'm late, guys."

"No worries," Gayle said. "You didn't miss anything. Joe and I just finished the rest of the samples from last night and we didn't find anything of interest. There was more *Sulfolobus acidocaldarius*, as well as some *Picrophilus torridus*, which is a thermoacidophilic species of archaea, but nothing else. Certainly nothing exotic that we haven't seen before. And nothing that could produce cyanide."

"How do you know that for sure?"

"I guess we don't, but there's been no cyanide in any of the samples. Not even a trace."

"Now what?"

"We're waiting for the second batch of samples. Robin, Ricky, and Eric started just after dawn, so they should be here soon."

"Where's Whitney?"

"Probably getting some well-deserved rest. She's hardly slept at all the past couple of days."

A few minutes before eleven, the collection team delivered the second batch of samples from the thermal features in the Upper Geyser Basin. This time there were no problems with the magic arm, and they arrived with all twenty-three vials intact. As they were placing them on the counter in the BSL-2 lab, Whitney showed up, and she brought the samples back with her into the BSL-4 lab while Robin, Ricky, and Eric headed out to collect the next batch.

When Whitney emerged into the BSL-4 lab, Gayle greeted her with a smile. "Hey, sleepyhead!"

"Just get back to work, okay? I was exhausted."

"Just kidding, boss."

Whitney winced. "I know. Sorry I snapped."

They settled in to analyze the new batch of samples, Sage working with Whitney and Gayle with Joe. They all had the procedures down pat by now.

Place a small portion of the sample into a sterile analysis container.

Insert the container into the receptacle in one of the automatic genetic sequencers.

Wait for the sequencer to do its thing.

Upload the results to BLAST to look for matches in the NCBI database for archaea.

Test a portion of the same sample for cyanide.

Repeat with the next sample.

By 2:55 p.m. they were almost halfway through the second batch of samples, and there was nothing new. No foreign or novel species of archaea. No cyanide.

Whitney called for a snack break. After everyone made their way through decon and collected their munchies, they gathered around the table in the middle of the BSL-2 lab.

"This is really discouraging," Gayle said.

"It is, but we've got to keep trying," Whitney said. "The next sample might be the one."

* * *

Robin, Ricky, and Eric brought the third set of twenty samples back at four o'clock and then the final set at nine, right before sunset. Exhausted, the three of them returned to the Old Faithful Inn for the night.

Whitney, Sage, Gayle, and Joe tested each sample for archaea and cyanide. Other than a brief break for dinner, they worked straight through the afternoon and into the night.

For each sample, the results were the same: no foreign or novel species of archaea and no cyanide.

"Twelve samples left," Whitney said at eleven thirty. "Let's meet back here in the morning to finish these up."

JUNE 15

Whitney arrived at the lab just after dawn, followed closely by Sage, Gayle, and Joe. The team resumed their analyses of the remaining samples and by nine they were done.

A total of eighty samples had yielded seven positive results for archaea. Four samples contained *Sulfolobus acidocaldarius* and three contained *Picrophilus torridus*. But no novel or foreign species of archaea. And no cyanide.

"What now?" Gayle asked.

Whitney replied with as much enthusiasm as she could muster. "We keep looking."

"Why don't we finish our paperwork and call it a day," Gayle suggested. "We could all use a break."

Whitney agreed. "And I think Sage and I should attend the morning FBI briefing. We missed both of them yesterday and we need to know what's going on."

* * *

FBI CLASSIFIED BRIEFING
YELLOWSTONE NATIONAL PARK COMMAND POST
JUNE 15 – 10:00 A.M.

Sage started up before everyone had settled into their seats. "Monica, why did you lie in the Daily Update yesterday?"

"About what?"

"About the reason people are no longer allowed to go outside."

"I didn't want to cause a panic."

"Don't you think everyone deserves the truth after being locked up for over two weeks?"

"There's no need to worry people unnecessarily."

"Unnecessarily? First everyone can go outside and now they can't. Don't you think they're already worried?"

Gus smirked. "It was *your* idea to let people go outside in the first place."

"I thought it would do everyone good," Sage snapped.

"And it was also *your* idea to revoke those very same privileges."

"True, but I still think people deserve an honest explanation."

"Let's move on," Monica said. "I understand we had another fatality this morning, but this new death appears to be unrelated to the others. Can you fill us in, Hank?"

"The details are still a little sketchy, but here's what we know so far. The new fatality is Ronald Brinkley, a seventy-six-year-old male who was on vacation with his seventy-three-year-old wife Ada. This morning was their fiftieth wedding anniversary, and they wanted to watch Old Faithful erupt, just like they did when Mr. Brinkley proposed to his wife half a century ago. At dawn this morning they headed out of the Old Faithful Inn to walk around Geyser Hill. They were stopped at the front door by National Guardsman Mark Ridley, who informed them that residents were no longer allowed outside. But the Brinkleys told him their story and pleaded with him to let them celebrate their anniversary watching Old Faithful. Guardsman Ridley eventually gave in and let them go outside on the condition that they would only walk around for an hour and then come back in.

"From his post at the entrance of the Old Faithful Inn, Guardsman Ridley kept an eye on the couple as they walked among the geysers and hot springs. After a few minutes, Old Faithful started to erupt, which diverted Ridley's attention. When he looked back, he could see Mr. Brinkley down on one knee facing his wife, as if he were proposing. They were in the middle of Geyser Hill, a couple of hundred yards or so northwest of Old Faithful.

"After Old Faithful's eruption was over, Guardsman Ridley proceeded on his usual patrol route along the boardwalk that curves around Old Faithful toward the Old Faithful Lodge. About thirty minutes later, he heard screaming from the parking lot in front of the Old Faithful Inn. He raced back and found Ada Brinkley kneeling over her husband, who was lying face down in the parking lot. She was screaming that he'd had a heart attack. Guardsman Ridley called for medical assistance and started CPR. When the medics arrived, they took over the CPR but eventually gave up, indicating that Mr. Brinkley was already deceased. Mr. and Mrs. Brinkley were transported by ambulance to the Old Faithful Clinic.

"A short time later, Ada Brinkley was interviewed by FBI investigators. She told them that while Old Faithful was erupting, her husband got down on one knee and reenacted his proposal in honor of their fiftieth wedding anniversary. After a quick kiss on the boardwalk, they walked around Geyser Hill for about a half hour before heading back to the Old Faithful Inn. Everything seemed fine until they got to the parking lot, when her husband starting gasping for air. He fell to his knees and then lurched forward onto the asphalt. She knew right away it was a heart attack because he'd had one about a year ago. He'd told her before this trip that he hadn't been feeling well, but he was determined to come to Yellowstone to renew their vows in front of Old Faithful.

"Guardsman Ridley's account matched Mrs. Brinkley's in almost every detail. He confirmed that there were no other people on Geyser Hill while the couple was walking around, and he didn't see anyone approach them at any time while they were outside.

"We've also reviewed video from the security camera that faces the parking lot from a position above the front door of the Old Faithful Inn, but it's not very helpful. You can just make out Mr. Brinkley falling to his knees, but the view is largely obscured by trees in the parking area."

Monica was irate. "Dominick, I thought we had one hundred percent coverage of all areas in Old Faithful Village!"

"So did I. I'll look into it right away."

Hank closed his notebook. "Ada Brinkley requested that her husband's body be flown back to their home in Indiana for services and burial. Since his death is not related to any of the others, we granted her request. A local funeral parlor will be transporting Mr. Brinkley's body, along with Mrs. Brinkley, to the airport sometime this evening."

"Has an autopsy been conducted?" Monica asked.

"No. Mrs. Brinkley refused to agree to an autopsy."

"I'd feel more comfortable if we could conduct one before his body leaves Yellowstone. Can you try again to see if Mrs. Brinkley will consent to one?"

"I'll do my best."

Monica continued. "The good news is that there have been no new deaths other than Mr. Brinkley. Almost all residents took advantage of the relaxed rules and went outside at least once, and no one died."

"That *is* good news," Ben agreed.

"That brings me to the next report. As you know, we've been holding press briefings every day since the evacuation."

"I *didn't* know that," Ben complained. "Why wasn't I told about these?"

"That was Maddie's call."

"I demand to be present at the next one."

"I'll relay your request to Maddie. Anyway, she informed me that the briefings haven't been going particularly well. The reporters have been getting more aggressive and more critical about the lack of information every day."

"Can you blame them?" Sage said. "We've been here for over two weeks and nobody knows anything."

Monica ignored Sage. "Maddie said that numerous media outlets have been demanding access to the park so they can report firsthand on the situation here."

Sage was livid. "Is that what you're calling this? A *situation*?"

Monica and Sage went back and forth for a good fifteen minutes discussing how much information should be provided to the press. Neither budged an inch.

Finally, Monica changed the subject. "Despite repeated efforts by the media to gain access to the lockdown area, the security situation is generally under control. Although there has been at least one drone intrusion every day, all have been successfully intercepted. While some of the UAVs have been quite small, others have had wingspans of fifteen feet or more. Most have been dispatched by news organizations, but an increasing number appear to be from private citizens trying to get pictures of our installation to post online."

"Maybe we should start holding up large signs for the drones," Sage bristled. "You know, explaining what's *really* going on here. Pictures of those would definitely go viral."

Monica continued. "A few people have tried to enter the park on foot, but they've all been apprehended within a couple of miles of the park border. Two reporters tried to sneak in by concealing themselves in the cargo area of a food delivery truck, but they were arrested as soon as they were discovered."

"Where was that?" Sage asked.

"Just behind the Old Faithful Inn when the delivery truck was opened for unloading."

"When did this occur?"

"About seven this morning."

Sage tried to revisit the discussion about providing more information to the press, but Monica would have none of it. "Let's move on, shall we? Whitney, have you found archaea in any thermal features?"

"We've identified two well-known archaea species—*Sulfolobus acidocaldarius* and *Picrophilus torridus*—in several features, but they've both been studied extensively and are not harmful to humans in any way. And they certainly don't produce cyanide."

"Have you found any *new* species of archaea?"

"No, but we're still looking."

Gus scowled. "I think Sage was completely wrong about this archaea thing. I suggest we stop this foolishness and focus our resources on finding the killer."

"And what exactly do you propose we do?" Monica asked.

"Interview everyone again," Gus replied. "Use polygraphs. Something. Anything."

"That sounds *really* scientific," Sage taunted.

"Oh yeah? Well, you've led us down one dead-end path after another. And for what? We've wasted a whole lot of time and we're no closer to finding the killer. How about we try it my way for once?"

"You can go to hell!"

"What did you say?" Gus stood up, his face beet red.

Sage stood up too. "Don't make me say it again!"

"Sit down, both of you!" Monica shouted. "I know we're all extremely frustrated, but let's at least try to be civil with one another. Does anyone have anything else? If not, I think we're done."

Sage spoke up. "Would you be willing to reconsider my request to return everyone's electronic devices? Now that people can't go outside anymore, they're getting really agitated."

"I've noticed that too," Monica said. "Let's go around the table and see what everyone thinks. Gus?"

"I think it's a terrible idea."

"Why?"

"I just do."

"I agree with Gus," Dominick said.

"Hank?"

"I think it's a good idea for the reasons Sage gave. And since we've blocked all electronic access into and out of the park— Internet, social media, e-mail, phone calls, texts, everything— there's virtually no risk of any information getting out."

"Whitney, what do you think?"

"I can't think of any reason not to return them. There aren't any medical risks associated with using electronic devices, and there are clear psychological benefits that will result from letting people use their devices to listen to music, play games, and watch movies. I'm in favor of returning them."

"How about you Ben?"

"If Sage and Whitney are fine with returning them, that's good enough for me."

"Okay, it looks like we've reached a consensus on this, except for Gus and Dominick, so I'm willing to return the electronic devices tomorrow morning."

"Let's do it tonight," Sage pleaded.

Just then, the trailer rattled for several seconds. The water in Sage's cup sloshed gently from side to side and several pencils rolled off the conference table. Though most everyone took the aftershock in stride, Gus's knuckles turned white as he gripped the arms of his chair tightly and let out a quick groan.

Monica smiled. "It seems as if Sage has control over the seismic activity here at Yellowstone, so we better do what she says. I'll order that all electronic devices be returned to the residents this evening."

* * *

As Sage, Adam, and Anaya walked into the dining room for lunch, they saw the announcement posted on both sides of the doorway.

THE YELLOWSTONE DIRECTIVE
SUPPLEMENTAL UPDATE
JUNE 15

ALL PERSONAL ELECTRONIC DEVICES WILL BE RETURNED IN THE LOBBY OF THE OLD FAITHFUL INN AT 9:30 THIS EVENING. RESIDENTS MUST BRING THEIR RECEIPTS TO CLAIM THEIR DEVICES.

ALL FORMS OF ELECTRONIC COMMUNICATION INTO AND OUT OF YELLOWSTONE NATIONAL PARK HAVE BEEN BLOCKED, SO IT WILL NOT BE POSSIBLE TO MAKE PHONE CALLS OR SEND E-MAILS OR TEXTS OR USE ANY TYPE OF SOCIAL MEDIA. THERE WILL BE NO INTERNET ACCESS WHATSOEVER. HOWEVER, RESIDENTS WILL BE ABLE TO LISTEN TO MUSIC, PLAY GAMES, AND VIEW PHOTOS, VIDEOS, AND MOVIES STORED ON THEIR DEVICES.

"What fun is that?" Adam said. "I want to call my mom."

Anaya slapped her forehead. "Haven't you guys got it by now? We're in a prison camp, plain and simple. This is their way of placating us so we don't stage an uprising."

* * *

The return of the electronic devices didn't start until almost 10:30 p.m. It was more than an hour after that when Adam, Anaya, and Sage finally got theirs back.

Adam cradled his phone and laptop against his chest. "I really wanted to call my mom, but at least I can listen to some music. What are you two going to do first?"

"Read," Anaya replied.

"Sleep," Sage said.

When they got back to their room, Sage turned on her laptop and instinctively tried to check her e-mail. "Damn! I forgot there's no Internet. What good is this thing if I can't check my e-mail?"

She tossed her laptop on the chair and plopped down on the bed next to Adam. While Anaya browsed her Kindle library on her iPad, Adam cued up his Mariah Carey playlist on his phone.

"Really?" Sage said. "We haven't had any music for over two weeks and that's what you're going to listen to?"

"Sure. Why not?"

"I may have to rethink our relationship."

Adam grinned. "What relationship?"

"Can you at least put on headphones or something so I can get some sleep?"

"I don't have any. Hey, Anaya, you have any headphones I can borrow?"

"I've got earbuds, but there's no way you're borrowing them— that would be gross."

Adam turned off his phone and snuggled next to Sage. They talked softly for a few minutes until they both fell asleep.

JUNE 16

The pounding on the door woke Sage with a start. She stared at her alarm clock until the numbers came into focus.

"Go away! It's only five a.m."

"It's Whitney! It's an emergency!"

Sage stumbled out of bed and opened the door. "What is it?"

"There've been three new deaths overnight! We've been ordered to attend an emergency briefing right now."

Suddenly wide wake, Sage pulled on some clothes, and Whitney handed her a surgical facemask.

"What's this for?"

"Just in case. Put it on."

They jogged to Trailer 2, arriving at the same time as Ben.

* * *

FBI Classified Briefing
Yellowstone National Park Command Post
June 16 – 5:15 a.m.

Monica started right in.

"As you all know by now, there have been three new deaths in the last few hours. On Whitney's advice, I'm ordering that all residents be quarantined, effective immediately. Everyone will be confined to their rooms and only allowed to leave to eat and use the restroom if they don't have a private bathroom. An emergency update is being circulated to all residents as we speak. Take a moment to look at it."

Monica sent copies of the announcement around the table.

THE YELLOWSTONE DIRECTIVE
EMERGENCY UPDATE
JUNE 16

DUE TO THREE NEW FATALITIES THAT OCCURRED OVERNIGHT, A FULL QUARANTINE HAS BEEN INSTITUTED FOR EVERYONE IN YELLOWSTONE.

ALL RESIDENTS ARE CONFINED TO THEIR ROOMS IN THE OLD FAITHFUL INN EFFECTIVE IMMEDIATELY.

RESIDENTS WILL ONLY BE ALLOWED TO LEAVE THEIR ROOMS TO EAT MEALS IN THE DINING ROOM AND TO USE THE PUBLIC RESTROOMS IF THEIR ROOM DOES NOT HAVE A PRIVATE BATHROOM.

RESIDENTS WILL NOT BE ALLOWED TO LEAVE THEIR ROOMS FOR ANY OTHER REASON.

AS AN ADDED SAFETY PRECAUTION, RESIDENTS ARE ORDERED TO WEAR SURGICAL FACEMASKS AT ALL TIMES, REMOVING THEM ONLY TO EAT, SHOWER, OR ENGAGE IN OTHER PERSONAL HYGIENE ACTIVITIES.

RESIDENTS ARE PROHIBITED FROM HAVING ANY PHYSICAL CONTACT WITH OTHER RESIDENTS, INCLUDING ROOMMATES. THIS INCLUDES TOUCHING, HUGGING, KISSING, HOLDING HANDS, OR ANY OTHER PERSONAL CONTACT.

THE QUARANTINE WILL ALSO APPLY TO ALL FBI AND NATIONAL GUARD PERSONNEL HOUSED IN THE TEMPORARY BARRACKS.

THESE QUARANTINE REGULATIONS WILL BE STRICTLY ENFORCED, AND ANY VIOLATIONS WILL BE PUNISHED SWIFTLY AND SEVERELY.

AT THIS TIME THERE IS NO ESTIMATE AS TO HOW LONG THE QUARANTINE WILL BE IN EFFECT.

"Everyone—and I mean everyone—must wear facemasks at all times, even in your rooms," Monica ordered. "Whitney brought facemasks for all of us. Put them on now."

The light blue surgical facemasks covered the mouth and nose and were secured by thin elastic bands that looped around each ear. Everyone quickly put one on.

"Why the facemasks?" Hank asked, rolling his watch around his wrist more rapidly than usual.

"In case it's contagious," Whitney replied.

"But I thought cyanide poisoning wasn't contagious."

"It's not. But if a microbe is producing the cyanide, it's possible that the microbe could be transmitted from person to person. Up until now, I thought the chance of human-to-human transmission was negligible because no one had died since the aborted evacuation eleven days ago. But these new deaths have changed everything. That's why I've recommended a full quarantine for all residents immediately."

"I thought this microbe was coming from some sort of thermal feature or animal, not from other humans," Hank said.

"That's our hypothesis about the *source* of the microbe, but once it has jumped to humans it could be contagious. Lots of zoonotic diseases are highly contagious."

"Zoonotic?"

"Diseases that jump from animals to humans."

"Like Ebola?" Hank asked.

"Yes. Also, the H1N1 virus."

"The what virus?"

"The Swine flu."

Whitney took a breath and continued. "Bacteria and viruses can spread among humans in many ways, including direct contact through kissing, sexual activity, or touching, droplet transmission from coughing or sneezing, airborne transmission, or even by touching contaminated surfaces such as counters and glassware. Of course, not all microbes can be transmitted in all these ways. The facemasks won't completely prevent human-to-human transmission, but they'll help. And if we limit all physical contact with other people, that should help too. Obviously we're dealing with a lot of unknowns here."

"How many facemasks do you have on site, Whitney?" Monica asked.

"Five cases with four hundred each. That should be enough for four masks for each person in the village. I'll make them available right after this meeting."

Sage shuddered as she glanced around the conference room. FBI agents were usually cocky and confident, but the eyes that peeked out above the facemasks in Trailer 2 revealed nothing but fear.

Queries flew from every corner of the conference room.

"What happened?"

"Why are people dying again?"

"Are we all going to die?"

"Settle down everyone," Monica said firmly. "There's no need to panic yet."

Gus's voice cracked. "Yet? I think it might be a bit late for that."

"Hank, tell us what you know so far," Monica said.

"At about one this morning, Marcia Pippen, a member of the kitchen staff, ran into the lobby screaming about her roommate. Two guardsmen raced to her room and called for medical assistance. When they arrived at Room 134, a Caucasian female was on the floor in full arrest. She was unconscious, unresponsive, and had no pulse. The guardsmen started CPR immediately and continued until medics took over about a minute later. One of the medics began an IV administration of the antidote from a Cyanokit. The female was transported to the Old Faithful Clinic where she was pronounced dead at one forty-five. Two FBI investigators interviewed Ms. Pippen at approximately two thirty. She told them that she had been awakened by her roommate who was making gravelly, gasping noises. Within moments, her roommate had lurched forward and dropped to the floor where she convulsed for a few seconds before becoming absolutely still. Ms. Pippen didn't know what to do, so she ran to the front desk for help."

"Sounds a lot like the deaths on the evacuation bus," Sage said.

Hank went on. "We were also notified about two other deaths that occurred sometime between two thirty and four this morning. My understanding is that both victims were found unresponsive in their beds by their roommates, one here in the Old Faithful Inn and the other in the temporary barracks housing the FBI and National Guard. We don't have an exact time of death yet since both incidents are still being investigated. I learned their identities right before coming to this briefing. One was a private contractor hired to work on electrical systems here in the village."

"And the other?" Monica asked.

"Dr. Walter Arnold, our profiler."

Gus gasped.

"I thought he'd left Yellowstone when he stopped coming to these briefings," Sage said.

"No, he was stuck here just like the rest of us," Gus said.

Monica turned to Hank. "Do we have any autopsy results on the new victims?"

"Not yet. They won't be available until later today at the earliest, but these new deaths look a lot like all the rest."

"We don't know for sure that it's cyanide poisoning this time," Gus said. "Maybe our killer has switched poisons."

"Are you still holding on to your sex killer theory?" Sage asked incredulously.

A National Guardsman burst into the conference room and handed a note to Monica. She scanned the folded piece of paper and looked up.

"Two more deaths have been reported in the last hour. That makes five this morning. One was a five-year-old boy."

"Calvin?" Sage screamed. "Was it Calvin?"

Monica looked at the note again to make sure. "I'm afraid it was."

"He was my buddy! His sixth birthday was in a couple of days!" Sage buried her head in her hands and pounded the table with her elbows. "He wanted to go to the beach for his birthday!"

Now even Monica started to panic. "Whitney, what the hell is going on?"

"I wish I knew."

Monica prodded Whitney again, her voice laced with fear.

"Tell me what you think is *really* going on. Not some watered-down official CDC statement. Just your honest, unvarnished, personal opinion."

Whitney straightened the papers in front of her into a neat pile, running her fingers carefully along all four edges.

"Whitney?"

Whitney cleared her throat and stared down at the stack of papers. "In view of these recent deaths, it's possible we're dealing with a brand new disease—one that's highly contagious and extremely lethal. In the best case scenario, we could lose a lot more people here in Yellowstone."

"And the worst case?"

Whitney took a deep breath and looked around the table. "If this thing somehow gets out of Yellowstone, we could be witnessing the beginnings of a global pandemic."

* * *

Sage had grabbed some extra facemasks from Whitney's supply before racing out of the briefing, and she handed them to Adam and Anaya as soon as she got back to the room. She didn't need to ask if they had read the Emergency Update—she could see it in their eyes. She told them everything she had learned in the briefing, her words spilling out uncontrollably. When she got to the part about Calvin, she buried her head under the pillow on her bed.

"I don't understand why people are dying *now*," Adam said. "If there really are archaea or some other poisonous microbes outside somewhere, why didn't we all die yesterday? Or the day before that?"

Sage sat up slowly, clutching the pillow to her chest. "Nobody knows. We don't even know if these new deaths were caused by cyanide poisoning. The autopsies haven't been done yet."

Adam began to shake. "This is it. We're actually going to die! All along I've been assuming that everything was going to turn out okay and we'd get to go home, but I was wrong. We're never going home!"

Adam's voice quivered as he looked at Sage. "I want to hold you, but the update said we shouldn't touch anyone."

"To hell with the update!" Sage said, throwing her arms around Adam and holding on tight.

* * *

Breakfast in the dining hall was miserable. No one spoke as they collected their food from the Spartan buffet tables. Packaged cookies and chips, small containers of yogurt, and bottles of water—that was it. No eggs, no muffins, no fruit. Only food that had been prepared and sealed off-site. The dining hall had become a giant vending machine.

Sage spotted Calvin's family at a table in the far corner of the room. They were all crying, and his mom was wailing uncontrollably. Sage wanted to go over and tell them how sorry she was for their loss, but for some reason she couldn't move. Frozen in place, she shared their grief from afar.

Everyone wore facemasks, even the National Guard soldiers. Sage looked around to see how people were managing to eat. Some had lowered their masks to their chin, a few had put them on their foreheads, while others had taken them off altogether. Sage opted for the chin position and furtively held Adam's hand under the table as she tried to make small talk about the weather. They did their best to pretend that everything was normal as they ate their yogurt and Fritos. But things were far from normal.

Suddenly a blood-curdling scream filled the dining room.

"Liz is dead! She just dropped to the floor. She's dead! She's dead!"

Sage looked toward the buffet table on the far side of the room and saw people gathering around a young woman lying on the ground.

"Get away!" someone yelled.

"What if she's contagious?"

"We could all die!"

As quickly as it had formed, the crowd dispersed, some people pushing and shoving to move away from the motionless woman.

"Somebody's got to help her!"

Sage rushed over to the woman and knelt down, hesitating before touching her. Just as Sage leaned in to see if she was breathing, the woman blinked a couple of times.

"She's alive!" Sage shouted.

A doctor and two nurses arrived just after Sage. As they huddled around the woman, Sage backed away to give them space. After a few minutes, the doctor stood up, pulled her facemask down, and addressed the crowd in the dining hall.

"It appears Ms. Williams simply fainted. I encourage all of you to finish your breakfast so the same doesn't happen to you."

Despite the doctor's assurances, the dining room emptied as most people headed straight back to their rooms.

Sage approached the doctor to thank her for her quick action. "My name's Sage."

"I'm Easton Blake."

"I don't think I've seen you before. When did you get here?"

"About four days ago. I've been working in the Old Faithful Clinic."

Sage rejoined her friends, and they all left the dining room with Ricky, who had been assigned as Sage's personal escort to ensure her ability to move about freely. Out in the lobby they saw two guardsmen carrying a sheet-covered stretcher. An arm fell out from beneath the sheet and bounced gently as the guardsmen made their way through the lobby. Everyone stared in silence.

Anaya sobbed quietly as they walked to their room. Sage tried to comfort her, but Anaya pushed her away.

Back in their tiny room, the three friends retreated into their own separate worlds—Anaya on one bed, Adam on the other, and Sage lying on the floor, her head cushioned by a pile of dirty clothes. Everyone needed comforting, but no one was up to the task. Instead, they all lay quietly, lost in their own desperate thoughts about what was going to happen.

I don't blame Anaya for giving up, Sage thought. *I'm ready to give up too. No matter how hard we've tried, we haven't found any poisonous archaea anywhere. Penny, Calvin, and so many other people are dead and nobody knows what the hell is going on. I'm so numb I don't even know if I care anymore.*

At 11:40, Whitney entered their room without knocking. "Monica's scheduled another emergency briefing at noon."

"You head on over," Sage said. "I'll meet you there."

She pulled herself up off the floor, splashed some water on her face, and got ready to go to the briefing.

"You feel any better?" Adam asked tentatively.

"Not at all. I'll probably go to the lab right after the briefing, and I have no idea when I'll be back. You two stay in the room while I'm gone. I don't want either of you getting sick."

"We'll be safe here," Adam said. "It's you I'm worried about, working in that lab with all those microbes."

"I'll be fine." Sage pulled her hair back in a loose ponytail and adjusted her facemask while Adam cranked up Mariah Carey on his phone. Anaya threw her earbuds at Adam, hitting him square in the face.

"I guess you can use these if you want."

"Thanks." Adam put the earbuds in, lay back on the bed, and closed his eyes.

Before heading out the door, Sage pulled her facemask down, then Adam's too. He opened his eyes and smiled. As she leaned in to kiss him lightly on the lips, she could hear "Emotions" emanating from the earbuds.

* * *

FBI Classified Briefing
Yellowstone National Park Command Post
June 16 – 12:00 p.m.

"Many of you have probably heard the news by now," Monica said, speaking solemnly through her facemask. "There have been seven more deaths since we met this morning. That makes a total of twelve today."

Sage could see that she wasn't the only one who hadn't heard the horrific news.

Monica continued, speaking deliberately. "At this point, I think it would be prudent to suspend all press releases and press briefings until we get a handle on what's going on. We'll issue a brief written statement today explaining that in order to protect the integrity of our investigation, all press communications will be temporarily suspended until further notice."

Even Sage didn't object to the new policy.

Monica drew a deep breath and steadied herself. "One of the new fatalities was Dominick Pagano, who passed away in his room this morning after our briefing."

Gus was stunned. "D-d-dominick? He and I disagreed about lots of things, but I really did like him."

"We all did. Let's take a few moments to remember our colleague."

Everyone sat in silence, eyes down; a few people sniffled. Sage looked up and saw Gus crying. She thought about trying to comfort him but decided against it.

After a few minutes, Monica cleared her throat. "Unfortunately, some of the other fatalities may be familiar names too. One was Kurt Becker, a park ranger, and another was a National Guardsman named Eric Thelin. Did anyone know them?"

Sage gasped. "I knew them both! Kurt was my trainer when I first got here, and Eric was one of the guardsmen helping us collect samples from the thermal features. I can't believe this is all happening. When did Eric die?"

Monica looked down at her notes. "About ten this morning."

Sage turned to Whitney. "Do you think he was exposed to archaea while collecting our samples?"

"Maybe, but there's no way to know for sure."

"But I thought you hadn't found any of this so-called archaea," Gus said sharply, anger creeping into his voice.

"We haven't—at least not yet," Whitney replied evenly.

Surprising even herself, Sage sided with Gus. "I hear you Gus. I'm starting to doubt my archaea theory too."

Ben leaned forward in his chair and cleared his throat. "There's another possible explanation, although it may seem a bit weird."

"Nothing's too weird at this point," Whitney said.

"Maybe it's not archaea at all. Maybe all the deaths have something to do with people's electronic devices."

Sage looked at Ben. "How?"

"I don't know, but the new deaths occurred right after everyone got their electronics back last night. I don't think that's a coincidence."

"But what about the first eleven victims?"

"Maybe they had electronic devices with them when they died. If I remember correctly, they were all quite young. Maybe they all had a phone or music device or something else."

"And what about the three people who died on the evacuation bus? They didn't have any personal electronics."

"I hadn't thought about that." Ben paused and looked at the ceiling. "But maybe there was some sort of electronic system on the bus that had the same effect."

"But how could electronic devices kill all these people?" Monica asked.

"I don't know. Maybe the electronics were programmed to kill somehow."

"By a serial killer!" Gus exclaimed.

"Hank, what do you think?" Monica asked.

"It's conceivable that electronic devices could kill through some sort of electronic pulse that stops a person's heart by interfering with the heart's electrical circuitry. We're getting into science fiction territory here, but nothing would surprise me anymore. As Dominick would have said, terrorists always seem to be one step ahead of us."

"But all the victims died of cyanide poisoning," Sage countered.

"I know," Ben said. "I'm just trying to come up with something here."

Sage's eyes brightened. "Maybe you *are* on to something! And just maybe my archaea theory isn't completely dead after all. What if it's electronics *and* archaea? Maybe there's something about an electrical field that changes the composition of archaea so they produce cyanide. Is that possible, Whitney?"

"I suppose so. Electromagnetic radiation can affect cellular functioning, so it's not out of the realm of possibility that an electrical field could alter the way archaea cells function."

"Let me remind you once again that no archaea have been found anywhere," Gus said firmly. "Not in any of the victims' bodies or in any of the thermal features."

"Strictly speaking, that's not true," Whitney responded. "We've found *Sulfolobus acidocaldarius* and *Picrophilus torridus* in several of the thermal features and we've identified *Methanobrevibacter smithii* in the intestinal tracts of most of the victims. But I get your point. None of these species are new, and none of them can produce cyanide."

"I think we should confiscate everyone's electronic devices again just in case," Sage said. "We've certainly got nothing to lose."

"And if the deaths stop, we'll know we're on to something," Whitney added.

"I agree," Monica said. "I'm going to order that all personal electronics be confiscated immediately. Hank, direct all available National Guard soldiers to go door-to-door and retrieve all electronics from everyone."

"What should they tell the residents?" Hank asked.

"How about the truth?" Sage suggested.

Monica thought for a second. "I agree with Sage. Instruct the soldiers to inform the residents that we think there's a possibility that electronic devices may be involved somehow in the deaths. My guess is everyone will turn over their electronics willingly."

Whitney turned to speak to Sage, but she was already gone.

* * *

Sage raced back to her room and burst in, yelling, "Put all your electronics away! They might be killing us!"

Anaya leaped up and met her at the door. "How?"

"It's complicated. I'll explain later. What's Adam doing?"

"He's taking a nap. He tossed and turned for a bit after you left and then fell fast asleep."

Sage yanked her facemask off and rushed to Adam's side. "Adam! Wake up!"

Adam didn't budge.

Sage shook him gently. "C'mon Adam, you need to wake up. It's really important."

Still there was no response.

"Adam! Get up now!"

Sage shook him harder.

"Why won't you get up?"

She tried to pull him up, but his head flopped backward.

"Damn you, Adam! Wake up this minute!"

Sage couldn't believe this was happening. Not to Adam. Her Adam.

Anaya had already run for help and returned with Ricky and a nurse. Sage was wailing and screaming at Adam.

"WAKE UP! WAKE UP!"

Sage turned to Ricky. "What's wrong with Adam?"

The nurse moved in, ripped Adam's shirt open, tore his facemask off, and began CPR immediately while Ricky tried unsuccessfully to wrestle Sage out into the hallway. A doctor appeared with a Cyanokit, started an IV infusion of the antidote, and took over the CPR.

Sage's howling and the doctor's CPR both continued for a full twenty minutes while the IV delivered its precious cargo. Ricky did his best to keep Sage away from Adam so the doctor could focus on her life-saving efforts, but Sage broke free of his grasp twice before he could pull her away again.

Every minute or so, the doctor put her stethoscope to Adam's chest. Each time, after listening for only a few seconds, she resumed CPR. No one asked the doctor whether Adam was going to make it. They didn't have to.

Once the IV bag was empty, the doctor searched for a heartbeat one more time. This time she listened for well over a minute, moving her stethoscope all over Adam's chest. Everyone—including Sage—watched in silence.

Finally, the doctor draped her stethoscope around her neck and looked at Sage.

"I'm sorry."

"What do you mean you're sorry?" Sage shrieked, her voice choked with tears.

Sage shoved the doctor aside and shook Adam again. She yanked out one of his earbuds and shouted directly in his ear. "Don't leave me Adam!"

Then the room started spinning. Slowly at first, then faster and faster. Sage's arms grew heavy and her knees buckled. Her vision blurred and narrowed until finally everything went dark. All she could hear were the faint sounds of Mariah Carey.

JUNE 17

"Turn off the light. It's too bright."

Anaya held Sage's hand. "It's okay. Everything will be okay."

Sage sat straight up, ripped off her facemask, and wailed. "He's dead! Adam's dead!"

"There was nothing anyone could do," Whitney said.

Whitney and Anaya were sitting on either side of Sage, an IV in her left arm.

"Why Adam? Why not me? It's not fair! It's just not fair!" Her chest heaved rapidly and her hands shook.

"Try to get some rest," Anaya attempted to push Sage back down on the bed, but Sage refused to budge. "At least put on another facemask."

"What time is it?" Sage said testily after donning a new mask.

"Eight forty-five."

"When did I fall asleep?"

"Actually you passed out right after …"

"Right after Adam died!"

"The nurse gave you a sedative so you would rest."

"So I've been asleep for almost eight hours?"

"More like twenty."

The despair started slowly, building up momentum until it was in complete control. There was little Sage could do except hold on as her emotions ran their course. Her sobbing and wailing came in waves. When it seemed the worst was over, her grief returned even more strongly than before. She cursed the world, the FBI, Yellowstone, and even herself for leaving Adam in the room while she attended the FBI briefing. Anaya and Whitney tried to assuage her guilt with reason and logic, but she would have none of it. Finally, the anguish gradually began to release its grip. She knew it would return, maybe in a few hours, maybe in a few days, but for now she welcomed the respite.

Then some of her resolve returned. "We have to keep going until we figure this out. We have to do it for Adam. And Penny. And Calvin. And everyone else who's died." Sage's eyes were so puffy she could barely see. "Where's Adam now?"

"The Old Faithful Clinic," Whitney replied. "They're keeping it there along with the other bodies awaiting autopsy. His will probably be later today. The coroner is really backed up because of all the new deaths."

"How many people died yesterday?"

"Last I heard it was sixteen."

"How did Adam die?"

"Same as the others, we assume. Several of the other autopsies have been completed and they all came back the same as before—massive doses of cyanide. Also, it looks like Ben was right about the electronics—the deaths stopped as soon as everyone returned their personal devices."

Despite her overwhelming sorrow, Sage's scientific curiosity kicked into gear. "But what about the people on the bus?"

"We still have to figure that out."

"And what about the first eleven victims?"

"We still have to figure that out too."

"But Anaya and I didn't die, and we used our electronics. Why didn't we die?" Sage started to sob uncontrollably again. "Why did *Adam* die? All he used was his phone. That's all—just like the girl we found on the trail."

"What do you mean?" Anaya asked.

"She was listening to her phone too." Sage's eyes widened. "With earbuds. Just like Adam! I remember taking one of her earbuds out to see if I could wake her up. Just like I did with Adam!" Sage paused. "Anaya, did you wear earbuds yesterday?"

"No. I gave mine to Adam. Remember?"

"I didn't wear any either. Maybe it's the earbuds! Maybe they're killing people somehow."

"But how could earbuds kill people?" Anaya asked. "Could they have been laced with cyanide?"

"I doubt it," Whitney said. "But maybe they can trigger archaea cells to produce cyanide like Sage suggested in the FBI briefing yesterday. I've no idea what sort of electromagnetic radiation earbuds emit, but I suppose it could be enough to alter cellular function. After all, some people think that cell phones can cause cancer."

Sage moaned. "But there's no archaea anywhere! Not in any of the bodies, not in any thermal features. We've wasted all this time and energy and gotten nowhere. This is all my fault! And now Adam's dead!"

Her whole body shook as she began to cry again.

Whitney held Sage's hand. "It's nobody's fault. We're all doing the best we can. And maybe earbuds *are* involved somehow. Let's go see if we can find some."

"But where?" Anaya asked. "They've all been confiscated again."

"Only from residents who are still alive," Whitney said. "Maybe there are some with the bodies that haven't been autopsied yet. If we can get those earbuds, we can test them for cyanide and archaea and anything else that might be interesting."

"How on earth will we get access to the dead bodies?" Anaya asked. "We'd have to get past security at the inn, then get into the clinic, then find the bodies."

"We could ask Monica for help." Sage pulled her facemask down and blew her nose loudly.

"That would probably take too long," Whitney said. "Medical examiners definitely do not like other people, no matter who they are, touching their cadavers. There would be lots of red tape and forms to fill out. We don't have time for all that. We need access to the bodies right now before they're moved. Besides, I still don't trust the FBI completely."

"Neither do I," Anaya said.

"Let's ask Ricky for help," Sage suggested between sniffles. "Maybe he can get us in to see the bodies."

Anaya stepped out into the hallway, found Ricky almost immediately, and brought him into the room. He sat down by Sage and took her hand. "I came by last night, but you were sleeping. How are you doing?"

"Not great."

"I don't understand why all of this is happening," Ricky said.

"None of us do." Sage squinted at Ricky through her swollen eyes, still moist with tears. "That's why we need your help."

"What can I do?"

Anaya explained the plan.

"I don't know. I could get in a lot of trouble."

"But aren't you supposed to take Sage anywhere she wants to go?"

"Yes, but to see dead bodies over in the clinic? How will we get in? The clinic's not under the control of the National Guard. It's just medical personnel in there."

"You could escort us over and say it's official business."

"I don't think that'll work." Ricky looked down at the floor for almost a minute before continuing. "I've got an idea. How about we pretend I've detained you for fighting and I'm taking you to the ranger station for questioning. The FBI has set up shop there as sort of a makeshift police station and temporary jail."

"Perfect!" Sage said. "The ranger station is in the same building as the clinic. We can sneak into the clinic just like Penny and I did."

"What? You and Penny?"

"I'll explain later."

"That just might work," Whitney said. "Can we go right now?"

"I don't see why not," Ricky said.

"Can you get someone to keep an eye on Sage while we're gone?" Anaya asked.

Sage kicked the covers off. "What are you talking about? I'm coming too!"

"No, you're not," Whitney said firmly. "You're going to stay right here and get some—"

"Like hell I am! Besides, I've been in the clinic before and I know where the bodies are."

"But you really need your rest," Whitney pleaded.

"Get a nurse in here right now to remove this IV or I'm going to yank it out myself."

* * *

Ricky played his part in the charade beautifully, yelling at his three charges several times as they left the inn and poking Sage with his nightstick for dramatic effect. Once they were outside, he continued to bark orders as they walked across the parking lot. They passed several other National Guard soldiers without incident; one soldier offered to help, but Ricky assured him that he had the situation under control.

Sage saw two guardsmen arguing with an FBI agent near the Visitor Center and she asked Ricky what was going on.

"It looks like they're telling the agent to put his facemask on."

"So what's the problem?"

"Not everyone likes being told what to do—especially FBI agents."

"This isn't the Yellowstone I know," Sage lamented. "And I'm worried it never will be again."

As they drew near the ranger station, Sage quietly explained to Ricky how she and Penny had snuck into the clinic along the narrow porch that spanned the front of the ranger station and the clinic while the entry guards had been distracted. Ricky decided to try a more direct approach.

He addressed the two guards at the front of the building. "Hello, officers. I've got some residents I've brought over from the Old Faithful Inn for questioning. Nothing serious. They were involved in a scuffle in the dining room. I've been told to take them to the clinic because the ranger station's being used by the FBI to conduct interviews."

"Who gave you those orders?" one of the guards asked.

"Captain Penny Phillips," Ricky said without missing a beat.

"You do know they've got lots of bodies in the clinic, don't you?"

"Yes, but we're just going use the lobby for a little bit. I need a quiet place where I can conduct my interviews and get them to sign a statement. It won't take long."

The two guards looked at each other. "If Captain Phillips approved it, then it's fine with us. You want one of us to go inside with you?"

"Thanks, but I can handle it." Ricky poked Sage with his nightstick again. "Let's go, ladies. I don't have all day."

Sage leaned close to Ricky and whispered through her facemask. "Can you stop poking me so much? That last one hurt."

"Sorry. I just want it to look realistic."

Once inside, they sat together on a long bench near the window. The clinic lobby was completely empty except for a nurse behind the counter.

"Who are you?" the nurse demanded.

"I'm Ricky Stabler with the National Guard. These residents got into a scuffle in the Old Faithful Inn dining room, and I'd like to use your lobby to get their statements. There's no room over in the ranger station."

"Well, make it quick. We've got a lot going on here."

"We'll do our best, ma'am."

"So what do we do now?" Anaya asked quietly.

"Follow my lead," Whitney said.

She stood up and spoke to Ricky loud enough for the nurse to hear. "I'll take this one over to the other side of the room while you conduct your interview here."

Ricky looked puzzled. "I don't understand—"

Whitney interrupted before he blew their cover. "We have to interview them separately, don't you think?"

"And who are *you*?" the nurse asked. "I thought you were one of the residents."

Whitney drew herself up to her full height. "FBI Agent Hughes. I witnessed the fight in the dining room this morning. I'm just helping Guardsman Stabler. The National Guard is a bit overstretched at the moment."

"I know what you mean. We're bursting at the seams too. At least the bodies have stopped coming in for now."

Whitney saw an opening and kept going. "How many have you got in here?"

"We're down to eleven now. The bodies are being moved one at a time to the temporary morgue for autopsy. They're going to keep them there until the FBI gives the okay to release them to the families. Who knows when that will be. It's good we've got two medical examiners working on them or we'd be here forever. Even as it is, the bodies are practically piled on top of one another in the cold storage room."

"These are indeed extraordinary circumstances." Whitney

grabbed Sage by the arm and pulled her up off the bench. "Let's go over here to talk. What's your name again?"

"Lucy Ledbetter."

Whitney guided Sage to two chairs on the far side of the lobby.

"Now *I* have an idea," Sage whispered. "This time follow my lead."

Sage stood up, pulled her facemask down, and waved both hands at the nurse. "Hey, madam nurse, I need to pee really bad. Where's the head?"

"All our bathrooms are restricted to medical personnel only."

Sage squeezed her legs together and hopped around. "If I can't use the head right now, there's going to be a puddle right in the middle of your damn floor!"

"Okay, okay. Down that hall, go around the corner, and then the second door on the left. And put your facemask back on immediately."

Sage started to shuffle down the hallway, but the nurse called after her. "Ms. Ledbetter, you can't go back there by yourself. Agent Hughes will have to escort you."

Whitney was only too happy to oblige.

As soon as they rounded the corner, Whitney gave Sage a quick high five. "Lucy Ledbetter? That's the best name you could come up with?"

"It's all I could think of on the spot."

"Okay, Lucy, we've probably got three minutes … four tops. Let's go find some bodies."

Although Sage had been down the hallway once before with Penny, she couldn't remember exactly which room the bodies were in. They tried the first door on the right—a small storage closet. The second door was locked. As soon as frigid air rushed out when they opened the third door, Sage knew they were in the right place. She motioned Whitney in and closed the door quickly behind them. Unable to see in the dark, they stood perfectly still, shivering in the ice-cold room, until shapes slowly started to emerge from the inky darkness. There were sheet-covered cadavers on gurneys everywhere, one not more than twelve inches away from Sage.

Sage felt carefully on the wall for a light switch and flipped it on. Bright lights blazed from overhead, so she quickly turned it off and tried the adjacent switch. This one activated a single floor lamp that emitted just enough light to guide them as they moved about.

Although this was the same room that Sage and Penny had looked into three weeks earlier, it was very different than before. The makeshift cooling system powered by bags of ice and noisy fans had been replaced by two enormous industrial cooling units.

"Time to get to work," Whitney said. "Let's see if any of these bodies have earbuds."

They began with the corpse next to Sage. After putting on a pair of latex gloves she had brought with her, Whitney pulled the sheet down to reveal a woman who looked to be in her forties, her sallow face frozen in a grimace. Sage looked away while Whitney felt gingerly around the woman's head and neck.

"No earbuds here. Let's move to the next one."

Whitney pulled the sheet off the next cadaver. Sage put her hand to her masked mouth and gasped loudly.

"It's Adam!"

She froze, transfixed by the sight of him lying on the stainless steel gurney—eyes closed and mouth slightly open—his waxy, pallid skin tinged pale blue. His pants and shoes were still neatly in place, but his light gray chambray shirt was ripped wide open, a result of the efforts to revive him. She reached out and stroked his disheveled hair.

"My dear Adam," she said over and over again.

Sage could feel the warmth drain from her body in the frigid room, and she was barely able to remain upright. *Why did you leave me Adam? I had so many plans for us.*

Whitney tugged Sage's arm. "C'mon, let's get out of here. Anaya and I can come back later and try again."

Sage stiffened. "I'm okay. Let's finish what we came here for." She spied an earbud lying on Adam's bare chest, exposed between the two tattered halves of his shirt. It was the earbud she had pulled out when she had tried to rouse him. The other one was still in his left ear, attached to the cord that joined the two earbuds together.

Whitney slowly removed the earbud from Adam's ear. As she pulled it out, a drop of viscous brown liquid slowly oozed down his earlobe.

"What's this? It looks a bit like syrup … certainly not like anything I've seen in an ear before. I better get a sample." She retrieved a small stoppered vial from her jacket pocket, collected several drops of the brown liquid in the vial, and replaced the stopper.

"You have a vial with you?"

"I work for the CDC. I'm always prepared."

Whitney wrapped the earbuds, cords and all, in two layers of tissue and placed them, along with the vial, in a clear plastic evidence bag that she secured in the inner pocket of her jacket.

"Let's find another set of earbuds and get out of here."

Suddenly they heard the squeak of rubber soles in the hallway.

"Someone's coming!" Whitney exclaimed softly. "Turn off the light."

Sage dove for the light switch and flipped it off. They crouched down among the cadavers, breathing heavily through their facemasks as the steps grew louder.

After what seemed like an eternity, the footsteps finally moved past the room and grew fainter. Sage and Whitney were about to get up when they heard the footsteps approach again, this time from the opposite direction. They waited another minute or so before slowly standing up.

"Let's get out of here." Whitney poked her head out the door, looked in both directions, and quickly moved into the hall. But Sage was not behind her. "Sage? We need to go!"

Whitney stepped back into the room and saw Sage leaning over Adam, her facemask pulled down.

"C'mon Sage, we have to go. *Now!*"

Sage kissed Adam on the forehead, pulled the sheet back over his head and gently tucked it in. Just before getting to the door, she turned around, tears streaming down her face, and blew a final kiss in his direction. "I'll love you forever."

When they got back to the lobby, the nurse was waiting for them. "Where were you, ladies? I just checked the bathroom and there was no one in there."

"We must have gone the wrong way after we came out of the bathroom," Whitney said. "It's like a maze back there."

"Are you crying, Ms. Ledbetter? Did this agent hit you?"

"No, no, I'm fine."

"Everything's fine," Whitney said. "I got Ms. Ledbetter's

statement when we were in the ladies room. She's just upset that she's caused all this trouble. She apologized for the fight and said it won't happen again. Guardsman Stabler, are you done?"

"Yes, we're good over here. Let's head back to the inn." Ricky looked at the nurse. "Thanks for letting us use your lobby."

"No problem. I hope those two young ladies have learned their lesson."

On their way back to the inn, Anaya and Ricky peppered Sage and Whitney with questions.

"We got one set of earbuds," Whitney reported. "But then we ran out of time. We also got some strange brown liquid from inside one of the ears. We don't know what it is yet."

"Must have been pretty rough seeing all those dead bodies, huh Sage?" Anaya said.

"One of them was Adam," Sage said softly. "The one with the earbuds—your earbuds."

"Oh my God! You okay?"

"Not really, but there's not much I can do about that now. We've got to focus on figuring out what killed Adam and everyone else."

As they neared the Old Faithful Inn, Sage and Whitney peeled off from the group.

"You guys going to the morning briefing?" Ricky asked.

"No time for that," Whitney replied. "We're heading to the lab. We've got to start analyzing this stuff right away."

* * *

Whitney and Sage sat quietly in the BSL-2 lab gnawing some energy bars and staring at the clear plastic evidence bag containing Adam's earbuds and the vial of viscous brown liquid from his left ear.

Finally, Whitney broke the silence. "Are you sure you want to do lab work today?"

"Yes, I'm sure. I need to do this for Adam."

"I'm just worried you might make some sort of mistake or something. Maybe you should just take it easy today. You've been through a lot."

"You don't think I can handle this, do you? You don't think I can put aside my personal feelings and be a professional."

"It's not that—it's not that at all—but you just lost a good friend."

"He was much more than that."

"I know, and I'm so sorry."

Whitney finished her energy bar and drained a small bottle of Gatorade. Sage only managed a small bite out of hers and pushed the remainder around in circles on the table.

"Why was Adam still dressed?" Sage wondered out loud.

"What?"

"Why was he still dressed on that gurney? And why was he still wearing that earbud?"

"I'm not certain," Whitney replied, "but I think in field operations like this the medics are instructed to transport the bodies exactly as they find them so they don't disturb any evidence. You never know what might be important."

"Like earbuds?"

"Like earbuds."

Sage nodded toward the evidence bag. "Do you really think the secret to all of this is in that tiny bag?"

"There's no telling, but there's only one way to find out."

* * *

Once they were inside the BSL-4 lab, Whitney opened the evidence bag carefully. "Let's begin by testing this brown stuff for cyanide. But before we start, I think I'll call for reinforcements."

Within minutes, Gayle, Robin, and Joe arrived in the BSL-2 lab. Gayle's voice came over the intercom. "What's up?"

"Not sure yet," Whitney said. "Why don't you and Robin come back and help us. Joe, can you wait out in the BSL-2 lab in case we need you?"

"Of course."

While Gayle and Robin proceeded through decon, Whitney tested the brown liquid for cyanide.

Twice.

Both times the test came back positive.

Sage and Whitney looked at each other.

"Do you think?" Sage asked.

"I do." Whitney said evenly.

Whitney took the sample vial to one of the fume hoods, placed a tiny portion of the viscous liquid into a sterile analysis container, inserted the container into the sample receptacle at the end of one of the genetic sequencers, set the controls, and sat down next to Sage. They stared at the sequencer in silence.

When Gayle and Robin emerged from decon, Whitney quickly brought them up to speed. The mood was decidedly subdued while they waited for the sequencer to finish; their hopes had been raised before, only to be dashed each time.

It wasn't long before the sequencer announced it was done. Whitney prepared the data file, uploaded it to BLAST, and everyone huddled around, waiting for the results.

"We've got something here," Whitney said in a measured tone. "Something unidentified."

"What is it?" Gayle asked.

"It looks like it might be archaea, but it's not an exact match with any archaea in the NCBI database." Whitney was surprisingly calm. "Its genetic makeup is similar to *Ignicoccus hospitalis,* an archaea species that lives in undersea hydrothermal vents near Iceland, but our organism is clearly different. It's definitely a new species."

"Could this be our killer?" Sage asked.

"There's no way to know for sure," Whitney replied. "But—"

"But it COULD BE, couldn't it?" Sage shouted.

"Yes, it could, but we need to confirm our analyses. Let's run another sample of the brown liquid through the sequencer."

A half hour later it was Whitney's turn to shout. "Same results as before! We definitely have a new species of archaea!"

The four scientists erupted into a spontaneous dance. Actually, it was more of an enthusiastic shuffle in their bulky pressurized body suits, but it was joyous nonetheless.

Whitney yelled above the din. "Let's go out to the BSL-2 lab and talk about our next steps."

As they all converged on the entrance to the decontamination area, Whitney sounded a note of caution. "Let me remind you that we've just handled an unknown biological substance that contains cyanide and a new microbial species that could turn out to be one of the most dangerous pathogens we've ever encountered. We need to be extra careful as we go through decon. We don't want to bring even one archaea cell out with us."

The trip through decon took a full hour. As captain of the ship, Whitney was the last one through, watching everyone else to ensure that all protocols were followed to the letter.

Once they had all emerged into the BSL-2 lab, they joined Joe at the table in the middle of the lab, everyone chattering excitedly through their facemasks.

Whitney held up her hand. "Let's not get ahead of ourselves … but I do have to admit, this really *is* exciting. Although we can't be certain yet, it looks like this microbe is a previously unknown species of archaea."

"*Now* can we give it a name?" Sage asked.

"Yes, we can." Whitney thought for a minute and then her face brightened. "I've got it!"

"Don't keep us in suspense," Gayle said. "What is it?"

"*Sagillium yellowstonii.*"

A flush crept across Sage's cheeks, barely visible above her facemask. "But species names are usually reserved for famous scientists or other important people. I don't deserve this."

"Of course you do!" Whitney said. "You've been our driving force. We wouldn't have gotten this far without you."

"If you say so …"

"I say so."

Whitney continued. "Since *Sagillium yellowstonii* and cyanide were both detected in the brown liquid, it appears that our new species of archaea may indeed be producing cyanide, just like Sage has been saying all along."

"And what exactly is the mechanism?" Robin prodded caustically. "I've never bought into the theory that archaea could produce cyanide."

"We don't know yet."

Robin was not convinced. "And just *where* is this mysterious poison manufacturing occurring?"

"In people's ears," Sage said softly. "The process is probably jumpstarted somehow by the electronic field emitted by earbuds."

"Was there any brown liquid in Adam's other ear, the one without an earbud?" Robin asked.

"In all honesty, I didn't notice," Whitney said. "We only had a few minutes with the bodies in the cold storage room. Did you see anything in his other ear, Sage?"

"Afraid not. I was focused on saying goodbye."

All eyes turned to Sage. Tears soaked the top of her facemask as she stared straight ahead.

Whitney place her hand gently on Sage's shoulder. "You okay?"

"I will be eventually."

Apparently oblivious to Sage's pain, Robin pushed on. "And just *where* is the *Sagillium yellowstonii* coming from?"

"From a thermal feature, of course," Sage said sharply.

To no one's surprise, Robin kept going. "But we haven't found *Sagillium yellowstonii* in any of the thermal features."

Gayle jumped in. "That doesn't mean they're not there. We just haven't found them yet."

Robin still wasn't satisfied. "And just *how* would archaea cells magically jump from a thermal feature into dozens of people's ears?"

"I ... we ... don't know," Sage admitted.

"There *is* another possibility," Robin said. "I know it sounds a little weird, but hear me out. Maybe someone coated some of the earbuds with cyanide, and people died when they put the earbuds in their ears."

"That's theoretically possible," Gayle said. "The lethal dose of cyanide is only about two hundred milligrams, which could conceivably be transported on a pair of earbuds."

"But how could that have happened?" Whitney asked. "The victims were located all over the Old Faithful Inn and the temporary barracks. No one could have put cyanide on all those earbuds."

"It would have to have happened before the electronics were returned to everyone," Robin replied. "And only one group of people has had access to the electronics over the past few weeks."

"Who?"

"The FBI."

Whitney tilted her head. "I'm the first to admit that I don't like the FBI, but this seems crazy to me. You really think the killer could be an FBI agent?"

"Why not?"

"But the killings started before the FBI even got here."

"They started before they *officially* got here. But a homicidal FBI agent could already have been here."

"Why would an FBI agent be a serial killer or a terrorist?"

"You know how sometimes arsonists turn out to be firefighters? Maybe it's the same thing here. Maybe the killer is a member of the FBI."

"And what about the *Sagillium yellowstonii*? How did *that* get into the victims' ears?" Whitney asked.

"I'm not sure," Robin replied. "But I think we should consider every possibility, no matter how far-fetched it seems."

The discussion continued back and forth for another half hour until everyone, except for Robin, agreed that Sage's archaea-earbud hypothesis was the most plausible explanation. Whitney concluded by stating the obvious. "Clearly we have a lot more work to do."

The outer door to the lab reverberated with a loud thump.

"Who is it?" Whitney yelled.

"Hank."

"And Ricky."

"And Anaya."

Whitney walked through the changing room, pulled the outer door open, showed them how to change into scrubs, and then ushered them into the lab.

"What are you all doing here?" Sage asked.

"I thought you could use some help," Anaya said. "So I asked Ricky to bring me over, and he suggested Hank might want to come too."

"Anaya told me about your boyfriend," Hank said. "I'm so sorry."

"Thank you," Sage said softly.

"Y'all came at a great time," Whitney said. "We've got lots to do, and we can use all the help we can get." After she gave the trio a brief rundown of the day's discoveries, she assigned the tasks ahead of them.

"We've got to examine the bodies still awaiting autopsy to see if they have any earbuds or brown goo in their ears. Hank, can you get us access to the bodies?"

"I'm afraid I don't have that kind of authority."

"Ricky, can you get us into the clinic again?"

"Don't think so. They'll never buy our story a second time."

"That leaves only one option."

"Monica," Sage said.

"Now that we've got plenty of evidence to show we're on the right track, she should be willing to pull some strings so we can get immediate access to the bodies," Whitney said. "Let's go see her as soon as we're done here. We also need to see if the first eleven victims had any personal electronics, earbuds, or brown goo in their ears."

"Don't forget about the three people on the bus," Sage said.

"I'll take a look at the first fourteen victims, including the three on the bus," Anaya offered. "We still have their FBI files, including the autopsy reports. I'll see if those are any help."

"And I can get the files and autopsy results for the most recent victims," Hank said. "How about I retrieve those and then meet you back at your room?"

Anaya blushed ever so slightly. "I'd like that."

"And we desperately need to find the source of the *Sagillium yellowstonii*," Whitney said. "I think it's time we start looking in Black Sand and Biscuit Basins and maybe even Midway Geyser Basin."

"But everyone who died yesterday was only in the Upper Geyser Basin over the past few days," Hank said. "I think we should focus there. Have you really sampled every single thermal feature in the Upper Geyser Basin?"

"No, but we hit all the major ones in the Old Faithful, Geyser Hill, and Castle-Grand areas—about eighty in all. There are dozens of other tiny features that we didn't bother with. Most of them are nothing more than a puddle or a small crack in the rock."

"Why not look at those?"

"We could make another pass, but I doubt it'll help. How would archaea jump from a small dormant pool or a tiny steam vent to a human?"

"Maybe if someone leaned down real close to get a better look or take a picture?"

"Perhaps. But do you think all the victims did that?"

"Probably not," Hank conceded. "But I still think you should go back and take samples from the smaller features. I don't think it's a coincidence that people started dying again after walking around the Upper Geyser Basin."

"You may be right," Whitney agreed. "Robin, how many thermal features did you skip when you took the samples?"

"There's no telling. Maybe twenty. Maybe sixty. I have no idea."

"How about you start back at Old Faithful and take a sample from every feature you skipped last time, no matter how small."

"Will do. Ricky and I will head out as soon as we're done here."

"While Robin and Ricky are out gathering new samples from the Upper Geyser Basin, Sage and I will collect earbuds and samples from as many cadavers as we can. Gayle and Joe, you get ready in the BSL-4 lab to look for *Sagillium yellowstonii* in the new thermal feature samples Robin and Ricky bring back and in any brown liquid Sage and I can get our hands on. Then there's one more thing we need to do. We've got to make sure we've really found a new species of archaea instead of some artifact of the sequencing process."

"How are we going to do that?" Sage asked.

"By doing something I haven't done in a long time—some good old-fashioned microscopy!"

"With a light microscope?"

"Not that old-fashioned! I'm talking about our scanning electron scope."

"I can help with that," Sage said.

"You sure you're up to it? The sample prep will probably take us all night."

"Absolutely. It'll take my mind off Adam."

"Okay everyone, let's do our very best to get everything exactly right," Whitney said. "Why don't we reconvene here in the BSL-2 lab at seven tomorrow morning so we can get a status check on our progress."

As they headed toward the changing area near the front door, Whitney turned to Hank. "It's almost five now, so the afternoon briefing is probably over. Where does Monica usually go after the briefing?"

"Back to the Visitor Center to fill in the rank and file agents as to what happened during the briefing. They always meet right after each briefing."

"I didn't know that."

"There's a lot you don't know about the FBI."

* * *

Sage and Whitney jogged to the Visitor Center in their scrubs, not bothering to change into their street clothes. They bolted past the two soldiers at the main door and burst inside where they were confronted by another soldier, a rifle raised stiffly across his chest. He stepped forward to within inches of Sage and Whitney.

"We need to see Monica immediately!" Sage said, panting loudly.

"Who?"

"Special Agent Velasquez. It's extremely urgent."

"She's in a meeting with FBI agents and cannot be disturbed. You'll have to come back in a half hour or so."

"To hell with that! We're going in now."

Sage and Whitney pushed past the soldier and through the door into the office. Monica was seated at a large rectangular table with about a dozen FBI agents, all wearing their light blue facemasks.

"We found the archaea!" Sage shouted, her facemask puffing in and out.

Monica glared at Sage. "Can't you see we're in a meeting?"

"But we found the archaea!"

Monica stood up briskly. "Everyone out of the room. I need to speak with Dr. Hughes and Dr. Maldonado privately."

The agents started to shuffle out.

"I mean now!" Monica barked.

The room cleared out in less than twenty seconds.

Monica closed the door. "Are you sure?"

"Yes. Almost definitely sure," Whitney said. She told Monica about the bodies, the earbuds, and the viscous brown liquid. Everything tumbled out in a barely intelligible muddle, but Monica appeared to get the gist of what she was saying.

"That's fantastic! You've finally discovered why people are dying!"

"Almost. But there's still lots of work to do," Whitney said.

"Such as?"

"We haven't figured out how the archaea produce cyanide."

"Anything else?"

"We don't know where the archaea are coming from."

"But you've seen them, right?"

"Not exactly, but we hope to view them sometime soon."

Monica's facemask didn't hide her scowl. "So you *think* you've found a new lethal species of archaea that produces cyanide, but you don't know *how* it produces cyanide, you don't know *where* it's coming from, and you haven't *actually* seen it. Have I got that right?"

"That's basically it. But if we're correct, we're probably only days away from figuring out how to stop all these deaths once and for all."

"And if you're wrong?"

"Then it's back to square one."

"Sounds more like square zero to me," Monica said. "So what's your plan?"

Whitney laid out their strategy as coherently as she could, with Sage interrupting every now and again to clarify details. Then she got to the crux of the matter.

"We need access to the bodies immediately to see if we can recover any more earbuds or brown liquid from their ears. When Sage and I were in the clinic this morning, there were eleven cadavers still waiting to be autopsied. There are probably only about seven or eight left by now. We need your help because the medical examiners and their staff won't let us anywhere near the bodies."

"But how did you get in there this morning? ... Never mind. I don't want to know."

"So can we go to the clinic?"

"I'm going to have to go through official channels first. My boss will need to contact the director of the Medical Examiner's Office and then—"

"We can't wait for all of that," Whitney complained. "We need to see the bodies right now!"

Monica clapped her hands once. "You know what? You're absolutely right! To hell with all those rules and regulations. This is no time for protocol. I'll just send Gus with you to make sure you have access to everything you need."

"Gus?" Sage said. "Please, anyone but him."

"He's the only agent I can spare right now. I know what you think about him, but his heart's in the right place. He wants to solve this just as much as you do. Just give him a chance. He may surprise you."

"I'll try."

"When will you two have more to tell me?"

"Probably tomorrow," Whitney replied. "Our team is meeting at seven in the morning in the lab for a status check. How about Sage and I come over here right after our meeting?"

"I've got a better idea. How about I attend your meeting? That way, I can hear everything firsthand."

"That would be great!"

"Will I have to wear one of those pressurized body suits I've been hearing about?"

"No. We'll be meeting in the BSL-2 lab. All you'll need to wear are scrubs like the ones we have on now."

"We're all set then," Monica said. "You can head over to the clinic with Gus to look at the bodies as soon as we're done. Anything else?"

"I think we've covered everything."

"Whitney, can I have a moment with Sage?"

"Of course. I'll wait out in the lobby."

After Whitney left, Monica spoke softly. "I've been informed that one of the fatalities yesterday was your boyfriend. I'm so sorry."

"His name is Adam—*was* Adam." Sage's eyes welled up with tears.

"I know this won't help ease your pain, but I understand how you feel. I lost my husband a while back. He was a member of the FBI's Criminal Investigations Division and he was killed in the line of duty. All he was doing was serving a search warrant on a white-collar suspect in a money-laundering scheme. Nothing dangerous. Just serving a damn warrant, and he was shot right through the door of a home. No warning, no nothing. His partner said his last words were 'FBI here to serve a warrant. Open the door please.'"

Tears rolled rapidly down Monica's cheeks and disappeared behind her facemask. "Can you believe it? His last word before he died was *please*."

"It's just not fair," Sage said. "Neither of them deserved to die."

Sage locked eyes with Monica, and they both continued to cry.

"Thanks for sharing, Monica. It actually does make me feel better. What was your husband's name?"

"Adam."

* * *

"It looks like you two may have solved this thing after all," Gus said on the way over to the clinic. "I must admit I'm impressed."

"We don't know for sure," Whitney said. "But I think we're getting close."

"I'm happy to help if I can. My mom, God rest her soul, once told me that life is a team sport."

Sage laughed out loud. "What is it with your moms?"

Gus looked confused. "What?"

"Never mind. I'll explain later."

It was much easier getting into the Old Faithful Clinic this time around. Gus did all the talking; Whitney and Sage just followed him in.

The nurse at the front desk eyed the two women. "Weren't you two here earlier this morning?"

"We were," Sage admitted.

"I don't understand."

Gus showed the nurse his credentials. "It's complicated, ma'am. We're here pursuant to direct orders from Special Agent in Charge Monica Velasquez, who is head of the FBI Command Post here at Yellowstone. We need to see the bodies that are still awaiting autopsy. Do you have any protective gear we can wear?"

The nurse retrieved a box of surgical gloves and three Tyvek hoods with plastic face shields from a supply cabinet. "Will these help?"

"Absolutely," Whitney said. "Thank you."

"Do you want me to take you back to the cold storage room?" the nurse asked.

Sage chuckled. "Thanks, but we already know where it is."

As they went down the hallway, Gus wanted to hear more about their earlier visit.

"It's complicated," Sage said. "We'll explain later."

"Here we are." Whitney approached the third door on the right.

Gus backed away. "Do I have to go in? Dead bodies give me the creeps."

"I thought you wanted to help us?" Sage teased.

"I do, but I think I'll go back to the Visitor Center and see if they need any help there."

"You're going to miss all the fun!"

As Gus headed back to the lobby, Whitney and Sage entered the cold storage room, and immediately the unmistakable stench of death wafted around them.

"Did you notice that smell this morning?" Sage asked.

"No. Maybe we were so nervous we didn't detect it."

"Or maybe the bodies are starting to decompose now. Let's get this done as quickly as we can."

This time they turned on all the lights and surveyed the room. "One, two, three, four, five, six. Six bodies still in here," Sage said. "Hopefully that'll be enough."

Sage scanned all the cadavers and let out a big breath. "It looks like Adam's not here anymore."

"How can you tell?"

"I tucked his sheet in right before we left." Sage's voice cracked just a bit. "I'm glad I got to say goodbye this morning."

"You okay?"

"As good as can be expected. Let's get to work."

They still had on their scrubs, and they donned the surgical gloves and Tyvek hoods the nurse gave them.

"Let's start over here." Whitney pulled back the sheet. "White female, probably in her thirties." She turned the woman's head slowly from side to side, her neck slightly stiffened by rigor mortis. "Pay dirt! Earbuds in both ears! It looks like they're wireless. I'll get a sample vial ready and you pull the earbud out of her right ear so I can collect whatever's behind it."

Sage reached around Whitney and put her thumb and finger on the earbud. "You ready?"

"Ready."

Sage slowly extracted the earbud, and there it was: the same brown liquid that had been in Adam's ear.

Whitney deftly captured three drops of the liquid in her vial and put the stopper in. "Let's see what's in the other ear."

There was more brown liquid in the second ear. After Whitney put both vials in an evidence bag, she collected the earbuds and put them in the bag too. She closed the bag, sealed it with evidence tape, and pulled out her pen. "We need to put a name or something on the evidence bag so we know which body this came from."

Sage located the ankle band on the corpse. "Her name was Evelyn Buchman."

"We'll just use her initials—E.B."

Moving clockwise around the room, they went to the next body.

"African American female. Probably in her late teens or early twenties," Whitney said.

When Sage looked at the woman's ears, she couldn't hide her disappointment. "No earbuds here. Let's move on."

"But we need to see if there's any brown liquid in her ears." Whitney pulled out a tiny flashlight and shined it directly into her left ear. "No liquid here, but there's a clump of dark rubbery material. This doesn't look like any earwax I've ever seen."

Expertly wielding a tiny scoop, Whitney took a sample of the mysterious material from each ear and put the two samples in separate vials.

Body after body, they followed the same procedure. Only one of the other bodies had earbuds still inserted in the ears. Her name was Helen Huntsman, and both of her ears yielded the bounty they sought—the viscous brown liquid they believed would be teeming with *Sagillium yellowstonii*. Two of the other bodies had the mysterious dark rubbery substance in both ears. The final body had the rubbery substance in one ear and regular earwax in the other ear. The final haul: one set of earbuds with cords, one set of wireless earbuds, and four samples of brown liquid from the two bodies with earbuds, and seven samples of dark rubber and one sample of earwax from the other four bodies.

* * *

When they emerged from decon into the BSL-4 lab, Sage and Whitney spread the evidence bags out on the table in the middle of the lab.

"Only two of the bodies had earbuds?" Gayle asked. "There goes Sage's earbud theory."

"Not necessarily," Whitney said. "That doesn't mean they weren't wearing earbuds when they died. The earbuds could have fallen out during CPR or they could have been removed before the body was transported to the clinic. Hopefully Hank and Anaya will be able to determine from the autopsy reports and the FBI records whether all the victims were wearing earbuds when they were stricken. Also, to be more precise, one body had earbuds with cords and one had wireless earbuds."

"You think that matters?" Gayle asked.

"I have no idea," Whitney replied.

"So what shall we do first?"

"Let's start with the brown liquid in evidence bags E.B. and H.H. There are two vials in each bag, one from each ear. Why don't you sequence one sample from each bag for *Sagillium yellowstonii*. Now that we know what we're looking for, this should be fairly easy. We can just BLAST any sequences we find to see if they match the *Sagillium yellowstonii* we identified in the brown liquid earlier today."

"What about the other bags?" Joe asked. "What's in there?"

"Not really sure. We got one sample of what appears to be regular earwax and seven samples of an unknown dark brown rubbery substance. All eight of those samples came from ears without earbuds. We can look at those after we finish with the samples of the brown liquid."

While Gayle and Joe were sequencing the new samples of the mysterious brown liquid, Whitney and Sage started preparing a portion of the brown liquid from Adam's ear for the scanning electron microscope. The process was tedious and involved numerous steps—cleaning, fixation, dehydration, mounting, and applying a conductive coating. Sage knew the basics, but she was used to working with inorganic samples such as volcanic pumice, so Whitney did most of the heavy lifting.

"*Sagillium yellowstonii!*" Gayle shouted. "There's *Sagillium yellowstonii* in the brown liquid from H.H.!"

Whitney and Sage rushed over to see the results for themselves.

"Well, I'lllll be damned!" Whitney exclaimed in her best Southern drawl.

"Also in E.B.!" Joe echoed a few moments later.

Whitney could barely contain herself. "We've found *Sagillium yellowstonii* in all three samples of brown liquid we've tested. There's no way this is just some sort of artifact of the sequencing process. But I still want to see these little suckers for myself. Once we can determine their structure, we might be able to figure out how they're producing cyanide."

"We also need to test the brown liquid from H.H. and E.B. for cyanide," Gayle said. "And after that, we need to sequence some of the brown rubbery stuff from the ears without earbuds."

"Do you think the rubbery stuff will contain *Sagillium yellowstonii* too?" Sage asked.

"My guess is it will," Gayle replied.

JUNE 18

The intercom crackled. "It's Robin and Ricky."

"It's after midnight," Whitney said. "Where have you guys been?"

"Out collecting samples."

"But it's been dark for hours."

"Ricky brought two monstrous lanterns the National Guard uses when the power goes out. We had plenty of light."

"How many samples did you get?"

"Twenty."

"Great! That should keep us busy all night. C'mon on back."

"But that means there will be five of us in the BSL-4 lab," Robin said. "We've never done that before."

"It'll be crowded, but we'll manage. You can use one of the spare pressure suits hanging in the corner of the suit room. Are you comfortable going through decon by yourself?"

"I'll be fine."

"What shall I do?" Ricky asked.

"Why don't you go get some sleep and come back at seven for the status meeting."

While Robin made her way through decon with the new samples, Sage and Whitney continued their prep work for the electron microscope, and Joe tested the two samples of brown liquid for cyanide. It didn't take him long to announce that both samples contained cyanide, just like the liquid from Adam's ear.

Robin emerged from decon and carefully placed a container holding twenty vials of water on the large lab table.

"You think we've struck gold with any of these samples?" Whitney asked.

"I've no idea. We started at Old Faithful and worked our way westward, taking a sample from each thermal feature we skipped the first time. We probably got about halfway done before we ran out of vials. Most of the features were so small we could barely see them as we walked along the boardwalk, but a few were a bit larger. Once it got dark we only took samples from features we could reach from the boardwalk with the magic arm."

"How did you label the vials?" Sage asked. "Most of these smaller features don't have names or even numbers."

"I put a small number in purple ink on the USGS map at the approximate location of each feature, and we labeled the sample vial with the same number. Also, Ricky took a picture of each feature after we collected the sample."

"Now that we have these new samples, let's get to work on them right away," Whitney said. "Robin, you can help Gayle and Joe sequence the new samples. We'll hold off on analyzing the rubbery material from the ears until we're done with this new batch of thermal feature samples. Gayle, do you think you can get through these twenty samples by noon tomorrow?"

"We'll do our best."

"Sage and I will continue to prep the brown liquid for the electron microscope."

Over the next few hours, the five scientists settled into a methodical routine, accompanied by the mesmerizing rhythm of clinking glassware, whirring centrifuges, and beeping instruments.

Just after 5 a.m., Gayle's earsplitting shriek caused Sage to drop the empty test tube she was holding, sending it crashing to the floor.

"*Sagillium yellowstonii* in a sample from one of the thermal features!"

"Are you sure?" Whitney asked.

"I'm sure!"

"Which feature?"

"Number 9."

"Robin, where is Thermal Feature 9?" Whitney asked.

Robin pulled out the USGS map with the tiny purple numbers. "Here it is, just down the boardwalk from Beehive Geyser. If I remember correctly, it's a vigorously bubbling hot spring about six or seven feet in diameter with a fountain of water in the middle."

Sage looked closely at the map. "I know that area pretty well, and I don't remember any large bubbling features around there. I think there are just a couple of small, quiet pools called Scissors Springs. One of them might bubble a bit, but nothing like you're describing."

"I'm fairly sure about its appearance, but I could be wrong. Ricky has the camera—we can check the picture of it when he returns at seven."

"Anyway, we've finally found the source of the archaea!" Sage tried to jump in her pressurized body suit but was only able to elevate an inch or two.

"It may not be the only source, though," Whitney cautioned. "We need to keep testing all the features. Maybe there's *Sagillium yellowstonii* in more of them."

Robin ran her fingers slowly over the USGS map. "There's probably about thirty more features in the target area we haven't tested yet."

"Hey, Joe," Whitney said. "Let's run a cyanide test on Thermal Feature 9."

"I'm way ahead of you. It's almost done."

"Let us know when you have—"

"Negative. Negative for cyanide." Joe sounded a bit deflated.

"Actually, that makes perfect sense," Robin said. "It means the cyanide's being produced by *Sagillium yellowstonii* in people's ears—not in the thermal feature. That's why no one has died on the boardwalk next to Thermal Feature 9. It looks like Sage was right after all. I must admit I was a bit skeptical at first—"

"Apology accepted," Sage said.

Robin looked confused. "What? You're welcome, I guess."

Sage moved in and hugged Robin awkwardly, two giant powder-blue marshmallows sharing a moment of mutual admiration and scientific discovery.

* * *

Robin, Gayle, and Joe went out to the BSL-2 lab to greet the morning arrivals while Sage and Whitney remained in the BSL-4 lab to finish the sample prep for the electron microscope.

Ricky was the first to arrive, just past six thirty. Robin greeted him in the changing area. "Did you bring the camera we used last night?"

"Yep, I've got it with me," Ricky said as he was unbuttoning his shirt. "Did you find something?"

"We did! I'll explain once everyone gets here."

A few minutes later, Hank and Anaya arrived with an oversized folder stuffed with papers.

Ricky finished changing into his scrubs and entered the BSL-2 lab just as Whitney and Sage emerged from decon.

"Hey, Sage," Ricky said. "What were you two doing back in the fancy lab?"

"We were completing the final prep of the brown liquid for the scanning electron microscope."

Monica showed up just before seven and brought two guests along with her.

"Ben! Gus!" Sage exclaimed.

Gayle pulled out another box of scrubs for the new arrivals and showed Monica and Gus where to stow their firearms. When everyone had finished donning their scrubs, the changing room was knee deep in pants, shirts, and shoes, looking a bit like a mudroom in a middle school.

Since there weren't enough stools to accommodate everyone, Sage, Monica, and Ben stood by the long counter at the side of the lab.

"This is quite a group we've got here," Sage said.

"I count eleven," Anaya said. "How about we call ourselves the *Gang of Eleven*."

Sage laughed. "Really?"

Anaya thought for a few moments. "Well then, how about the *Yellowstone Eleven*?"

"I kind of like that," Ricky said.

"Then it's settled," Anaya said. "From now on we're the Yellowstone Eleven!"

Sage laughed heartily. "Now that's the Anaya I know!"

Whitney took charge of the meeting. "We've got a lot of exciting news to discuss. But before we start, I've got some new facemasks for us." She opened a large box containing several dozen white facemasks with small valves near the center of the mask. "Everybody take one."

Gus removed his old facemask and donned the new one, making sure it was snug against his face. "Are these better than the ones we've been using?"

"They are," Whitney replied. "These N95 facemasks are much more effective at protecting us from minute airborne particles. Standard surgical facemasks only protect against large-particle splashes, sprays, or splatters. N95 masks can filter out much smaller particles. I thought we should wear these from now on in the BSL-2 lab since we're in an especially high-risk environment in here."

"What about everyone else in Yellowstone?" Gus asked.

"We've requested hundreds more of the N95 masks," Whitney said, "but they won't be here for another day or so. The surgical facemasks should be fine for now."

Whitney continued. "Let's get on with it. To begin, we've found *Sagillium yellowstonii* in the samples of brown liquid we collected from the ears of three of the victims. That means this is no artifact, no mistake. It's the real deal. It's a brand new species of archaea. We also found cyanide in all three samples."

"Have you seen what this new species looks like?" Gus asked.

"Not yet. We should get our first look at them sometime today."

"Were the victims with the brown liquid in their ears wearing earbuds?"

"Yes, all three had earbuds. Two sets had cords and one set was wireless."

"Did all the victims have earbuds?

"No. We saw a total of seven bodies yesterday, but only three were wearing earbuds—Adam and two others. The other four weren't."

"Was there any brown liquid in the ears without earbuds?"

"No. But there was some unusual rubbery material in all but one of those ears."

"Have you tested that stuff yet?"

"No, we haven't had a chance to. But that's on our plate for today."

"Since the four bodies without earbuds didn't have the brown liquid, how did they die?"

"We don't know yet," Sage said. "But just because the bodies didn't have earbuds when we saw them doesn't mean they weren't wearing any when they died. We're hoping Hank and Anaya can shed some light on that."

Anaya pulled out her notes. "Before I talk about the earbuds, I want to share one other interesting finding. As best as we can determine from the information in the FBI files, all of the victims spent time on Geyser Hill at some point before they died."

Sage was impressed. "Adam and I had already determined that each of the first eleven victims had walked somewhere in the Upper Geyser Basin, but you've been able to narrow that down to Geyser Hill specifically?"

"We have. And the same applies to the three people on the evacuation bus. Yellowstone's maintenance records show that the two private contractors on the bus had been repairing boardwalks on Geyser Hill for three days right before the lockdown was instituted."

"And Penny spent time there with me," Ricky said softly. "Almost an hour."

"In addition, all of the most recent sixteen victims had walked around on Geyser Hill during the time the quarantine rules had been relaxed," Anaya said. "So every single victim had been on Geyser Hill at least once in the days before they died."

"Thermal Feature 9 is on Geyser Hill!" Gayle exclaimed.

"What?" Anaya asked.

"Sorry! I'm getting ahead of myself. Tell us what you found out about the earbuds, and then I'll tell you about Thermal Feature 9."

"For the most part, the information in the FBI files supports the earbud hypothesis. The FBI inventories of the personal effects of each of the first eleven victims include personal electronic devices of some type, mostly phones and a few MP3 players. Seven of the inventories mention earbuds—four wireless and three corded. The other four inventories list headphones—two large wireless over-ear headphones and two smaller ones like the kind you used to get on airplanes."

"The same holds true for the sixteen most recent deaths," Hank added. "FBI reports have only been filed on eight of these, but all eight inventories include electronic devices. Five of the inventories list some type of earbuds and the other three mention headphones."

"Circumstantial evidence," Gus said. "Highly suggestive, but circumstantial nonetheless."

"There's more," Anaya said. "Some of the FBI files contain pictures of the deceased at the death scenes. In most of those cases, earbuds can be seen in the pictures, and in a couple of others, headphones are visible." Anaya pulled out two photographs and laid them on the lab table. "For example, these pictures of the couple who died in the backcountry campsite at Mallard Lake clearly show earbuds with cords, which are especially easy to see because both of these victims were naked when they died. Some of the pictures of other victims show wireless earbuds, and headphones can be seen in a few others. But earbuds or headphones are not visible in all of the pictures, and not all of the files have photographs of the death scenes. Of course, the absence of earbuds or headphones in the other pictures doesn't mean that the victims weren't wearing them when they died. As I learned from one of my college professors, *the absence of evidence is not evidence of absence.* It's possible they were removed or fell off before the pictures were taken."

"Did any of the autopsy reports mention the contents of the ears?" Sage asked.

"No," Anaya replied. "None of them mentioned brown liquid, rubbery substances, or anything else in the ears. And no toxicology tests were conducted on anything in the ear canals of any of the victims."

"That doesn't make sense," Sage said. "As soon as Whitney took out Adam's earbud she noticed the brown liquid. Wouldn't the medical examiners have noticed that sort of thing?"

"They should have," Whitney replied.

"So why didn't they?"

"My guess is that they were under tremendous pressure to process all the cadavers as quickly as possible, which could have caused them to miss some things. And if you're going to overlook something in an autopsy of a murder victim, ear canals would be high on that list. There's usually nothing forensically interesting in people's ear canals."

"Except this time," Sage added glumly.

Whitney exhaled loudly. "You can't really blame them. They've had so many bodies to deal with. Don't forget, I was careless too. I should have been looking for archaea all along, but I didn't think it was necessary, just like they probably didn't think it was necessary to look in the victims' ears."

Whitney's shoulders slumped and her chin dropped down almost to her chest. "Too many bodies for them, too much data for me. It's no different really. They should have slowed down and so should have I. If we'd all been more careful, maybe we would have solved this thing days ago."

"Don't beat yourself up over this," Monica said gently. "You've been doing your best. We've all been doing our best. I'll instruct the medical examiners to look for earbuds and headphones and collect samples from the ear canals of the victims in all future autopsies."

"Unfortunately, one big problem remains," Anaya said. "The three victims on the bus didn't have any earbuds or headphones, and we're not sure what to make of that."

"Were there any other unusual sources of electrical activity on the bus?" Ben asked.

"None that we could find. But here's where it gets interesting. There were some discrepancies in the witnesses' statements about what happened on the bus."

"How so?" Monica asked.

"Two of the witnesses gave inconsistent or evasive answers in their FBI interviews about what they were doing when the three people died."

Monica leaned forward. "Do you think they might have been involved in the deaths?"

"Hard to tell," Hank said. "The agents who interviewed them thought they were just shaken up, so they didn't put too much weight on the inconsistencies."

"What do *you* think?"

"I'm not sure. I'd like to conduct follow-up interviews with both of them to see what I can find out."

"Can you do those now?"

"I'm on it. Anaya, wanna come?"

Anaya's face brightened. "Of course!"

Hank grabbed her hand and they headed toward the changing room.

Gayle went next. "We've finally found the source of *Sagillium yellowstonii*! It's coming from a feature that Robin and Ricky labeled Thermal Feature 9."

Robin unrolled the USGS map lying at the end of the table. She pointed to a tiny purple "9" on the map. "Here it is, about twenty-five yards or so west of Beehive. Ricky, let's look at the picture."

Ricky was already peering at his camera. "I'm looking, I'm looking ... Here it is! Number 9."

Everyone crowded around Ricky, but it was difficult to discern anything on the camera's tiny screen.

"Put it up on the monitor," Whitney said.

Ricky popped the memory card out and inserted it into the computer. He quickly found Picture 9—a photo of a hot spring sporting a vigorously bubbling fountain of water in the middle.

"Yep, that's it," Robin confirmed. "It was splashing a lot while we were there, kind of like a giant pot of boiling water, and a couple of times it let off a burst of steam while we were collecting the sample. It's near a slight bend in the boardwalk not far from Beehive. There's a railing on the side of the boardwalk right next to it."

"Why is this thermal feature not on the USGS map?" Sage asked.

"We wondered that too. It's right next to Scissors Springs, but we skipped it the first time because it wasn't on the official USGS map. We thought we should stick to our original plan of just collecting samples from the features listed on the map."

"Is there a date on the map?" Ben asked.

"None that I can find," Robin replied.

"There's no telling how old that map is," Ben said. "It might be outdated or incomplete."

Sage studied the picture carefully. "Still, though, I don't remember seeing this at all. I spent a lot of time on Geyser Hill in my first few weeks here, and I didn't see anything like this next to Scissors Springs."

"Maybe you just didn't notice it before," Robin suggested. "I can assure you it's the one that tested positive for *Sagillium yellowstonii.* The numbers on the map, on the picture, and on the sample vial all match. It's definitely Thermal Feature 9."

Sage continued to stare intently at the image on the screen. "Wait a minute ... now I remember it!" Her lips trembled.

"What's wrong?" Ricky asked.

"This is where Adam and I shared a long kiss while we were watching Old Faithful erupt when we went outside the other day. It was so romantic." Sage pointed at the side of the image. "We were standing right by that railing. It was a beautiful day, and steam was coming up all around us."

"Where was the steam coming from?" Ricky asked gently.

"I don't know."

"Could it have been coming from the bubbling hot spring in the picture?"

"Maybe. I don't know. We were kissing and watching Old Faithful and ..." Suddenly the color drained from Sage's face. "This is where he was exposed to the archaea! Adam died because I kissed him right by that railing! I killed him!"

"That's ridiculous!" Ricky said. "You didn't kill him. The archaea did."

"Yeah, the archaea that's named after me! The one I exposed him to!"

Sage picked up the closest thing she could find and threw it against the wall. Ricky's camera broke into a dozen pieces, some of them bouncing back and landing at Sage's feet.

"Damn it! Damn it! Damn it!"

No one dared say a word.

Sage stared down at the scattered pieces on the floor for the better part of a minute and then mumbled, "Sorry about your camera, Ricky."

"No worries. It's not mine anyway. It belongs to the National Guard. Besides, we already took the memory card out so we've got all the pictures." Ricky picked up the largest piece and handed it to Sage. "You wanna throw it again?"

Instead of replying, she just gave Ricky a big hug.

Then Gus shouted what everyone else silently feared. "You know what this means? We probably all walked by that bubbling hot spring when we were outside! We've all been exposed to the deadly bugs! We may die any second!"

"No, we won't," Sage said, trying to reassure Gus. "Have you worn any earbuds or headphones at any point in the last few days?"

"I don't think so."

"Then you're probably safe." Sage looked around the lab, making eye contact with everyone. "Has anyone else worn earbuds or headphones?"

They all shook their heads.

But it wasn't enough to mollify Gus. "Hey, Whitney, you think we all have those bug things in our ears?"

"There's only one way to find out."

* * *

Whitney collected samples from both ear canals of all nine people in the lab, including herself. Each sample was placed in a separate vial, marked with the donor's name, and put into a large cooler packed with ice. When she was done with the last two samples, she exhaled loudly.

"At least none of us have any brown liquid or that mystery rubber stuff in our ears. All we have is good old-fashioned earwax."

Gayle and Joe took the cooler with the eighteen samples into the BSL-4 lab to test for *Sagillium yellowstonii*.

* * *

"We've been waiting for forty-five minutes," Gus complained. "How long is this sequencer thing going to take?"

"It probably took Gayle and Joe about a half hour to go through decon," Whitney replied. "My guess is they started sequencing the samples within the last ten minutes or so."

Right on cue, Gayle's voice came over the intercom. "The first two samples have been loaded into the sequencers. We expect the results within thirty minutes."

"Whose samples are first?" Gus asked.

"Sage's. Now we'll commence the secondary analyses."

"What secondary analyses?"

"We're also testing everyone's earwax for cyanide."

The wait in the BSL-2 lab was excruciating. Almost fifteen minutes passed in complete silence.

Finally the intercom blared again.

"Secondary analyses are negative for both samples! I repeat—secondary analyses are negative!" The intercom screeched with feedback from Gayle's shouting.

Gus relaxed just a bit. "Negative is good, right?"

"Yes, that means I don't have any cyanide in my ears," Sage replied. "And since I probably spent more time near Thermal Feature 9 than any of you, it's likely that none of you have any cyanide either."

"Is the sequencing done?" Whitney asked Gayle.

"Not yet."

It wasn't long before Gayle reported back to the group. This time she was more subdued, and the news was decidedly less sanguine.

"We've detected *Sagillium yellowstonii* in both of Sage's samples."

"What does *that* mean?" Gus squealed.

"It's too early to tell," Whitney replied calmly. "We know there's some archaea in Sage's ears, but we don't know how much. It could just be a trace amount. We'll have to use real-time quantitative PCR to find out how much. We've got the most advanced PCR equipment in the world right here in our BSL-4 lab, but it will take a while to set everything up, so I suggest we keep sequencing the other earwax samples for the time being."

Whitney could sense the growing panic in the room. "Remember everyone, there's no cyanide in Sage's ears. None. Zero. It's the cyanide that's killing people, not the *Sagillium yellowstonii*."

Whitney called back to Gayle and Joe. "Let's test all of the samples for cyanide first. Then you can move on to the sequencing for *Sagillium yellowstonii*."

"We're on it," Gayle said.

"Do you think Sage is in any danger?" Gus asked.

"I don't believe so," Whitney replied, "but we'll watch her closely."

Sage touched her right ear lobe. "I feel fine. Really."

Whitney continued. "Also, we have several Cyanokits right here in the lab. Because the previous deaths were so quick, no one was able to administer the antidote in time. But if Sage shows even the slightest symptoms of cyanide poisoning, we can start the antidote protocol immediately."

"Why not just give her the antidote now?" Gus suggested.

"Actually, that's not a bad idea," Whitney said. "I haven't run an IV line in a while, but it shouldn't take me too long to get one going. What do you think, Sage?"

"I'm fine with whatever you recommend."

True to her word, Whitney was able to begin the antidote infusion within minutes, and when it was finished she extracted the empty IV line from Sage's arm.

"There. It's done. Keep in mind that the protection from the antidote is short lived—it's only effective for about sixteen to twenty-four hours."

"You feel any better?" Gus asked.

"I was fine before and I don't feel any different now," Sage replied. "But thanks for asking."

In a little over an hour, Gayle reported the news everyone had been hoping for. "No cyanide in any of the samples!"

"You've just made a whole bunch of anxious people very, very happy," Monica replied.

"Now we're moving on to the genetic sequencing of the rest of the samples," Gayle said.

"So what do we do now?" Gus asked.

"We wait," Whitney replied. "It'll probably take Joe and Gayle four or five hours to run them all, so just try to relax and stay calm."

At roughly half-hour intervals, Gayle announced the sequencing results for *Sagillium yellowstonii* over the intercom.

"Monica: Negative for both ears."

"Whitney: Negative for both ears."

"Ben: Positive for one ear. Negative for the other."

Ben sighed nervously. "But I don't have any cyanide in my ears so I should be fine, right?"

"That's correct," Whitney replied.

Gayle continued her reports.

"Joe: Negative for both ears."

"Ricky: Positive for both ears."

Ricky dipped his head into his hands. "I'll be okay, I'll be okay," he said softly.

"Robin: Positive for both ears."

"Ricky and I must have been exposed when we were out collecting samples last night. Sorry about that, partner."

"Gayle: Negative for both ears."

There was only one set of samples left. Finally, Gayle announced the results.

"Gus: Positive for both ears."

It took the combined strength of Ben, Sage, and Ricky to restrain Gus as he went into full-blown panic mode. He wriggled free from their grasp and started hyperventilating as he bounced up and down. Ben tackled him in the corner of the lab and held him down while Whitney jabbed him in the thigh with a sedative.

His chest heaving and his face dripping with sweat, Ben's massive frame lay on top of Gus waiting for the drug to take effect. Finally, Gus relaxed and Ben rolled off him, still breathing heavily.

Gus sat up slowly, and Sage helped him to a chair.

"I'm sllorrrry everyone," he mumbled through his facemask. "I'm really, really sllorrrry."

Sage put a hand on Gus's shoulder. "We're all scared, Gus, but we're going to be fine."

"Can I get one of those Slanokit infllusion things like Sllage got?"

"I don't think you need it, but I don't see why not," Whitney said. "Will it make you feel better?"

"Yessssss."

Whitney followed the same protocol with Gus's infusion as she had with Sage's.

As Sage gazed at Gus lying on the cot, his fists clenched tightly and his facemask puffing rapidly in and out, she no longer saw a caustic, self-centered FBI Agent. Instead, she saw a slightly chubby, vulnerable, middle-aged man who was just as scared as everyone else.

A loud knock on the outer lab door signaled that Hank and Anaya had returned. They quickly changed into their scrubs and joined the rest of the group just as Gayle and Joe were emerging from decon.

"It's good to have the Yellowstone Eleven back together again," said Anaya.

Whitney told Hank and Anaya about the results of the earwax testing and took samples from both of them and stored them in the lab refrigerator, assuring them the testing would be done as soon as possible.

"We do have a bit of good news," Hank announced. "The earbud hypothesis is alive and well. It seems that all three victims on the evacuation bus were wearing earbuds when they died, just like the other victims."

"How is that possible?" Monica asked. "All their personal electronics had been confiscated."

"You may remember that the evacuees' electronics were stored in a trunk at the back of each evacuation bus. A couple of passengers on Bus 4 convinced the National Guardsmen on their bus to let them have their electronics for the long ride to the airport. After the guardsmen reluctantly agreed, about half of the passengers retrieved their electronics, including the three who later died.

"After the three evacuees died, it took a while for the ambulances to arrive at Bus 4's location. While they were waiting, the two guardsmen asked everyone to return their electronics to the trunk because they didn't want to get into trouble. They even retrieved the electronic devices and earbuds from the three victims. At that point, of course, no one had any idea that earbuds might be involved in the cyanide poisonings."

"How did you find this out?"

"From one of the passengers who had given inconsistent statements during her FBI interview. She admitted to us that she hadn't been completely truthful about the electronics in her first interview because she didn't want to get the nice National Guardsmen in trouble. Anaya and I also interviewed both of the guardsmen who had been on Bus 4, and they confirmed that they'd allowed the evacuees to take their electronics from the trunk and then tried to cover it up."

"It's all come together perfectly!" Sage exclaimed. "Think about it. *Who's* most likely to wear earbuds or headphones? Young people, which is why the majority of the victims were under thirty. And *when* are people most likely to wear them? When they're alone outside … or when they're traveling on a bus and want to be left alone … or when they're in their room and don't want to bother their roommates … or any other time they want to listen to music. All of the victims were in one of these situations. Now there's no doubt that earbuds and headphones somehow contributed to the deaths of all these people."

"But how?" Ben asked.

Whitney sighed. "We still have no idea."

* * *

Whitney, Sage, Gayle, and Robin headed back into the BSL-4 lab just before 3 p.m. to see if they could determine the amount of *Sagillium yellowstonii* in the earwax samples from Sage, Ben, Ricky, Robin, and Gus. The rest of the Yellowstone Eleven waited out in the BSL-2 lab.

The four scientists began with the earwax sample from Sage's left ear, taking it from the refrigerator where the samples were being stored. After removing a small portion of the earwax for the quantitative PCR analysis, Whitney put the capped vial containing the rest of the sample in a biosafety storage container at the back of the lab.

Sage remembered some of the basics of quantitative PCR analysis from her undergraduate biochemistry and virology courses but had long forgotten most of the technical details. "Let me see if I understand what we're doing here. Real-time quantitative PCR is not much different from regular PCR, except it allows us to monitor the accumulation of DNA from the PCR reaction in real time."

"Very good!" Whitney said.

"Therefore, we can use real-time quantitative PCR to estimate how much of a specific sequence of DNA from *Sagillium yellowstonii* there is in a biological sample, and from that information we can estimate how many cells of *Sagillium yellowstonii* are in that sample. Have I got that right?"

"That's basically it. There are a lot of assumptions involved, so whatever estimates we come up with will be very rough."

"How long will it take?"

"The whole process, including sample prep and analysis, used to take hours, but with our cutting-edge equipment, which automates every step, it'll only take us about twenty to thirty minutes."

Sure enough, in less than a half hour Whitney announced the results with a flourish.

"Looks like we have about five hundred cells of *Sagillium yellowstonii* in the sample from Sage's left ear—barely even a trace amount."

"That makes me feel a little better, I think," Sage said.

"Time to replicate. Let's do it again with another sample from the same ear." Whitney retrieved the vial from the biosafety container at the back of the lab and let out a sharp yelp. "Get over here quick, everyone! Right now!"

Sage rushed over. "What is it? What's wrong?"

"Look at your earwax!"

"That's not my earwax. That's the brown liquid we found in some of the victims' ears."

"But it *was* your earwax!"

Whitney turned the vial around so Sage could see her name on the label.

"I don't understand," Sage said.

"Me neither."

"What happened?"

"It looks like your earwax turned into the brown liquid."

"But how? The vial wasn't wearing any earbuds." Sage attempted a weak smile.

"Let's run a quantitative PCR on the brown liquid," Gayle suggested. "Maybe that'll give us a clue."

Whitney took half of the brown liquid for the PCR analysis and left the other half in the vial in case they needed it for further testing. When the analysis was complete, Whitney studied the data carefully before announcing the results.

"This tiny amount of brown liquid contains about nine hundred thousand cells of *Sagillium yellowstonii*!"

Gayle spoke for everyone. "How is that even possible?"

Whitney took a stab at it. "Since this sample started with just a few hundred cells of *Sagillium yellowstonii* when it was earwax, the *Sagillium yellowstonii* must have multiplied over a thousand fold in less than forty minutes. That's unheard of! Some bacteria and viruses can multiply rapidly, but not nearly that fast. And during that same time the earwax somehow transformed into a brown liquid. Let's test the other half of the liquid to make sure our calculations are correct."

Whitney spied the vial at the end of the counter. "The cap's not on the vial!" Her voice crackled with anger. "Robin, I thought you were going to cap it!"

"I thought Gayle was going to do it."

Whitney was shouting now. "How could you be so sloppy? We might have *Sagillium yellowstonii* all over the lab!"

"I'm really sorry." Robin picked up the vial, quickly screwed on the cap, and held it up to the light. "Boss, you need to take a look at this."

"What now? Did you spill it?"

"Just take a look."

Whitney snatched the vial from Robin. "Well, I'lllll be damned!"

"What? What?" Sage yelled.

"Now we've got the brown rubbery stuff we found in some of the victims' ears—the ears without earbuds or headphones."

Sage took a moment to catch her breath. "So we started with earwax. The earwax turned into brown liquid. And then the brown liquid transformed into the rubbery stuff?"

"Exactly!" Whitney exclaimed. "This is incredible!"

"So the vial's cap really *was* its earbud!" Sage said.

"But the cap's not electronic," Gayle said.

"Indeed," Whitney said. "But maybe it doesn't have anything to do with electromagnetic radiation, or electric impulses, or anything like that. Maybe it's not so complicated. When we put the cap on the vial and stored it in the biosafety container, there was no light and no outside air supply, just like when an earbud or headphone covers an ear canal. That's when the number of *Sagillium yellowstonii* cells exploded and the earwax turned into the brown liquid."

"So why didn't the other earwax samples change into liquid?" Sage asked. "They were in a dark, enclosed container too."

The lab fell silent while the four scientists pondered Sage's query. After a few moments, she answered her own question.

"The other samples were in the refrigerator! It was too cold in there. My sample only changed into liquid after it warmed up. So the darkness and warmth and lack of air circulation allowed the *Sagillium yellowstonii* in my sample to multiply incredibly rapidly while at the same time the earwax was changing into that viscous brown liquid. And when the brown liquid was exposed to a fresh supply of air it congealed into this brown rubber."

"Do you think the rubber contains *Sagillium yellowstonii*?" Gayle asked.

"I'll bet it does," Whitney replied.

"And what about cyanide?"

"Let's find out."

While the team was running real-time quantitative PCR on the rubber sample, they also tested a portion of the rubber for cyanide.

It didn't take long to get the results of both analyses. The rubber sample had approximately 970,000 cells of *Sagillium yellowstonii*, roughly the same amount as in the brown liquid. Even more frightening, the rubber contained about 300 milligrams of cyanide—well above the amount that would be lethal to a human.

Gayle gasped. "This is truly terrifying."

Whitney stared at the results in silence. Finally, she found her voice. "Before we announce this to everyone else, let's replicate just to make sure."

They ran the exact same sequence of tests on one of Gus's samples and also tested for cyanide at each step. They took the earwax sample from Gus's right ear and divided it in half. While they ran the quantitative PCR and the cyanide test on one half of the earwax, they stored the capped vial containing the other half in the same biosafety container where they had placed Sage's sample. When they retrieved Gus's earwax from the container after forty minutes, it had changed into viscous brown liquid just like Sage's had.

They tested a portion of the brown liquid for *Sagillium yellowstonii* and cyanide, intentionally leaving the remaining portion in an open vial, as they had done by mistake with Sage's sample. Gayle and Sage watched the brown liquid closely. Nothing happened for almost twenty-five minutes, but then it started to congeal into a rubbery state, a process that took about five minutes. They tested the brown rubber for *Sagillium yellowstonii* and cyanide.

"You know what, Whitney?" Sage said. "This happened to the liquid from Adam's ear when we were prepping it for the scanning electron microscope."

"What do you mean?"

"When we were working with the liquid, it started to congeal just like the liquid did here."

"Oh my gosh, you're right! I didn't think anything of it at the time."

"So how come the samples of liquid from Adam and the other two victims didn't change into rubber when we were sequencing them or testing them for cyanide?" Sage asked.

Whitney thought for a moment before responding. "I think I might know. When we were conducting the sequencing and cyanide analyses, the liquid was exposed to the air for only a few minutes at a time, and it looks like it takes at least twenty or twenty-five minutes for the state change to commence. But when we were prepping the liquid for the electron microscope, it was exposed to air for much longer, which is why it started to congeal."

After all the analyses of Gus's samples had been completed and the results double-checked, they gathered around the table in the BSL-4 lab to review the data.

Earwax: 450 cells of *Sagillium yellowstonii* and no cyanide.

Brown liquid: 850,000 cells of *Sagillium yellowstonii* and 263 milligrams of cyanide.

Brown rubber: 875,000 cells of *Sagillium yellowstonii* and 271 milligrams of cyanide.

* * *

Out in the BSL-2 lab, Whitney summarized the results of the tests for the rest of the Yellowstone Eleven while Gayle stayed behind in the BSL-4 lab to clean up.

"In conclusion, there is ample evidence of a direct, linear relationship between the amount of *Sagillium yellowstonii* and cyanide in these samples, which means that…"

Sage finished Whitney's thought. "*Sagillium yellowstonii* produces cyanide as it replicates. And it seems to replicate best in a dark, warm, oxygen-free environment, which is exactly what occurs when an ear canal is covered by an earbud or headphone."

Whitney slowly strung out her words. "And if that isn't scary enough, the rate of replication of *Sagillium yellowstonii* is much, much faster than any microbe I've ever encountered, which means it can produce large amounts of cyanide in a matter of minutes."

No one said a word, not even Gus.

Finally, Anaya broke the silence. "This really *is* scary!"

Just as Anaya finished speaking, the lab started to shake. It began with a slow rolling motion and concluded with a single sharp jolt, causing the glassware to rattle noisily.

As soon as the shaking ceased, Sage's face lit up. "That's it! It was the earthquake! I should have figured this out before, but earthquakes are so common in the Yellowstone Caldera it didn't occur to me that they would be involved in all these deaths."

"I don't understand," Monica said.

Sage turned to Anaya. "You remember the big earthquake we had a couple of weeks after we got here?"

"Of course."

"It was a 5.9 temblor centered up in Norris. Do you remember *when* it occurred?"

"Not exactly."

"Well, I do. It happened on May 26th."

"The day before people started dying!" Ben exclaimed.

"Precisely! Seismic events can change the plumbing that feeds the thermal features in Yellowstone. Geysers can go dormant, hot springs can dry up, and new features can appear where there were none before. It all has to do with how and where underground sources of water can get to the surface."

"Sage is right," Ben said. "The infamous 7.2 magnitude Hebgen Lake earthquake that occurred in 1959 caused all sorts of changes to existing thermal features. It even created dozens of new ones."

Sage couldn't contain her excitement. "So the big earthquake three and a half weeks ago must have changed the plumbing beneath Geyser Hill!"

"Now that you mention it, I seem to remember some of our rangers reporting changes in thermal activity the day after the quake," Ben said. "Normally we'd conduct a full survey of the thermal features in popular tourist spots like Geyser Hill after a moderate or large earthquake, but this time we didn't have time to do a survey because that's when people started dying."

"So the earthquake on May 26 created Thermal Feature 9?" Anaya asked.

"Exactly!" Sage exclaimed. "That's why it's not on the USGS map and why I hadn't seen it before. And that's why people hadn't been dying before the last couple of weeks."

"I still don't understand," Monica said. "Can you explain this in a little more detail for us lay people?"

"Sure. In order to have thermal features you need three things: super-hot magma near the earth's surface, an underground plumbing system, and a readily available supply of water. Yellowstone National Park is one of the few places on earth that has all three.

"Just beneath the surface of Geyser Hill—and all geyser basins in the park, for that matter—is an incredibly complex system of fissures, pipes, chambers, and pools that allow water to flow in many different directions. Some of these chambers are isolated while others are interconnected. As the huge magma plume beneath the Yellowstone Caldera heats the underground water, the water expands and tries to rise to the surface. In some places, the water finds a crack in the rock that allows it to rise directly to the surface, where it forms a thermal pool, hot spring, or mudpot. In other places, there's not enough water to form a pool or a hot spring, so the water vaporizes and is released as steam in a fumarole, more commonly known as a steam vent.

"Geysers occur when there is a constriction in the plumbing that prevents water from rising easily to the surface. As the water is trapped below the surface, it's heated by the magma below, and the pressure increases as it tries to expand. Eventually the pressure builds up enough so that water and steam burst forth in an explosive manner, which is what we call a geyser. Then the process starts all over again. There are several different types of geysers, but I won't go into that now. Is everybody with me so far?"

"I think so," Monica said.

"Good, 'cause now I'm getting to the important part. As I said a few minutes ago, an earthquake can change the underground plumbing, which is probably what happened here. Earthquakes can open up new chambers or cracks and close up old ones. They can connect previously isolated underground features and separate ones that used to be interconnected. As a result, geysers might stop erupting or hot springs might drain. Or new thermal features might appear. What apparently happened after the 5.9 earthquake a few weeks ago was that a new bubbling cauldron featuring a splashing fountain suddenly appeared next to Scissors Springs."

"Okay, that explains why this new thermal feature appeared overnight," Hank said. "But how does it account for the completely new species of archaea? An earthquake can't create a new species of archaea, can it?"

"No. But an earthquake might help release a species that's never made it to the surface before. Let me preface this by saying that now we're getting into speculative territory. What I'm about to suggest is theoretically possible, but I have no way of knowing if it's what actually happened.

"Archaea have existed on Earth for at least a billion years, probably even two or three billion. Who knows how long they've been in the Yellowstone area. It's safe to assume they've been here for millions of years. The last major eruption of the Yellowstone Super Volcano was approximately 640,000 years ago. That eruption created the basic geology of the Yellowstone Caldera as we know it today, which includes thousands of underground chambers and pools, many of which could be home to archaea. Maybe a few species, maybe dozens, maybe even hundreds.

"Since that last major eruption, there have been countless seismic events in the Yellowstone area ranging from major earthquakes to numerous smaller ones. One of those earthquakes may have created an isolated chamber beneath what we are now calling Thermal Feature 9. If that chamber contained archaea and was not connected to any other plumbing features under Geyser Hill, the archaea it housed would have evolved in isolation over many thousands of years to adapt to the unique chemistry and geological architecture of that chamber, eventually resulting in a new species of archaea. That's one way new species can evolve. For example, it's how the various species of finches that Darwin cataloged on the Galapagos Islands developed different beak sizes, shapes, and functions.

"So we can speculate that this new species of archaea remained hidden underground for eons until the earthquake three and a half weeks ago. The earthquake probably altered the plumbing under Geyser Hill so that the water from that isolated chamber surged up to the surface, creating the bubbling hot spring we've named Thermal Feature 9. And that new water source is bringing with it *Sagillium yellowstonii*, a previously unknown species of archaea. Like all archaea, *Sagillium yellowstonii* are incredibly small, probably only a few microns across, so they can easily hitch a ride on steam particles as they rise into the air from Thermal Feature 9.

"If those steam particles enter someone's ear canal, they can deposit a few cells of this previously unknown species of archaea, and when the conditions are right, such as when the ear canal is covered by an earbud or a headphone, those few *Sagillium yellowstonii* cells multiply explosively, producing massive amounts of cyanide in the process. Finally, the cyanide enters the bloodstream through the capillaries in the exceptionally thin epidermal lining of the ear canal and kills its victim within seconds."

Sage looked around the lab, proud of her scientific tour de force.

No one said anything for a full minute.

Finally, Monica broke the silence. "So how can we keep everyone safe?"

"First, we need to make sure no one has access to any earbuds or headphones of any type," Sage replied.

"That shouldn't be too hard. Everyone's electronics have already been confiscated again."

"That's what we thought before, but look what happened on Bus 4 during the evacuation. Just to be sure, I think we should notify everyone about the danger of using earbuds and headphones. Second, we need to keep everyone away from all thermal features, especially Number 9."

"We'll just keep everyone inside," Monica said.

"How about we seal Thermal Feature 9?" Hank suggested. "Close it permanently."

"How would we do that?" Monica asked.

"Just pour in concrete and keep going until it fills up."

"That might be dangerous," Sage said, "and I don't think it would work anyway. The water's got to go somewhere, and if we seal Thermal Feature 9, the water that's feeding it might bubble up somewhere else—maybe create a new feature or join up with an established one that's nearby."

"Like Beehive," Robin said.

"Or Old Faithful!" Anaya exclaimed.

"We want to avoid that no matter what," Sage said. "Can you imagine trying to seal Old Faithful?"

"So what *can* we do?" Monica asked.

"How about we build some sort of tower over Thermal Feature 9 so the steam vents high into the air?" Hank proposed.

"That just might work," Monica said slowly. "I'll ask the National Guard engineers to take a look. Anything else?"

"We should test everyone's ears for *Sagillium yellowstonii*," Whitney said.

"How long will that take?" Monica asked.

"To collect samples from everyone still here in Yellowstone? Probably a couple of days."

"And to analyze them?"

"If we run both sequencers twenty hours a day ... about ten days or so, maybe longer. But we'll need to do real-time quantitative PCR on any samples that test positive for *Sagillium yellowstonii*, and we'll also need to test all the samples for cyanide. So maybe ... three or four weeks total."

"That's way too long."

"I've got an idea," Ben offered. "This may seem way too simple, but how about we just wash out everyone's ears? Get rid of everything in the ear canal—earwax, dirt, dust, and most importantly, all the archaea."

"Would that actually work?" Gus asked.

"I don't see why not," Whitney replied. "We know that *Sagillium yellowstonii* is entering the body through people's ears, and it doesn't appear to go any further than that because none of the victims had archaea anywhere else in their bodies. Although the cyanide readily enters the bloodstream through the lining of the ear canals, *Sagillium yellowstonii* seems content to stay put in the earwax."

Whitney paused before continuing. "Since the only place we've found *Sagillium yellowstonii* is in people's ears, if we evacuate all the earwax and everything else in the ear canals, that should do the trick. The beauty of this plan is that we can start immediately. We don't have to wait for any test results. We can just wash out everyone's ears. I'll bet if we get all the medical staff working on this, we can get everyone done in a single day."

"Can we set up all the equipment we'll need overnight?" Monica asked.

"I believe so," Whitney replied. "We can create a bunch of ear-cleaning stations in the hallway right outside our lab. That way we can keep samples of earwax for testing later on. Also, if there is any sort of emergency we can handle it immediately inside the lab. It'll probably take the medical staff about six or seven hours to set up the ear-cleaning stations and develop a cleaning protocol. Then we'll need to test everything to make sure it works—all of us can be the guinea pigs for the testing." Whitney glanced at the clock. "It's almost seven now, and if everything goes well we should be ready first thing tomorrow morning, say about six."

"I'll ask Maddie to write an emergency update detailing the ear-cleaning procedures," Monica said.

"I've got a better idea," Sage offered. "How about we hold a public meeting where we explain everything?"

Monica chuckled. "You really are into transparency, aren't you? Well, for once I agree. Let's have a public meeting tonight at nine."

The intercom came alive. "Hey, it's Gayle. I'm still back in the BSL-4 lab. Boss, I hope you're not going to be mad at me."

"Why would I be mad?" Whitney asked.

"After I cleaned up in here, I went ahead and loaded the sample you prepared into the scanning electron microscope."

"That's great! Our tiny microbe is finally ready for its close-up!"

"Here's why you might get mad. I know how much you wanted to be the first one to see *Sagillium yellowstonii*, but I've already taken a look. I just transmitted the first images to the computer out in the BSL-2 lab."

Whitney almost tumbled off her stool. "What does it look like?" She rushed over to the computer as everyone gathered around her. No one said a word as she peered intently at the monitor.

"There it is! *Sagillium yellowstonii!*"

On the screen were several corrugated corkscrew-shaped organisms, each about a micron across and sporting a long, thin flagellum at one end.

Gus shook his head in disbelief. "I can't believe those little things have killed over two dozen people."

* * *

When Sage and Anaya returned to their room, the Emergency Update was already taped to the door.

THE YELLOWSTONE DIRECTIVE
EMERGENCY UPDATE
JUNE 18

AT 9:00 THIS EVENING, THERE WILL BE A PUBLIC
MEETING IN THE AUDITORIUM OF THE OLD FAITHFUL
VISITOR CENTER. AT THIS MEETING, THE FBI AND
THE CDC WILL PROVIDE AN UPDATE ON THE STATUS
OF THEIR INVESTIGATION AS WELL AS ESSENTIAL
INFORMATION ABOUT THE NEXT FEW DAYS.

ATTENDANCE AT THIS MEETING IS MANDATORY FOR
ALL RESIDENTS.

BEGINNING AT 8:30, NATIONAL GUARD SOLDIERS
WILL BE AVAILABLE TO DIRECT RESIDENTS TO THE
PUBLIC MEETING. ALL RESIDENTS MUST USE THE
GROUND FLOOR EXIT AT THE END OF THE EAST WING
OF THE OLD FAITHFUL INN AND THEN PROCEED
DIRECTLY TO THE VISITOR CENTER.

AS A REMINDER, FACEMASKS MUST BE WORN AT ALL
TIMES.

* * *

FBI PUBLIC BRIEFING (*NOT CLASSIFIED*)
YELLOWSTONE NATIONAL PARK COMMAND POST
OLD FAITHFUL VISITOR CENTER AUDITORIUM
JUNE 18 – 9:00 P.M.

The auditorium in the Visitor Center was filled to the brim with a
sea of anxious, masked faces. Every seat was occupied, and people
were standing two and three deep all around the perimeter of the
room. The noise of the chatter was deafening.

On the stage at the front of the auditorium were Monica,
Whitney, and Sage. After asking for quiet, Monica began by
thanking everyone for their patience and cooperation during the
previous three weeks. Then she made the announcement everyone
had been waiting to hear.

"If all goes according to plan, everyone will be going home the day after tomorrow, except for a core group of National Guard soldiers, FBI agents and analysts, CDC scientists, and Park Service support personnel, who will remain in the park to complete our investigation."

The audience erupted into cheers, hoots, and hollers. There was shouting, hugging, and more than a few tears.

As the din slowly died down, someone in the back of the auditorium pulled down his facemask and shouted, "We've heard this story before! The last time you told us we could go home, three people died on a bus heading out of here, and then things got even worse. What makes this time any different?"

Over the next forty-five minutes, Monica, Whitney, and Sage explained why this time was indeed different. They took turns holding the microphone as they told the assembled throng what they had learned over the past few days.

They talked about the discovery of *Sagillium yellowstonii* and where the archaea were coming from. They went into detail about the viscous brown liquid in the victims' ears and assured everyone that only people who had worn earbuds or headphones after being exposed to *Sagillium yellowstonii* had died. Most importantly, they explained that the best way to prevent any more deaths was surprisingly easy—everyone was going to have their ears thoroughly cleaned out.

"So there's no serial killer?"

"No serial killer," Monica replied.

"No terrorist?"

"No terrorist."

"Just some tiny bugs?"

"That's it—just some tiny bugs."

Finally, Monica described the ear-cleaning procedure in detail. "As we speak, preparations are underway so that the ear cleaning can commence at six tomorrow morning in the main hallway of the Old Faithful Snow Lodge. National Guard soldiers will show you where to go in the morning. If everyone cooperates, we believe we can have you all processed by tomorrow night."

"Then what?"

"Then you can go home."

JUNE 18 TO JUNE 19

It took all night to gather the requisite supplies from a local hospital in Jackson Hole, set up ten ear-cleaning stations in the hallway outside of the CDC lab, and perfect the cleaning procedures. All the medical personnel, as well as the Yellowstone Eleven, went through the ear-cleaning process until it was deemed completely ready. Gus had insisted on going first.

The process began with standard over-the-counter earwax removal treatments, supplemented by handheld low-pressure water nozzles. After softening the cerumen with carbamide peroxide, a water nozzle was used to clean out the loosened earwax. The softening and cleaning process was conducted two more times. Soften, rinse, repeat. After each cycle, a doctor visually examined each ear canal under high magnification to determine if any earwax remained. For almost everyone in the test group, two cycles of cleaning removed all visible earwax, but a third cycle was needed for a few people. A sample of earwax from each person was saved in a vial and labeled for possible future testing.

The next step involved disinfecting the ear canal with hydrogen peroxide and two other powerful topical disinfectants. Finally, a cocktail of liquid antibiotics was administered directly into each ear, and each person also took an oral dose of antibiotics as an added precaution. Although no one knew if antibiotics would kill

Sagillium yellowstonii, it was worth a try since archaea and bacteria are somewhat genetically similar. Finally, a doctor examined each ear canal one more time.

At first, the entire procedure took about forty-five minutes per person, but by the end of the night each of the two-person medical teams had reduced the time to about twenty-five minutes. Whitney calculated that with ten cleaning stations going non-stop they could clean the ears of everyone in Old Faithful Village by midnight or a little later.

While the ear-cleaning stations were being set up, the CDC team finally had time to sequence the earwax samples from Hank and Anaya. As with the other members of the Yellowstone Eleven, their samples did not contain any cyanide. Although both of Hank's samples were negative for *Sagillium yellowstonii*, both of Anaya's were positive. Since her ears had been cleaned along with everyone else, she accepted the news with equanimity.

Two other preparations were made overnight to ensure everyone's safety. The National Guard had constructed a tunnel out of a non-porous fabric leading from the East Wing entrance of the Old Faithful Inn all the way to the main entrance of the Old Faithful Snow Lodge, where the ear-cleaning stations were located. The huge fabric contraption, which looked like a gigantic version of a tunnel that hamsters and guinea pigs might use, allowed residents to move between the Old Faithful Inn and the ear-cleaning stations in the Old Faithful Snow Lodge without going outside and risk being exposed to *Sagillium yellowstonii*.

The other big change was that Thermal Feature 9 had been temporarily contained. Instead of building the large tower suggested by Hank, Whitney had come up with the idea of using a giant BioBubble containment system like the one in the decontamination area between the BSL-2 and BSL-4 labs, and she had arranged for one to be brought in by helicopter overnight. The enormous transparent dome had been placed over Thermal Feature 9 to capture any steam it emitted. It was a satisfactory solution that would do until something more permanent could be constructed.

By five thirty, the ten ear-cleaning stations were ready to go, each one staffed by a doctor and a nurse. Satisfied that the ear-cleaning process was completely effective and that all possible safety precautions had been put in place, Monica gave the go-ahead to commence the cleaning operation just before six.

Residents had started arriving at the Old Faithful Snow Lodge well before dawn, and by the time the ear-cleaning stations opened, over a hundred people were already in line. The lobby of the Snow Lodge looked a bit like the waiting area for a ride at an amusement park, with roped-off lanes zigzagging back and forth.

No one had priority for the ear cleaning; it was first come, first served. Scattered along the queue were park guests, FBI employees, Park Service rangers and employees, National Guard soldiers, and concessionaire employees. When each person was done, they were given a large, bright yellow happy-face sticker and instructed to wear it prominently on their clothing until they left Yellowstone. No one would be allowed to board an evacuation bus without a yellow sticker. They were also given a small piece of paper.

```
You may remove your facemask at this
time, as it is no longer needed. Please
deposit your facemask in one of the blue
bins near the exit of the Snow Lodge.
```

* * *

After the ear cleaning of the residents had begun in the early morning, Monica had ordered the Yellowstone Eleven to grab something to eat and get some sleep before returning to the lab at five that evening.

Everyone arrived at the lab by 4:45, eager to hear how things were going.

Monica gave them the good news. "I'm happy to report that the ear cleaning is going even faster than we'd anticipated. It looks like everyone will be done by eleven or eleven thirty this evening. In addition, the doctors have been cross-checking each other's work, and they're certain they've been able to extract one hundred percent of the material from everyone's ear canals."

Sage raised her hand.

"What is it, Sage?"

"Won't people's ears start producing new earwax as soon as the cleaning is finished?"

"They will, but that won't be a problem since the new earwax won't be contaminated with *Sagillium yellowstonii*. Thermal Feature 9 has been completely contained, and there are no other sources of the microbe that we know of. And just to be absolutely sure, we will keep everyone inside until they board the buses for the airport."

Monica looked around the table. "Any other questions?" After pausing for a few moments, she continued. "All right then, it looks like we're good to go. The evacuation will commence at eight o'clock tomorrow morning."

* * *

Sage and Anaya headed back to the Old Faithful Inn arm in arm, overcome by a potent mixture of sadness, exhaustion, excitement, and anticipation. When they entered the inn, they were greeted by dozens of identical notices posted throughout the lobby.

THE YELLOWSTONE DIRECTIVE
FINAL UPDATE
JUNE 19

THE FINAL EVACUATION OF YELLOWSTONE NATIONAL PARK WILL BEGIN AT 8 A.M. TOMORROW.

THOSE WHO HAVE VOLUNTEERED TO REMAIN IN YELLOWSTONE WILL DEPART AS SOON AS THEIR PORTION OF THE MISSION HAS BEEN COMPLETED.

EVERYONE ELSE MUST BRING THEIR SUITCASES AND BELONGINGS TO THE LOBBY OF THE OLD FAITHFUL INN NO LATER THAN 7 A.M. ALL PERSONAL ELECTRONICS WILL BE RETURNED AT THAT TIME. THERE WILL BE NO SECURITY SCREENINGS AND NO BUS ASSIGNMENTS. YOU MUST BE WEARING YOUR YELLOW STICKER IN ORDER TO BOARD AN EVACUATION BUS.

A PRESS RELEASE WILL BE ISSUED IN THE MORNING WHEN THE EVACUATION BEGINS SO YOUR FAMILY AND FRIENDS CAN MAKE ARRANGEMENTS TO MEET YOU AT YOUR FINAL DESTINATION.

HAVE A SAFE TRIP HOME.

JUNE 20

Sometime after midnight, there was a loud banging on the door of Room 231. Sage woke with a start. "Who is it?"

"Monica. I need to speak with you immediately!"

Sage stumbled to the door. As soon as she turned the handle, Monica burst in.

"We need to have an emergency meeting. Let's gather in Trailer 2 in fifteen minutes."

"But the evacuation starts in just a few hours!"

"That's why I woke you in the middle of the night. I'll get Ricky and ask him to round up Ben, Hank, and Gus. You and Anaya bring Whitney, Robin, Gayle, and Joe."

"What happened?"

"I just received a very troubling report that may change everything."

Before Sage could say anything more, Monica was already running down the hall.

* * *

FBI Classified Briefing
Yellowstone National Park Command Post
June 20 – 12:40 a.m.

All of the Yellowstone Eleven were present in Trailer 2 except Ricky, who'd sent word with Monica that he'd be a few minutes late. Not everyone had bothered to get dressed for the emergency meeting. Whitney, Gayle, and Robin had just thrown robes on over their nightclothes, and Ben was still wearing his grizzly bear pajamas.

Monica's voice trembled. "A report I received a few minutes ago is quite disturbing. It concerns the death of Ronald Brinkley, the seventy-six-year-old man who died of an apparent heart attack in the parking lot of the Old Faithful Inn five days ago. Some of you may remember that his wife Ada had initially refused to allow us to conduct an autopsy, but she eventually consented to one after speaking with Hank later that evening. Mr. Brinkley's autopsy was scheduled for the next day, but that was the same day all the new deaths occurred. Because everyone assumed he had died of a heart attack, his autopsy was delayed until all the others had been completed." Monica waved a report above her head. "His autopsy and toxicology analyses were finally completed a few hours ago. It turns out that Ronald Brinkley didn't have a heart attack after all. He died from cyanide poisoning, just like everyone else."

"Why is that so troubling?" Whitney asked.

"Because he wasn't wearing any earbuds or headphones. There's no mention of them in the autopsy report, and you can't see any in the coroner's photographs. No electronic devices of any type are listed in the inventory of his personal items, and his wife didn't mention any phones or music devices in her interview with the FBI."

"Maybe the medical examiner missed them in the autopsy," Whitney suggested.

"That's doubtful. Two days ago, I instructed the medical examiners to look for earbuds or headphones and to inspect victims' ear canals carefully in all future autopsies. According to his autopsy report, Mr. Brinkley didn't have any earbuds or headphones, and he didn't have any brown liquid in his ears. However, he did have the brown rubbery substance in both ear canals."

"Does this mean the earbud theory is off the table?" Sage asked.

"I don't know," Whitney said. "But if it is, we have a real conundrum on our hands. It's pretty clear that simple exposure to *Sagillium yellowstonii* doesn't kill people in and of itself. Otherwise, many of us would already be dead. Something else must be contributing to the deaths. But if it's not earbuds or headphones, then what is it? I'm afraid we're going to have to put the evacuation plans on hold until we figure out what's going on."

Just as Whitney finished speaking, Ricky entered the conference room. "Monica, I have the guest you requested."

"Please bring her in."

A slight, elderly woman stepped out gingerly from behind Ricky and entered the room. She addressed the group with a quavering voice.

"I'm Ada Brinkley."

Monica smiled warmly. "Please have a seat, Mrs. Brinkley. I'm Monica."

Gus stood up and offered her his chair. Ada Brinkley's eyes were red and her gait unsteady as Ricky guided her to the chair, making sure she was comfortable, and then he remained by her side.

"Thank you so much for coming," Monica said. "We're very sorry for your loss."

"I'm glad someone is finally willing to listen to me," Ada said softly. "I've been in the park ever since Ronnie passed away and nobody will tell me anything. I allowed them to conduct an autopsy and do some other tests, but that was the last I heard about it. I miss him so much." She dabbed her eyes with an old-fashioned embroidered handkerchief. "Can you tell me what happened to Ronnie? I thought he died of a heart attack."

"So did we, until just a little while ago. It turns out he didn't have a heart attack. He died of cyanide poisoning, just like everyone else."

"How could that be?"

"That's what we are trying to find out. Would you mind telling us what happened that day so we can figure this out together?"

"I'll do my best, ma'am."

"Please call me Monica."

"And you can call me Ada."

Guided gently by Monica, Ada recounted what had happened the morning her husband died. They had all heard the story of Ronald Brinkley's death before, but it was much more poignant coming directly from his wife.

"Did your husband own a smart phone or music listening device?" Monica asked when Ada was done.

"No. He was kind of hard of hearing, and he didn't like all that noise that passes for music nowadays."

Monica smiled. "Neither do I, Ada. You said your husband was hard of hearing. Did he have any hearing aids?"

"He got some about six months ago, but he couldn't stand wearing them. He said they made him feel old."

"Were they the kind that go completely inside the ear?"

"Yes. They're sort of like those bud things the teenagers wear. They fit in the ear, and you can hardly see them at all."

"Was he wearing his hearing aids the day he died?"

Ada started sniffling. Ricky crouched down and held her hand.

"When we headed out to watch Old Faithful that morning he wasn't wearing them because he wanted things to be just like they were fifty years ago when he proposed to me. But he kept the hearing aids in his pocket in case he needed them. As I already told you, we walked around the geysers waiting for Old Faithful to erupt. I think we were somewhere near Beehive Geyser when Old Faithful started up. Ronnie immediately got down on one knee and asked me to marry him again."

Caught up in the moment, Sage couldn't help herself. "What did you say?"

"What do you think, young lady? I said yes!" To Sage's relief, Ada broke into a half smile.

"After Ronnie got up, we had a quick kiss and then started to walk around. We tried to talk but Ronnie couldn't hear me, so I asked him to put in his hearing aids. At first he said no, but then he gave in. We walked around for twenty or thirty minutes before heading in. That's when …" Ada's voice trailed off and she started to cry.

"Just a few more questions, Ada, and then we'll be done," Monica said softly. "I've read the autopsy report for your husband, and it doesn't mention any hearing aids."

"That's because I took them out."

"When did you do that?"

"He hated those things so much, I just couldn't bear the thought of him being buried with them. So as we were riding in the ambulance to the clinic I took them out of his ears. I straightened his hair and tried to make him look nice."

"What did you do with them?"

"I don't know. I probably threw them away. I certainly didn't want to keep them."

"Thank you so much, Ada. You have no idea how helpful you've been."

Ada gazed at Monica with tear-filled eyes. "But none of this will bring Ronnie back."

Monica took a deep breath. "No, it won't. I'm so sorry."

* * *

Two hours before the evacuation began, a long line of hearses quietly took the remaining victims to the airport. Monica and Sage arrived at the temporary morgue just in time to see the bodies off. Somewhere in the somber procession were Penny, Calvin, and Adam. As the victims began their final trips home, FBI agents around the country were delivering the horrible news to their next of kin.

At six thirty, the lobby of the Old Faithful Inn began to fill. As the excited residents waited to board the evacuation buses, they exchanged phone numbers and addresses, fully intending to stay in touch. Some talked about TV appearances and book deals; a few even dreamed of starring in a movie about their ordeal. But most just longed to be with their families and return to a sense of normalcy.

As soon as the residents got their phones and laptops back from the FBI, they immediately contacted friends and loved ones. Shouts of "I've logged on!" ... "I'm in!" ... "The Internet's working!" filled the cavernous lobby of the Old Faithful Inn. The enthusiastic exclamations were quickly followed by tears, laughter, swearing, and lots of chatter as everyone finally made the human connections they had so desperately longed for during their three-week confinement.

The evacuation buses started arriving at seven forty-five and entered the staging area one at a time. During the night, the entrance to the Old Faithful Inn had been enclosed in a gigantic, improvised BioBubble. With the sprawling second floor balcony serving as the top of the enclosure, the sides had been covered with impermeable plastic sheeting with massive entrance and exit flaps at each end for the buses. Whitney had argued that the enclosure wasn't necessary given all the other precautions they had taken, but Monica decided it would help put the departing residents at ease.

The evacuation went off without a hitch. There was no pushing, no shoving, no altercations. A few residents showed up without their yellow stickers, but the CDC was ready for them, as they had set up two ear-cleaning stations at the far end of the lobby of the Old Faithful Inn. Within an hour, the sticker-less residents were on their way.

The final evacuation bus left just before ten, leaving behind a group of FBI agents and analysts, National Guard soldiers, CDC scientists, park rangers, doctors, and support personnel, all of whom had volunteered to stay. Not surprisingly, all of the Yellowstone Eleven were among the volunteers.

After the buses departed, Sage and Anaya sat on Old Faithful's spectator benches and chatted for over two hours, watching the iconic geyser erupt twice. After the second eruption, Sage clapped politely. "I could sit here forever watching Old Faithful. Notice how each eruption is a little different than the others?"

"Not really," Anaya replied. "They all look the same to me."

"Oh no. Some are taller, some last longer, some are more intense. The differences may be subtle but they're real."

They sat quietly for a few minutes before Anaya broke the silence. "So how are you doing?"

"Not so good. Will I ever start feeling better again?"

"Of course. It's just going to take some time."

Sage started to cry. "I can still feel his arms around me and hear how his voice cracked when he was excited or nervous. I can even smell his hair. I miss everything about him. I don't believe in soul mates or that sort of stuff, but if I do have a soul mate, it's Adam."

Anaya and Sage held hands and stared at the steam rising from Old Faithful.

* * *

The Yellowstone Eleven reconvened in the BSL-2 lab at 4 p.m.

"What's that stack of boxes in the corner?" Gus asked.

"The N95 masks I ordered a couple of days ago," Whitney said. "There's two thousand of 'em."

"Shouldn't we wear them in here?"

"I don't think they're necessary anymore."

"Mind if I wear one?"

"Of course not. Go for it."

Gus opened the top box and pulled out a handful of masks. "Anyone want to join me?"

After it was clear there were no takers, Gus tossed the masks back in the box. "I guess I don't need one either."

Sage smiled. "Good for you, Gus."

"We still have a lot of work to do," Whitney said. "Our first task will be to figure out how *Sagillium yellowstonii* produces such large quantities of cyanide in such a short amount of time."

"How long will that take?" Monica asked.

"To reach some tentative conclusions? Less than a week, I hope. After that, we need to determine whether any other thermal features in the Upper Geyser Basin contain *Sagillium yellowstonii.*"

"And how long will *that* take?"

"Maybe another week or two."

"And how long will it take to test all the other thermal features in the park?"

"The *entire park*? You really think that's necessary?"

"I do."

"So do I," Ben added. "The Secretary of the Department of Interior has informed me that she won't allow Yellowstone National Park to be reopened to the public until we're absolutely certain there's no *Sagillium yellowstonii* anywhere in the park."

Whitney took out a piece of paper. "Sage, how many thermal features are there in Yellowstone?"

"About ten thousand, give or take a couple of hundred."

Whitney scribbled some figures on the paper and thought for a few moments. "It'll probably take us at least a year, maybe even two, to test them all."

"That's what I thought," Monica said. "I think we'll plan to keep the park closed for a full year while you keep testing all the other thermal features, and then we'll reevaluate the timeline at that point."

"Fine by me," Whitney said. "I've always wanted to spend a winter in Yellowstone."

Monica smiled. "It looks like you're going to get your wish."

JUNE 21 TO 24

Over the next four days, Whitney, Sage, and the rest of the CDC team worked day and night to determine how *Sagillium yellowstonii* multiplied so rapidly in the ear canal and how it produced such massive quantities of cyanide.

Based on analyses of samples of the liquid and rubber from the ears of some of the victims, and incorporating extrapolations about the amount of liquid or rubber that had been in the victims' ears, the CDC team calculated that the total amount of *Sagillium yellowstonii* that had been present in the ear canals of the victims when they died ranged from approximately 6,000,000 to 11,500,000 cells.

They tested the effects of more than thirty different combinations of air, light, and temperature on the growth rate of *Sagillium yellowstonii* and determined that the optimal conditions for replication were a dark, moist environment with an organic food source at a temperature between 35 and 38 degrees Celsius and with virtually no airflow—the exact conditions present in human ear canals covered by earbuds, headphones, or hearing aids.

Their experiments demonstrated that in these optimal conditions, a *Sagillium yellowstonii* cell could divide once every 112 seconds, which meant that a single *Sagillium yellowstonii* cell could multiply into more than 65,000 cells in approximately thirty minutes. Thus, if an initial colony consisted of only 100 cells, after thirty minutes in ideal conditions that colony could grow to approximately 6,500,000 cells.

Although this explosive rate of division was much faster than any known bacteria or archaea, Whitney hypothesized that the unique shape and genetic makeup of *Sagillium yellowstonii* made the rapid rate of multiplication possible.

They also discovered that in less than perfect conditions, *Sagillium yellowstonii* cells divided much more slowly or even not at all. Such conditions might occur if earbuds, headphones, or hearing aids were loose fitting and did not cover the ears completely or if they were dislodged during sleeping or physical activity. Even the brand of earbud, headphone, or hearing aid could affect the replication rate, as some brands fit the ear more snugly than others, thus impacting the levels of light, airflow, and temperature in the ear canal.

The team also found that other factors had an impact on the total number of *Sagillium yellowstonii* cells in the victims' ears when they died, including the number of cells deposited in the earwax during the initial exposure, whether the cells were deposited in one ear or both, and whether the exposed person wore earbuds or headphones on both ears or only one.

All of these factors, and undoubtedly others that had not yet been identified, helped to explain why there were large variations in the amount of *Sagillium yellowstonii* in the samples of brown liquid and brown rubber recovered from the victims. It also helped solve a conundrum they'd only recently become aware of. Although most of the victims had died within a half hour to forty-five minutes after covering their ears with earbuds or headphones, some had survived for several hours before succumbing, including a few who had died in their sleep during the night after the electronics had been returned. It turned out that several of these victims had fallen asleep while wearing earbuds or headphones and had likely dislodged them slightly as they slept, thus creating conditions that slowed the rate at which *Sagillium yellowstonii* replicated and produced cyanide.

In addition, Whitney noted that although the conditions in which they stored Sage's and Gus's earwax samples were conducive for replication of *Sagillium yellowstonii*, they were not ideal because the temperature in the enclosed biosafety container was considerably lower than in a human body. She believed this explained why the amounts of *Sagillium yellowstonii* and cyanide in Sage's and Gus's samples were much less than in the brown liquid and rubber from the victims who had died.

The scientists tried growing *Sagillium yellowstonii* in cultures of saliva, lacrimal fluid, and nasal secretions under a variety of conditions. After all these attempts proved fruitless, they concluded that *Sagillium yellowstonii* only survived and replicated in earwax, which meant that even if *Sagillium yellowstonii* cells were to enter someone's mouth, nose, or eyes, the cells would die within minutes. This finding also explained why no *Sagillium yellowstonii* was detected anywhere else in the victims' bodies

Their next task was to determine the total amount of cyanide that had been produced by the *Sagillium yellowstonii* in the victims' ears. These calculations were quite complex and involved numerous assumptions, as most of the cyanide had already been absorbed into the bloodstream at the time of death, so the resulting approximations were rough at best. The final estimates ranged from 1,820 to 3,590 milligrams, both amounts far, far above levels that would be fatal within thirty seconds. They also computed that the amount of cyanide varied linearly with the number of *Sagillium yellowstonii* cells.

Once their analyses were complete, Whitney drafted an executive summary of their working hypothesis explaining how *Sagillium yellowstonii* produces cyanide.

Working Hypothesis About The Production of Cyanide by *Sagillium Yellowstonii*

- Hydrogen cyanide is a simple chemical compound (HCN) that can be manufactured from the organic compounds found in cerumen (common earwax).
- *Sagillium yellowstonii* can survive in a dormant phase in cerumen for an undetermined period of time—probably at least a week and possibly even longer.
- When an ear is covered by an earbud, headphone, or hearing aid, it creates

the perfect conditions for *Sagillium yellowstonii* to exit its dormant phase and begin replicating, using cerumen as its food source.

- It seems certain that *Sagillium yellowstonii* is an anaerobic organism, but it is not yet clear whether it is an obligate anaerobe, meaning it is poisoned by oxygen, or is an aerotolerant organism, indicating that it can tolerate the presence of oxygen.
- When a *Sagillium yellowstonii* cell divides into two daughter cells, it releases a minuscule amount of cyanide during the process of binary fission.
- The presence of glycine in the cerumen acts as a catalyst for the production of cyanide by *Sagillium yellowstonii*.
- As these chemical reactions occur, the cerumen is converted into a viscous brown liquid.
- If the temperature of the viscous liquid drops below an as yet-to-be-determined level, the *Sagillium yellowstonii* ceases to replicate.
- The viscous material remains in a liquid state unless it is exposed to a fresh supply of oxygen, in which case it congeals into a dark rubbery substance.
- By itself, the amount of cyanide released by a single cell of *Sagillium yellowstonii* during binary fission is negligible.
- However, millions of cell divisions, which can occur in as little as 30 minutes in ideal conditions, or over a longer period of time in less than ideal conditions, can produce enough cyanide to kill a human instantly.

Satisfied with their working hypothesis, Whitney called a meeting of the Yellowstone Eleven for the afternoon of June 24 in the secure conference room in Trailer 2.

* * *

FBI Classified Briefing
Yellowstone National Park Command Post
June 24 – 4:00 p.m.

At the beginning of the meeting, Whitney reported that she had just finished testing the new earwax samples she had collected from everyone in the Yellowstone Eleven.

"And?" Monica asked nervously.

"All samples were negative for both *Sagillium yellowstonii* and cyanide."

"So the ear cleaning really did work!" Monica exclaimed.

"Was there ever any doubt?" Sage asked.

"No, of course not … but this still makes me feel much better."

Then Whitney distributed a three-page handout describing the work of the CDC team over the previous four days. The last page contained their working hypothesis.

After everyone had finished reading, Gus posed the first question. "Are you done?"

"Far from it, but I think we're off to a pretty good start."

"That's good to hear," Monica said, "because you're going to be presenting your results tomorrow afternoon to a big group. I'd like you to prepare a formal scientific presentation with PowerPoint slides, handouts, the whole works."

"I can't pull all of that together in less than twenty-four hours."

"You're going to have to. I'm sure Sage can help."

"We can all help," Anaya and Gus said simultaneously.

"And who's going to be at this big meeting?" Whitney asked.

"Lots of people. Lots of important people."

"Such as?"

"For starters, our bosses—the Directors of the FBI and the CDC."

Whitney gulped. "Is that all? Anyone else?"

"The Secretary of the Interior and the Secretary of Homeland Security."

"Couldn't the President make it?"

"She wanted to attend, but she's in Europe at the moment and couldn't make it back in time."

Whitney gathered her papers and stood up. "C'mon everyone, we've got lots of work to do."

JUNE 25

FBI Classified Briefing
Yellowstone National Park Command Post
Old Faithful Visitor Center Auditorium
June 25 – 2:00 P.M.

The special briefing was held in the auditorium of the Old Faithful Visitor Center to accommodate all the visiting dignitaries.

The Secretaries of the Departments of the Interior and Homeland Security were present, as were the Directors of the FBI and CDC. Each of the four leaders was accompanied by a retinue of undersecretaries, aides, and staff members. The Yellowstone Eleven were joined by Maddie Spurlock and numerous other FBI agents and analysts.

Security was extremely tight. National Guard soldiers were posted at the main entrance and at all emergency exits of the Visitor Center, and explosive-sniffing German shepherds were constantly on the move with their handlers throughout the facility.

Monica commenced the meeting more formally than usual.

"May the record reflect that this classified briefing is being videotaped and will be archived at the Federal Bureau of Investigation. Let me begin by thanking all of our special guests for taking time out of their busy schedules to travel here to Yellowstone. We are here to present our preliminary report about The Yellowstone Incident. The presentation will be led by Dr. Whitney Hughes from the CDC and Dr. Sage Maldonado from the National Park Service. There will be ample time for questions after they have completed their presentation. The floor is yours, Drs. Hughes and Maldonado."

Aided by a polished PowerPoint presentation, which had taken all night to prepare, along with a fifteen-page handout compiled by the Yellowstone Eleven, Whitney and Sage spoke for over an hour about what they had discovered concerning the thirty-one cyanide deaths in Yellowstone.

Whitney began with a technical summary of everything her team had done. She expounded on the automatic genetic sequencers, the scanning electron microscope, real-time quantitative PCR, and a host of other scientific tests and analyses. Then she and Sage took turns explaining their findings, with Whitney handling the genetics and biochemistry and Sage the geology and seismology.

Whitney concluded by emphasizing the groundbreaking nature of their discoveries. "Although the scientific literature does not describe any species of archaea that are toxic to humans, some experts have argued that there could be unknown species that might be dangerous or even lethal. I believe we have discovered just such a species right here in Yellowstone National Park."

She placed the remote control on the table at the front of the auditorium. "That concludes our presentation. Are there any questions?"

After a polite round of applause, the questioning commenced with a few preliminary softballs. The intensity of the questions quickly escalated, with many of the attendees challenging assumptions or offering alternative interpretations of the data. Representatives from the FBI and Homeland Security inquired whether people could harness *Sagillium yellowstonii* as a biological weapon of mass destruction, while the scientists from the CDC asked technical questions about the structure and functioning of *Sagillium yellowstonii*.

Whitney and Sage did their best to answer all the questions, with Monica jumping in occasionally.

Dr. Amanda Gaines, director of the CDC, had a question for Whitney. "Dr. Hughes, I'm not sure I understood what you said about the optimal conditions for *Sagillium yellowstonii* to grow and multiply. Could you go over that again?"

"Of course. To our surprise, *Sagillium yellowstonii* exhibits its most explosive growth, and produces the largest quantities of cyanide, in complete darkness with virtually no supply of gaseous oxygen. We're not certain whether *Sagillium yellowstonii* is an obligate anaerobe or is aerotolerant, but we're leaning toward the former. Either way, the incredible rate of replication of *Sagillium yellowstonii* in the absence of oxygen and light is astounding, which is what makes it so incredibly dangerous."

Dr. Gaines nodded. "Indeed. Although some bacteria are obligately anaerobic, including some in the *Actinomyces*, *Peptostreptococcus*, and *Veillonella* genera, I don't know of any that can replicate nearly as fast as you've described here."

"Neither do I," Whitney agreed. "The same holds true for archaea. Although a few species of archaea are anaerobic, such as *Ignicoccus hospitalis*, which has been found in hydrothermal vents off the coast of Iceland, *Sagillium yellowstonii*'s growth is much more explosive than *Ignicoccus hospitalis* or any other anaerobic archaea. Keep in mind that *Sagillium yellowstonii* evolved for eons in complete darkness in an underground chamber with little or no air, which likely explains its ability to thrive in such conditions."

"And you say that the cyanide is produced during binary fission?"

"That's our working hypothesis."

"Fascinating! Cyanide production in bacteria like *Pseudomonas aeruginosa* appears to occur as a byproduct of regular metabolic processes—not as a result of replication." Dr. Gaines leaned forward, her words tumbling out. "This truly is a revolutionary discovery!"

As the questioning died down, a new voice ascended from the third row. It was Anna Baildon, Secretary of the Interior.

"I commend you all on a job well done. This could have been a catastrophe of unimaginable proportions, and it appears your small team was able to contain the threat with only a minimal loss of life."

Sage winced. *Over thirty deaths? A minimal loss of life?*

"In a way, we were lucky," Whitney said. "Because *Sagillium yellowstonii* can only survive and replicate in cerumen, it doesn't appear to be subject to human-to-human transmission. All the deaths here in Yellowstone can be traced to direct exposure to Thermal Feature 9, not to contact with other people."

"So what's the plan going forward?" Secretary Baildon asked.

"Actually, there are several plans," Monica replied. "The team from the CDC, led by Dr. Hughes, will remain in Yellowstone to test water samples from every thermal feature in the park to determine if any more of them contain *Sagillium yellowstonii*. My understanding is that it will take the CDC at least a year, possibly even longer, to complete the testing. They will also continue their groundbreaking research on *Sagillium yellowstonii*.

"Of course, our most immediate concern is containing Thermal Feature 9, the only known source of *Sagillium yellowstonii*. As you saw during your tour of our facilities before this briefing, Thermal Feature 9 has been temporarily sealed with a BioBubble containment system, but there is no consensus yet as to how to seal it permanently. A team of engineers and geologists is assessing the situation in order to come up with a more permanent solution. Meanwhile, a barbed wire fence is being constructed in a fifty-foot radius around Thermal Feature 9 to deter vandals and curiosity-seekers. That fence will be patrolled by National Guard soldiers around the clock until Thermal Feature 9 is permanently sealed. If any other thermal features are found to contain *Sagillium yellowstonii*, the same procedures will be followed for them.

"We are proposing that Yellowstone National Park remain closed for at least a full year while we work to seal Thermal Feature 9 permanently and while the scientists from the CDC verify that there are no deadly microbes anywhere else in the park. Approximately sixty National Guard soldiers will be deployed in the park for the next year, mostly guarding the entrances and patrolling the perimeter of the park. We considered erecting a fence around the entire park, but that idea was rejected as impractical given the enormous size of Yellowstone and the treacherous terrain in many of the wilderness areas near the park borders. Does that answer your question, Secretary Baildon?"

"It does, but I also want to hear directly from Dr. Hughes and Dr. Maldonado. When do the two of you think it will be safe to re-open Yellowstone National Park to the public?"

Sage and Whitney looked at each other; then Sage spoke for both of them.

"It will be safe to open the park when the threat from *Sagillium yellowstonii* has been completely eliminated."

"And when will that be?"

"We don't know."

Monica jumped back in. "I recommend that this group reconvene every three months for a progress report on the ongoing efforts to make Yellowstone National Park safe again."

"Agreed," Secretary Baildon said decisively.

The other agency leaders nodded their assent.

Monica cleared her throat. "Before we wrap up, I'd like to make a statement for the record. From the very beginning of this investigation, all of us in the FBI thought we were dealing with some sort of serial killer or bioterrorist, and we clung stubbornly to our theories even in the face of mounting evidence to the contrary. We were paranoid about everyone and everything because we didn't have a clue about what was actually happening. It took the hard work and unflagging determination of these two brilliant scientists"—Monica gestured toward Whitney and Sage and gave them a broad smile—"to show us just how wrong we were. We would not have solved this mystery without their leadership and dedication, and I'd like to acknowledge their immense contributions, which undoubtedly saved countless lives."

Monica stood and started the applause. Soon the rest of the auditorium joined in, the thunderous ovation punctuated by hoots and hollers from the Yellowstone Eleven. Their eyes gleaming, Sage and Whitney smiled as the applause echoed around the room. When it finally died down, Sage got Monica's attention.

"Special Agent in Charge Velasquez, before we adjourn I have something I'd like to add, if I may."

"Of course. Go ahead."

Sage's final statement was simple. She read aloud the names, ages, and hometowns of all thirty-two Yellowstone victims—the thirty-one souls who had died of cyanide poisoning and Steve Musk, who had hung himself in the shower. For each victim, she added a tidbit of personal information she had gleaned from the FBI files.

She saved Penny, Calvin, and Adam for last, but when she tried to recite their information her voice trembled and she disintegrated into a cascade of tears. As Sage covered her face, Anaya came to the rescue and finished for her.

* * *

As the crowd filed out of the Old Faithful Visitor Center, Anaya took Sage's hand and they headed toward Sage's favorite spot in the village, the Old Faithful viewing area. Monica and Whitney joined them, and they all huddled together on one of the benches that formed a semicircle around the most famous geyser of them all. On a normal June day, the viewing area would have been packed with thousands of spectators, but on this day it was just the four of them.

"I know life will go on," Sage said, "but it's hard to see that now."

"It'll get easier, I promise," Anaya assured her.

As if on cue, Old Faithful started to erupt and the four women watched in silence.

When the eruption had run its course, they talked about their journey together over the past four weeks.

"I've seen a lot during my time with the FBI," Monica said. "But this is one for the books. We spent tens of millions of dollars chasing down phantom serial killers and hypothetical bioterrorists when all we had to do was wash out everyone's ears. We were all convinced that we were dealing with some kind of high-tech twenty-first century murderer when in fact the actual killer turned out to be a tiny microbe billions of years old."

Whitney smiled. "We weren't *all* convinced."

Monica leaned forward. "Sage, I've got a question that's been bothering me all day. Could earthquakes release *Sagillium yellowstonii*, or some other lethal microbe we haven't even discovered yet, into other thermal features in Yellowstone sometime in the future?"

"It's definitely possible."

"So will Yellowstone ever truly be safe again?"

"I honestly don't know."

"I've got a question for you too, Whitney. I don't know much about genetics, but I've been wondering whether *Sagillium yellowstonii* could evolve to be even more dangerous than it is today. Do you think that's possible?"

Whitney stared at the thin column of steam rising slowly out of Old Faithful's majestic cone.

"I do."

JUNE 26

Sage looked back through the rear window of the bus and watched the Old Faithful Inn recede slowly into the distance. "I can't believe we're actually leaving."

The bus was a little over half full for the two-and-a-half-hour trip to Jackson Hole Airport. On the bus were National Park Service employees, FBI agents, doctors, nurses, and a few other personnel.

They were leaving behind Monica, Hank, Gus, Whitney, Gayle, Robin, and Ricky, sixty National Guard soldiers, two doctors and one nurse, and a few additional support personnel. And of course, Ben. After all the VIPs had departed for the airport the day before, Monica gathered everyone left in Yellowstone for a brief ceremony in which she officially returned control of Yellowstone National Park to Ben.

As the bus bounced along toward the South Entrance, Sage and Anaya stared at the lodgepole pines rushing by.

"I thought this day would never come," Anaya said.

"Me neither. But now that it's finally here I'm incredibly sad. We may be going home, but Adam and Penny aren't. And neither is little Calvin. I still can't believe they're all gone. Every morning I wake up half expecting Adam to be lying next to me."

Sage cradled her treasured gold pendant gently in her hand. "I wish I'd left this with Adam so he'd have something to remember me by. My parents wouldn't have minded."

"Have you talked to Adam's parents yet?"

"I called them a couple of days ago and we spoke for over an hour. They seem really nice. I'm going to Portland to help them bury Adam. After that, I'll fly to Hawaii to see my mom and dad. What are you going to do before grad school starts in the fall?"

"I'm heading back to Mumbai to be with my family. They've already told me they want me to stay in India and go to grad school there."

"Is that what *you* want to do?"

"I'm not sure yet. I got to know Hank a little bit over the last week, and we might get together when he's done here in Yellowstone."

Sage managed a weak smile. "Look at you!"

Anaya was staring out the window when she gasped. "Hey, look! Is that a grizzly over there?"

"Where?"

"About twenty yards past that small stand of lodgepole pines."

"How about that—a real life grizzly!" Sage yelled toward the front of the bus. "Driver, can you stop the bus for a second so we can look at the grizzly?"

Either the driver didn't hear her or just ignored her, as he didn't slow down at all. Sage and Anaya tried to keep the grizzly in sight as long as they could.

"Ever since I got here I wanted to see a grizzly, and now I finally get to see one on our way out of the park," Anaya said. "Better late than never, I guess."

The next twenty miles passed quietly as they both just looked out the window. When the bus slowed down to go past the South Entrance, Sage sighed audibly.

"I'm leaving a big piece of me here. Goodbye, Yellowstone. Goodbye, Penny. Goodbye Calvin. And goodbye, Adam. I will miss you all."

After a moment she added softly, "See you later, alligator."

Anaya pulled a manila folder out of her backpack.

"What's that?" Sage asked.

Anaya smiled. "I borrowed it from the FBI."

"Where'd you get it?"

"I saw it in the same steel security box in the Visitor Center where I found the other reports, and I took it for old times' sake."

"So what is it?"

"Don't know yet."

"Let's take a look."

Anaya opened the folder on her lap and they read it silently together.

FEDERAL BUREAU OF INVESTIGATION
YELLOWSTONE NATIONAL PARK COMMAND POST
CLASSIFIED REPORT

REPORT NUMBER: YNP.6.24-1

APPROVED BY: Special Agent in Charge Monica Y. Velasquez

TITLE: Suspicious Fatalities Related to The Yellowstone Incident

SYNOPSIS: This report briefly summarizes nine deaths related to *The Yellowstone Incident*. Complete details of these fatalities are contained in Classified Reports YNP.6.24-2 through YNP.6.24-10.

==

VICTIMS WHO VISITED YELLOWSTONE NATIONAL PARK AND DIED AFTER LEAVING THE PARK

Four people who departed Yellowstone National Park on their own on May 28 or May 29 (before the lockdown went into effect) perished after leaving the park.

- Victim T.L. died on May 30 in Rochester, New York.
- Victim M.C. died on June 1 in Baton Rouge, Louisiana.
- Victim P.R. died on June 4 in Nashville, Tennessee.
- Victim R.G. died on June 5 in Darien, Connecticut.

Two people who departed Yellowstone National Park on June 5 (as part of the first evacuation) perished after leaving the park.

- Victim R.Z. died on June 8 in Milwaukee, Wisconsin.
- Victim S.S. died on June 15 in Tampa, Florida.

One person who departed Yellowstone National Park on June 20 (as part of the second evacuation) perished after leaving the park.

- Victim C.B. died on June 23 in Sunnyvale, California.

All seven of these victims died as a result of cyanide poisoning. Six were wearing earbuds and one was wearing headphones at the time of their deaths.

VICTIMS WHO DID NOT VISIT YELLOWSTONE NATIONAL PARK
Two people who did not visit Yellowstone National Park also perished recently from cyanide poisoning.

- Victim M.S. died on June 19 in Tampa, Florida. She was the wife of Victim S.S.
- Victim L.S. died on June 21 in Tampa, Florida. She was the daughter of Victim S.S.

Although both of these victims died as a result of cyanide poisoning, neither was wearing earbuds, headphones, hearing aids, or any other ear coverings prior to, or at the time of, their deaths.

RECOMMENDED ACTION
It is recommended that no further action be taken at this time.

AUTHOR'S NOTE

Writing about an iconic location familiar to millions of people is a daunting task, and I strove to be as faithful (pun intended) as possible to Yellowstone National Park and its countless wonders. Of course, it was necessary to take liberties with some details (mostly small, a few more substantial) in service of the fictional account contained in these pages.

YELLOWSTONE NATIONAL PARK
With a few minor exceptions, the descriptions of Yellowstone National Park and all of its thermal features are as accurate as possible. Any inaccuracies are solely my fault.

THE OLD FAITHFUL INN, THE OLD FAITHFUL LODGE, THE OLD FAITHFUL SNOW LODGE, THE OLD FAITHFUL VISITOR CENTER, THE RANGER STATION, AND THE CLINIC
The descriptions of these beautiful and historic buildings are generally accurate, although the configurations of some interior spaces have been altered due to plot considerations.

EMPLOYEE HOUSING
To protect the privacy of employees who work in Yellowstone National Park, the employee housing described in the book is completely fictional.

THE FBI AND THE CDC
All details about the FBI and CDC were obtained from publicly available sources. Any inaccuracies are entirely my fault.

SCIENTIFIC APPARATUS AND PROCEDURES
Out of necessity, many of the scientific analyses have been shortened to fit within the time frame of this narrative. This was accomplished primarily through the invention of fictional instruments that automate and condense complex scientific analytical procedures. It is likely that many of these next-generation instruments, which are essentially extrapolations of equipment already in existence, will be available in the very near future and may even seem antiquated within the next decade.

ACKNOWLEDGMENTS

I'd like to thank my editor, Averill Buchanan, for her dedication, expertise, and tireless work in editing *The Yellowstone Directive*. She was instrumental in turning an interesting idea into a polished finished product, and she proved to be an invaluable resource every step of the way. Andrew Brown and his team at Design for Writers produced a powerful, dramatic cover that is both exciting and mysterious. Amanda Baildon and Easton Gaines, former students of mine at Lafayette College, offered candid feedback and keen insight on an early version of *The Yellowstone Directive*, for which I am truly grateful. Thanks also to Dr. Lisa Gabel and Dr. Robert Kurt, who served as scientific consultants concerning microbiology, toxicology, and other scientific topics.

Most of all, thank you to my wife, Carolyn, and our children, Carson and Kendall, not only for their helpful comments on several drafts of *The Yellowstone Directive*, but also for their continuous love and support.

ABOUT THE AUTHOR

John Shaw is a psychology professor at Lafayette College in Easton, Pennsylvania. He lives in Bucks County, Pennsylvania, with his wife, Carolyn, and their two children, Carson and Kendall. *The Yellowstone Directive* is John's second novel.